Protecting Elvis

Charlotte Morgan

Printed by CreateSpace, An Amazon.com Company

Available from Amazon.com and other retail outlets

This novel is entirely a work of fiction.
From "Elvis lore" and research I have borrowed names, but my imagined version of the characters and events are my complete fictional creation.

Patrick Harry Brown and Pat H. Broeske's **Down at the End of Lonely Street** (1997), Peter Guralnick's **Last Train to Memphis** (1994) and **Careless Love** (1999), and Patricia Joe Pierce's **The Ultimate Elvis** (1995) were particularly useful in my research and study of Elvis Presley, the man and the myth.

Cover design by Elizabeth Davis assisted by Miranda V. Morgan

Text copyright ©2013 by Charlotte Gregg Morgan
Cover copyright © 2013 by Charlotte Gregg Morgan
All rights reserved.

ISBN: 1494460068
ISBN 13: 9781494460068
Library of Congress Control Number: 2014903432
CreateSpace Independent Publishing Platform
North Charleston, South Carolina

No part of this book may be reproduced, or stored in a retrieval system, or transmitted in any form or by any means, electronic, mechanical, photocopying, recording, or otherwise, without express written permission of the author.

For Miranda

who took the Tennessee Tour with me

and for
Frankie

who made a place for me

"... Twenty years since pills
and chiliburgers did another in,
they gather at Graceland, the simple believers,
the turnpike pilgrims from the sere Midwest,
mother and daughter bleached to look alike,
Marys and Lazaruses, you and me,
brains riddled with song, with hand-tinted visions
of a lovely young man, reckless and cool
as a lily. He lives. We live. He lives."

from "Jesus and Elvis"
by John Updike

"Elvis at three is an angel to me."
Howard Finster, Man of Vision

Protecting Elvis

Table of Contents

Prologue
Gladys Love Presley
1912-1958   *xi*

J. Velis Emerson, Tupelo

Velis
June 12, 1972   *1*

Velis
June 12, 1972, later   *11*

Velis
June 13, 1972   *19*

Velis
June 13, 1972, later   *33*

Velis
June 14, 1972   *43*

Velis
June 15, 1972   *49*

Velis
June 15, 1972   *59*

Velis
June 16, 1972   *67*

Charlotte Morgan

Velis
Tape Talk #1   *81*

Velis
Tape Talk #2   *83*

Velis
Tape Talk #3   *85*

Velis
Tape Talk #4   *87*

Velis
June 17, 1972   *91*

Satnin
Summer 1972   *93*

Priscilla Johnson, Durham

Priscilla
January 9, 1973   *101*

Priscilla
January 10, 1973   *115*

Priscilla
January 10, 1973, later   *129*

Priscilla
Sunday, January 12, 1973   *143*

Priscilla
January 12-13, 1973   *161*

Priscilla
January 13, 1973   *177*

Satnin
April 1973   *189*

Notary Midgette, Memphis

Notary
July 1, 1975 — *193*

Notary
July 2, 1975 — *205*

Notary
July 3, 1975 — *219*

Notary
July 4, 1975 — *235*

Satnin
July 1975 — *249*

Graceland
August 18, 1977 — *253*

Satnin
August 18, 1977 — *263*

She Devil — *265*

Acknowledgements — *267*

Prologue
Gladys Love Smith Presley
1912-1958

SATNIN

"Elvis? You hear your Satnin Mama, sonny boy? You listening? Oh please, darlin boy, please answer me. I'm 'bout to worry myself into a state, it's been so long since you got down on your knees and talked to your Satnin Mama. She's sick at heart, bitty one, worrying about her one and only Elvis. Him hear? Elvis?"

Velis
June 12, 1972

Velis picked up the phone on the second ring: "Tupelo Fan Club, Birthplace of Elvis."

"I'd like to see about joining."

"Yes ma'am. We have three levels of membership . . ."

"I wanna see about the one in last Sunday's paper, I got the ad right here, the one offers a signed pitchur of Elvis. . ."

"That would be our introductory trial six-month membership? With the King's brand new signed photo from the Madison Square Garden show, a schedule of his upcoming tours and club events, and a complete mailing list of other Elvis fan clubs in the state of Mississippi."

"Yeah. That's it. I want the new pitchur. Says in the paper he signed it hisself, that true?"

"That he did. Elvis Presley himself. Exclusively for his loyal Tupelo fans." Velis could hear the woman take a deep drag on her cigarette, then let out the smoke. "Now if you'd like to go for the year's enrollment, you'd also get an Elvis pocket calendar . . ."

"Well how much it cost, with the mailing and all? The special in the paper. That's the one I want. I could drive by and pick it up if that'd cut down on the price. You right over there in Tupelo ain't you?"

Velis' throat tightened, her breathing came short and jumpy. Come here? Of course not. She hated to cough into the receiver, so she made an effort to swallow, to take a slow relaxing breath. "Oh, no ma'am, that won't be necessary; the club absorbs all mailing costs. The dues pay, actually. Pardon me a moment, please." She breathed in, a long deep breath, breathed out slowly like the doctor said, rattling a paper on the desk in a businesslike fashion. "So all you send is five dollars even for the introductory special. That covers it all."

"You don't say. Bout how long before I get my pitchur?"

"I'll see that your membership packet, along with your six-month membership card and the color photo of Elvis, goes into the mail first thing in the morning. You should have it the day after tomorrow. Oh wait—that's Sunday. You can count on it coming in your Monday mail. And if you decide you would like to . . ."

"Don't I hafta send you the money first?"

"Oh no. Elvis fans are always wonderful people. Trust is our policy. Elvis wouldn't want it any other way. Like I said, if you . . ."

"I got a two-month old squalling in his crib. You wanna take this stuff down or not?"

Velis cradled the phone in its black shoulder nest, held her pale petite fingers above the typewriter keys, ready. Despite her tiny hands she could type more than 80 words a minute. "You go ahead then, ma'am. Full name?"

After she took all of Mrs. Sadie Jo Long's mailing information and entered the first and only note in her phone log for June 12, 1972—Mrs. Long had agreed to send in the five dollars; she lived on Rural Route 1 outside Tupelo proper, just beyond East Tupelo in Lee County; she would be interested in getting information about future concert tickets or bus tours to Memphis—Velis stood and moved her shoulders back and forth, to loosen the tight neck muscles.

Her arm brushed the dark brown curtains on the tiny window to the side of her desk; Velis jerked away. Her mother had made those curtains five years earlier, when Velis was a sophomore at Tupelo Consolidated and her nerves started up. Blackout curtains. She'd sewed them for every room in the house, even the bathroom, from a big remnant bolt they found in the basement of Woolworths. Velis had wanted black, but dark brown was the best they could do. Chocolate Fudge, the tag said; more like chocolate sludge. The tidy office pleased Velis, except for the color of the curtains, but her motto had always been you do what you have to do so she lived with the disagreeable brown. This had been her Mama's sewing room, until she'd turned it into Velis' home fan club headquarters; the safe feel of the small, narrow space relaxed her. It was her favorite room in the house. They'd covered the walls with Elvis posters and glossies, did that together in her Mama's last year, when Velis was elected corresponding secretary for the Tupelo club. Her beloved eight by ten, the one he'd signed "to Velis back home, Love Elvis," she kept framed eye level just above her phone and typewriter. Elvis in his black leather outfit for the 68 Special. He looked so handsome it took her breath. Almost four years ago, now. How could that be?

She lined up her pencil with the notebook, put the cap back on her fountain pen, checked her Bulova: fifteen minutes till As the World Turns. She missed her Mama every single day, but especially around now and in the morning. They'd get the paper first thing and read Rona Barrett, scanning for some tidbit about Elvis and whoever he was seeing in his latest movie. Ann Margaret had been her mother's favorite, but Velis much preferred Debra Paget. To Velis' mind Elvis needed more of a wholesome, hometown girl than the glamorous starlet. He had a flighty nature himself. Least that's what folks said. Course if everybody knew Elvis who claimed to he wouldn't know a stranger in all of Mississippi.

She reached up to straighten the picture and then lined up the phone with the edge of her notebook, letting out a long breath. If she could ever work up her courage to go outside again, maybe one day she might apply to be a secretary at Graceland. Certainly Elvis could use somebody with good office skills and a pleasing telephone voice. Plus she was short—only five two in her stocking feet—and tiny built. Not much more than a hundred pounds. Everybody knew Elvis favored little women like his own Mama Gladys. Called her his pretty bitty Satnin Mama. And look at Priscilla. No bigger than a minute. Velis kept herself neat, dressed only in proper office attire, straight skirts and ironed blouses and flats. None of those mini skirts and crocheted tops and outlandish platform shoes for her, goodness no. Thanks to Pigeon's willingness to come to the house one evening a month she was able to keep her sandy pageboy trim and smart-looking, too. Plus she could keep a secret 'til the end of the world, a prized trait in a confidential secretary. Didn't Elvis value privacy and loyalty above all else, didn't she know that? Velis was nothing if she wasn't loyal. She would make a excellent secretary at Graceland, she knew she would, if she could ever leave Tupelo. If she could ever leave the house. A big if.

She'd gone out like everybody else most of her 21 years. Why she'd been to see Elvis every single time he'd appeared in Tupelo, even times she was too little to remember, but she'd been. Had the ticket stubs to prove it, in the first Elvis scrapbook her Mama started for her. Her Mama had been a fan since she was ten and she and Elvis had gone to Assembly of God together; she'd talked on and on about going to Milam Junior High with him, Elvis wearing those pink shirts and singing "Old Shep," how sweet and shy he was, so sweet the hoody guys picked on him. Velis and her Mama probably talked more about Elvis than they did her own dead Daddy, till sometimes Velis got the feeling she was the one who'd gone to church with him. Her Mama'd actually known Gladys, too, from working at the nursing home together that little while. Said Gladys couldn't talk about another thing except her boys. Both of them, Jesse and Elvis, though Jesse never drew breath. It was common knowledge around Tupelo that all those Presleys were high strung.

A car pulled into the driveway; Velis flinched. The crunching gravel was like grinding her teeth; it gave the inside of her head that same clenched sensation. She stood stark still. Nuttall's delivery? It wasn't Wednesday, it was Friday, couldn't be the grocery guy—what was the new man's name, Dudley something? Nope, couldn't be him. She'd checked the last order twice and everything was there, so he would have no reason to double back. Especially not in the afternoon. That was her rule, all deliveries before ten in the morning. Nuttalls knew that. They only brought the non-perishables, which could set out until after dark. Hal and Helen got the milk and bread and eggs for her. Sometimes ice cream.

Probably somebody turning around. She listened, didn't hear a car back out. Had she ordered any office supplies? She didn't think so. No, she certainly hadn't, she'd gotten a big order just last week. Mailman? But why—he'd already come at nine, like always. Special Delivery? Could be that, some new club promotion. She'd gotten the new packet of signed photographs just yesterday, though. A different driver? But Elvis Enterprises usually called and alerted her, let her know to expect a package. They probably notified all the fan club secretaries, not just her. She forced herself to touch the fake velvet fabric—what had they called it at the store, rayon velvet? Had a slimy feel, really, not plushy like her Mama tried to convince her. Slimy and slick. Ugh. She made herself hold the edge of the curtain between her thumb and middle finger. She could do it. She could. Velis counted one two three, pulled the curtain back a crack, but when the sunlight stabbed into the room she dropped the cloth like she'd been whacked on the head. Panic hit in a flash. She didn't get so much as a glance to see who'd driven up.

Shaking, her breathing quick and shallow, Velis plopped down on the edge of the daybed they'd never taken out of the room, not even checking to be sure her fanny didn't smush something. The bed held boxes of Elvis pictures and membership cards and current schedules—all her Elvis supplies, plus her special club stationery. No matter how many times she panicked, each time was as bad as that first time, walking home from school, when she was afraid she'd fall down on the sidewalk and die before she got to the house. She'd been a freshman then, and her Mama was still working, and she could remember just as clear what she was thinking right before it happened: *When I get home I'll start supper and sit down at the table and get my algebra out of the way.* That was it. She never could figure what brought that spell on, maybe a tire backfiring, or the sun so hot and bright, or the fact that she'd had a speed typing test the last period of the day. Whatever it was, she was sure she was dying that first time. Now, her breath started coming in gasps and her palms felt so hot and sweaty she started to shake them, like she was shaking off ants. She closed her jumpy eyes and made herself close her mouth, too. Deep breath, deep breath, deep breath, she told herself, still shaking her fingers. Deep breath, deep breath, deep breath.

At first she thought the doorbell ringing was the ringing inside her head, but then it got through, somehow: doorbell. Her hazel eyes popped back open, hyper alert. Ohmigod, ohmigod, ohmigod. She shook her hands faster. Whoever it was, he didn't know she couldn't answer the front door; he didn't know to come to the back, inside the screened porch, to knock at the back. Ohmigod, ohmigod, ohmigod, make him go away. The doorbell kept up its rising, falling bing bonging and Velis kept shaking her hands and making herself take slow deep breaths. She said to herself: Picture the front porch empty. Picture the car gone, the driveway empty.

When the doorbell stopped she must not've noticed. She had no idea how long she sat there in a quiet house, her throat dry, her eyes closed, willing the person on her front porch to go away. But he was gone, and now she knew something was sitting there waiting on her porch. She just knew it. What could she do? She hadn't opened the front door in almost three years. No one had. The problem was too big for her to deal with at that moment, she was too wrung out. Too tired to even walk to her own bedroom. Clearing a place on the daybed Velis stretched out, her breathing slowed. Exhausted, she fell asleep as soon as her head hit the mattress.

The dream, the one she always has, the one that's more real than any actual day she can remember: They're both on stage. She's standing in the wings, holding their capes and extra silk scarves, white and orange and black, watching and waiting while they're singing the last number of the encore. Sometimes it's "Unchained Melody." Tonight it's her all-time favorite, "How Great Thou Art." In minutes they'll come off and she'll hand them their dark glasses and they'll look at her and Elvis will ask, "How'd we do?"

She waits and watches, the scarves floating out over the audience. Floating, like slo mo, the audiences' arms stretching toward them. E & J are frozen onstage, arms above their heads. E is smiling, natural, loving the audience loving him. J makes himself smile, waits just long enough before he can bolt offstage. She watches them from the wings, thinking: They're my babies, like I'm their Mama or big sister. Elvis will ask "How'd we do?" Jesse won't. He's moody as all getout. Elvis is her secret favorite, but she still loves Jesse despite his own sourpuss ways. The first born is always the moody one, they say. She doesn't blame Jesse. In many ways he's smarter than Elvis, truth be told. He's better at making business decisions, that's for sure. He's the one who fired the Colonel, for which she thanks her lucky stars. Elvis goes on gut feeling; Jesse uses his head. All this flitters through her mind while she watches them, arms lifted, singing that last sad song.

She swells up inside, watching them, so proud she could pop. The Presleys: anybody who's drawn breath the last twenty years knows them. That's what the lights in the backdrop spell out, The Presleys. She stands in the dark wings, listens all the way through this number, watches them stretch out their white winged capes, claps, says to herself, "Way to go, E and J." She's the only person who can tell them apart, with Gladys gone; it's their little inside trick. Their buddies will say, real stunned-like, "How in the world can you do that, Velis?" cause those brothers are alike as two nickels. It's easy.

They sprint from the stage, sweat pouring, coal black hair soaked. She hands them fresh white towels. "You think we gave them their money's worth, Little Vel?" Elvis asks, that half-curl on his lip that means he's teasing. That look still drives the women wild.

"Money couldn't buy it, E. You know that. You two gave the fans a piece of heaven tonight. A pure piece of heaven."

Elvis smiles; he can never get his fill of compliments. He's like a kid about that. Now Jesse don't care a bit what people say. Or the press either, for that matter. She ignores all that dirty talk the papers and movie magazines print. She hasn't ever thought about them being sexy one way or another, except when they're considering new stage costumes or making a movie. Then she has to evaluate how they look, their sex appeal, in a strictly businesslike way. So to her that curled lip is no more than a typical Elvis tease. Part of his boyish magic. She smiles back.

"Want some juice, J?" He shakes his head no, doesn't even look at her. Jesse's voice isn't what it once was. Elvis says maybe they should give up performing, but Jesse claims they can go on forever, long as they pack the house, long as his voice don't get no worse. See, with two they can cover up a lot. Elvis carries him. With twins it balances out. She's never seen two people closer, not even other spittin-image identicals.

"Y'all ready?" she asks, throwing Jesse's black satin cape around his shoulders.

Elvis winks and puts on his glasses. "Ready as we'll ever be," he says, striking a dramatic pose. "TCB, Little Vel." That's just E.

The three of them pass through the stage door, single file, to the waiting limousine. It's dark, so dark she can't breathe, so dark she thinks she must be dead.

When Velis woke in a panic the room was pitch black. For an instant she thought she was in the limousine, inside the dream, that she hadn't even opened her eyes yet. She had this dream a lot, at least once a week, and it was always twice as hard when she woke up like this, in the dark, with them both gone. Two times as hard, and then some. Her mind scrambled between here and there. Why didn't the driver turn on the lights, and why wasn't Elvis going ape, since he hates the dark so much, almost as much as she does. But then her eyes started to adjust and she gets it: she was in the sewing room. By herself. All by herself, like always. Elvis was safe, alive; Jesse never had been. What time could it be? She must've fallen asleep some time around three, maybe closer to four. Missed her show. The memory clicked in: a package on her front steps. She was guessing a package. Something. Somebody had been on her front porch. Who? What could it be?

She propped up on her elbows, head pounding, mouth dry. Her skirt and blouse had to be a wrinkled mess in back. She hadn't hardly moved while she slept, so the front was the same, but the back felt crushed and sleep-sweaty. Sleeping in her clothes was a no-no. She almost never took a nap, but when she did she stripped to her whole slip. Even though Velis lived alone, even though she went days without seeing a single soul, she didn't let herself go. She dressed every morning, did her hair, put on nylons, made herself up in a businesslike manner to do her club work. She took her responsibilities seriously. And her grooming.

The phone rang again and she startled, then got up to answer before it could ring a third time. She punched the desk lamp on at the same time she said, "Tupelo Fan Club, Birthplace of Elvis."

"You need anything, Velis? I'm going to Giant in a few minutes."

Her next-door neighbors Hal and Helen Chandler had started looking out for her when her mother was so sick. They'd really been her Mama's friends, not hers, but she'd inherited them. Velis'd grown up thinking of them like the perpetually old, like they both had one foot in the grave, when really they were only in their seventies now. She could not imagine either one of them less than grayed and wrinkled, could not put either of them in a teenager's body. After her Mama died the summer she graduated Tupelo Consolidated, Hal and Helen kept on watching out for her. Called themselves her lookouts. "I don't need a thing from the store right now, Helen, but somebody came to the front a little bit ago. . ."

"I saw the car."

"You did?"

"Yes I did. We both did. I'm no good at that kind of thing, so I said 'Hal, come here, somebody's in Velis' driveway.' It was a new-looking car. A convertible. Hal said, 'Who's that knocking on Velis' front door. Don't he know she don't come to the front?'"

"He?"

"Young fella. Never seen him in Tupelo before. Had on blue jeans."

Velis' breathing got jumpy. "He leave anything, you see?"

"Looked like he might've left a note. Hard to see, but he went to his car for a minute or two, see, wrote out something, maybe on a envelope, looked like to me, stuck it inside the screen. Could've just been a letter."

"You get it for me, stick it by the back door?"

"Sure. That Hal – he didn't even think to look at the license tag. But he didn't recognize the young man or the car. You want anything from the Giant?"

"No, not a thing."

"I've got a bag of tomatoes for you anyway. And some soup I got on sale. I'll do it before we go."

When Velis hung up the phone her hands were sweaty. She reached for a Kleenex, wiped them dry. Must've been some salesman, a Bible salesman or home improvement. That's who it was. Or maybe somebody got her mail by accident.

She busied herself getting the membership packet together for Mrs. Sadie Jo Long, so she'd have it ready for the mailman in the morning.

Would Mrs. Long adore Elvis the way she did, the way her Mama had? Velis had to wonder; sounded to her like she was more into having that "pitchur" as she called it to show around to her friends, though who could say? And who was she to judge why people joined the club? Maybe Mrs. Long'd save that signed photograph and pass it along to that baby of hers one day. Or put it in a frame out in her living room. Elvis made so many people happy, in so many different ways, that was a fact. He brought more happiness into the world than probably he could ever imagine. Hadn't he already given her more than she could ever give him?

Velis
June 12, 1972, later

Arranging her knife and spoon side by side on the ironed turquoise placemat, situating the fork just so on the folded matching napkin, Velis jerked her head toward the door when she heard three soft knocks. Helen. Their signal.

She glanced at the clock: 6:47. Never ever open the back door before 9:30 at night. An important rule. Since this daylight savings time mess, the sunrise and sunset all confused, she never ever opened the back door before 9:30. Tonight, a bag of tomatoes from Hal's garden. Friday night was milk night, too. Maybe a one-pound bag of Hershey's Kisses: Helen bought those for her, her little treat, at least once a month; she hadn't gotten a new bag in a while. Helen'll put it all on the shelf next to the back door. Right there, where they belong, where Velis can reach them without taking a step out the door. She could count on Helen. Remember: Put the membership packet out, with the postage. Hal would get it in the morning. This other. This stranger. Helen said a note. She'd put it on the ledge, too. Not important. Not important.

Velis turned to the stove, wiped her hands on the clean embroidered apron—daisies, her mother had stitched yellow and white daisies, they were beginning to wear a bit, to fray—and stirred the soup warming in the saucepan. Friday supper: cream of chicken soup; cottage cheese with pineapple rings; red Jell-O plus two Oreos. A delicious, hearty supper. Then her favorite TV shows. The Partridge Family, best of all. Room 222. Summer re-runs, but still. Why couldn't they make new shows all year long? Didn't make sense. A small glass of cold milk before bed, two more cookies. Tomorrow morning typing, the Chamber of Commerce job. Five hundred envelopes. Always club business, every day. Sometimes more on Saturdays. Laundry. Ironing. And this other unexpected note thing.

She filled the yellow Fiesta bowl, her mother's everyday dishes, that's what she'd called them, her everyday dishes, turned off the burner, placed the soup bowl in the center of the placemat, untied her apron, dropped to her knees when the doorbell rang, bing bonging even louder in the kitchen than before, bonging, bonging right here at her ears, bile rising up in her throat. She grabbed onto the chair, tried to steady herself, still the doorbell bing bonged.

The phone started to ring. Helen? Still on her knees, the apron crumpled in front of her, Velis stumbled on her kneecaps to the wall, pulled herself up with one hand, the other covering one ear, picked up the receiver, heard, "Velis? You okay Velis?"

She couldn't speak.

"Velis, it's that same fella on the porch. I can see him. You want me to come over there and talk to him?"

She could barely get out "Please" before she crumpled against the wall, slid to the floor, the receiver dangling beside her. The doorbell ringing stopped, she tried to catch her breath, it started again, bing bong, bing bong, bing bong. Sweat spurted from her forehead. Helen will make it stop. Make it stop!

It stopped again. Silence. Velis sat there, the smell of chicken soup causing her to gag. She closed her eyes, gulped in air, started to cry in gasps and jerks. She held her sides and rocked. Go away. Go away. Go away.

Three soft knocks at the back. Then quiet. Velis breathed deep. Three soft knocks. Helen needed to talk to her. Breathe in, breathe out, breathe in, breathe out. She rubbed her eyes and nose with the apron, looked at the clock. Only 6:54. Can't open the door. Helen knows that. Three soft knocks. Okay, she'd have to crawl to the door, open it a crack. Just a crack. It must not be bright out or Helen would never make her do this. She could trust Helen. It's okay. Okay.

On hands and knees, her skirt stretched taut so she almost stumbled, Velis crawled to the door, reached up for the knob, turned it, closed her eyes, turned it, pulled ever so slightly, waited. No light streaked in. Maybe it was raining? She couldn't smell rain.

"Velis honey, it's all right Velis honey.

She hung there, her hand on the knob, eyes closed, taking deep breaths.

"Velis, it's a guy from some paper. Not the Tupelo paper. A big paper. Not a newspaper, really, he said, but like a national newspaper. Or maybe he said a magazine. He talked so fast. Anyway, he wants to talk to you about you and your Mama and Elvis, about starting the fan club and all."

"No."

"I told him you wouldn't do it, honey. I didn't tell him any of your business, I swear, but I told him you wouldn't do it."

"Patsy."

"That's exactly what I said, Velis. I said, 'You need to talk to Patsy Taylor, she's the president, she can tell you anything you want to know.' But you know what he said? He said he was more interested in talking to *real* fans. Early fans. People who knew Elvis when. He's writing this article . . ."

"No."

"That's what I said honey. My words exactly. I told him it wouldn't be possible. But he seems nice enough; he's left his card. Gracious, I could just look at this card to see what magazine. Hold on."

Velis could hear Helen fumbling, probably in the pocket of her plaid cotton blouse. Helen lived in plaid cotton blouses.

"*Rolling Stone*. That what it says right here. Never heard of it, honey, have you? His name's Marc Collins. That's what he said. I remember now, Marc, with a C."

Velis hung on, breathing more like normal now. "I can't."

"Course you can't. Don't worry one bit, he's gone for good. That's what I wanted to tell you. I made him promise he wouldn't come back here to the house. He promised, honey."

"Thank you."

"But he made me say I'd give you his card, and this note he left today. When he came earlier."

"Leave it. Please. I can't."

"Oh I know you can't open the door right this minute, Velis. I just wanted you to know he won't be back. He promised. So you can watch your shows and take your bath and relax, okay? I got the Kisses."

"Thank you, Helen." She crawled closer to the opening, could actually smell the humid evening air. She almost gagged again. "What would I do if something happened to you and Hal?"

"Oh, honey, Hal's too hateful and ornery for anything bad to happen to him, you know that. So you just go eat your supper and . . ."

"Thank you, Helen."

"Good night, Velis. I'm just leaving this stuff on the shelf."

Velis closed the door, heard the latch engage, turned the safety lock. She leaned against the frame, exhausted. Thank goodness Helen had made this reporter—what did she say his name was, Marc something?—go away. Reporters had nothing to do with her and Elvis. Reporters had said so many ugly untruthful things about him, lately, and him a family man now. Plus a lifelong Christian. A hometown boy who'd never gotten above his raising. That's what made them all so jealous, he'd come from little old Tupelo and risen to the top. And stayed so humble, his Mama raising chickens right there in the back yard of Graceland, him taking care of his Grandmama Dodger, his Aunt Delta, all those friends and relatives on the payroll. Even cousins. What could she tell some reporter he didn't already know—that she and her mother had loved him like their own, like their own little boy? That some people in Tupelo hated his guts, said horrible things about him and Gladys and Vernon behind their backs? Even poor Gladys, dead all these years, they still had to say those awful things about her and him. Well that was none of this Marc Collins' business. *Rolling Stone* or no *Rolling Stone*. What kind of a name was that, anyway, for a newspaper? She'd rather walk naked in broad daylight than talk to some reporter about Elvis.

Velis started to tremble inside. She reached down to pick up her apron, all dirty now from the floor. She folded it just so, tucking in the ties. Tomorrow she'd wash it by hand. And iron it, take care not to ravel any of the loose threads. Pulling herself up with the chair, she stared at the table, at the ruined soup and salad. She'd never be able to eat any of this ever again. The sight of it made her sick to her stomach, the smell made her heave. She picked up the bowl, poured the thick milky soup back into the saucepan, walked to the pantry for a jar to throw it out in. Maybe she'd have some toast later. Maybe the Jell-O. Once her stomach settled. She scraped the cottage cheese and fruit into a paper bag, rolled the top, tossed it into the garbage beneath the sink along with the jar of soup. Rinsing the dishes, the warm water soothing her shaky hands, she wondered: Why in the world had some reporter showed up at her door, ruined her Friday night supper, scared her half to death trying to butt his nose into nobody's business? Maybe this is how Elvis felt, a tiny little bit, holed up there in Graceland. It made her sad for him, and sorry.

Saturday started all wrong. She hadn't hung the phone up the night before; she'd seen it dangling there the second she walked into the kitchen to make her morning tea. That off kilter phone made her uneasy right off the bat. Things weren't supposed to be out of place. What if someone had tried to call about fan club business and gotten a busy signal? She put the phone back on the receiver, irritated with herself. And then she'd realized she hadn't brought in the bag of tomatoes Helen had left. Or the milk. It would surely be sour by now in this heat.

She stopped, the loaf of bread halfway out of the breadbox: she hadn't put out the membership packet for Mrs. Sadie Jo Long. That man. That note. He'd thrown everything out of balance.

Velis checked her watch. She could still get the packet to Hal; they'd have to use the emergency procedure.

Listening for a dial tone—thank goodness the phone still worked—she dialed Hal and Helen's. It only rang once before someone picked up. She spoke before they could even say hello. "Helen? Is Hal still home?"

"Can't seem to get rid of him this morning, Velis. What you need?"

"I'm gonna go up to my office and shut the door . . ."

"Okay, honey, he's got his key."

". . . and I'm gonna leave this membership packet on the kitchen table."

"You need him to mail it?"

"I do."

"When you going upstairs?"

"How bout in ten minutes? Wait a minute; let's make it fifteen. I haven't boiled the water for my tea yet."

"That'll be perfect. It'll get him outta my hair. And I'll have him set the other stuff on the kitchen table for you. I can see it still there on the back porch. Guess you haven't read that note yet?" A rustle let Velis know Helen was actually peeking out the window over her sink, where she had a clear view of the screened porch. "I'll have him pick up some more milk for you."

Velis scurried to make her peanut butter and banana toast, the weekend breakfast. She hated the hurrying, but she had to be sure Hal got the packet to the post office on time. She'd promised. Elvis fans counted on her.

15

Charlotte Morgan

As she was cutting the banana rings onto her toast the phone rang. Helen again? When she picked up, said "Hello," without thinking, the realization blinked through her brain just as she was saying the "'lo" syllable, *I should've said Tupelo Fan Club, Birthplace of Elvis*, but then it was early, she was so sure it was Helen, everything was so out of whack this morning...

"Is this the Elvis Fan Club secretary?" a male voice asked, in an accent she couldn't place. All these snappy sharp sounds. Not from around here.

"Yes." She couldn't back up and say the proper greeting. That would still be wrong.

"This must be Velis Emerson then?"

"Yes, this is Velis Emerson, Corresponding Secretary." She hated the sing songy way this conversation was going, hated having it so out of sync. And this man said her name in a way she'd never heard it said. More like VUH-lis instead of Vel-is.

"This is Marc Collins. With the *Rolling Stone*? Did you get my note? I spoke with your neighbor, Miz Chandler?"

She dropped the phone. Why was he calling her? Hadn't Helen told him to go away? She put her hand to her throat.

"Miss Emerson? Miss Emerson? You still there?" She could hear his voice, muffled, like he was in some other room of the house calling her.

Her heart pounded. Was this official fan club business? Was she obliged to speak to him if it was fan club business? She hadn't thought of that last night. What was her obligation here, as corresponding secretary? As a representative of the club, of Elvis' good name, did she have to interact in a professional manner with anyone who called on club business? What would a responsible secretary do?

"Miss Emerson? Please? You still there?" The little far-off voice insisted.

She lifted the receiver, put it back to her ear, bringing his peculiar voice into normal range again. "How might I help you, Mr. Collins?"

"Hi there. Can you hear me now? I thought for a minute I'd lost the connection. This motel phone, you know. Can't always be sure about them. Did you get my message? I'm sorry I missed you yesterday."

"My neighbor, Mrs. Chandler, told me you'd stopped by." This in her most businesslike voice.

"Patsy Taylor gave me your name and address, said I should talk to you since you and your mother both grew up in Tupelo and..."

"Is this official fan club business, Mr. Collins, or a personal matter?"

"I guess you could call it fan club business, Vuh-lis, since I'm on an assignment with *Rolling Stone* to do an Elvis roots piece."

"And how might the corresponding secretary of the Tupelo Fan Club, Birthplace of Elvis, be of use?" She wanted to make it crystal clear to this reporter that she was speaking to him strictly in her official capacity.

"Actually, I've heard that your mother knew Elvis from elementary school..."

"My mother is deceased, Mr. Collins."

"I'm sorry, I knew that. And please, call me Marc, okay? I understand you have quite a collection of memorabilia, quite a few first-hand stories..."

"My mother's personal belongings are not available to the public, Mr. Collins. There are those in Tupelo who..."

"I was wondering if we could talk, set up a time..."

"Is this about fan club business, Mr. Collins?" Her throat felt dry. "I'd be happy to send you a membership packet. Right now we have three levels..."

"Look, Vuh-lis, I'm going to be in Tupelo for some time. I have a number of people to talk to. But I was really hoping you and I could get together..."

"Perhaps Mrs. Taylor didn't tell you that I only conduct club business on the telephone?"

"Actually, she did mention that..."

"I've never given an interview on Elvis Presley." Her breathing started to get jumpy. "I'm absolutely certain I never will. That would be so... wrong. So please, if you're not interested in one of our membership packages..."

"Come on, Vuh-lis, take pity on a reporter a long way from home. Meet me for coffee? I promise I won't bite."

"Mr. Collins, I don't drink coffee. If you'll excuse me, I have a lot of work to do this morning."

"It's Saturday. Don't you take it easy on Saturdays? I'd love to treat you to breakfast. You name the place."

"Would you like me to describe our three levels of membership?"

"Tell you what, Vuh-lis, I'm gonna try to track down some of these other folks on my list. Let's just say if I don't get everything I need I'll give you a call back some time next week. How's that sound?"

"I'm sure you'll get plenty for your article without me, Mr. Collins. Believe me, you'll find more than enough people here in Tupelo who'd love to talk a reporter's ears off about Elvis. Just don't believe everything you hear."

"Don't be surprised if I call back. Or if you change your mind you could call me over at . . ."

"Good-bye, Mr. Collins."

She heard a faint "I'll be talking to you soon I hope, Vuh-lis," as she moved the receiver from her ear to hang it in its cradle. Imagine this total stranger asking to see her mother's Elvis collection. She'd never even laid eyes on him. When he didn't know her from Eve. How in the world had he found out about their collection in the first place? People do talk, that's a fact. But Patsy? Certainly not Patsy. He wouldn't have to snoop too far around Tupelo to get an earful, though.

She'd known this day had started all wrong, and now this. Well, she'd sent him on his way in no uncertain terms: firm but polite. Wouldn't Mrs. Coleman be pleased—what was the name of that class Mrs. Coleman taught, Proper Manners in the Workplace? She'd gotten an A in that class. Maybe she'd send her teacher a note. In fact, wasn't it Mrs. Coleman herself who'd talked about the power of the note of appreciation? Add that to her to-do list. That'd been such a good class. Seemed like forever ago, though, when it was really only what, three years? Closer to four. Meanwhile, she'd have to throw out her toast, start over.

The back screen door creaked. "Hal?" Had to be Hal. Had it been fifteen minutes already? "Wait!" she called, running to be certain that the safety lock was still in place. "Wait, Hal! I haven't even put the packet on the table yet!" she yelled through the door.

"Take your time, Velis." Hal's voice had its familiar lilt, a blend of southern and cigarettes and old. "Helen's been trying to push me out the door all morning. I'm a few minutes early anyway. Don't you fret. I've got nothing but time."

The screen eased back into place. "I'm gonna run up and get that packet, Hal. Just hold your horses, okay?" Velis looked around the kitchen, saw the jar of open peanut butter, the half-cut banana, her breakfast toast cold on the counter. How had this day gotten so out of control? She'd just have to count to ten and start over: you do what you have to do.

Velis
June 13, 1972

"Velis, honey, what did that man from that magazine thing have to say to you?"

Patsy Pinckney Taylor, President of the Tupelo Fan Club, was the only person Velis knew who started talking before she even said hello. Before the one answering the phone even got to say hello. No need to identify herself: her perky voice came at you like nuts hitting a tin roof. She was like that in person, too, never still or quiet for a second.

"Why in the world did you give that reporter my number, Patsy?"

"He wouldn't give me a minute's peace till I did, honey." She was drinking her morning Pepsi while she talked, probably the tenth one. Velis could hear her smacking her lips. "Besides, he'd have found it one way or the other. He didn't bother you, did he? I specifically told him not to bother you."

"If you call coming to the door and calling me on the phone not bothering me, well then he didn't."

"I swan. You cannot trust a Yankee to keep his word. Not for a New York minute. I told him not to go near your house, I could tell him any little thing he needed to know about Elvis myself, but he was stuck on talking to you for some little old reason he couldn't tell me. Or should I say wouldn't?"

Elvis's "Stuck on You" echoed in Velis' head. Not among her favorites. "I talked to him a few minutes on the phone, out of club courtesy. I asked if he wanted me to send him membership information."

"You are such a riot, Velis. Without even trying to be. Did he say he'd join? Wouldn't that be something." Patsy was big on "something." In high school

19

Charlotte Morgan

she'd been head cheerleader, Vice President of the SGA, and chairman of the Christmas Ball Committee and Prom Planning. For Senior Superlatives Patsy Pinckney was voted the Get It Done Girl PLUS Most Likely to Succeed. She still skittered from activity to activity like some mama Chihuahua with a litter of pups. She was skinny like a Chihuahua, too, with a scrunchy thin face and little dark eyes that were constantly checking things out. The only thing big and still about Patsy was her bottle blond hair—teased six inches out from her head and hairsprayed to a stiff, immovable fare thee well.

"Goodness no, Patsy. You know better than that. He doesn't care a thing about our club, not really. He's just another one of those snoops trying to dig up dirt on Elvis. Just cause he's from some big-deal paper in New York doesn't make him a bit different than the other nosy Parkers who come around asking a million questions." Velis wanted to swallow her words; for a blink she'd forgotten how much Patsy hated people saying Nosy Parker.

Patsy didn't miss a beat, though. "You ever heard of his magazine? Must have something to do with that ugly-looking rock band called Rolling Stones, I'm guessing."

"You're probably right. I mean, let's face it, it's not like he's from *TV Guide* or something. Not that I would've talked to him even if he was. Oh, I almost forgot: Helen said he left a note."

"Well I told him right off the bat you weren't about to have strangers over, that he was wasting his breath, but he seemed to think otherwise. Real pushy-like, you know?"

"I guess I know. But it didn't do him a bit of good."

"I could've told him that. Anyway, I've got something really big in the works that I'm gonna present at the next meeting. You sure you can't come? This is really something." Patsy was forever trying to get Velis to come to some social event, like a barbecue at her house or an Avon party at Pigeon's, like she didn't get the fact that Velis *couldn't* come out of the house. People didn't generally say no to Patsy. Around Tupelo she was known as a take-charge person as well as the town expert on Elvis. She'd met him more than once, even had her picture in *Photoplay* with him the last time he'd been back home. She swore he called her on the phone any time he wanted to catch up on what was happening in town. She was forever saying Elvis this and Elvis that.

"Patsy, you know good and well . . ."

"You can't condemn a girl for asking, now can you? I've just gotta tell somebody, though. You swear you won't breathe a word?"

"When have I ever? Besides, who would I tell? Hal and Helen?"

"Well, you just have to promise. This is the biggest thing that the club's ever done. Bigger, even, than when they opened the birthplace."

"That would've never gotten off the ground if Mama hadn't . . ."

"You are not going to believe this, sweetie. Elvis has invited the entire Tupelo Fan Club to come to Graceland."

Velis didn't make a sound. It felt like her heart didn't even beat. The club was invited to Graceland?

"I know, honey, you bout to faint, aren't you? I felt the exact same way when his cousin called to tell me. Or ask me, I guess I should say."

"When?"

"When did she call? Just a couple a days ago. I like to dropped dead when she said it. They gonna have a cookout, see, to celebrate his coming back home and all from this big tour he's on now—let me look at my calendar; where is he right this minute? That would be Evansville, Indiana, wherever that is, somewhere close to Chicago, I'm betting—anyway, kind of a homecoming. I'm guessin' with Priscilla and little Lisa Marie gone, coming home to Graceland is bound to be kinda sad for him, don't you reckon? So the staff is planning . . .?"

"When?"

"That's what I'm telling you now, silly." She crunched ice like a machine. "The weekend right after Labor Day. He's finishing up in Las Vegas on September 4, then he'll drive the bus back across the country, and they want us there for a big welcome home Elvis cookout that next weekend. Do you believe it?"

Three months. In three months the club was going to Graceland. To have a cookout with Elvis.

"Anyway, you can bet I said yes right off the bat. Anybody who doesn't like me not putting it to a vote can just kiss my skinny butt, you know? I mean anybody who'd even think for a second about saying no to Elvis might as well hit the road." I could hear Patsy working the adding machine; she never did just one thing at a time. "What we've gotta figure out now is how to raise the money to charter a bus there and back, you know. And motel rooms for everybody if we decide to spend the night. All those details. My goodness, it's a gigantic task, bigger than anything I could've imagined. Something I would've never even dared to dream, don't you know?" I could hear her chair rolling away from her desk, the file cabinet opening and closing. "We surely do need your help with this, Velis honey. Your organizational skills. Plus I swear, Velis, you can't miss a once-in-a-lifetime opportunity like this, now can you? Graceland! A cookout with Elvis himself in his own back yard!"

"Patsy, you know I'll help y'all every single way I can . . ."

"Don't you dare say no, you hear me? Who knows what could happen between now and then. You might could go. We'll just have to wait and see. So I'm calling an emergency meeting of the executive committee Tuesday night: me and Pigeon and Alice can come. Course I didn't tell them WHY yet, so they're about to pop with curiosity, so you know they'll be on time. I haven't been able to get Scooter yet, but I'll track him down even if I have to go to the hardware to talk to him. I need some vermiculite anyway. Does Tuesday night suit you?"

The executive committee met at Velis' house once a month, the first Tuesday. That worked all right, since of all her TV shows she minded missing Bonanza the least. She could re-arrange the chores that one night, scrub the upstairs bathroom after they left and move the vacuuming to the next night. That worked, once a month. It was on the schedule. But they'd already been over in June for the regular session. Her throat felt all tight at the thought of changing her evening routine again, and her hands were getting sweaty. Too much all at once. Too much.

"Velis? That all right with you, honey? Really, this is the biggest thing that's ever happened to the club. Wouldn't your Mama just bust a gut?"

Her Mama started the club, was founder and president until the day she died. She'd be dancing around the kitchen right this minute, belting out "All Shook Up" as loud as she could. Mama was a card, and she was nothing if she wasn't a fool for Elvis. Why couldn't her Mama be here for this?

"Maybe you all could meet without me this one time . . ."

"Don't even think about such a thing. We NEED you, you hear? Don't you know correspondence with the membership will be a critical factor in pulling this whole thing off? Plus notifying the radio stations. We're just gonna be depending on you a lot to make this work."

"Talk to Scooter . . ."

"I'll do that. And I'll tell him to be at your house at the regular time. We'll come on in the back. Course I'll call first. And don't you worry about dessert this time, honey. Since it's a extra session I'll pick up something at Belle Bakery or get Pigeon to make a pan of brownies. Okay?"

Velis tried to say something, to tell Patsy *I just don't think I can handle this right this minute, with everything all upside down with this reporter fella bothering me and all*, but she couldn't make a sound. She rubbed her damp hands on a tea towel.

"You know, I'm thinking one bus probably won't be enough for all the members. We might have to have a drawing or something for seats. I have no idea what hiring a bus even costs, you know? The Baptists have a bus, don't they? Bet they wouldn't lend it, though. I tell you, soon as word gets out we're gonna be swamped with new members. Oh, I just have to pinch myself to be sure I'm wide awake and this is happening for sure. This beats being crowned Rescue Squad Sweetheart my senior year, and I didn't think anything could ever in my life thrill me more than *that*. Not even the day I married sweet ol' Parker Taylor. But this beats all, I can tell you that right now, beats it all to town and back."

That's how they'd talked about Parker Taylor their whole lives, calling him by his full name, Parker Taylor. Even his Mama and Daddy did it. Velis didn't know if it was cause he was an only child or what, but it's how everybody always said his name. She could well believe the day Patsy married him wasn't as exhilarating as being invited to Graceland. He was as calm and easygoing as she was high energy, downright dull, some would say, though Velis considered him more shy and sweet than boring. Everybody'd known they'd get married since about sixth grade, so the actual event was no cause for excitement, though Patsy did put on an elaborate reception the likes of which Tupelo had never seen before. No, Parker Taylor didn't even try to keep up with Patsy; he just sat back and cheered her on from the sidelines in his own quiet way. He knew her first love was Elvis and he wasn't a bit jealous. He kinda loved Elvis, too. They all did.

"Anyway," Patsy went on, barely stopping for breath, "we're counting on you, Velis. You know the executive board does all the work. Hell, let's face it, you and I do most all the work. Pardon my French. So don't even think about saying no, honey."

"I can't . . ."

"We'll see about that when the time comes. For now, let's just keep this under our pretty little hats and get busy making it happen, okey dokey? By the way, sweetie, what did that reporter's note say anyway?"

"I don't know."

"What do you mean you don't know? Haven't you read it?"

"No. Not yet."

"When did he come over, honey? He was here at the cleaner's day before yesterday. I guess he's staying out at the Tupelo Towne. Least that's what Alice said. She talked to him, too, you know. And he stopped in at the hardware to see Scooter. Anyway, I'd be about to pop if I was you. Go get it right this minute and read me what he had to say."

Patsy was always about to pop. "I just forgot about it. It's still on the porch I guess. Hal was supposed to bring that stuff in this morning..."

"Goodness gracious, you won't even get your hands on it till tonight then, will you? Want me to come over after lunch and bring it in to you?"

"No. Please, no thank you. I told that guy on the phone I couldn't talk to him any more, not to bother calling again."

"Wouldn't you just love to know what he's got to say, though? I thought he was right cute myself, in those tight bluejeans. Can you imagine wearing bluejeans to work? Parker Taylor don't wear nothing but khakis to the cleaners. Oh, that Marc Collins was just itching to meet you, I can tell you that."

"He only wanted to pry, is all. I've gotta get to my typing, Patsy."

"Course you do, honey. And these books ain't going to balance by themselves. Parker Taylor's gotta do the quarterly taxes and course he can't do a thing till I finish the damn books. But anyway, we'll see you Tuesday evening."

"Okay." She couldn't argue with Patsy. It took too much energy, and right at that minute Velis had about as much energy as a Kleenex. "Bye, Patsy."

"DON'T HANG UP, VELIS!" Patsy was screeching just as Velis was about to hook the phone back on the receiver. She lifted it to her ear again. "Guess what?"

"What?"

"Petey's coming home!"

"When?" Petey was Patsy's big brother; he'd been a medical corpsman in Viet Nam over a year.

"In two weeks. He's supposed to come into Oakland, California two weeks from today. Then he'll fly home a couple of days after that, as soon as he gets out."

"Oh my. That's really good news." Petey was the closest thing to a boyfriend Velis had ever had, and they'd only gone out one time. He'd asked her to write him while he was away. He'd even written her four or five times, but she'd never answered him once. Just the sight of those thin blue letters from that terrible place halfway around the world made her cry and cry. She couldn't bear the thought of him in the midst of all that suffering and commotion and craziness. So she'd never written him back. He probably wouldn't even want to hear her name when he got to Tupelo.

"We'll throw some kind of party when he gets home, Velis. You've just got to come. Mama and Daddy won't take no for an answer. Parker Taylor can come get you after it gets dark."

"You know I can't. Besides, . . ."

"Listen, I've gotta run. The shop's backed up and Parker Taylor's hollering for me. I'll talk to you later, sweetie." And she hung up.

Velis checked her watch: 11:37. This morning had been all ragged. The kitchen, finally, looked orderly like she kept it. Still, her schedule was off kilter. Lunch at one. Grilled cheese and tomato soup on Saturdays. Quick and easy. She set the can of soup on the counter, then made herself go to her study and continue typing envelopes for the Calvary Baptist Church monthly newsletter until a quarter to one. She hadn't even fixed herself a glass of iced tea, which was the reason she'd gone to the kitchen in the first place, before the phone rang and Patsy had gotten her all stirred up. She absolutely *had* to finish those envelopes today. This was the last time the registration form for Vacation Bible School was going out, and they needed the job in the mail by the first of the week. Normally Velis didn't type after lunch on Saturdays, but she'd promised the church these envelopes and even though they'd been late getting her the updated address list she was bound to keep her word. So if she didn't finish by one she'd just have to come back after lunch, then hurry the afternoon chores. The hand washables never took all that long, so surely by supper she'd feel caught up.

But right this minute her head was a jumble, and she had the hardest time concentrating while she worked her way through the R's. Calvary Baptist sent out over 700 newsletters, and she'd only finished a little over 500 envelopes. She tried to maintain her best speed but her fingers were behaving like she was wearing mittens. She had to pull out the Mr. and Mrs. Charles Allen Ritchie and Family envelope and tear it up and start over. She'd managed to misspell every single word except the second "and"; it wasn't worth the time it would take to use the correction tape on that one. Deep breath. Deep breath. She forced herself to slow down and focus on her typing—back straight and leaning slightly forward, elbows out just above the waist, fingers curved, feet flat—but Patsy's voice kept battering away inside her head: "Elvis has invited the entire Tupelo Club to come to Graceland!" "Petey's coming home!" Those two sentences scrambled, back and forth, like some pinball bouncing off those unpredictable flippers.

Velis plowed through the Rudds. About a hundred Rudds lived in and around Tupelo, and all of them were faithful members of Calvary Baptist. Most days she liked typing envelopes, the rhythm and monotony tended to soothe her, to steady her nerves. Plus she made good money, and the neatness of moving blank envelopes from one box and typed envelopes into another gave her satisfaction. She knew good and well this wasn't solving the problems of world Communism or working towards equal rights for women, but she liked doing it anyway. She needed the work, of course. Her Daddy had been smart enough to take out some kind of insurance that paid up the house free and clear when he died, and after he was buried his policy left enough in escrow, Mama said, to pay taxes for as long as they lived. Only Mama hadn't lived very long, as it turned out, and they'd used most of her savings for medical bills when she got so sick. The rest went to bury her. So Velis had to watch what she spent: the phone bill, the electric bill, the water bill, her food: it added up. Luckily she hadn't been sick a day, herself, since her Mama died. Not so much as a cold in three years. Staying in the house had its advantages. And thank goodness she didn't have to buy gasoline, either. Mama's old yellow Volkswagen bug just sat in the garage out back since Velis had never bothered to get a driver's license. She could walk to school or church or the store, back when she still went out. Even when she was sixteen and not nearly so skittish, though, the thought of driving a car made her sick to her stomach. Her Mama begged Velis to at least get her learner's and give it a try when she got so sick and was going back and forth to the hospital all the time. Hal volunteered to teach her himself. But she had to say no to her Mama about this one thing. She just couldn't do it.

And now the club would be going to Graceland without her. And Elvis would be there. It would no doubt be her one and only chance to meet him face to face, not like some autograph-hungry fan but more like a family friend. He'd probably show her around the mansion himself. What she wouldn't give to see his music room. Sit around and listen to records. Maybe he'd even play the piano and they'd all sing along. Him so sad and lonesome, coming home to a empty house: Wouldn't the two of them have a lot in common? He'd never gotten over the death of his mama Gladys, not in all these years. Some said that touch of sadness in his eyes was because of that. Now he'd lost Priscilla, too. She didn't see how he could bear to sing "Are You Lonesome Tonight," how he could get through it without crying every single time. Oh, meeting Elvis and trying to take away a little of his loneliness, wouldn't that be the most wonderful day of her life? Wouldn't her Mama just have a fit? Mama would expect her to find some way to go to Graceland, that's a fact, even if they had to knock her out with drugs and put her in a straight jacket to get her there. How in the world could she pass up this chance—but how could she possibly go?

And Petey: She knew in her heart he would want her to spend time with him once he got home, whether she'd written to him or not, whether she went out with him or not. Hadn't he come over after her Mama died, night after night, and sat right on the sofa beside her and watched TV, not saying a word, just sitting there with her? Wonderful World of Disney, Gunsmoke, Bonanza, Carol Burnett Show, The Waltons, Sonny & Cher, All in the Family, then Disney again. Every night, like clockwork, he'd stop in at quarter to eight, bring her some little sweet: a Peppermint Patty or a box of Milk Duds or sometimes an Almond Joy. He'd set it down on the coffee table, ask if he could get her a glass of milk or a Pepsi, then turn on the TV and not say another word until he said, "Well then, goodnight, Velis. I'll see you tomorrow if that's okay. Anything I can bring you?" And then he'd been drafted and sent off to his training at Fort Benning and that was that. It wasn't like they'd promised one another anything. He'd never even asked her anything. But he had let her know in his own quiet way that he cared about her.

Her Mama used to say that Petey probably learned to be so quiet after Patsy was born, but Velis was inclined to think it was just his way. Mrs. Pinckney called Petey and Patsy her Irish twins, since Patsy came along exactly nine months after Petey. Their mother swore Patsy said her first sentence before Petey said a word. They'd held him back a year in school, he was so late talking, so he and Patsy and Velis were all in the same grade. She and Petey were a lot alike, only now he'd been halfway around the world and she hadn't walked out her door the whole time he was gone.

Not that she'd hung out with Patsy all that much while they were in school. As kids they'd gone to one another's birthday parties, since their Mamas were friends, but Petey and Velis were always the ones in the back of the snapshots with their heads half-ducked while Patsy was the one on the front row looking straight at the camera saying cheese. In high school Velis and Patsy were in D.E. Secretarial together. Patsy took all the prizes while Velis plodded along and earned mostly B's. She was forever getting graded down because she couldn't type or take dictation fast for those blamed timed tests. Patsy was friendly enough to her, always said hi when they passed in the halls or chose Velis when they had a project in class, but they never ate lunch at the same table, and Velis certainly never went to the drive-in in East Tupelo that Patsy and all her laughing, loud-talking gang headed to every night in the summer.

No, Velis didn't date or go to parties or out to the lake to dance. She didn't really want to, so it was okay that she wasn't invited. The thought of so much noise, so many people not sitting in desks or following a schedule of any sort, made her whoozy. The kids at school weren't hateful to Velis or anything. She just didn't fit in as a teenager, and neither did Petey. Ever since she'd been a little girl she'd been solemn. It probably had something to do with her Daddy drowning like that when she was so young. Her Mama always teased that Velis was like the grown person and she was like the kid. It was true, too, until Nelly got so bad sick.

When her Mama had the idea to start the Tupelo Fan Club, from the first Velis wanted to be the Corresponding Secretary. She didn't want to be Recording Secretary; that job involved reading aloud the minutes from the last meeting, of having people make additions and corrections to her work. No, she liked the idea of sending out the pictures and membership forms, of organizing the new members' lists, of typing the newsletter, of calling the office at Graceland to talk about Elvis' schedule and any new promotions the Colonel had going. Her Mama thought of forming the club in January of 1969, kind of a New Year's Resolution after the December Special had been such a big hit on the TV and everybody all over town was talking about how much they'd always loved Elvis and how they'd said all along he was the King. Seemed like that December you couldn't go in a store that didn't have some sign up: Elvis Spoken Here; Wanna Know About Elvis? Ask Me!!! Plus bumper stickers everywhere you looked: Honk If You Love Elvis; I ♥ Elvis; Welcome to Tupelo, Elvis Country. It made Nelly Emerson mad enough to spit, all these people claiming Elvis who no more than a month before had had nothing but something nasty to say about him and his kin if they'd thought about him at all.

That's when Nelly made up her mind, even though she was so sick most days she could hardly get out of bed: she wasn't going to be a fair weather fan. It was a downright disgrace—Tupelo needed its own official fan club. Wasn't he born right here in East Tupelo, the exact same year she herself was born? Nelly'd been a member of the Memphis club for years, but after all the TV show hoopla she got busy right from her sick bed and organized a home town group.

Of course Patsy was one of the first people she called. Even though Patsy and Velis were only high school seniors at the time, they were rabid fans. Elvis lovers knew no age boundaries around Tupelo. Plus Patsy's get-up-and-go was a necessity, since Nelly was practically housebound and Velis was so shy. Patsy would make the perfect First Vice President. Nelly got her best friend from school, Margaret "Pigeon" Smith, to help get things rolling, too. Pigeon claimed kin to Elvis through his Smith relatives, but none of them had ever been able to get her to explain exactly to their satisfaction how that second cousin once removed connection worked. In any case, having an inside Elvis link would be a big advantage, and Pigeon was thrilled to help with the start-up. Between the four of them they had a membership list and their first big project—buy back the birthplace and open it to the public—going by the end of February.

Velis actually got a charge out of talking on the phone to other club presidents and secretaries all over the place, not just the south. Elvis was more popular than the President of the United States; he was certainly more beloved. Plus speaking to a voice on the telephone turned out to be a real strength for

Velis. Most people got the impression that she was a grown woman, a take charge kind of person, in view of her mature-sounding telephone voice. She'd talked to Daddy Vernon himself on more than one occasion. Nelly cherished getting The Tupelo Fan Club off the ground. It gave her a world of pleasure, when she was so sick and knew she was going soon, to think she'd given birth to Elvis' home town organization. Let the hippies have their Bob Dylan; let the flower children have their Peter, Paul and Mary; Elvis still had his loyal fans, too, and Tupelo was going to let the world know he was adored back home, no matter what the gossip mill wanted people to believe.

Velis was so proud she and her Mama had worked together making this one last dream of Nelly's come to life. They started having the executive committee meetings at the house because of Nelly being so sick, not because of Velis' skittish nature. She never intended to stay inside, to make the world come to her door. After graduation, she'd spent almost all her time taking care of Nelly. That's when she took up the typing, too; she could do it at home, any time. Supposedly, though, it was temporary, until her Mama had passed and she could go out and find a regular secretarial position. Her recommendations from her teachers were excellent. They said her seriousness would be appreciated in an office.

But somehow, as taking care of her Mama dragged on for months, she got used to her home typing business, and goodness knows she had plenty of customers. The Chandlers were the best neighbors in the world, too. Hal would drive Nelly to the hospital for treatments and Velis would ride along, just to have as much time as possible with her Mama; Velis would go to the doctor's whenever Nelly had to go, too. Got to be, though, that those hospital and doctor trips were the only times she went out. Helen started getting the groceries, just to help out, and Velis stayed in with her Mama more and more. Plus as corresponding secretary she could do all her work from her home office, and that got busier and busier. She got in the habit of working alone, of being in the quiet house, of locking the doors and calling Hal and Helen if she needed anything. It made life so much calmer.

After the funeral that sunny May day in 1969, when she was soul weary and sad enough to disappear, Velis decided to go on upstairs and rest, she'd clean up after all the relatives and neighbors and church people and friends left. All that week Helen kept saying, "Just you rest, honey, I'll get your mail," or 'Hal'll run that certificate on over to City Hall for you, Velis" and she just never came out again. It just kinda happened.

Now she couldn't go to Graceland. Or Petey's coming home party. Now she couldn't imagine going outside, not ever again. Not even for Elvis.

Velis
June 13, 1972, later

As it turned out Velis was able to finish up the hand washables and sit down and watch "All in the Family" on schedule. Edith Bunker always made her laugh out loud. But why couldn't Gloria be a little more considerate of her Mama? Didn't they both have to put up with Archie and his grumpy, bigoted ways? After her show Velis took her bath and put her hair up in curlers and before she knew it it was 9:46 and she was brushing her teeth when it hit her: I have to get the stuff off the back porch. I can't let another bottle of milk go sour. That kind of wastefulness went against her grain. She wasn't made of money.

She put on her Daddy's old plaid robe and tied it tight around her waist and went back downstairs through the dark house. She'd already cut out all the lights down there, but it wasn't that hard to make her way through the dim living room and dining room to the kitchen; she could probably do it blind folded. Why were people so afraid of the dark? It was the bright light of day that was scary.

Unlocking the dead bolt, Velis turned on the back light and peeped out. Sure enough, Hal had set a cardboard box with all her supplies on the shelf right by the back door. She leaned out just enough to reach it, hauled it in, smelling the muggy night air for no more than a minute. As she bolted the door again a big sigh burst out her mouth, like she'd been holding her breath the whole time.

Much as she didn't want to, she turned on the kitchen light to see to put her provisions away. Milk in the fridge. The bag of tomatoes in the basket on the counter. Kisses in the canister. Bread in the breadbox. Canned goods in the cabinet. This day had started off weird and it was ending the same way.

Charlotte Morgan

Velis was relieved when she'd stacked the last can of Campbell's Soup in the cupboard, glad she could finally go to bed and go to sleep so she could start over on the right foot the next morning.

She was putting the empty cardboard box beside the back door when she saw it: a stark white envelope with her name in blue ink the size of a headline.

The letter from the reporter. What was his name? Marc Somebody. Marc with a C. She stared at that envelope for at least a minute. She could leave it in the box and Hal would throw it out for her. She wouldn't even have to ask him. Patsy would never let her forget it if she didn't read it, though. She could leave it and let Patsy read it Tuesday night when she came over for the special executive committee meeting. Knowing Patsy, she'd probably tear it open and read it out loud right there without even reading it to herself first. What if there was something personal in there, about her Mama and Elvis, for instance? Not that there *was* anything about her Mama and Elvis, but still, Velis wouldn't want anything read out loud until she'd had a chance to see it for herself.

The longer she stared at the envelope the less bothersome it became. She was used to opening letters from strangers every day. On occasion the club had even gotten what was known as hate mail—it was certainly hateful, she knew that for a fact. Saying awful things about Elvis being fat and unfaithful. People could be so cruel. The nuisance now was that it was past her bedtime and she didn't want to deal with another single out of place thing. The reality, though, was that if she didn't somehow deal with it tonight—at least make a decision about how to deal with it—it would serve to start tomorrow off out of whack, too. Best handle it now and get it over with: You do what you have to do. She took three deep breaths.

Velis picked up the #10 business envelope—this Marc Collins was, perhaps, more businesslike than she'd given him credit for earlier—and pulled out the silver drawer for a knife to slit it open. Might as well go ahead and read it right here in the kitchen. After all, the envelope only said Velis Emerson, it didn't say Velis Emerson, Corresponding Secretary, Tupelo Fan Club.

The letter was handwritten in the same blue ink as on the envelope. The writing wasn't quite as big, but it was still what she'd call bold. Velis was a bit taken aback that the whole thing wasn't typed. Wasn't Mr. Collins on assignment for his magazine? Shouldn't he use a portable typewriter to conduct his business? But no, this was handwritten. Standing in the middle of the kitchen floor she read:

June 12, 1972

Dear Velis *(Why did he think he could address her like that when he'd never even met her? Such an address suited personal correspondence, but was way out of line for professional interaction. Her hands began to shake just the slightest bit.),*

I'm sorry you weren't home when I knocked just now. *(Of course: he'd written this in his car after she didn't come to the door; that's why it wasn't typewritten.)* Patsy Taylor led me to believe you'd be in, though she did discourage me from stopping by.

I work for *Rolling Stone Magazine* and right now I'm assigned a hometown piece on Elvis Presley. It's going to tie in with a major cover story on the roots of rock and roll. Everyone I talk to around here mentions your name, and your mother's.

I'd very much like to sit down with you and see what you might contribute to the story. I understand you're the corresponding secretary for the Tupelo Fan Club, and that you and your mother are actually the ones who started it.

Could we talk? I'd be pleased to take you to lunch or dinner. Whatever suits you. Please call me at the Tupelo Towne (RI 3-7764, Room 16). I'll be waiting to hear from you.

Regards,
Marc

He could just wait 'til Hades freezes over.

A card dropped to the floor. Velis picked it up. He'd included his business card; she definitely approved of that. It was that eggshell white color, heavy stock, with the logo Rolling Stone in raised letters just like the title of the magazine. Seeing it on the business card like that Velis realized she *had* seen that magazine somewhere once before—her mother must have had a copy at least once. Was Elvis ever on the cover? That rang a bell. She'd have to look in the magazine collection. Plus Marc Collins, and a New York address and phone number. Velis ran her fingers over the letters, all raised. Printed. Very classy, really. Why would this Marc Collins who had such a refined business card wear bluejeans to come to meet someone he hoped to interview? It didn't make a bit of sense.

She tucked the letter and the card back into the envelope, put it in the pocket of her bathrobe. She'd give it to Patsy on Tuesday, that's what she'd do. Patsy would like nothing better than to take this Marc Collins all around Tupelo and tell him her neverending Elvis stories. His ears would throb, he'd be so tired of hearing Patsy talk. Both of them would get what they needed: Patsy would no doubt be quoted in a rock and roll magazine, probably even have her picture included if she had her way, and Marc Collins would get enough Elvis info to write a book. Least Patsy's stories would have a grain of truth, and wouldn't be all that nasty gossip. Velis patted her pocket, satisfied she'd come up with the right solution, pleased she'd gone ahead and faced up to this situation so she could get up in the morning and get started on the right side of the bed.

She bout jumped out of her skin when the phone rang. Three rings, then it stopped. She stared at it, hardly breathing, thinking it has to be the Chandlers, and sure enough it started up again. Hal and Helen. Velis looked at the kitchen clock: nine fifty nine. What in the world were they doing calling so late? She picked up the phone. "Hal? Anything wrong?"

"That's what I was going to ask you, Velis honey. Helen saw your kitchen light on and it like to scared her to death."

"I had to get the groceries in is all. I was just a little late getting to it."

"That's what I told her. I said, 'Don't go scaring me half to death, Helen. Velis is probably just a little late getting her things off the porch.'"

She could hear Helen saying something in the background, but she couldn't make out the words. "Thanks though, Hal. You go on to bed now. Good night."

"Wait a minute, Velis. Helen is bound and determined to talk to you. I told her she ought to wait till morning, I said . . ."

"Put her on, Hal. It's all right. I'm wide awake now." For some reason that was true. Velis wasn't even slightly sleepy right this minute, though only a little bit ago she could've gone to bed and gone on to sleep without even reading her library book. Probably the unexpected ringing of the phone breaking the stillness of the night kitchen.

"Velis? You all right?"

"I told Hal I was just a little slow moving this evening is all."

"You sure? I can come over there if something's wrong." Helen's voice sounded more worried than made sense.

"Course not. I'm sorry to worry you."

"Listen, Velis honey, I've gotta tell you something you're not gonna like one bit. I was gonna tell you in the morning, but I don't think I'd get a wink of sleep if I didn't just go ahead and get it over with right now."

"Well sure, Helen. You and Hal are okay, aren't you? You're not sick?" Velis pulled out one of the kitchen chairs and sat down. The thought of anything happening to one of the Chandlers made her hands start to sweat and her throat get that tight, itchy feeling. She glanced all around the orderly kitchen: everything in place. Everything all right. Deep breaths. Deep breaths.

"No, it's nothing like that. I don't mean to scare you, honey, so I'm just gonna go ahead and say it. Marc Collins came over here tonight to see me and Hal. There. That's it."

Thank the good Lord nothing was wrong with them. On the other hand, just when she was starting to think this Marc Collins might be more nuisance than harm here he was snooping around her neighbors. Velis started twisting the phone cord with her right hand. "Well what in the world was he thinking of, bothering you two?"

"He's a sweet young man, Velis. I swear he is. Not a bit uppity like you might think. I gave him a piece of my homemade peach pie and he like to died, he thought it was so good. Can you believe he ate a second piece?"

"But what did he want, Helen? How long did he stay, anyway?"

"He wanted to talk to us about Elvis, I think. Though we didn't have much to tell him on that score. Hal used to see his daddy Vernon and his Uncle Vestor around town, which he told him, but since we went to First United Methodist all these years instead of Assembly of God, we didn't have much occasion . . ."

"Well did he ask anything about me and Mama?"

Helen paused. "You know I'd never tell a living soul your business, Velis . . ."

"But did he ask?"

"Yes, he did. He wanted to know how well your Mama knew Elvis, and all about her collection of Elvis stuff."

"What did you tell him?"

"That he'd need to take that up with you. Of course."

"Thank you, Helen. I appreciate that."

"And Hal said the same thing, you can go to the bank on that."

"Course he would."

"But Velis: I think you should call him."

"Why do you say that? You know as well as I do there's plenty of people here in town he can talk to without talking to me."

"Well, yes, I do. But I get the impression he truly wants to get to know about Elvis Presley as a human being, not as some rock star."

"What in the world makes you think that? Are you telling me he snowed you, Helen? I can't hardly believe it."

"Could be. But Hal's a pretty hard sell, as you well know, and he agrees with me. Don't you Hal?" Her voice faded as she must've leaned away from the phone. Velis could hear Hal's muted voice chiming in with a "I told you what I thought, Helen. The boy seemed fine to me." "Did you hear that Velis?"

"I did. I could hear him just fine."

"And this is the part you won't believe. Marc Collins is divorced—I don't guess anybody bothered to tell you that?—and he's got little twin boys, only get this, one of them's a dwarf."

"What?"

"I swear. He showed me their pictures. Gavin and Gabe Collins. They turned three right before he came, and he showed me snapshots from their birthday party. It was the cutest thing. They had a astronaut theme with a little rocket on the cake. Anyway, Gabe's the dwarf. Mr. Collins said it's okay to say that, to say that he's a dwarf. Anyway, he don't look that different from his brother right now. His head's a little bigger, is all, and his little arms are right short. Marc don't seem the slightest bit sad or embarrassed about it, says just as normal as nuts, 'Gabe was born first; he's a dwarf.' Now don't he sound like a nice young man?"

"That is surely a surprise, Helen, I have to say." Velis had a soft spot for twins, no doubt about it. Her mother had been a twin, only Velis had never known her aunt Nancy. She'd died of polio when they were sixteen years old. Everybody thought they were too old to get it, and they'd gone swimming in the lake, and her Mama said Nancy came down with it and died faster than you can say Jimminy Cricket. It was so sad. And of course Elvis was a twin; she and her Mama had talked hours and hours about what it might've been like if Nancy had lived and Jesse Garon had lived and they'd all gone to school together. That would've been so sweet. And she had that dream at least once a month about Elvis and Jesse, the two of them. Usually more often.

"So he made me promise I'd talk to you about seeing him, Velis. I hate to tell you this, but I told him I would." Now it seemed like Helen was holding her breath. Velis could hear Hal grumbling in the background.

"You know I can't do that."

"I know. I told him so. But I said I'd ask so I'm asking. He was gonna call tomorrow around lunch time . . ."

"Was gonna?"

"Well, yes. But I told him to come on over and eat with us. Hal and I enjoy a bit of company. Plus I could tell he'd love to have another piece of that pie."

Velis kept on twisting the phone cord. "You do that, Helen. Just be sure he don't set foot on my porch again, you hear?"

"Course, honey."

"I don't want to talk to him on the phone or anything; no more pushy phone calls, you hear? Nothing."

"You don't have to say another word."

The silence went on for a few seconds. Velis could hear the light by the sink start to buzz. "And thanks again for the Kisses."

"You're welcome. You need anything tomorrow?"

"No. I'm fine." The buzzing seemed to get louder. She'd have to ask Hal to take a look at it soon. "You say you saw a picture of those twins?"

"I did. They're as cute as two brass buttons, Velis. Marc says it like to killed him, getting the divorce, that it won't his choice, but being as he's on the road so much, and being as little Gabe made his wife Paula so sad all the time, well, it was just one of those things. He is the sweetest man, Velis, he really is. You want me to see if Marc'll let me bring the picture over to show you?"

The fact that Helen called him Marc just as natural as new money made Velis cringe just the slightest bit. She'd like to see that picture, she really would, but there was no way she was going to start up any kind of communication with Mister Marc Collins, even if it was just a picture-looking kind of event. One thing always did lead to another, and she wasn't about to be tugged into talking to that man by some snapshot of his little twin boys. "That won't be necessary, Helen. But thank you for asking." She couldn't keep the formal edge out of her voice. She realized that if she didn't make herself talk in that corresponding secretary voice she might start crying.

"Okay, honey. It was just a thought. Well, good night then. Hal's about to shoot me dead, the way he's looking at me. You sure you don't need anything tomorrow?"

"Not a thing. Thanks, though. Night." Her hands were all slippery when she hung up the receiver, so she wiped them on the clean tea towel hanging from the handle of the stove. The irritating noise from the light only added to the jumpy feeling she had inside her chest. She had straightened this kitchen to a fare thee well, but Helen's phone call and the sound coming from that connection made it seem like the place was a wreck, a ruin, a disorderly shambles. She cut out the light and stood there in the blackout quiet. It was dark as dirt. In that complete deep cave peacefulness her breathing came easy again.

Wiping any thoughts of the day from her mind like scrubbing the tub, Velis made it through her house, walking through the pitch black rooms as though every light in the house was on. When she hit the bed she fell into a deep slumber right away, like a baby who's cried so hard she doesn't have an ounce of energy left to fight off sleep.

The dream comes, the exact same way as always: They're both on stage.

She's standing in the wings, holding their capes and extra silk scarves, white and orange and black, watching and waiting while they're singing the last number of the encore. Sometimes it's "Unchained Melody." Tonight it's her all-time favorite, "How Great Thou Art." In minutes they'll come off and she'll hand them their dark glasses and they'll look at her and ask, "How'd we do?"

She waits and watches, the scarves floating out over the audience. Floating, like slo mo, the audiences' arms stretched toward them. E & J are frozen onstage, arms above their heads; E is smiling, natural, loving the audience loving him; J—J is tiny, no bigger than a Tiny Tears Doll. He looks and sounds exactly the same, except he's not even as big as Howdy Doody.

Velis hears screaming. The dream is all wrong. She wakes up in the pitch dark and she can still hear the screaming. Plus crying. It takes her almost a minute to realize that it's her: she's the one who's screaming like she's screaming for dear life. She's the one crying like her Mama and Daddy both just died two seconds ago. She keeps on crying, cries so hard she must cry herself back to sleep, because next thing she knows it's Sunday morning and damned if the phone isn't ringing off the hook again.

"Tupelo Fan Club. Birthplace of Elvis." It was all Velis could do to keep her voice calm, after running all the way to her office, but she knew presenting a dependable club presence was one of her major functions and no matter what happened she was determined to do that job and do it right. Still, she didn't usually get club calls this early on Sunday.

"You doing all right, Velis?" Pigeon's soft voice was almost as familiar to her as her own Mama's, as light as meringue, which was right odd, since she weighed close to two hundred pounds.

"Oh. Hi, Pigeon. You going to Sunday School?"

"Course I am, honey. I was just wondering if you were bout ready for your trim?"

"Is it time?" Velis glanced at her calendar. Sure enough, it said "Pigeon, Trim, Monday evening, 7:30." She wrote the next appointment down every time as a matter of habit. Pigeon always came at 7:30.

"It sure is. You think this time you might want to come to the house and have some supper with me and Mama, then watch TV after I finish? Mama said the other day she'd sure love to see you, it'd been way too long, and you know her arthritis is getting right bad." Without fail Pigeon tried to talk Velis into coming out. One time she'd suggest her coming to the shop so she could see Pigeon's new wallpaper. Another time it'd be coming on over to Patsy's so she could do a make-over and they could all visit. Every blessed time she tried to lure Velis out of the house some tempting way. Course it never worked, but she kept on trying.

"Tell your Mama maybe another time. And give her a hug from me, okay? If you don't mind, though, I need to stay close to the phone in case somebody calls about the fan club. With this new promotion and all . . ."

"Oh it's no trouble, honey. I'm glad to come on over. I'll see you tomorrow evening then."

"Sure thing."

"And the next night, too. I guess Patsy's called you?"

"She did. Just yesterday. Has she talked to Scooter yet?"

"I think so. I think we're all set. I'm gonna make us some brownies. And maybe a batch of peanut brittle if I get the chance. You have any idea what this is all about? Patsy was all in a swivet when she called me."

"Me too." Velis couldn't bring herself to tell a fib, so she just sidestepped the question. Pigeon didn't seem to notice.

"Well, I'm sure she'll blurt it out as soon as we all get there. I'm gonna pick up Scooter myself, to be sure he's on time."

Charlotte Morgan

"That's a good idea, Pigeon."

"Well then, I'm off to Sunday School. You heard anything from your Uncle Carl lately?"

"Nothing since my birthday." Uncle Carl was Mama's closest brother. He lived in Richmond, Virginia, though, and worked at Phillip Morris doing something with tobacco. Velis got a card and check every Christmas, a card and check on her birthday, and every now and then a phone call to see if she needed any money. Other than that she never heard a peep from Uncle Carl. He was kinda quiet, anyway, unlike her Mama, who'd been what was known as a live wire in her day. Uncle Carl adored his baby sister, and he'd do anything for Velis if she asked, but she never asked. Both of them missed Mama too much to talk to one another; her absence between them was too sad. Carl had had a crush on Pigeon when they were kids. Mama said she'd been too self-conscious about her size to go out with him, and after he'd gone on to Richmond that was that. Neither one of them ever married anybody else. Mama had never told Velis the whole story, and she always wondered why Pigeon and Carl hadn't gotten married, if it was only the weight, but she figured it was too much of a sore spot so she hadn't tried to worm it out of Pigeon. "You hear from him?"

"Oh no, honey." Her voice was even quieter than usual. To hear Pigeon on the phone you'd think she was no bigger than a minute. "How bout Petey coming home, though? Isn't that just the greatest thing? I've prayed for him every single night, and looks like all our prayers are gonna be answered."

Velis
June 14, 1972

The back door clicked as Pigeon let herself in. "Yoo-hoo, honey, it's me," she called out as the door latched shut. Pigeon was reliable as the Reverend Billy Graham; if she said seven thirty, you could set your watch by it. Velis could hear her friend adjusting the deadbolt. She was sitting in a kitchen chair in the middle of the living room floor, newspaper spread beneath her, waiting. She'd already wet her hair and brought down a towel, in preparation for her haircut.

The day had about worn her out, and she was glad to just sit quiet for a minute, pleased Pigeon would be fiddling with her hair. It was so relaxing, having her mess with it. But she'd be glad when Pidge was gone, too, so she could stretch out on the sofa and watch her show. Gunsmoke tonight. One of the best. She loved Miss Kitty. She and her Mama were sure Matt Dillon would marry Miss Kitty, but he never did. Not yet. Thank goodness she'd finished the envelopes that morning and gotten them out of the house. The church secretary Della Dowdy came on in after lunch to pick them up and leave her money. Velis didn't let all the church secretaries come in the house, but Miss Dowdy had gone to school with her Mama. She'd brought two pecan pies when her Mama died. She'd never take liberties. She did things exactly the way Velis said and left the sweetest notes along with the money. The Baptists opposed rock and roll, but Miss Dowdy didn't hold that against Velis.

Plus the phone had rung off the hook all day with requests for fan club membership because of all the Madison Square Garden publicity. The Sunday paper had carried a big article about Elvis' press conference, him so cool and funny with those New York reporters, then the shows selling out, so Tupelo folks were jumping on the Elvis bandwagon big-time. About time. Velis had gotten together a dozen packets for Hal to mail. She'd have to remember to put them on the porch after the show. That was one of the best days ever for the club. Twelve new members. Why, she'd talked to seven more people who were considering joining and just called for information. And folks didn't even know, yet, about the trip to Graceland. Wait till that got around.

"Yoo-hooo. It's me, honey." Pigeon's little quiet voice whispered, again, through the dining room to where Velis was waiting in the front room. Thank goodness they'd kept that swinging dining room door, never taken it down like so many families did when they stopped having the maid serve the mid-day meal. Her Mama liked that swinging door, liked the old-fashioned things, and now Velis thanked her lucky stars for it. That way no light crept into the living room when the few people Velis let in opened the kitchen door. As long as she wasn't surprised she was safe.

"In here," she called back. Her voice sounded funny to her, out in the open like that, all loud and sharp in the quiet room, not soft like it sounded when she was talking into the telephone receiver.

Pigeon swung through the dining room door into view. "How's my girl?" she called as she walked toward Velis, who half-stood to welcome her hug. Pigeon was a world class hugger. Stout as she was, she wasn't a bit squooshy; no, her heft was solid and her embraces were like being encircled by Cassius Clay. Nothing at all sissy about those hugs. They were state-of-the-art. And she always hugged, coming and going, every time she saw you. As she pressed up against Pigeon's soothing bulk Velis wondered, not for the first time, how her Uncle Carl could bear to give up such breathtaking, warmth-producing hugs.

"I see you're all set for your hair-cut, hon." Pigeon dropped her canvas bag and embraced Velis, her own hair smelling of Prell, her moist skin emanating Ivory soap and Jergens lotion. Who could ever choose to forgo a lifetime of Pigeon's hugs?

Velis plopped back onto the straight-backed chair she'd dragged into the living room. The newspaper she'd put down crinkled as Pigeon picked up her bag and began taking out her supplies. "It's been a day, Pidge. I'm so glad you're here."

"Really?" With military precision Pigeon set out her beautician's tools on the coffee table, first spreading out a fresh hand towel. "Busy typing?"

"I finished the Cavalry Baptist envelopes this morning, thank goodness. You know what a big job that is. I don't have to start the Methodists till Wednesday, so I get a little break. But the club business has been non-stop all day."

"You don't say. People must be wanting that signed picture of Elvis in Madison Square Garden, don't you think?"

"I guess. That plus the piece in the paper. I signed up twelve new people just today. And one lady on Saturday."

"No kidding." Pigeon started combing through Velis' damp hair. Velis leaned against the chair back, her shoulders relaxing. "You want me to do anything different? Try a shorter cut?"

"No thanks. Just the regular trim."

"You've got the thickest, prettiest hair. What I wouldn't give for your hair." It was true; Pigeon's brown hair was so thin and fine it wouldn't even take a permanent. She started twisting clumps of Velis' hair into aluminum clips. "That reporter fella call you any more?"

Velis tensed. "Not today. I guess he got the word. How bout you? He been bothering you?"

"I told you I had a cup of coffee with him, didn't I, sweetie? On Saturday?" She began trimming the neck layer.

"You didn't say a word about it when you called." It was all Velis could do to keep from turning around to glare at Pigeon.

"I didn't? Goodness gracious, I don't know why I didn't. Must've been so excited about Petey coming home and all. I thought sure I told you." She kept combing and clipping, letting layers down one at a time.

Velis counted to ten inside her head. She didn't want to be the one to ask what he'd had to say, so she made herself sit still while Pigeon combed and cut. She was wondering if this Mr. Everywhere Marc Collins had asked about her and her Mama, was curious to know if he'd shown Pigeon the pictures of his twin boys he'd shown the Chandlers, but she bit her tongue to keep from asking.

"So did anybody tell you this Marc Collins is right cute, honey?"

"What do you think? Patsy was practically drooling when she called, and Helen's ready to adopt him."

"You don't say. Well, I don't know if I'd say he made me drool, but he is right easy on the eyes, and sweet as can be."

"How so? I swear, sounds like he's snowing every single soul in Tupelo." Velis couldn't help herself.

"He wears these skin tight bluejeans. And he don't talk like one of them New Yorkers, you know what I mean? He don't say youse guys or anything like that."

"His voice sounded kinda sharp-like to me."

"You talked to him?"

"Only on the phone."

"Well he talks almost normal, if you ask me, and plus he takes his time, you know? More like somebody from, say, Virginia or Maryland than from New York City."

"Is that a fact?"

"Turns out he's not from New York, originally, anyway, which sorta explains it. He's from, let me think, I guess it's Ohio. Or is it Iowa? To tell the truth, he doesn't sound like anything, really, I guess when you get right down to it."

"Is that where his wife is?"

Pigeon stopped mid-cut. "Wife? We didn't talk about any wife."

"You didn't? Hal and Helen did."

"Well tell me." She snip-snipped again.

"I don't know all that much. He's divorced, I guess. Recently. Least that's what Helen said."

"You don't say. Divorced. My, my." Pigeon came around to Velis' front and started pulling the side hair out with her hands, standing back and gauging how much needed to be trimmed. "He really just wanted to talk to me about Elvis. Not personal stuff."

"Like you and Elvis being related and all? And going to elementary school together and all that?"

"Exactly." She was trimming around Velis' face, staring at her hair, not looking into her eyes at all. "You can't hardly explain to somebody who's not from the South about second cousins; and forget once removed. He asked me so many questions about it that finally *I* was confused."

"I know. No telling what he'll have to say in his magazine about you all being kin. So did he ask to see your old school pictures? That kind of thing?"

"Right." She stood back and pondered, as though this haircut might be the factor deciding the Cold War. "That looks real good, honey. I swear, it's impossible to mess up that hair of yours."

"Did he ask about Mama? Or me?"

"Course he did." Pigeon was putting her equipment back in her canvas bag. She never hairsprayed Velis. Velis couldn't stand the smell. "I let him have our fourth grade class picture. And that picture of you all."

Velis nearly fell out of the chair. "Which one?"

"The one of you and your Mama and Elvis at the state fairgrounds, that last time he performed at the dairy show. Remember that picture?"

"Course I do. Mama loved that picture." Velis had a copy upstairs, framed, in her Mama's room. "It's right after that gal he was engaged to gave him that big kiss and people in the crowd went crazy. I can still remember the noise, mostly. The Colonel hustled me and Mama up on stage. I always thought it was cause he wanted Elvis to look like somebody's big brother instead of somebody's boyfriend. Had him pick me up and kiss me. That's the picture, right?"

"That one. You're bout seven years old and cute as a bunny."

"Thing is, I don't remember Elvis kissing me at all. Just all that noise." Velis could see the picture in her mind's eye, Elvis holding her in his arms, planting the kiss on her right cheek. Or would it be her left? Didn't the camera reverse? She touched her finger to that cheek, wanting to feel something there, but couldn't.

"I hope you're not mad at me."

"Oh," she smoothed her hair with that hand. "I do wish you hadn't given it to him. That's all. But I'm not mad." She could see her mother clear as Saran Wrap, too, smiling to beat the band, young and vibrant and just so happy she could pop up there on the stage beside Elvis Presley. They were all young and happy, frozen in that snapshot, only not frozen at all.

"I've got to be going, then. Mama likes me home before Gunsmoke starts, you know."

"Course. Thanks for the trim."

"Don't say a word. Least I can do. You let me know if you need anything at the store or anything, all right?" She held her bag over her stomach. "And think about coming over some time soon for supper, you hear? Maybe the next Avon party?"

"You hug your Mama and tell her hi for me, will you? Tell her I hope that arthritis gets better." Velis stood, was caught up in another of Pigeon's hearty embraces.

Pigeon stepped back and held onto Velis by the shoulders and stared into her eyes, her own brown eyes somber. "I swear, I think Nelly would be proud to have that picture in an article about Elvis. Don't you?"

What would her Mama want? She'd want Pigeon to be happy, that's for sure. And Velis. And she would no doubt be proud, that's probably true, for people to see Elvis kissing her little girl. "I'm not mad at you, Pigeon, honest. Just surprised is all. This Marc Collins seems to be getting to everybody."

"Okay, hon. I'm off then." She lumbered through the dining room, pushed out the swinging door, leaving the faint scent of shampoo and soap and hand lotion in the empty room. Velis heard Pidge let herself out the back. She balled up the newspaper, waited a couple of minutes, then went to set the deadbolt.

Three minutes until eight. She wouldn't vacuum until after the show. Then put the packets out. She'd maybe scrub the bathroom first thing in the morning, after breakfast, since she didn't have any typing to do. She'd dust again, too, and make some sweet tea, since the executive committee would be coming over to talk about the trip to Graceland. Goodness, things had certainly gotten out of control in just a matter of days. And it had all started with this Marc Collins coming to town. It was true: she wasn't mad at Pigeon. Who could be mad at Pigeon? But she was unnerved. It was like Marc Collins was circling her house, getting closer and closer no matter how many times and ways she said no to him. Like some vulture.

Well, to heck with Marc Collins and his snooping. He'd gotten his picture; he'd gotten all his Elvis stories. He could just go back to New York and leave her and the Tupelo Fan Club alone. Good riddance. She had no intention of talking to him again. And certainly would never meet him. She'd just go turn on the TV and watch Gunsmoke and forget he ever even existed. Maybe Matt Dillon would propose to Miss Kitty tonight. But one thing she couldn't deny: she surely would like to see that snapshot of those little twin boys of his, that was a fact.

Velis
June 15, 1972

Patsy insisted that Pigeon wait to serve the refreshments until after the new business. Scooter had a sweet tooth, and Pigeon's peanut brittle was a particular favorite of his, so he was a little out of sorts with this shift in procedure. He'd already suggested "Can't we have a plate of peanut brittle and wait on the brownies and tea?" but Patsy had brushed aside his proposal. They always had dessert and iced tea first, then settled into the business meeting, but she couldn't possibly wait a second more to tell them the new business. He sat back on the sofa, skinny arms crossed in front of his chest, dark eyes glowering behind his Buddy Holly glasses. Patsy was not to be overruled tonight.

"Thank you for those minutes, Pigeon. Any additions or corrections?" Patsy's businesslike voice snapped. She was somewhat on edge tonight, but then when wasn't Patsy edgy? The **Elvis Now** album was playing low in the background. They played Elvis at every meeting, usually the most recent release. Velis loved this version of "Hey Jude" and strained to hear it. Pigeon's minutes were unfailingly flawless, so she hadn't really paid attention.

The group sitting around Velis' coffee table didn't make a peep. Patsy leaned forward in the blue brocade wing chair, where she always sat for executive committee meetings, the regal line of the seat adding to her position of authority. Velis sat next to Scooter on the sofa. Alice lounged in the plaid overstuffed chair her Mama used to sit in to watch TV, her slender legs propped on the matching ottoman (Did she have on pantyhose? In June?). Pigeon had pulled an armchair in from the dining room and was taking notes in the club notebook propped on her sizable lap.

Charlotte Morgan

"Velis, would you please give the Corresponding Secretary's report?"

She was ready, had it typed in duplicate, one for Pigeon's minutes, one to read herself. She cleared her throat.

"I move we dispense with all other reports until the regular executive session, and proceed to new business," Scooter intervened, his brisk voice startling Velis a tad.

"Any objections?" Patsy crunched ice from her Elvis souvenir cup; she always brought her own Pepsis to the meeting. Patsy would never go anywhere without a Pepsi.

Again, no one else in the room made a sound. Velis could tell that Patsy's ice crunching was irritating Scooter, by the way he kept breathing deep and blowing out his nose, but she didn't let it bother her. Scooter usually found something to be irritated about.

"Second?" Patsy could've been a tape recording of Roberts' Rules of Order.

"I second," Pigeon whispered.

"All in favor indicate by saying aye."

Four "ayes" peppered the room.

"Any opposed?"

Silence.

"So moved." Patsy set her cup on the floor beside the chair. "Well then, let's proceed with the new business." She checked the binder on her lap.

As though she has to check, Velis thought. She was practically holding her breath, thinking that the others had no idea what was about to hit them. She wriggled just the slightest bit on the sofa cushion. Wait until they heard: an invitation to meet Elvis and have a cookout with him at Graceland.

"We have two items of new business, and I suppose we'd better dispense with the Marc Collins item first."

Marc Collins item? Everyone looked at Velis, who stared at Patsy, a "What?" escaping her mouth unwilled.

Patsy continued. "As you all know, Mr. Marc Collins of the **Rolling Stone** magazine has come to Tupelo on assignment, to write a roots piece on Elvis Presley."

The others nodded; Pigeon took notes. Velis stared. Who'd ever heard of a "roots piece" until right this minute?

"Mr. Collins has properly introduced himself to each and every one of us, is that correct?"

Even Velis had to nod assent to this question. He had called her to introduce himself, that was true. And he'd given her his card.

"So, he has asked that I bring a proposal before the executive committee tonight, as an item of new business at the special called session."

"How did he know we were meeting tonight?" Velis blurted.

Patsy gave her a disapproving look. "Velis, honey, could I continue with the item of new business before we bring it up for discussion?"

She nodded, her hands starting to sweat. She reached for a Kleenex on the end table, pressed it between her damp palms. What in the world did this have to do with the Elvis cookout?

"In any case, because we are the Tupelo Fan Club, and because this is the birthplace of Elvis Presley, Mr. Marc Collins would like to have a photograph of our executive committee in session for his article."

Ohmigod, ohmigod, ohmigod. Velis looked from person to person. Not a one met her eyes except Patsy, who faced her confused look with her own confident, steady gaze.

"He is waiting next door, at Hal and Helen's, for our decision as to whether he can come over to take the photographs."

Velis stood. "You all knew about this? You all practically invited this reporter to my house without asking me? To our meeting?"

Pigeon wouldn't look up. Alice and Scooter stared at Patsy, who barreled on. "Listen, Velis, please just sit down and let me finish, please. Scooter, would you help Velis sit down?"

Scooter made a feeble attempt to take Velis' arm but she shook him off.

"You can't possibly think I'd let this stranger come into my house, could you?"

"Velis, honey, sit down right this minute so we can continue with the new business."

Something about the bossy tone in Patsy's voice must've reached Velis' obedient citizen trigger because she did slump back down on the sofa, dazed. These people knew her, knew her home was her safe place, her sanctuary. They knew she didn't want to talk to Marc Collins, much less have him come right into her living room like he was some trusted friend or neighbor. Goodness gracious, she wasn't even certain she'd be able to let Elvis Presley himself come into her house unannounced.

"Listen here, honey, nobody's done a thing yet so just calm down. Promise me you'll calm down."

Velis stared at Patsy. Scooter edged toward the arm of the sofa on his side. Elvis was singing "Put Your Hand in the Hand." She felt distracted, confused. This reporter was next door, at Hal and Helen's? So they knew all about this, too. He wanted to come here? To the meeting? Tonight? Right now?

"Mr. Marc Collins would like to come in and take a roll of film during our meeting. He has promised me that he would not say a word. He would come in the back, with Hal, . . ."

"With Hal?"

"Velis, honey, please . . ." Patsy gave her an arch look. "Let me finish. And Hal would bring him into the living room where he would take his pictures, while we conduct our business, then Hal would take him out again. That's it. Simple as pie. If we all agree, that is. Including you, Velis."

Now they all did stare at her. Velis felt like her heart would beat right out of her chest. Her hands were all sweaty, the Kleenex no more than a shred, and she couldn't concentrate: What are the words to that song Elvis is singing right now? "Until It's Time For You To Go"? Not one of her favorites. Deep breaths. Deep breaths. Deep breaths.

"Velis, honey? Are you with us? It's time to make the motion. Then we can talk about it."

All she could do was shake her head no.

Pigeon looked up, looked at Velis. "Honey? Say something, okay? We won't do this if you say no."

Velis still couldn't speak.

"Let's forget it, Patsy. Okay? This just isn't gonna work."

"Be still, Pigeon. Does anybody want to make a motion?"

Alice spoke for the first time. Alice Alexander was the newest member of the board. She hadn't even grown up in Tupelo. Her husband came to town to start up the new Chevrolet dealership, and she met Patsy at her cleaners and they got to be friends in the Junior Woman's Club and before you knew it she was on the executive committee of the Tupelo Fan Club. Velis was always surprised that Alice had wanted to join them. She wore fourteen carat gold jewelry and diamond stud earrings and skirts with matching tops from the Neiman Marcus catalog—Patsy told Velis all these details after she and Alice got to be friends—but she'd loved Elvis her entire life and had every record and album he'd ever made plus she'd actually seen him live in Las Vegas five times. So Patsy convinced the others that Alice would be an influential member of the board, someone who could raise support with people in town who had looked down on Elvis in the past. She'd only been with them six months and she'd hardly said six words in all that time. Velis barely knew her, but a true fan of Elvis was automatically okay in her book.

"Madam Chairman, if I may?"

Surely Patsy loved the firm, orderly way Alice addressed the chair. "Yes?"

Alice took her legs off the ottoman, leaned toward Patsy. "I'm rather uncomfortable with this item of business. I mean, after all, this is Velis' house, and if she doesn't want Mr. Collins to come to our meeting tonight I say we table the whole idea."

Pigeon nodded agreement. Scooter crossed his arms again and gazed at Patsy with an I-told-you-so look.

For a moment Patsy appeared stunned, but she regained her composure almost instantaneously and directed her imperial gaze at Alice. "Is that in the form of a motion?"

Alice didn't miss a beat. "I so move."

"Second?"

Pigeon said "Second" almost before Patsy had finished saying it herself.

Patsy leaned back in the wing chair. "Any discussion before I put the motion to a vote?"

Velis had to speak, forced herself to make the words come out of her mouth. "I want to say something." Her throat was so scratchy she could hardly form the sounds.

"You don't have to say a thing, honey. It was a bad idea is all and that's that." Pigeon fidgeted in the chair, like she wanted to jump up and go over and hug Velis right in the middle of the meeting.

"Pigeon, please," Patsy insisted. "Velis has the floor."

Clearing her dry throat, Velis reached for another Kleenex and balled the used one up into it. "What I want to say is, or ask, I guess, is, did all of you know about this and agree on it before you came over here tonight?"

Even Patsy didn't say a word.

"And Hal and Helen too?"

Still not a syllable, not a breath.

"But . . . why?"

Patsy's voice was defensive. "I mean, Velis, look at it this way, it wasn't a decision or anything, just a proposal. Okay? I mean, if you didn't want us to do it we weren't going to."

"Honey, I was worried how you'd react, I really was, but it seemed like such a good idea for the club . . ." Pigeon's usually sunny face was clouded over like she might cry.

The phone rang, three rings. "I'll get that," Pigeon said, half out of her chair, but it stopped.

"It's Hal or Helen," Velis said, and sure enough it started up ringing again.

"You want me to get it, honey?" Pigeon asked, and Velis nodded her okay.

They waited in silence, only Scooter's noisy breathing disturbing the quiet. Everyone could hear Pigeon's murmurs from the kitchen but couldn't make out her words. Patsy wiggled in her seat, adjusted the hem of her miniskirt, but even Patsy didn't say a thing.

When Pigeon came back they all stared at her while she picked up her notebook and pen, sat down, opened to the minutes, until she finally said, "Hal's gonna just wait. I told him to just wait for somebody to call."

"What did he say?" Patsy snapped.

"He said Mr. Collins said it's okay, not to feel like we had to or anything, he understood Velis . . . he said Miz Emerson, actually, Hal said . . . he understood Velis might be uneasy with this whole thing and it was kinda a blindsided punch . . . that's what Hal said he called it . . . wasn't that thoughtful, honey?" She turned to Velis, her soft voice pleading, "and not to worry about it one bit if it don't work out."

They all sat, stunned. Velis wrung the Kleenex in her damp hands. This is what it means, damned if you do and damned if you don't. Her Mama always said that; she'd forgotten it until right this very moment. Somehow her heart calmed down, remembering that. It wasn't a comforting phrase at all, but she realized her heart was calming down and she could breathe easier. You do what you have to do. Wasn't that her very own motto?

The Elvis record ended and the needle made that scratchy sound over and over. Scooter jumped up to put on a new album; he was in charge of music at the meetings.

"I tell you what." Everyone froze, like they were playing swinging statues. Velis took a mouthful of air. "Maybe this would work. How about we have the refreshments and start over," she had to take another quick breath, and "after the refreshments, Patsy, you call the meeting to order, okay? and maybe then Hal could bring Mr. Collins in, if nobody says a thing about it, and we just go on about our business and don't say a single solitary thing about it and he could take his pictures and leave. For the club. For my Mama." She could hardly catch her breath she'd said so much so fast. Nobody else spoke a word either. "What do you all think of that?"

Pigeon did get up this time and leaned over the coffee table to hug her. "Why Velis, I think that's the best thing I've heard since Elvis announced his comeback special. Nelly would be tickled to death." Then she got all flustered, dropping her pen on the table, almost dropping the notebook, maybe because of what she'd said about Nelly, but Velis understood.

Patsy looked anxious and pleased all at the same time. "This proposal is definitely out of order, certainly irregular, but maybe me and Pigeon can confer later and figure out how to do the minutes."

Alice said, "Let me help with the refreshments," and that was that. It was decided without a motion or a second or a vote. Marc Collins was coming over to Velis' house in just a few minutes to take pictures of the Tupelo Fan Club's special called meeting of the executive committee.

Scooter called, "I'm putting on the greatest hits," and for some reason they all laughed, even Velis.

The back door opened while Patsy was in the process of reading the official invitation from Vernon Presley on Presley Enterprises stationery inviting the membership of the Tupelo Fan Club to come to Graceland for a cookout with his son Elvis the Saturday after Labor Day. Velis felt lightheaded. Even Patsy's businesslike demeanor could not keep Pigeon and Scooter and Alice from all talking at once. Still, Velis could hear the mens' footsteps more clearly than anything the committee members were saying, though they both seemed to be walking quietly, maybe even tiptoeing. Velis kept her eyes on Patsy, willing

Charlotte Morgan

herself not to look toward the entrance to the dining room, so that when they came into the room she would not even notice "Mister" Marc Collins, would not so much as glance his way. While she couldn't pretend that he wasn't there, she could will her mind to make him invisible.

"So, if I could have your attention, is there a motion on this invitation?"

They went through the normal routine in a flurry, and when Patsy called for discussion even Scooter could barely contain himself. They all talked over one another and Patsy kept insisting on order and taking turns but this was bigger than she was and they all knew it. Velis was aware of Hal leaning against the frame of the pocket doors—he'd made little waves, trying to catch her attention, when he first came in, but even though she couldn't help seeing what he was doing from the corner of her eye she'd avoided making eye contact with him and now he stood still as stone. Dear Hal: he would never upset her on purpose.

Marc Collins moved quietly around the room, his camera clicking. He'd started off behind her, and she could hear him moving but had no trouble ignoring him, pretending he wasn't even there, though that was only outward. Inside she noted every bend of the knee, every movement of the arms, each snap and wind, any little sound to indicate his presence and actions. When he went behind Patsy to take shots from that angle, she could see him clear as day. She forced herself to keep her face still, to not make so much as a flicker of recognition in his direction.

What had people said, that he wore tight bluejeans? He certainly did. But nobody had mentioned that they looked like he'd been wearing them, steady, for about the last five years. They were practically worn through at the knees. And that he was cute? Well, maybe. Cute was a stretch. He had on wire-rimmed glasses but she couldn't really see his eyes because of the camera. His hair was brown and wavy, kinda light brown, and long, like he needed a haircut. Too long, if you were to ask her, and in need of a brush. She liked the blue oxford shirt rolled up at the sleeves—must not be as hot in New York in June as it is here—but that looked like it could've used an iron. All in all he was not so much cute as not ugly, actually, if anyone were to ask. And he was in need of tending. That, somehow, made Velis a bit more calm, a bit less worried about whether he was taking them all for a ride or not. Though he could still be, that's a fact, she could see that he didn't come across so much as hotshot big city reporter. More like the kid in high school who was forever taking pictures at every school event, so busy doing all the documenting that he was always on the fringe, never actually took part in anything. She'd felt simpatico with that boy in her class; what was his name? Eddie Clark? Eddie Carter? That's it; he was one of the Carter boys. Thinking about Marc Collins in those terms put Velis' mind at rest. Her breathing steadied. Though she still had no intention of talking to him, he didn't seem quite so threatening a presence in her living room.

Whatever Patsy had been saying required a vote.

"I beg your pardon?" Velis said, when it was clear they were all looking at her, expecting her to say something.

"Well do you agree, is it unanimous, that we accept the invitation on behalf of the club?"

"Of course. Yes. Aye."

Marc Collins snapped a picture then. She thought it was bound to include her, given where he was standing, and hoped she didn't look too prune-faced or ill tempered or stiff. She could've smiled, actually, and not been smiling at him, but she hadn't. She'd been so busy keeping her face emotionless that she probably looked mad or mean or just plain blank. She made a conscious effort to relax.

"Velis, you'll need to write the official acceptance letter right away, then." Patsy passed the invitation to Pigeon to pass to her. Velis took the letter in her clammy hands.

This was not the first correspondence she'd touched that had actually come from the mansion office, but no matter how many times she opened a letter from Mr. Presley or Elvis' cousin Patsy Presley, who acted as secretary to his daddy, she still got a tingle of energy, like a little electrical shock. She stared at it, respectful of the connection, the near brush with greatness. "I'll write the letter of acceptance first thing in the morning. Hal'll take it right to the post office, I'm sure." She didn't look in his direction, didn't need to. She could count on Hal. No doubt that confident mention of his name and his willingness to help her sent the message she intended: she wasn't mad at him for his involvement with this Marc Collins' thing. Maybe it would turn out all right in the end, after all. Maybe.

Velis
June 15, 1972

Another envelope, her name written in that masculine handwriting, big and unavoidable. Smack in the middle of her clean kitchen table, propped against the turquoise sugar dish. Velis, of course, hadn't gone into the kitchen until Patsy called "I'm the last one out, honey. All clear. Talk to you in the morning." And she heard the door latch. And counted to ten. The committee members always put their dishes in the sink and went on, so she wouldn't have to wait by herself too long in the living room. She could take her time washing and drying the dishes, putting the kitchen straight. Now that envelope sat begging to be opened like the Academy Awards, bold as buttercups right there on the table.

Velis stared. Not a one of them had brought it in to her or come back in the living room and said a thing about it, though they couldn't have missed it. Probably knew he was gonna leave it. She got the distinct impression her friends were somehow joining forces with Marc Collins—what did the detective shows call it? In cahoots? Accomplices?—to force her to meet him. But not a one of them was coming right out and saying so. Well, Helen had hinted, sort of. And Pigeon had, too, in her own timid way. Still, they could've been more open with her. Pigeon had been right here in the living room cutting her hair just last night. She could've talked to her about it. It made Velis' skin prickle, thinking of them all planning her business and keeping it a deep dark secret from her. Her dearest friends. Her Mama's friends. And why in the world were they all so in love with this Marc Collins in the first place? Up close he was more ordinary than hotshot, nobody's pretty thing, seemed to her. Or was it his magazine that drew them, the idea of piggybacking onto Elvis' fame, some rock and roll wishful thinking? Well she certainly didn't want any tiny portion of that crazy celebrity for herself. Didn't it cause Elvis himself plenty of headache and heartache? She got trembly inside just thinking of all that idiotic attention. Poor, poor Elvis. She leaned against the counter, so tired she didn't even want to start the rinse water, but she had to. You do what you have to do.

The hot sudsy water was actually soothing, and going through the familiar, steady motions of washing and drying and putting away the dessert dishes and forks and glasses helped Velis regain a tad of her composure. As she did her chores she thought: Shouldn't they be satisfied now? She'd survived having Marc Collins in her house for that little bit, had let him take his pictures so they could all be in his article. Lord, you'd think he was writing a book of the Bible, the way they'd been carrying on since he came to town. She had to admit he'd behaved himself exactly like he'd promised while he was in the room, had been as invisible as it's possible for a man who's close to six feet tall to be, easing out when he finished without so much as a peep. She'd been anxious every second he'd been in the house, even if he hadn't made any effort to catch her eye or talk to her, though she had to admit having him there hadn't turned out to be more than she could bear. She'd gotten through it without a single bad breathing spell. But that was that, or so she'd thought.

Now here he was again, practically screaming her name in that blue block handwriting of his. VELIS EMERSON. Like he kept circling closer and closer to her personal life. Which didn't have a thing to do, in any kind of direct fashion at all, with her responsibilities as corresponding secretary. Or his magazine article, either, for that matter. What did he want from her, really? She hung the damp dishtowel over the back of one of the kitchen chairs, stretched it taut so it would dry better.

The letter sat there. It couldn't have been much more unnerving if it could talk or move across the table on its own like one of those Disney characters, the dancing broom or flying/talking elephant. Maybe she'd leave it until the morning. Tonight had already presented more than enough surprises. Velis was worn to a nub. Let Mr. Marc Collins wait until morning. What commandment said she had to read his old letter anyway? Maybe she'd just throw it in the trash then, after she'd gotten some sleep and could consider how to handle it when

Protecting Elvis

she wasn't so jangled. She turned out the kitchen light, relieved to bring the day to a dark close.

Unable to sleep, Velis flipped the pillow over to the cooler side and plumped it. The fan's steady swoosh, usually something she didn't even notice, made her teeth clench. The evening had drained her and agitated her at the same time, and not just because of Mr. Collins. They'd decided on committees and come up with a slate of committee chairmen to bring before the full membership at the next meeting. Of course Velis wouldn't be at that meeting. Or at the cookout, either. Dear Lord, wouldn't her Mama have a conniption fit, planning this trip to Graceland? Wouldn't she be the first one on the bus, the first one off, happier than happy birthday, smiling so hard her face would get sore?

Velis turned from her stomach to her side, pulled up her knees, kicked off the sheet. Sometimes she missed her Mama so much she wanted to evaporate, to disappear like I Dream of Jeannie only never come back. She never *ever* let herself think about going out of the house, just like she'd never actually made a decision not to. But all this planning to go to Graceland had forced her to face the facts: she was stuck, like some invalid or prisoner or lost-in-space astronaut.

Nosiree Bob, she wasn't about to let herself dwell on that nasty thought. What useful purpose could it serve? Velis swung her legs over the side of the bed, her pale pink Barbizon nightgown contrasting with the deep dark of the room like one of those undersea creatures on Lowell Thomas. In the bathroom at the end of the hall a tiny shell nightlight glowed, not so much because she needed it or wanted it or was afraid of the dark but because her mother had always left it on at night, as long as she could remember. Force of habit. From where she sat that dim ghostly glow gave Velis reassurance, like a pat on the top of her head. This evening her habits and routines had gotten all out of whack, and the soft faint radiance from the nightlight provided comfort. She'd get a glass of cool water, maybe take one aspirin. Just the walking to the kitchen and back might get rid of some of this nervous energy so she could rest easier.

The refrigerator cast a door-shaped patch of light onto the floor when Velis opened it to get the water bottle. Hurrying, she took out the quart jug, set it on the table, and shut the door. Light would only cause her to wake up more, and the goal was to get to sleep. As she picked up the bottle to pour her water, her hand hit the envelope. The envelope. She startled, jerked her hand away, lost her hold on the slippery glass and spilled the water. "Noooo," she moaned. "Noooo," as the chilled water ran onto her nightgown, the fabric so thin the liquid hit her legs instantly and almost made her cry, it was such a shock. Plus it was spilling all over the table, all over the floor.

She had to turn on the ceiling light to clean up the mess. The bottom of her gown was soaked, she was chilled to the bone, the table and floor were drenched, but the envelope sat there perfectly dry on the table, the water running away from it like some invisible shield protected it. Velis felt like screaming. She had the urge to say damnit, damnit, damnit, something she'd probably never said out loud once in her life, but she only whimpered "No, no, no, no, no!" into the quiet room. Righting the near-empty bottle, she grabbed the dry dishtowel off the back of the chair and put it down on the puddle on the tabletop. She'd have to run to the linen closet for a bath towel for the floor. She was wide awake, more upset than when she'd initially tried to go to sleep.

After she'd changed her nightgown and cleaned up the water she felt more out of sorts than before, sitting at the kitchen table in the bright room staring at the envelope. Until she read it she'd be agitated, she could see that now. Might as well get it over with and hope to get some sleep afterwards. Go ahead, do it Velis. Open it.

When she picked it up, finally, she was surprised by its rigid feel. Obviously more was inside than one piece of paper like before. Velis hesitated: open the dab-blamed thing, or you're gonna be sitting up all night and tomorrow you'll be nothing but a living/breathing pile of nerves.

She stretched behind her to the utensil drawer, pulled out a bread knife, slid it into the edge and made a clean slit from one end to the other. As she lifted the folded paper out she could tell right away that it was wrapped around something stiff. Probably some Elvis thing. A picture, maybe. Or more likely a subscription form for the magazine. Lord she was getting sick of that magazine, and she'd never even read it. But when she unfolded the single sheet a color photograph of two little boys dressed in astronaut outfits fluttered to her lap.

Velis picked it up right away, like she didn't want to hurt them by letting them fall. Holding it close to her face, using both hands, she stared. Anybody could tell they were twins; they had the exact same unruly white-blond hair and they were dressed alike and they were the same size. But as she looked close it was as if the face of the boy on the right squinched up, like maybe her eyes crossed just a bit while she was focusing on him. And she could see his head was a little bigger, and his features were a bit closer together, and his stumpy arms reaching for the spaceship piñata were surely shorter than his brother's. Gabe? Is that you, Gabe? she thought. Just look at him laughing. He was the sweetest, most precious little boy she'd ever seen in her entire life. More than anything she wanted to sit him on her lap and hug him so he stayed happy like he was in that picture forever.

Velis rubbed the surface of the photograph, to be sure there was no dust or lint on the children, then propped it against the sugar bowl where she could still see it while she read the hand-written note. Goodness gracious those words leaped off the page. He must've written in a hurry, the letters were so . . . lively:

June 16, 1972

Dear Velis (*she guessed it was okay if he called her that, now; he had been to her house this evening*),

I'm over here with Hal and Helen (*Hal and Helen? When did they get to be Hal and Helen to him?*) hoping I'll be able to see you in person at the meeting tonight. One way or another, they said you wanted to see the snapshot of my little boys, Gavin and Gabriel (we call him Gabe; did Helen tell you?), so here it is.

Plus I wanted to say thank you, ahead of time, for even considering letting me come over. The people here in Tupelo have all been extremely helpful and totally friendly, especially the executive committee members. I have learned *a lot* I didn't know about Elvis. I'm sure I have enough information for my article and then some. I have a better understanding, after talking with the Chandlers and the other members of the board, of what a key figure your mother was in generating respect for Elvis in his own hometown. Also of your on-going role in making the fan club such a lively, vital organization.

So, I'd still like to talk to you, but if that's not possible, well, then, I accept your decision. If I get to take the photographs this evening (our photographer went back to New York a few days ago, before I found out about the called meeting, but I'm not too bad myself), thank you for allowing that to happen. If I don't, well, sorry as I will be I understand and respect your privacy.

Charlotte Morgan

Again, here's my number at the Tupelo Towne Inn (RI 3-7764, Room 16). I'll be here finishing up odds and ends for the piece for a couple of days. You can give the picture back to the Chandlers after you've looked at it. Aren't those little guys cute, if I do say so myself? Helen tells me you and your mother had a soft spot for twins, since she was a twin and of course Elvis had a twin, too (I looked for Jesse's grave and couldn't find it), so I hope you get a kick out of my little boys. They're pretty great. <u>Please</u> call if you think we could talk, even if it's only on the telephone.

Marc (*just Marc; not Marc Collins this time*)

The note was polite enough; Velis gazed at the picture again. Gavin and Gabe Collins. She would sorely love to meet those two twin boys, especially that precious grinning Gabe.

The fluttery sensation inside her entire body, the breathing like she'd been running to answer the phone from two rooms over, the sweating hands: Why were they acting up now? Here in her still, safe kitchen. She looked around the room: everything was put away, straight. Just the knife on the table, this envelope and letter and picture. That's it. Everything in order. Had to be all the unrest tonight. All the confusion. Deep breath. Right now she didn't care a hoot about Marc Collins. She realized he was not any danger at all to her, not really. He struck her as kind of nothing. But he was the daddy of those sweet boys, and more than anything she wanted to find out about them.

But how? If she depended on Hal and Helen talking to him, they'd never ask the things she wanted to know. Even if they did, they'd forget things. Or change them, not on purpose, but change them all the same. She'd have to do it herself some way. She'd have to call Mr. Collins at his motel room in the morning and try to figure out some way to talk to him. Course she couldn't go out, that was out of the question—deep breaths, deep breaths, deep breaths—and he could never come here by himself to visit. Lord no. She knew that for a fact, sure as taxes. It wouldn't look right, period, and besides, she couldn't possibly sit in the same room and talk to him face to face, casual as you please, like he was some long lost cousin on her Mama's side. Even if Hal and Helen were here, too, she couldn't do it. But she had a desperate urge to find out about those boys of his, an urge

64

Protecting Elvis

like needing to eat or drink or lie down when you're weary. What Elvis wouldn't have given to have his own sweet brother Jesse to play with and talk to all these years.

What would she say to him, though? How would she do it? She could call like any other fan club business. She could do that. After all, hadn't he proved to her tonight he was willing to abide by her rules? She practiced in her head: *Mr. Collins? This is Velis Emerson, Corresponding Secretary of the Tupelo Fan Club. You suggested I call?* Then what? The rest would be so . . . unpredictable. She wiped her hands on her gown. He only wanted to pump her about Elvis. That was what he was after. But she was wanting something completely different. Those darling boys: Which one learned to walk first? To talk? Could Gabe keep up with Gavin? Would people make fun of them when they started getting older and Gabe didn't grow as fast as his brother? Did he feel self-conscious already about being smaller, a little different? What did his voice sound like? Oh, she'd love to see them both, to hold their dear little hands, to make a tent under the dining room table and read them make-believe stories. Play her Elvis records for them.

Or she could write Mr. Collins a note. That was another possibility. Less uncertain. Just send a note over to the hotel. Hal would take it for her. What would she say, though? She couldn't just come out and ask all that about the boys. Not at first. And she certainly wouldn't use club stationery. She could still type it, though. Handwriting would look too personal, that's for sure. But some of it *was* personal. That was the problem in a nutshell. This needing to get involved with people you didn't even care a whit about just to be able to get to what you really wanted. Oh, why did it have to be so hard? Meeting new people was not for her. The boys, though, that was a different story altogether. Little children, their Mama and Daddy getting a divorce, turning their world inside out like that. She needed to know every little thing about them, almost as much as reading about Elvis and Priscilla and little Lisa Marie in *Photoplay* or Rona Barrett. Writing a note would be easier on her nerves, that's a fact. But then she'd have to wait for an answer. That might be even more nerve-wracking than talking on the telephone. Oh, it was never easy, no matter how she tried to keep things simple. Her Mama had warned her of that more times than she could count: "Life's no pickle boat, Velis. You've got to learn to take the good with the bad."

Charlotte Morgan

This night was a muddle on top of a mess, and she was so exhausted there was no chance she could think straight, much less make a decision. She'd have to do something, write or call Mr. Collins, and she'd need to do it first thing in the morning. That was all there was to it. She picked up the picture again, and now it felt like she already knew the twins, and they knew her. Almost like she knew Elvis. They were a part of her now, in that mysterious way people connect in a flash. Like Twilight Zone.

Velis
June 16, 1972

"Wooo-hoooo, honey, I've got the envelopes."

Helen shouted up from the bottom of the stairs. Velis could barely make out what she was saying over the new Elvis album she was re-playing, since she'd hardly gotten to hear it at the meeting the night before. Elvis' voice always had a soothing effect on her, but this morning she'd listened once through and was still agitated, so she'd started it over.

Helen was dropping off her church's order. That was the agreement: Helen came in the back with the envelopes for the Methodists. Usually she left them on the kitchen table and scooted, unless she had something particular she had to tell Velis or some little something she'd found at a yard sale that she wanted to show her. Today Velis needed to be left alone, though. She was companied out, what with the extra committee meeting and the reporter in her house. Leaning over the bathtub, she paused mid-scrub to holler back. "Thanks, Helen. Talk to you later." Her voice echoed in the tub like she was under a bridge.

"I brought some coffee cake, too. You 'bout ready for a break?"

Velis was still trying to figure out what to do about contacting Marc Collins while she scrubbed out the sink and tub and toilet. So far she was no closer to a decision. Phone call or letter? She'd figured that the reason she was stuck was because the house was still out of order from the special session. Not so much messy, cause she'd cleaned up and put everything to rights, but off kilter because her timetable had gotten all switched around. Clearly that was making her mind discombobulated, too. Everything, including her thinking, would be off until she got herself back on track. So she was using the morning time she usually spent typing catching up the chores. If the phone rang she could still handle the club business. She could count on her professional tone of voice to cover for the fact that she didn't have on a proper secretarial outfit yet. Cause she couldn't bear feeling uneasy like this in her own house, in her own skin, so she'd decided: No more tinkering with her daily to-do list, no matter how much Patsy begged. And Patsy would be begging non-stop, no doubt about it, with this ultra-special event in the works. Thank goodness she didn't have to start the Methodists till tomorrow morning. She could use today to get her life settled. But now here was Helen. With coffeecake.

"You hear me up there, Velis? I brought you a treee-eeeeat."

Wasn't the house usually downright quiet? Most weeks, she'd go without seeing a single living soul except for the people on her shows, except of course Hal and Helen. Seemed like for days now the traffic in and out of the house wouldn't stop. And here was Helen, right when Velis was trying to reclaim some semblance of order, with one of her dried out coffee cakes that Velis could hardly choke down. Helen was a terrible cook, but she was a doubly dreadful baker. She never ate her own sweets, had to watch her sugar, so she had no idea how awful her goodies turned out. Her cupcakes never sold at the church bazaars, which always came as a surprise to her. They were Hal's favorites, or so he claimed, to keep the peace.

"You coming down?"

Velis leaned back on her heels. Could she dare yell down and say she was too busy? Imagine Helen's face, letdown. Besides, they could maybe talk about Gavin and Gabe. Helen might know more, since she'd gotten so chummy with Marc Collins all of a sudden. Pulling the yellow plastic gloves off, Velis called, "Be right there. Would you go ahead and get the plates out for us while I wash my hands?" Daggone: Here she was, doing it again, leaving her chores unfinished, getting off the plan. The Comet was bound to get crusty in the tub. Well, somebody had told her—was it Pigeon?—that if you left it on a while it cleaned better. Still, in no more than a morning's time she was already guilty of what she'd promised herself she wasn't gonna do any more: fiddle with the routine. But this wasn't her fault. She couldn't turn Helen away, not after everything she did for her. She might have to lock herself in the office for a week if this kept up, though. She understood exactly how Elvis felt, wanting to close himself up in his room to get away from all the commotion. Who could blame him?

Helen sat at the kitchen table with her little red aluminum and sandbag ashtray in front of her—she took that ashtray everywhere—staring at the snapshot of the boys. She held her cigarette down towards the floor, cause she knew Velis didn't like her smoking, as if hiding it would make it one bit better. She'd turned the stove fan on low, too. Velis insisted on running the fan to get rid of the cigarette smell. Helen couldn't go ten minutes without a cigarette, which is why she volunteered at every one of her church's activities but never went to Sunday services, so it was a given that she'd smoke when she came over. Velis would never allow anybody else to light up in her kitchen, but she'd never think of asking Helen to stop, either.

"I cut you a hunk of coffeecake, honey. It's there on the counter." Helen nodded her head in the direction of the sink. "Ain't these two precious? Didn't I tell you?"

"Thanks. I don't know if I can eat all that. I already had breakfast a while back."

"Don't be like that. Everybody needs a little treat now and then. You got any coffee left?" One thing was for sure: Helen never changed. There she sat in her plaid cotton shirt and elastic-waisted polyester pants, smoking her everlasting Kool long, the same wavy permanent in her white-gray hair she'd had as long as Velis could remember, the same blue plastic glasses, the same heavy fuschia lipstick, a little smeared on her front teeth.

"Let me fix a pot." Velis took her time getting the coffee ready, not wanting to come to the minute where she'd have to eat at least some of Helen's cake.

"Hal and I are right proud of you for letting Marc take his pictures last night."

Bristling a bit at the sound of Helen calling Marc Collins Marc, all this buddy-buddy stuff, she wiped her hands on a tea towel. "I couldn't hardly let the executive committee down, now could I? They were crazy to get their pictures in a magazine."

"I talked to Pigeon this morning and she said . . ."

"You did?" Velis sat, used a fork to cut off a bite-sized triangle of cake, crumbled it and pushed it around the plate.

"I called over to the beauty shop to see if Pigeon had gotten my Avon order in yet, and she said . . ."

"So did Mr. Collins talk to you much about his twins while he was at your place?"

"I guess he did." Helen smashed her cigarette butt in her ashtray, stood to check the coffee. As usual she was wearing her latest pair of faded terrycloth slippers. Helen never put on shoes unless she was going to town. "Dang your pot's slow. I should've brought some of my own." She sat back down and lit another Kool. "Anyway, course he did. That's practically all he talked about. Hal, of course, had to bore him to death talking about fishing. As if Marc cared. But he's too polite to his elders to ever stop him. That's a trait you don't see all that much any more."

"What did he say?" Velis shoved the plate away.

"I tell you this, you'll never find a prouder Daddy." Helen stared at the stove, but the coffeepot wasn't perking.

"Did he show you any other pictures?"

"He's got one in his wallet of them in little plaid vests and matching bow-ties. That must've been their Christmas picture. I think that's what he said."

"I'd love to see that. Is it as cute as the birthday party?"

"Well, honey, he'd be happy to show it to you if you asked. You'd be surprised at what a sweet young man he is. Not the least bit snobby. Last night he even offered to help Hal put a new battery in the car."

Velis picked up her fork and started tracing on the tablecloth with it.

"Velis, honey, what's the matter?"

The coffeepot burbled as the strong smell of brewing coffee filled the kitchen; Helen stood, again, and this time poured herself a cup, then lifted the pot in Velis' direction. "You want any? I can't wait another minute." Velis shook her head. "All this to-do over the magazine article getting to you, honey?"

Nodding, Velis said, "I been thinking about Mama a lot lately."

"Lord, Hal and I miss Nelly. Every day. More than every day. Every time I turn around, seems like."

"Me too."

"That Nelly, she had a laugh could make everybody in the room laugh too. Remember her laugh?"

"Course I do."

Helen drank her coffee and stared at the picture of the boys while Velis sat still, not even playing with the fork any more.

"I don't know. This reporter coming to town, all this stuff going on with the fan club—I promised not to tell anybody, not even you, but it's a really big deal, take my word—and now these little boys. It's like it's all making me sad and I don't know why."

"Honey, I hope you don't mind that me and Hal been having him over. We get kinda hungry for company, you know? But if you want me to talk to Marc I know he won't bother you no more about Elvis and the fan club. He said so last night, while he was waiting to hear what y'all decided."

"He said as much in his letter there—" Velis pointed at the envelope propped between the salt and pepper shakers—"but that's not the trouble. I'm not sure what the trouble is. I know I want to find out about little Gavin and Gabe. I know that much. But I'm not even sure why. Sounds idiotic, but soon as I saw them I felt like they were family. You know? They look so precious."

"Them astronaut outfits are darling, weren't they? I asked Marc where he got them . . ."

"It's gotten so jumbled up and I think if Mama was here she could help me sort it all out again. I thought I had everything straight, but more and more I can barely get my breath . . ."

Helen sat her cup on the counter and leaned down and put a firm hand on each one of Velis' shoulders. "You listen to me, girly. Me and Hal loved Nelly like she was our own daughter. And you?" She put her head right up against Velis'; Aquanet hairspray and cigarette mingled with the scent of face powder. "Good Lord, I held you the day you were born, changed your diapers when Nelly brought you home from the hospital, made every Halloween costume you ever put on your back. Anything bothering you, Velis, anything at all, why you know me and Hal gonna be right here."

"I know." Velis reached up and patted one of Helen's hands. "What would I do without you?"

Helen stood and reached over Velis for her pack of Kools. When she'd lit one with the BIC lighter she carried in her pocket, she blew out a long puff of smoke in the direction of the back door, then poured herself a fresh cup of coffee. "Anybody talk to you yet about Petey coming home?"

"Patsy told me last week." Velis stood to scrape the coffee cake into the trash. Helen didn't seem to notice that she hadn't eaten a single bite. As she was washing the plate and fork she leaned forward and rested her elbows on the counter. "Course Patsy'll plan a celebration to beat the band and invite all her friends and all the Pinckneys' friends and any of Tupelo she's looking to impress."

"Don't you know."

"And Petey will be counting the minutes till he can get out of there."

"I reckon." Helen sat down again. "Course, you never know. People say you never can tell how that Viet Nam's gonna change a boy. Petey so quiet and all." She shook her head. "All kinds of talk about drinking and drugs and I don't know what all."

Velis pictured him sitting next to her on the sofa, hardly even smiling at the funny parts of Carol Burnett or Mary Tyler Moore. Petey was as solemn as Patsy was outgoing. How could Viet Nam make him any less serious? Seemed to her it was bound to work the other way.

"Wasn't no secret that Petey was sweet on you, Velis."

"He was a good friend is all." And she knew that's all he could ever be. Imagining herself Helen's age, she couldn't envision still sitting on the sofa beside Petey, year in year out, like neither one of them had ever moved an inch, like two aging rocks. He probably wouldn't want to see her again anyway, but if he did, well, they'd only be friends. No more.

"Oh, honey, I wish you wouldn't shut yourself off from other young people like you do."

Folding and refolding the tea towel, Velis stared at her hands. "People can be downright hateful, Helen, and you know it. Look at how they treated Elvis right here in his own home town."

"But they can be nice too, Velis. Nice as can be."

"I guess."

"I know you don't want to hear it, but Marc is as nice a young man as I've ever met. And even if you don't want to talk to him about Elvis—that's your perfect right, honey, and if that's your decision well, that's that—I still would bet my bottom dollar he'd be happy to talk to you about the boys. Want me to ask him?"

"I wouldn't know what to ask, Helen. That's part of the problem. I been thinking about it all morning. I don't really want to talk to him myself that much. I'd get so nervous I'm afraid I'd clam up and then I wouldn't really be able to carry on a personal conversation. Even on the telephone. You know how I get. But if I write a letter, then I'd have to wait. And I don't know, I'm not sure I want to write down a bunch of questions about the boys. Like 'Which one talked first?' 'What's their favorite things to eat?' I mean, writing stuff like that out would look downright dumb, wouldn't it?"

"Well talking would probably be easier, more natural, I guess . . ."

"That's right. IF I could sit down and talk to him. Which I can't. So we're right back to where we started."

"Want me and Hal to find out what you want to know?"

"Thanks, Helen." Velis smiled. "I know you'd do that for me. I even thought of asking you. But then what if you forget some of the stuff he says? Maybe that'd be the very stuff I wanted to know."

They sat a moment, Helen smoking the last of her cigarette, Velis rubbing her hands on her housecleaning apron.

Helen leaned forward. "You still got that tape recorder?"

"I do. It's up in the office."

"We could talk to him, and tape what he says, and you could listen. Here in the house, by yourself, safe as Santa Claus."

"That's a pretty good thought, Helen, I never thought of anything like that, but wouldn't that be kinda like eavesdropping, in a way?"

"Don't be ridiculous. I wouldn't think of doing it without telling Marc first."

"I don't know. Wouldn't you feel self-conscious?"

"Lord no. Hal would get a kick out of it. You know how he loves gadgets."

"You think Mr. Collins would do it?"

"Won't hurt to ask. He's got a tape recorder himself, come to think of it. I remember he brought one the first time he came to the house, when he interviewed me and Hal about our Elvis recollections."

"Wonder if his tapes would work on my machine?"

"Ain't they all the same?"

"I don't know. Mine's pretty old and he's probably got a brand new one."

"Well we won't know till we find out, now will we?" Helen was emptying her ashtray into a paper towel. Velis didn't like her to leave the ashes in her trash can cause the stale smoke smell lingered.

"That's a fact."

"So I'll ask him what he thinks of this and let you know. I'll call him soon as I get in the house." Helen stacked her cigarette pack on top of the ashtray.

"And you just keep the rest of that coffeecake. I cut Marc a big piece before I left. I was planning to call him anyway."

"I appreciate the thought, Helen, I really do. Maybe I ought to think this idea over and give you a call later . . ."

"What's to think about? Nothing ventured, nothing gained, right?"

Velis shrugged.

"You just get on back upstairs and I'll let myself out. I haven't been this keyed up since the Pinckneys asked me to do the costumes for Patsy's Miss Tupelo pageant. Remember?"

"Don't we all. Your evening gown was the best thing about that fiasco."

"I'm gonna talk to Hal and talk to Marc and call you, so listen for the phone, okay?"

Again Velis shrugged, nodded, mumbled "Okay" as she pushed the swinging door into the dining room. She could hear Helen bustling around the kitchen and letting herself out. She'd start the Elvis album again and go back up and finish the bathroom. What was she letting herself in for, with this notion of Marc Collins tape recording? But Helen was right: What harm could it do? It wasn't like she was going to have to meet Marc Collins face to face. She would so much like to know about the boys.

Her hand on the hi-fi dial, she stopped: She wasn't agitated, not one iota. Her breathing was steady, perfectly normal. Her hands weren't the slightest bit sweaty. She was calm: calm as a cucumber. Now wasn't that something? Here she was, cooking up a plan with the Chandlers to communicate with Marc Collins, and she wasn't at all nervous. Wonder why, she thought, pushing the automatic on button. Elvis sang to her, that soft mellow voice like no other, and she smiled: "Take the ribbon from your hair; shake it loose, let it fall . . ."

Three rings. Rubbing the towel through her wet hair Velis waited. Pause. Then ringing again. Helen. Or Hal. She checked the wall clock: 9:24. Helen would never give up. Most nights Velis was grateful she could count on Helen to check up on her if any little thing changed at the house, like the kitchen light came on at odd hours or some unknown car showed up in the driveway. Tonight she took her time picking up the phone. "Hello? Helen?"

"Oh honey, I could hardly wait till Carol was over to call. Won't she a riot tonight? Then I knew you'd be washing your hair . . ."

"I just got done a couple of minutes ago."

"I know. I was looking out the window at the light, thinking you were probably done, hoping you'd had enough time. Oh, I've got the best news." Helen's voice sounded like she'd just been picked for the Ted Mack Amateur Hour.

"What's that?" Velis put the damp towel over the back of the chair and ran her fingers through her wet hair.

"He thinks it's a great idea. He's gonna do it, Velis. Do you believe it? We can start tomorrow."

"Tomorrow?"

"He's gonna bring his tape recorder. And he says for Hal to get yours and he'll check it out to be sure they'll, you know, both play the same tapes and all. He says they probably will, but we oughta check. Isn't that terrific?"

"So he's willing to talk to you two about the little boys? And tape it?"

"Course he'd rather talk to you himself, but since that don't seem like it's gonna work, well, he said he'd thank heaven for small favors. Just exactly what he said."

"No kidding."

"Plus, oh yes, I almost forgot—I'm telling her right now, Hal—he says you can certainly look at the picture from his wallet. He took it out soon as I asked. Hal's gonna bring it over and leave it by the back door. In a envelope, of course."

"Tonight?"

"Yeah. In a few minutes. Hal's looking for his slippers right now. I tell him all the time not to walk around the house in his sock feet, he's gonna slip and break his neck, but you know Hal. Anyway, he's gonna put it on the shelf for you tonight. Didn't I tell you Marc's the nicest fella?"

About a million times. "Yes. You sure did." She took her big black comb out of her robe pocket and started pulling it through her tangled hair.

"Well it's a fact."

"I'm not so crazy about this idea, Helen. I'm not so sure it's gonna work."

"We're gonna do it. That's that. Plus—and this is the best part, you ask me—Marc says maybe he'll bring the boys on down to meet us, when he gets some time off, he's feeling so, how did he put it? feeling so at ease with us and all. Like we were his own grandparents. Turns out he never knew either one of his granddaddies and his one grandmother was mean as a snake. He and Hal have really struck it off. Ain't that the nicest thing you ever heard, him saying that about us?"

"Really? Bring the boys here to Tupelo? He said that?" She stopped combing.

"You know good and well I wouldn't tease you about something like that." Helen's voice sounded a tad quiet, like her feelings were hurt. Or maybe she was just leaning back from the phone lighting a Kool.

"Oh, Helen, I'm sorry. I didn't mean YOU were kidding. But do you think HE was kidding?"

"Course not. He wants Hal to show them how to fish. Maybe not this year—they're just three right now, you know—but some time, when they're a little bigger. Marc don't know a thing himself about the outdoors."

Velis leaned against the fridge, wrapping the phone cord around the comb.

"You still there, honey?"

"What I don't get is *Why*? Why would he do this?"

Helen took a long drag. "Thing is, Velis, he wants you to make a tape too."

She almost dropped the phone. Her comb was all twisted up in the cord now.

"Velis? You hear me? See, the reason he thinks it's such a good idea—I'm telling her, Hal—is cause he likes the idea of you taping your thoughts for him. About Elvis growing up in Tupelo and all. Said 'Now why in heck didn't I think of that myself?' only he didn't say heck. Said, you know, h-e-double-l. I didn't much like him saying h-e-l-l, but Hal says I was being a fuddy duddy, the boy just got excited. Says Preacher Hall uses it all the time. Anyway, Marc apologized, said it slipped out, but still."

"He wants me to make a tape for him?" Her shaky hands had a hard time unraveling the comb. When she got it she tucked it back in her pocket.

"Well, honey, I wouldn't make too much of it. You don't have to say a thing you don't want to say—don't let the blamed screen door slam, Hal, you hear!—ain't that a lot better than having to talk to him face to face?"

"I don't know if I could do that, Helen."

"Hal's on the way with the picture, honey. We can talk about it some more in the morning, okay? I just couldn't wait to tell you is all. And in a few minutes you can get the picture off the porch. It's not as good as the other one, I don't think—had it made in a studio, for his parents and her parents last Christmas, when they was still together—and I don't think the boys look natural like at the birthday party. But it's still mighty cute."

Velis could hear her porch screen slam, could make out Hal's slippered feet moving across the screened-in porch toward the shelf next to the back door. He swoosh swoosh swooshed on the porch floor then slippered away, the outside door banging not so hard the second time.

"Velis?"

"I'm here. Hal's on the way back. You tell him thank you for me, okay?"

"All right, honey. And you get your tape player out and put it on the shelf, will you? Before you go to bed? Hal can get it in the morning, but go ahead and put it out tonight, so Marc can take a look at it."

"I know where it is."

"Good night, then, Velis. Isn't this gonna be fun?"

"We'll see. Bye now."

As she hung up the phone, in slow motion, holding onto the receiver, Velis thought: *Fun?* Helen thinks I'd have *fun* talking into a tape recorder to Marc Collins? I'd have more fun cleaning the basement. Or going to the dentist. And she hadn't been to the dentist in over three years. Could she refuse, though? Just give up the idea of making contact with little Gabe and Gavin? Pressing her lips together, taking in a big breath, she turned out the kitchen light and eased the back door open.

The muggy night air was heavy. In the haze she could smell the strong scent of the rambling rose out back. For a minute she stood there, the door cracked, and closed her eyes. Her Mama had loved that rose, would cut blooms and bring them into the house as soon as it started to blossom. She'd say, "Velis, honey, come here and look. Have you ever seen such a red? Candy heart red. Just come in here and smell that first rose smell, honey." And they'd have to change them every few days. They opened fast, so they looked more like wallpaper than those florist roses. Velis'd have to get Helen to cut some for her in the morning. Put them in that blue vase, set it in the middle of the dining room table. Where was that vase? She couldn't remember the last time she'd seen it. Goodness gracious, had she gone all this time without bringing any roses into the house?

With her right hand she felt along the shelf and there was the envelope, feeling light, almost empty. She shut the door and bolted it, stared at the blank place where her name should've been. No Velis on the front of this one. It looked so . . . empty. Hal must've gotten one of Helen's envelopes from her kitchen desk. That's right: Marc Collins took the picture out of his wallet and gave it to them, so he wouldn't have had an envelope with him. Still, he could've at least put her name on the front. Or some little message about the boys.

She slid the wallet-sized photo from its cover and held it up: Oh. They took her breath, they looked so dear. Gavin stood behind Gabe, his hands on his brother's shoulders. Gabe held a small teddy bear in his tiny hands—probably one of those studio props. Their blond hair was combed in that stiff Christmas-picture way. But their smiles lit up the room, they were smiling so natural, so full of running outdoors in the sprinkler and taking baths together and knocking over block towers. She could swear she knew exactly how they were laughing right when the picture was taken. The goofy photographer probably held up the other bear, one just like the one Gabe was holding, so he got them to both look up like that right at that instant. And he no doubt said something silly like "Smokey the Bear wants you two to say *Santa Claus is coming* right when he says three. Okay, little guys, look right here at Smokey: One . . . two . . . three: *Santa Claus is coming!*" Oh, Velis could hear their little laughs clear as a Christmas bell, as if she'd heard them a million times already.

Gabe's features weren't so very different in this shot, and Gavin was plainly proud of his brother. Velis could see he'd look after him. But Gabe didn't look like he needed a bit more looking after than his twin. Anybody could tell he was a hundred percent boy. Why, he didn't have the slightest little sad look in his eyes. Not at all.

What could she do? She leaned the photo beside the other one: She'd have to make a tape of some sort. What would be the harm? Surely she could talk about Elvis a little bit into a tape recorder. Stuff everybody around town had probably told Marc Collins already. Course she'd never show him the scrapbooks or her Mama's private collection: Elvis signing her 6th Grade autograph book (U-R-2-Sweet-2-B-4-Gotten, from Your Friend, Elvis); the note after the first time he sang "Old Shep" at the Dairy Show (What did you think, Nelly? Was I too nervous? Did you think I would win first place? Elvis); the Get Well Card and all the Christmas Cards from Graceland, with personal notes to Nelly. And the Teddy Bear he'd sent for her own eleventh birthday, with a heart tag on the ribbon that said For Velis, and on the back of the heart, Love, Elvis. Her Mama never knew why he sent a present for that one birthday. She'd sent him a school picture every year, and most years he sent a card, but that year he surprised her with the bear. That was Elvis, though—unpredictable. Probably cause of the song going Number One. And the snapshots at the Hayride, some of her favorites: real snapshots, not the publicity photographs the Colonel sent out. (Here I am at the Hayride, Nelly! Do you believe it? Did you listen? Your old friend, Elvis NOT the Pelvis). She'd never ever tell about those. But the other stuff, the Tupelo stuff, she could tell him what she knew about all that, maybe even set the record straight on some things, since half the so-called facts people said were closer to lies anyway. Her Mama would like that.

Helen said the boys might actually come here. To Tupelo. That's what she'd do then: she'd make a tape of some sort for Marc Collins. It'd be worth it, to have Helen bring those little guys over here one day. She'd make them frozen juice icecubes in the ice tray like her Mama used to make her when she was little. And bring down the Lincoln Logs from the attic. And put on "Hound Dog" and let them dance around the living room and jump on the sofa and crawl under the dining room table. Oh, they'd have the best time. Maybe they could even sleep over, once they got to know her and got comfortable in the house, and she'd make a tent under the dining room table and pull down a mattress and read stories by flashlight. She'd get Hal to get them each their very own little flashlight from the hardware. They'd have the best time.

Grabbing her towel and comb Velis headed for her Mama's room, to get the tape recorder and put it out for Hal. Right that minute, before she lost her courage. Nothing ventured nothing gained: How many times had Nelly told her that? She frankly couldn't believe she was actually going to venture this, though, but she was. Oh my yes she was.

Velis
Tape Talk #1

I'm not really sure what you want, I mean Helen told me you just want me to tell you anything I remember about Elvis and growing up in Tupelo and all that, so I'm just gonna talk, so here goes.

I was in the D.E. program at Tupelo Consolidated. Of course Elvis never went there, but you know that. He was in Memphis by high school. Anyway, I was the first person in my family to finish high school, just like Elvis. A lot of people don't know what D.E. stands for. Some of the Tupelo first families, so-called, their kids would look down their noses at the girls in D.E. Secretarial. Like it's training to be a lifelong idiot. Kinda like they've always looked down on Elvis, you know? But being a capable secretary takes a lot of skills—multiple skills, they told us in class. And personal grooming. And a knack for dealing with the public, kinda figuring out human nature on the spot. So if you think about it it takes a lot. I'm proud of my Distributive Education diploma. I can tell you it gave my Mama a lot of comfort there in her last days, to know I had a reliable vocation to fall back on. Even if, by then, I was hardly going out. Still, knowing she'd passed down the house free and clear, I think that and my diploma gave her a lot of peace. Plus Elvis' greatest hits. She never got tired of hearing "Love Me Tender," "Loving You," "Heartbreak Hotel." The tears would stream down her face whenever she'd get to the end of her favorite album and he'd be singing "Can't Help Falling in Love." Happy tears. Not sad. Like aren't I lucky to hear Elvis, to have grown up here in Tupelo and known him from the first. I know just how she felt.

That's about all I can think of to say right now. Remember to tell Helen anything you can think of about the boys. Just anything at all. Do you have any other pictures? I'd sure like to see some more, okay?

Oh: Did Hal and Helen already tell you this?

Mama couldn't name me Elvis—only one Elvis. Plus it's a boy's name. And she couldn't name me *after* Elvis, cause what would people in Tupelo think, in their sick little minds? So she named me Velis, for Elvis, Elvis lives. Said I was one of a kind, like Elvis, to her. Plus she named me Jesse, too, cause she'd never seen a person love a child like Gladys loved Elvis and Jesse, even though Jesse was stillborn. Not until she had me did she see how a Mama could love a child like that, she said, so it struck her to name me Jesse, too, for that one-of-a-kind tenderness she felt for me the instant I was born. That's how I got to be named Jesse Velis Emerson. Mama said we might even be kin to Elvis, cause we have Tennessee Loves in our family tree and so do they. But I think that was just wishful thinking on her part, though I do have high cheekbones and my hair is the exact same sandy color as his before he dyed it. My official signature, for club business and checks and any tax purposes, is J. Velis Emerson. I've never been known as Jesse.

There's the phone. Be sure you put in how much the Tupelo club is growing when you write your article. Plus the special event coming up that we can't even tell you about yet. Talk to Patsy. Bye.

Velis
Tape Talk #2

Hal and Helen Chandler live next door. You know that. I don't know why I even said that. This thing makes me a little uneasy. Anyway, they were both born right here in Tupelo, so they know all there is to know about the goings-on in town. They've seen it all. He's retired from the Tupelo Hatchery. First shift supervisor for the last eight of his thirty-five years. He knew Vernon a little bit, but not much. Claims he was shiftless, to tell the truth. More the ladies man than people let on. Helen knows everybody in town but she never knew Gladys Presley or any of her kin, the Loves and the Smiths, I guess cause they were all mostly out there in East Tupelo. Every now and then she would see Gladys in Piggly Wiggly. Always had Elvis with her. He'd be neat and clean in those old worn clothes of his, but skinny as a stick. Helen said some sad, shy look about him made her want to take him home, but those two were always kinda set apart. Didn't pay much attention to anybody else. Gladys was a strange one, both my Mama and Helen said that, not quite right, and she kept Elvis right with her all the time. Seemed like she couldn't hardly let him breathe.

Helen never had children of her own, she didn't work, see, and most of the time Gladys didn't either. At least not after Elvis was born. Helen would've been a good Mama, that's for sure. Not near so protective as Gladys, I don't think.

Hal was a good provider, too. He wanted Helen at home, but she had to be doing something all the time, still does, so she hired out sewing. Made costumes for pageants and school plays. Some of the Tupelo upper crust families would pay her to make Halloween costumes for their children. Not the Presleys, of course. I remember once she made a Good Witch gown and crown and the whole deal, scepter and all, that turned out more beautiful than Glenda's in the movie. I could've spit when Ann Carol Allison won the Parade of Costumes that year. Helen's costume deserved the prize, don't get me wrong, but Ann Carol didn't. She was way too hateful to be a good witch. Helen made perfect cowboy outfits, too, like Roy Rogers and Dale Evans. You couldn't tell them from the real thing.

One year for Christmas she made me my own mouseketeer outfit, ears and all, with my name Velis embroidered on the shirt. I loved that outfit, I can't tell you how much. I thought I looked exactly like Annette's little sister in it, except my hair's not near as curly. Or as dark. Still, I felt like Annette's little sister anyway. Whenever I wore that costume I wanted to be on the TV show in the worst kind of way. I'd be singing "Today is the day that is filled with surprises" like the studio audience was right in front of me, the cameras were on. I knew exactly what it felt like to be a mouseketeer, to be a star. Like Elvis. Helen could sew anything, didn't even need a pattern.

She and Hal would have me and Mama over to eat once a week, every Thursday. Helen wasn't much of a cook. Mama would bring dessert so she'd know we'd have one thing I liked. But despite the dry meat loaf or runny spaghetti sauce I loved eating supper at Hal and Helen's cause they kidded one another all the time. Silly stuff. She'd say, "Don't come into my kitchen smelling like some catfish, Mr. Chandler" and he'd say "This is one catfish you were lucky to catch, Mrs. Chandler." Like that. I'd imagine my Mama and Daddy, happy like that, teasing, since I don't have a single memory of the two of them together. I don't have any memory of him, really, except from photographs and Mama saying "You remember the day we did such and such." But I don't. He died when I was four. It's hard to miss somebody you didn't ever know.

I probably shouldn't even send you this, ought to just go ahead and erase it. I got off on the Chandlers, I guess, and they already talked to you about Elvis. I'll try again tomorrow. But could you send on another picture? The Christmas one was so cute. I do love the birthday party best, but I'd sure like to see some more. Do you have any of them dressed up for Halloween?

Velis
Tape Talk #3

It like to killed Elvis when his Mama died. His people here in Tupelo, her people, the Loves and all, none of them even went to Memphis to the funeral. Course her sister Cletes and Vernon's brother Vestor—you know all about the Love sisters marrying the Presley brothers, I'm sure—anyway, they were already there. Vestor worked at Graceland at the gate. By the end there Gladys had gotten too sad, with Elvis gone so much of the time and Vernon with his wandering ways. Said she felt like a prisoner there at Graceland. She didn't keep in touch with her own kin back home there at the end. Plus it happened so fast.

I know about fast. My father died when I was four. He drowned. Me and my Mama were right there at the beach, she always told me, but I don't remember, and he drowned. Mama had walked me to a little stand to get a treat, to get a snow cone, is what she always said, and when we got back to the blanket a crowd had gathered and the people were pointing, looking out at the gulf, and my Daddy had drowned. Just like that. I've never been back to the shore, not once.

When Mama died, over three years ago, I remember every bit of that. The going to the hospital. The glare of the lights, day or night. The ambulance coming, all hours, five times in all. Riding to the hospital in the car with Hal and Helen, the window cracked, the cold fresh air coming in so they wouldn't get carbon monoxide poisoning, according to Hal. Waiting in the waiting room. People smoking. Strangers coming and going, crying, some of them, or fussing with one another. "How come you didn't call Uncle Carl and tell him 'bout

Nelly being so bad?" I remember every second of all this, closed inside the house, safe.

I don't remember ever kissing my father, either. I see a man in a photograph kissing a baby, holding her up over his head and kissing the air in front of her face. It's a black and white snapshot, the white edges scalloped like little shells. When I look at that snapshot—the man in profile, his lips puckered, the baby, arms mid-flail—it could be any man, any baby, but my mother always told me that it's me and my Daddy when I'm six months old. That day my Daddy came home from work—he still has on a white shirt from the insurance office, but he's not wearing a tie, the collar's open—Mama says he's just gotten home and he picked me up right away, as soon as he came in the door, and he swore I said "Da-Da" so he made Mama run and get the Kodak and snap a picture right away of the day I said my first word. Only I don't remember any of it—the feel of his hands picking me up, the sounds of his voice or his laugh, him saying my name, Velis, out loud even once. He smoked Camel cigarettes, Mama told me; he'd get me to blow out the matches. But I can't remember any of it—not the smell of the cigarettes, not the matches flaring close to my face, not even what flavor snow cone I was eating the day he drowned.

Besides, the smell of a cigarette makes me gag.

You don't smoke, do you? Please don't smoke around those little boys. It's not good for them.

Velis
Tape Talk #4

I didn't tell you about getting this tape recorder, did I? Right now I can't think of anything else to say.

When I was in fifth grade I made a best girlfriend, Elsie Jane Giancatterino. Mama had been so pleased—up till then my report cards would be straight A's, but under comments the teacher would write something like "Velis would benefit from greater socialization skills" or "I wish Velis would make more attempts to make friends with her classmates." Like that. I'd go to Vacation Bible School and Saturday Morning Explorers at the county rec, but I wasn't the kind of girl that other girls came up and talked to or invited to birthday parties unless their Mama made them.

Elsie Jane was a bit pudgy, really the tallest girl in the room. Her one grandmother lived in New Jersey and didn't speak a word of English, she swore to me, but her Mama was from Tupelo and her Daddy got a good job at the electric company so Elsie Jane started school here in fifth grade. She sat next to me and we got to be best girlfriends. Most afternoons we would play Monopoly on the screened back porch at our house. I never did go to her house. I don't know why. Elsie Jane spent the night a few times and Mama made popcorn balls and green Kool-Aid and we got to stay up late and watch Laugh-In.

Summer after fifth grade right after school let out Elsie Jane had to go to New Jersey to visit her other grandmother and go to the shore for a month. Mama bought us both little tape recorder machines. Course we could write letters and send picture postcards, but Mama thought we would really have fun sending one another tapes. Something extra special for best girlfriends.

Goodness, Mama spent all that money to surprise me and my girlfriend. I don't remember ever being more excited about a present.

I took a lot of time making that first tape. I said something into the microphone every day for a week. And recorded songs I liked from the radio, put the little microphone right up to the Bel-Tone and it sounded pretty good. Three Elvis songs: "Little Sister" and "Can't Help Falling in Love" and our newest favorite, "Return to Sender." We both adored Elvis. I didn't like the sound of my own voice at all, but I couldn't wait to get a tape back from Elsie Jane so I did it. Sent it to the house in Newark where Elsie Jane's grandmother lived. I didn't have the address for the shore. Decorated the thick brown envelope with drawings of our Monopoly pieces: Elsie Jane was always the Scottie dog; I got the top hat. But I never did get a tape back from Elsie Jane. Not even one. Or any postcards either. And that fall Elsie Jane didn't come back to Tupelo for school. Her family stayed in New Jersey, somebody said.

Once that next Christmas I saw Elsie Jane's Tupelo grandmother in the Piggly Wiggly, but she must not've seen me cause she didn't say hello.

After Mama died, when I was getting the house organized, I found this tape recorder with its little microphone in its box in one of Mama's bedside tables. It still had one new tape in the package. Instead of putting it out for Helen to take to the charity box at church, I kept it in my office. I had the idea that maybe some time I might use it for club business. I wasn't sure what, but thought it might come in handy. Waste not want not. Besides, Mama wanted me to have it and I know it cost her a lot. Then one late afternoon, when I hadn't gotten a single club call all day, when Hal and Helen had gone to see Helen's sister in Memphis for a couple of nights, when I was all alone without the sound of a single voice, I took the little tape recorder out and started reading the booklet about how to use it. It had been so long, since fifth grade, about nine years. I didn't even know if it would still work. But it did. I plugged it in and just played with it, talked into it like testing one two three, that kind of thing, and it still worked. So I began talking into the tape recorder, just saying whatever came to mind. That was what? About eight months ago. I never play back what I say, just some nights, when I haven't talked to anybody much during the day, when my TV show's over and I'm feeling restless for some reason, I take it out and talk to the tape recorder. I always rewind the tape and start over, tape over whatever I said the last time. It isn't like a diary or anything. Just company. Just sometimes.

Only now I'm sending them to you. Will you play them when you see Gabe and Gavin? I like to think of them recognizing my voice. I wouldn't mind at all if they called me Velis. But if you don't approve of them calling a grown person by her first name, maybe Aunt Velis would work.

This was way off the track. I just thought you might be curious about how I got this tape player. Elvis had a little radio, but I know he never even had a record player, they were so dirt poor. Mama said when they were in school he always knew the words to the latest hillbilly songs from the opry. He could memorize anything but he'd be too shy to get up in front of the class and sing them. He'd do it on the playground, though, for some of the girls like my Mama, even before he got that little guitar of his.

You probably want me to tell you more of what my Mama had to say about knowing Elvis, but that feels too much like invading his privacy, and goodness knows there's been enough of that. I will say she thought he was a sweet boy, and not at all stupid like people try to make out. Not necessarily book smart, but the kind of boy who could tell if you were upset over getting a whipping but you didn't want anybody to know. That kind of smart. No matter what you write about Elvis, please don't give people the idea that he's dumb. That's simply not true.

Velis
June 17, 1972

Velis startled awake to banging at the front door. The front? She sat up. Marc Collins? The last time someone came to the front it was Marc. No, he wouldn't be there now. Not this early. Not now. Now that he sorta knows about me.

More hammering. What time was it? She looked at the clock while the pounding continued. 6:22. When had something besides the alarm gotten her up? Banging, knocking to wake the dead. She bunched the top sheet in her fists, tried to breathe. Deep breath. A burglar wouldn't knock. Who could it be? Couldn't be any kind of confused delivery guy. It was way too early even for that. What day was it, anyway? Tuesday?

Knocking non-stop. Be still. It'll go away. A mistake, surely. Then she heard the hollering. "Velis! Velis! You've gotta open up, Velis!" It was Hal, and he sounded frantic, like he might have a heart attack. She jumped out of bed and raced down the stairs in her gown, not even stopping to pull on her robe.

"I'm coming, Hal!" she shouted while she struggled with the deadbolt. He kept on pounding and yelling. "What is it? What's wrong?" He was making such a racket he probably couldn't hear her through the door. When she opened it the dim morning light stunned her, and she blurted "What?" jerked a hand up to cover her eyes. Hal grabbed the other hand before she could say a word and pulled her out the door. "Helen can't get outta the bed. I think she's had a stroke! Oh please, Velis, hurry—I was afraid to leave her there in bed alone. Ohhh, she's all alone. I need your help."

Velis thought she might die: Not Helen! Please God, not Helen. Unable to say a thing, she squeezed Hal's hand hard as he pulled her behind him, thinking *she* might have a heart attack. The concrete porch floor, the steps, the sidewalk—gritty and cold on her bare feet. "Is . . . she . . . breathing?" she finally forced out.

"Oh, Velis, I swear I don't know what I'll do if something's wrong with Helen. You've got to make her get up." His voice had a whimpering/crying sound Velis had never heard before.

She kept her eyes covered, felt the damp morning grass on the bottom of her feet as they stumbled across the Chandlers' yard to their front porch. She could hardly breathe, strained to take a deep breath but couldn't. Who was gasping? Was that panting her or Hal or both of them? "Did you call the rescue?" she managed to get out, but her voice was so ragged she could've been crying herself. Every nerve scraped.

"They're coming. Good Lord where in the world could they be? They should be here by now."

They were inside the house and on the stairs in seconds. Velis still couldn't open her eyes or take her hand away, and they were struggling to run, so the going was clumsy.

"Velis is here, Helen! Hold on, honeybunch, it's gonna be all right," Hal yelled as he dragged her behind him.

When she heard Helen's muffled crying, not words, whimpering like some hurt child, Velis opened her eyes and she ran.

Satnin
Summer 1972

Satnin, oh my itty bitty Nungen, your Satnin Mama's so blessed happy you finally got down on your knees to talk to her tonight.

She's been worried sick, the Satnin Mama has. She taught her baby boy cutie pie to say his prayers every single night, didn't she, no matter where he was or who he was with or how dark it got in his room? To get on his knees and talk to his Lord?

You been a good boy, too, I know you have, even if you haven't talked to your itty bitty Mama in a such a long long time. Why baby boy you always was one to say your bedtime prayers, even when you was over there in Germany in that army. But seems like now you're straying from your Bible and your prayers these days, son. And I get powerful fretful when you forget. It's been way too long, Baby Boy.

Nungen just can't imagine how his little Mama frets when she don't hear from him.

You know I'm not mad at you, Baby One, I could never be mad at you for a single second, but it like to worried me sick, you in New York City all that while for them shows and all. Temptation in your face every minute of every day. No matter what you think, bitty boy, a Mama never gets over worrying about her Nungen, not even here.

I'm not saying it won't a big honor and all. Singing in Madison Square Garden. Dear Lord in heaven what a hullabaloo. You never said a word to me the whole time you was there, though. Far as I could tell you never gave your Satnin Mama a thought. That says a lot. Don't get me wrong, I knew you'd be busy every minute with all of them interviews and rehearsals and them crowds of people after you. Ask me there's too many of em crazy to see you and grab at you and try to touch you. They scare me to death. One of these days them wild crazy fans is bound to hurt you, I can't stop worrying about that. And when it's all said and done, Baby Boy, singing in one place ain't that very different from singing in another, now is it?

Your Daddy Vernon ain't been in touch with his widdle wife much lately either. He never was one for praying, though, not like me and you. That don't surprise me one bit, that's he's about give it up, with him so high and mighty now. Married to that cheap trashy blond. I'll never get over that, not from here to eternity, him running around with a married woman before my earthly bones was cold in the ground. Them laid up together there at Graceland in Satnin Mama's prettiest purple room Nungen gave her. I like to cried myself sick. I didn't expect that, not after I stuck by him, fought to get him out of jail after he did that stupid check thing. Waited for him almost three years that time. And you just a precious baby boy. Looked the other way all those years, too. You know what I mean, Nungen. Where's his respect? But don't you go and hold that against your Daddy now, you hear? He's all the blood family you got now, him and little Lisa. You two gotta stick together, so don't hold that blond hussy against him. You such a sweetnin to buy your Daddy that house and move him out of the Satnin's own room. Him always was her sweetest boy. I don't never expect to hear much from Vernon, though you might be surprised how often I do, but I can't hardly stand it when you don't keep in touch, Litt'lun.

She like to cries herself crazy, the Satnin Mama does.

I have to say, hearing your Satnin voice tonight washes away a world of worry, I can tell you that much, Baby Boy. Still, ain't nobody there in that crazy New York City can feed you right, I don't care what big price you pay for a meal in some fancy restaurant where they don't even cook the meat all the way. Whenever you get back to Graceland I'm just so relieved. Don't you feel that way yourself, that coming home is better? I can see looking at you that you ain't been eating right, so much time on the road. Them bags under your eyes ain't right. And all that poofiness. That ain't my Elvis Aron. That ain't my Nungen. Something mighty wrong. You look so tired, Baby Boy.

Them blues eyes of his is still his Satnin Mama's beautiful bright eyes. That'll never change in this world or the next.

Tomorrow promise me you'll tell V-O 5 to fix you up a meatloaf and one of my coconut cakes, you hear? She's the only one can do it right, now Dodger can't cook no more. I can tell just by looking at you you ain't been eating right.

You still there, darlin boy? Me and Jesse been talking, Satnin. He's every bit as worried as I am. Oh he's the handsomest little bitty boy you've ever seen, next to you. I know I've told you that ever since I've been here with him, but I still can't get over it myself, even after all this time. The spittin image of you, only he don't have no problems with food. That's one concern we don't have, neither one of us now. Or his bowel track either. I can't tell you what a heavenly relief that is. If you could see him you'd take such comfort, Bitty Boy. I don't know what I'd do without him. Funny how, when I was with you I thought about Jesse all the time, wondered if he was all right, and now I'm here with Jesse I worry about you. Ain't that peculiar? Preachers say you're free of worry once your earthly days are over, but there ain't a shred of truth in that. What do they know?

Anyway, it pains me to say this but neither one of us thinks much of that Linda gal you're seeing so much of now. Littlin, you know I never was one to mess in your business, and I was no fan of Priscilla, though she could be a sweet little thing, but having that Linda there in Graceland, well, that's not setting right with me. Hearing your voice tonight, and seeing you so clear propped up there in your big bed at home—oh dear Lord I want to reach over and hug you tight in the worst kind of way; can you tell?—I like to lost my grip when I saw her perched up there beside you, pretty as you please, talking so sweet like she was lady of the manor. You still married in the eyes of the Lord. Think about the sin, Baby Boy. Think about the sin. Besides, you never was one to favor a blond, never have been. And that gal's tall like a man. That ain't for you, Son. Something's blinded you, that's a fact. I wish you'd just think about that, Nungen. I swear, I ain't trying to meddle in your business, but I can't tell you what a start it gave me seeing her there with you, like she belonged in our house. Almost as bad as the day that Priscilla went up in the attic and put on my clothes. Dear Lord I'm not gonna dwell on that.

So let the Littlest Mama say this while she's got his attention: ain't nothing else for you to do now that you ain't already done, you know what I'm saying. God give you a gift and now you've used it. I wish you'd think about what I said such a long time ago: settle down and quit all this running around. I guess it ain't possible for you to buy a furniture store now. I can see that. And it ain't no use thinking about setting your Daddy up in hardware. He's had too much of a taste of being a big shot. I can see that clear as day. But Satnin, you don't have to do all this making TV shows and movies and concerts no more. People like that Tom Parker and this new Linda woman and some of the boys—I know you don't want to hear this, but listen to your own Satnin Mama for a minute—them people don't care a bit about your health. I can see that so plain. All they want is for you to keep bringing in the bags of money and the attention and the fancy cars and all. That hairdresser you put so much stock in, he's bad as the rest, Baby Boy. Ain't nobody down there looking out for you less it's Alberta and Ernestine and Notary. Maybe Vestor, but he ain't all there, which I'm sure you know. Plus the booze confuses him, too. Don't I know? The others, they've gone money mad, Elvis. Won't none of them tell you the truth. Won't none of them say what you don't want to hear.

Wait a minute. I ain't gonna say another word about that woman and that other business. I promise. Precious Jesse wants to say something. He says remember that time you saw him when you was young? Saw him clear as day there talking to you by the side of the house? What was it he said to you, remember?: "Care for other people, put yourself in their place, see their point of view, love them." Remember that, when you was just a tiny bitty boy of four? How you come running to me and crawled up in my lap and cried and cried, and for the longest time I couldn't get it out of you what all that crying was about, thought your cousin Gene had smacked you or something, and when you could talk you said you'd seen your own brother and he looked smack like you, same size and all, hair, teeth, everything, how he'd growed right along with you, he wasn't a little dead baby at all, and how he spoke directly to you like he was right there in the yard. And you told me just what he said and you said, "That's what I'm gonna do, Little Mama, I'm gonna care for people, I'm gonna love 'em just like my blessed baby brother said." Like a little man. Scared you half to death, like God was talking straight to you, you said, only it was your very own twin brother up in heaven.

Well now, Elvis boy, Jesse wants me to tell you he said exactly that and he meant every white word of it at the time, that what he said was God's own truth, but he don't want you thinking loving folks and giving 'em a handout is the same thing. He don't want you to think you gotta pay the bills for every person calls himself friend. You see what I'm saying? He says he wants you to stop and think is all, stop and think about loving little Lisa your own flesh and blood and taking care of yourself and trying to make things work with Priscilla—though she won't Jesse's choice and she sure won't mine, neither, but I ain't going into that again cause I know how agitated it makes you—and maybe stepping back from all this fame and fortune thing. Filthy lucre he calls it. Where does a baby get such words? He wants to be sure you know that ain't what he was talking about at all, footing the bills for all these hangers-on and con-men like this hotshot Tom Parker. I didn't like that man's shifty looks from the minute I laid eyes on him. You know that's a fact.

Don't go, Baby Boy. I ain't seen you near enough this time. I hate to see that pitiful sad look on your pretty face. You know I'm here, Satnin. Any time you need me. You so blessed tired, Little Boy. I'd give half of eternity to spend another night at Graceland with you, or better still back in Tupelo, make you a coconut cake, rub your feet, those sore itty bitty sooties, talk soft to you so you can fall sound asleep. And tuck little Lisa Marie in, just once, hear her say her prayers, touch that pretty hair of hers. Do you think she looks a little like me?

The Itty Bitty needs to get his sweet rest now. Can he hear his Satnin Mama saying good night? Her wuvs him. Her knows you need those pills right now to get your sleep, darlin' boy, but maybe if you'd stay home a bit and eat right maybe you wouldn't need so many of them sleeping aids, all those . . .

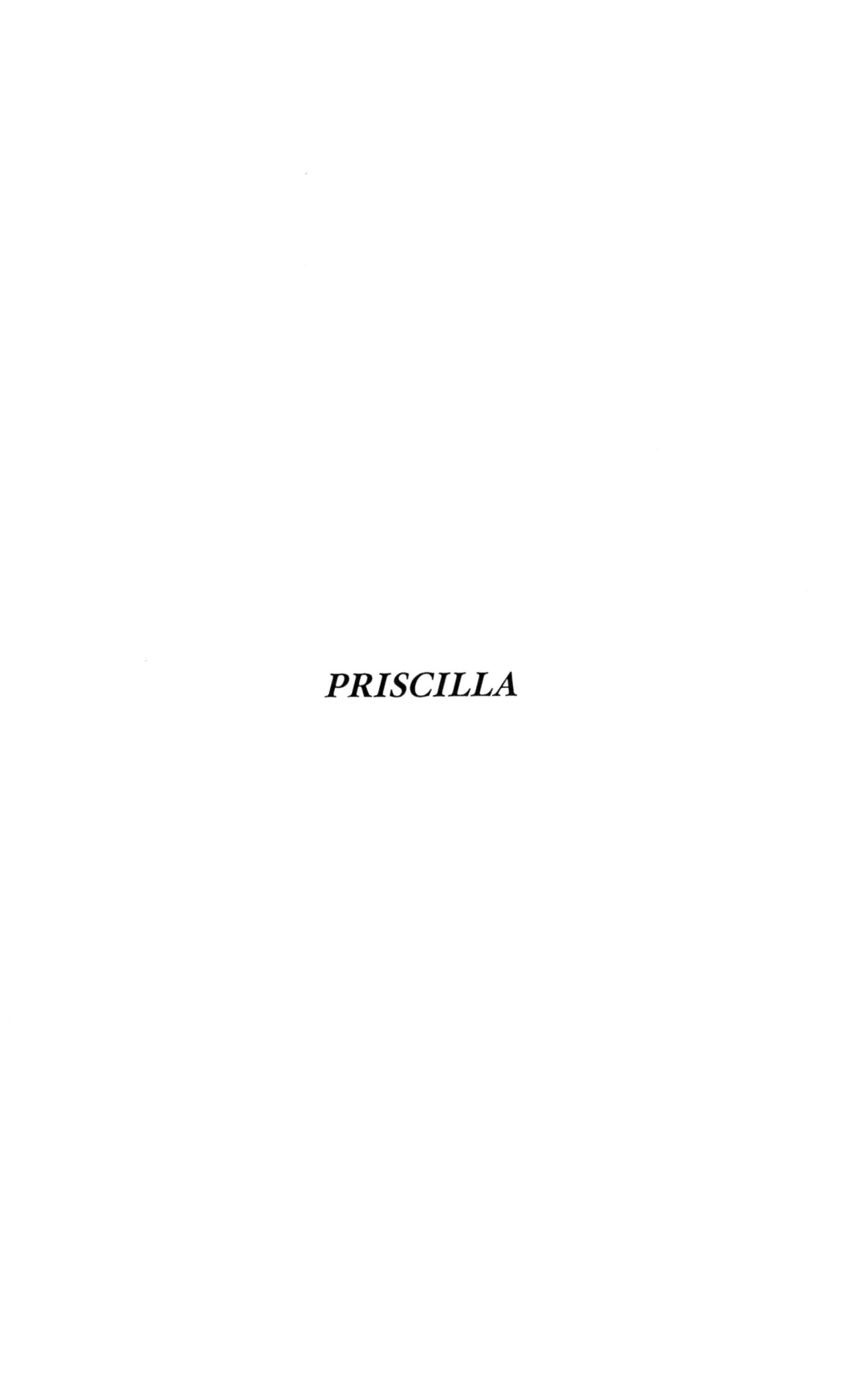

PRISCILLA

Priscilla
January 9, 1973

Priscilla clenched the set of shiny new car keys in her sweaty palm.

How in God's name was she gonna tell Kendall that she'd gone out and gotten herself a red Mustang convertible? He'd think she'd lost her feeble mind. One sure thing: she'd never ever be able to so much as hint that Elvis Presley had *given* it to her out of the blue—his parting surprise among a week's worth of surprises. She couldn't even imply to Kendall in any little way that E.P. was a patient at the diet clinic. Those initials were about as subtle as a heart attack. She'd never betray patient confidentiality anyway. Not this patient's or any other's. Besides, even if she told him, he wouldn't believe Elvis Presley would give *her* a car. She could hear him now: Kendall would pick at her, "What's a big shot old rich rocker doing carrying on with a little nobody like you?" Taunt her about flirting with that fat bloat-ox has-been who wouldn't look her way if she was the last pathetic female on the face of the earth. Then he'd lose it.

For a flash she'd considered saying no to Elvis, giving the car back. Imagine *her* saying no to Elvis Presley. It would've been something to see the shocked look on his pretty face. He was the one who shocked people, not her, not some registered nurse nobody in Durham, North Carolina. Anyway she wanted the car the second he handed her the keys and said, "Got a little good-bye something for you, Miss Priss." In that voice of his that was like a song. Those go-to-bed eyes. That come-here-and-hug-me-darlin' smirk. She'd looked at that famous face and looked down at those keys and for a blink she thought: I have to say no. I can't take this car. But for just a blink. She hadn't said a word, hadn't even choked out a thank you, and Elvis had laughed and swept out of the room, that Brut of his practically gagging her. Grand exit. Red had told her where the car was parked, described the features (as if she had any idea what a V-8 engine was) while she just stood there, mouth open, like a dope. By then it was too late to refuse. He'd checked out. Elvis had left the building.

Right this minute he and those creepy so-called pals of his were already on the airplane (imagine – his own airplane) on their way to Hawaii (imagine – Hawaii). She couldn't give the car back now, even if she wanted to.

Priscilla took out her cloth purse and slammed the locker door, still clutching the new keys.

"Your shift go okay, Priscilla?" That was Evelyn Tucker's squeaky-whiny voice. Evelyn had a locker two down from Priscilla in the tiny nurses' lounge. She worked nights, too. Sometimes Priscilla gave her a ride home.

Not this morning. Please, Lord, not this morning, Priscilla thought as she dropped the keys into her carcoat pocket and grappled in her bag for the set that went to the Corvair.

"Priscilla? Knock knock?" That whine.

"Oh, yeah, went fine, Evelyn. No excitement." Ha! Like any old uneventful night the King of Rock & Roll gave her a convertible. No big deal. She pulled on her brown corduroy coat. "How 'bout you?" She had to ask, obligatory chitchat. When really all she could think was *What in God's name am I gonna do about this car?*

"Same. Fatties sleeping like babies." Evelyn sighed. Her life revolved around this job.

"Right. Me too. No contraband Hershey bars on my hall." Priscilla forced a friendly smile.

"I heard" – leaning closer and whispering – "Elvis checked himself out." Wounded. Like why didn't you tell me?

"Oh, yeah. Has some big concert thing in Hawaii. That was sorta exciting I guess, him going all of a sudden like that."

"I'll bet. The Rice King would've never let him come if he'd known he was only gonna stay what? Eight days? No way."

"No doubt." Priscilla was on the verge of making her getaway, pulling on her tan like-leather gloves.

Evelyn touched her arm. "Say, you going to the Ivy Saturday night?"

"Probably. I'm not on this weekend, and Kendall's playing."

Protecting Elvis

"Maybe I'll see you there, then." All hopeful.

"Maybe." Evelyn was fishing for an invitation to sit with them, about as subtle as a bedpan. So she could maybe hook up with one of the band guys. But Kendall couldn't stand Evelyn. Said that voice of hers grated on his musical ear like rocks in a bucket. Said all she ever did was bitch and whine and babble about meaningless crap. Priscilla wished he wouldn't talk like that, but she had to admit: Evelyn was a bore and a snore. Plus she was Episcopalian.

"So I'm off tomorrow, too."

Good grief. Evelyn could change from whining to downright begging in a heartbeat. "Right."

"So I won't see you. I'll call, though. Okay?"

"Sure thing, Evelyn. Give me a call." Priscilla rattled the keys. "Listen. I gotta get going. Gotta stop by A&P on my way home. I promised Angie I'd bring her some donuts before she left for the hospital." She looked at her watch.

"Well then."

She couldn't walk out with Evelyn. She wouldn't even be able to *look* at the car if she walked out with her and Evelyn tried to bum a ride. "Bye," she called, waving, practically running for the door.

Out in the cold morning air Priscilla hustled, heart pounding, toward the staff parking area. Truth was, she didn't have a plan. All of this was so out of whack with her calm-as-custard everyday life. Elvis checking himself out, when nobody even knew he was going until a couple of hours before he left. In the middle of the night, no less. "Taking care of business, Little Bit. That's what a man's gotta do," he'd said. Plus the car. Even though he'd left at four – he didn't seem to think it was the least bit strange to take off at four in the morning; he was up all night anyway – she hadn't sorted out any kind of plan between then and now. Had concentrated on charts and change-over. Her head was way too muddled to do all that and make a plan at the same time. The car was parked on Seminary Street, that's what Red had told her. Locked. If she stood on tiptoe she could probably see it right this minute. Title in the glove compartment. Made out to her. Gas tank full. Just like that, like giving her a box of Whitman's.

She unlocked the door to her Daddy's brown Corvair. Even though he'd been dead for five years, she still called it her Daddy's car, not hers. And it still smelled of his Camel cigarettes, though the first thing she'd done when her Mama gave it to her was empty the ashtray. He'd been so proud of this hideous car. "Drive the USA in your Chevrolet." She could hear him now, belting out that jingle in his gospel voice while he waxed the ugly thing, like some TV dad. Only that image was about as real as some TV dad. Her Daddy singing in the driveway. Mr. Good Guy. He'd loved that car more than anything else she could remember. The day he drove it home he grabbed her and her Mama and pulled them out on the front stoop and stood there beside his new car like he'd just bought a Mercedes Benz, so proud he could've been a turkey gobbler in a yard full of hens. The first thing she'd thought: Why would anybody buy a car the color of doo-doo?

She turned the key in the ignition. What the heck was she gonna do with this car now, give it to Kendall? He hated it. He had a blunter name for the color, said anybody who'd drive a Corvair in the first place didn't have the sense God gave a pissant. Course he borrowed it all the time, but he made it clear he'd never buy a Corvair himself if it was the last car on the lot. What in heaven's name was she gonna do? She could take it to the used car dealer and take whatever they offered, put the money in savings. But she had no idea what a fair price would be, and she had to admit the car ran like a charm, and it only had nineteen thousand miles on it, even if it was eight years old. She was bound to get ripped off. And wouldn't Kendall see it around town and wonder? Maybe ask? Durham could be so small sometimes.

Of course, she could try to tell a little white one and say she traded it in for the Mustang. That made sense. But lying was a sin, and her Mama always said she wore a lie on her face plain as a scar. Plus she was supposed to be saving every extra penny for their wedding and reception and honeymoon. Soon as Kendall sold a song, they were doing it. So he'd think she was out of her teensy-tinsy mind to take on a car payment, even if she made good money working at the diet clinic. He'd accuse her of hanging around hotshots too much, getting the big head. All those so-called bigshots in and out of the diet clinic, all telling her how wonderful she was. A real Florence you-know-who. If there was one thing Kendall couldn't stand it was some nobody with the big head.

She eased out of her parking spot, checking the rear view mirror. Thank heaven Evelyn wasn't standing on the back porch looking all abandoned. Priscilla would have to tell her to hop in. She would hate herself if she drove off and left her friend standing there. Not that Evelyn was a real friend, but she was about as close as Priscilla had, besides her two roommates, who weren't exactly friend friends either. But Evelyn's daddy must've picked her up out front this morning. She still lived at home with her parents, poor thing.

About to pop out of her skin, Priscilla turned down Seminary and there it was, her car, the most gorgeous brand spanking new Mustang, red as rouge, the white top like a lady's Sunday gloves. Oh my! Hands trembling, she eased the Corvair into the spot behind it and sat there, engine idling. Would you look at that. She'd never been one to pay all that much attention to cars, but this one took her breath, it was so gorgeous. And it was hers. She closed her eyes, rested her head on the steering wheel, and offered up a silent prayer of thanks: Thank you, Lord, for letting me get to know Elvis Presley. He's a good man. Stranger than strange, I'll grant you, but he's got a good heart. Please look out for him, Lord. He's brim full with sadness. And, God, thank you for this car. I don't know why such fortune has come to me, so I'm gonna try to accept it with a humble heart. Guide me in the path of righteousness. Thy will be done. In Jesus' name I pray. Amen.

She felt calmer after giving thanks, but still her insides trembled. What she'd do: she'd get the donuts and take them to Angie, then she'd change clothes and come on back. By then she'd maybe be ready to actually sit in the driver's seat, maybe even drive it around the block. Surely by then she'd have a clear plan. Good grief, Angie and Maria would flip when they saw this car! Nobody, but nobody, would believe it was hers. Her Mama would disapprove for sure: The extravagance, Priscilla Jane. Your Daddy would turn over in his grave. And what have you done with *his* car? Well, she'd cross that bridge when she got to it. Let's see now: It was Thursday, so Kendall would be sleeping in, then giving guitar lessons. She wasn't supposed to even talk to him till around supper time. She was picking him up to take him to supper. That was it. They were going to the Top Hat for burgers. So she had plenty of time to figure this out on her own, practically all day. No way could she sleep, not with this to deal with. She could do it. She'd have to.

Priscilla stared at the Mustang, her very own Mustang, so glad she hadn't said no. Happy she'd met Elvis Presley, even though it had been one of the strangest weeks of her entire life. "Thank you, Elvis," she whispered. "Thank you for the car."

"You get my donuts?" Angie yelled from the bathroom. No doubt she was applying the tenth layer of mascara to her eyelashes. Angie and Maria went to work looking like they were characters on General Hospital, they were that fixed up. Both of them were as glamorous as Priscilla was plain. Both of them intended to marry doctors, no ifs, ands, or buts. They flirted like mad with Kendall, but they would no more hook up with him than they'd go to work without make-up. They had bigger fish to fry. When he gave Priscilla a promise ring for Christmas – her birthstone, a turquoise set in sterling – they oohed and aahed and called it the sweetest, most romantic gift. But neither of them would settle for anything less than a one-carat diamond set in fourteen-karat gold. Everybody loved Kendall: he was so handsome, such a gentleman, so talented with his singing and songwriting. Priscilla was lucky as all get out to find him, a good Christian man and all. But marry him? No way would her roomies give that a second thought.

Angie and Maria both worked days at the hospital, Angie rotating labor and delivery and maternity, Maria in peds. Angie still wore whites, so she looked like the model for Barbie, the Nurse version. Long legs, tiny waist, breasts up high and perky. The med students lined up to take her out. Maria, dark and petite and proportionally voluptuous, more like Barbie's friend Franny, had been dating the same doctor, on the sly, for months. They practically lived together. But he was engaged to a resident. Compared to his harried fiancée he had plenty of time. He made endless promises to Maria, but Priscilla had her doubts, though she'd never say so.

"Priss?"

"I got them. Exactly what you wanted. On the kitchen table."

"You are a doll." Angie came bustling out of the bathroom blowing a kiss in her direction. Priscilla was anything but a doll and she knew it. Most days she felt invisible, which was fine with her. Her Mama should've named her plain Jane, not Priscilla Jane; that would've suited her unremarkable looks better.

"You sleepy, hon?" Angie called from the kitchen, where she was leaning over eating a chocolate cream-filled donut standing up.

"No. Not really. Exhausted, but not the least bit sleepy."

"Mr. Big keep you talking all night?" That was one plus of rooming with nurses, they could talk shop.

"He left."

"Left? He just got here."

"Yeah. Checked out."

"I'll bet Big Doc goes wild over that."

"He'll probably be glad. Our star was a pain in the butt as a patient, you know. Not exactly a program kinda guy."

"Yeah, well." Angie sashayed into the living room, dabbing at her lips with a paper napkin.

"Where's Maria?"

"Went in early. You know who had early rounds. She was hoping to grapple him some in the meds room before her shift."

"Right." Priscilla never got used to how overtly sexy Maria and Angie were. Where she studied, at the North Carolina Baptist Hospital School of Nursing in Winston, the girls were a lot more like her, more lady-like, her mother would say. Here in Durham most of the nurses were like her roommates, wild as stray cats.

"You gonna see Kendall tonight?"

"Course."

"Y'all have fun. Give him a kiss from me. I've got the *cutest* date after work. A cardiac specialist." She raised her eyebrows, pulled her full-length black leather coat from the closet, slid into it like it was her skin, and hustled off.

"See ya," Priscilla called after her. Without looking, she knew Angie hadn't closed the donut bag. Or put the top back on the toothpaste. Or picked up her underwear on the bathroom floor. Priscilla and Maria, both neat to the point of being old-maidish, shared one of the bedrooms in the two-bedroom apartment. Angie had her own. Neither of them could room with her, she was such a slob. She didn't just have a week's worth of dirty clothes all over her space. She had a lifetime's worth of her wardrobe spread on every surface. When she left in the morning she looked immaculate, the proverbial neat as a pin nurse. The domestic disaster she left behind bore no resemblance to the tidy portrait she presented to the world.

Priscilla sat on the sofa, still wearing her coat and gloves. What now? What next? She was supposed to sleep from ten until six, but she could no more lay down now than she could find a cure for cancer. She needed to figure this thing out, to come up with a way to tell people she had a new car without lying, without betraying her patient's confidentiality, and without making Kendall mad or disappointing her Mama. Ever since she'd walked into the Rice House New Year's night, ever since she'd found out Elvis Presley had signed himself

Charlotte Morgan

into the program, her life had been more complicated than she could've imagined. He was gone now, though. She'd probably never hear from him again. And nobody but her medical colleagues would ever even know she'd met him. But he'd left this great big problem smack dab in the middle of her life. And she'd never been one to handle great big problems. She thought of that Marty Robbins' song: "This Time You Gave Me a Mountain," one of her Mama's favorites. That's how it felt. Like a mountain was crushing down on her, and she couldn't breathe. Well, sitting like a lump on the sofa wasn't gonna solve anything. First things first: she'd take a bath, change, and go drive that new car of hers. She had to smile: she'd never driven a Mustang before, never even been in one. Good thing it's cold out, Priscilla thought, or I'd have to put the top down. Then I'd need to disguise myself, wear a scarf and sunglasses, like some incognito movie star. What a ridiculous picture, her dressed like a movie star. Elvis would get a big kick out of it. Even Kendall would have to laugh at that one.

The Corvair was so easy to sell Priscilla had been stunned: $1,250, just like that. Already deposited in her savings account at Farmer's Trust. Driving the Mustang down I-85 it had come to her, plain as peanuts: she'd take the old car to a used car lot in Chapel Hill, which was so obvious once it struck her. Kendall never went to Chapel Hill, couldn't stand all those preps, he called them, UNC TarHeels wearing Gant shirts and loafers without socks. Durham was bad enough, he said. The dealer had taken that old ugly Corvair without batting an eye, had gotten one of the secretaries to run her back over to Durham during her lunch hour. That was one problem down, two big ones to go. Easing the Mustang along Mangum towards Kendall's rooming house, radio blaring, she felt a glimmer of optimism for the first time that day. Something else had hit her like a rock upside the head while she was driving around: Kendall was bound to love this car. Sitting in the white leather bucket seat, gripping the leather-covered steering wheel, turning on the radio to WIZS and hearing the stereo sound, she realized he had to love this Mustang, even if he gave her grief for buying it. Once he drove it he'd be crazy about it, nuts about how he looked in it. The whole time she was driving everybody who passed her honked and gave her the high sign, like super-cool car. That would suit Kendall to a T. She wouldn't lie to him – she'd made up her mind about that. And she wouldn't betray Elvis, that was a given. So she'd rely on the Lord to help her surprise Kendall with the truth – not the whole truth, but nothing but the truth. She'd prayed for divine guidance, so now she'd have to trust and obey and walk in the dark with faith. She could get through this. Somehow, with God's help.

When she parked in front of The Estate not a soul was outside on the long, wide porch. No surprise, since it was close to freezing out. She didn't pull into the driveway. There were six or seven cars on the gravel, and plenty of room for more, but she didn't want to take a chance of anybody blocking her in. Or dinging her new ride. People were always coming and going, all hours of day and night, at The Estate. She wanted to get Kendall into the driver's seat and on the road as fast as she could. Mostly musicians lived in the big old rambling rooming house, one of about a dozen grand homes gone to seed where the new crop of Southern rockers and bluegrass hopefuls came to be discovered. A couple of stained glass artists rented there, too, and one gal who was a clogger/actress/waitress. Everybody left the doors unlocked, even with all the instruments and equipment all over the place. Somebody was always awake, somebody was always sleeping, at The Estate.

Still, Priscilla locked her car door. Maybe she was just putting off the inevitable that one last second. Plus she'd never in her life owned anything so valuable, so of course she'd lock it. That was only sensible. But it was true, too, that she was stalling: she never knew what to expect from Kendall. He could be the sweetest, most loving person in the world. Or . . . she didn't like to think about the or.

When she walked into the vast shabby entrance hall she could hear Kendall's deep voice off to the right, in the old parlor that still served as the communal living space. He was finishing up his lesson. She couldn't tell what he was saying, but the up and down of his voice had that finality to it. She stood still, waiting, the car keys in one hand. She'd never interrupt a lesson. Two sets of feet stood, two sets of footsteps moved toward her, and then there he was.

"Hey there, Priscilla. You a little early ain'tcha?" Kendall walked toward her and kissed her on the cheek. "This here's Tommy Tyler. Tommy, this is my girl, Priscilla Johnson."

"Hi there, Miss Johnson." The gawky kid dipped his head.

"Hi, Tommy." She beamed as Kendall grabbed her hand, basked in that "my girl."

Charlotte Morgan

"See ya next week then, Tommy, same time. Work on them progressions like I showed you, every day, you hear?"

"Sure thing, Kendall. You bet." And the tall skinny boy was gone and Kendall had both arms around her waist and he was kissing her hard on the mouth.

"You look good enough to swallow whole, Priscilla," he said, burying his head in her neck, smelling deep, like he loved her scent. "Good Lord am I glad to see you."

She could hardly get her breath. No matter how long she went out with Kendall, she never got over that tremor whenever he kissed her, that near-electric shock when he pulled her close to his taut body. "I got a surprise for you outside."

"You surprise enough, babe."

She pulled back. "This is a BIG surprise."

"You don't say. I better get a move on, then. Let me grab my jacket; don't go away. Promise?"

"I promise." He bounded up the stairs, those lean legs of his taking the steps two at a time. She stood there, face flushed, a plain nobody in a brown corduroy car coat, wondering for the millionth time why a handsome, talented guy like Kendall Kennedy would look twice at her, let alone ask her to marry him. That Tommy must've thought what everybody always thought when they saw them together: What the heck is HE doing with HER?

The first time she saw Kendall, at Assembly of God, she thought *That is the cutest guy I've ever seen.* He was playing guitar, looking as natural as if that instrument was a God-given part of his body. His wavy chestnut brown hair was downright pretty, almost like a girl's it was so clean and shiny, and usually she didn't care much for a beard, but his was trim and full and suited his high forehead and slim face. Those full lips of his were moving just the slightest bit to the words of the hymns, and the look of rapture on his face made her think of the colored pictures of Jesus in her Bible. She could see he wasn't real big, wasn't real tall, that he was slender and muscular but not a size that would overpower a small woman. Even then, that first time, before he even spoke a word to her, she got that trembly feeling looking at him. Her: brown eyes, straight brown hair (brown brown; not dirty blond, not auburn-tinted, not dark brown, just brown brown), five three and right next door to skinny,

110

plain as a penny post card – guys never looked twice at her, even guys no more exciting to look at than she was. Somehow, she'll never figure out how unless it was Divine intervention, he looked up at the end of "Do Lord" and caught her eye and smiled that knocked-out smile of his right directly at her. She couldn't hold back a grin herself, remembering, knowing if ever the Lord had answered a prayer it was at that exact second in church that Sunday morning.

"What's that self-satisfied look about, babe?" Kendall was practically skipping down the steps, pulling on his old leather jacket.

"You'll see."

"Let's go, then." He started to pull her toward the door.

"Wait." She held his hand and he stopped. "I got to tell you something first."

"What?" An edge of impatience crept into his voice.

"I got a new car."

"What?" He looked at her like she'd grown a second nose.

"A new car. A Mustang."

He laughed. "Now I know you're pulling my leg." And kept on laughing.

"No. Really. A brand new Mustang." She couldn't bring herself to say convertible.

And like somebody had hit a power switch he stopped laughing. "Seriously?"

"Yep. It's right out front. I . . ."

He pulled her to the door, peered through the glass. "Damn. That red convertible out front?" He spoke, staring out the glass, not turning toward her.

"I told you it was a big surprise."

He turned and glared at her. "You just test driving it, right? You ain't outright bought that car?"

"It's mine all right." That was the Lord's truth.

"Yours?" He practically spit the word.

"What I mean is, it's for *us*." His hardened tone of voice made her anxious. She was having a tough enough time saying anything at all, much less speaking in a way that wasn't an accidental backhanded lie.

"Without so much as asking my opinion?"

Almost a whisper: "I wanted it to be a surprise is all. I didn't mean any harm."

He grabbed her by the shoulders. "You listen to me, girl, and listen good. When a man and a woman are like husband and wife, when they've made a Christian promise to one another, she don't go out and buy no car without so much as a hint to him. The man is the ruler of the household."

"I know that, but . . ."

"Don't say a word, Priscilla. Don't say another word or you're gonna make me lose my temper, and Lord knows I don't wanna do that." He dragged her over to the steps. "Sit down a minute. Let me think a minute."

She sat, mute, staring at him.

"Hand me the keys."

She held them out to him. "Here."

"Damnit, didn't I say don't say a word?" He snatched the keys, glowering. He paced back and forth in front of her, the heels of his boots clicking on the worn wooden floor. Priscilla could barely breathe. "What I'm gonna do is this: I'm gonna go drive that car, try to think, clear my head. How could you do a thing like this without consulting me first? I'm so mad at you I don't think I can trust myself to stay calm. Nope, I'm gonna drive that car around, and I want you to go into the front room there by yourself and close your eyes and pray to the Lord for forgiveness. You hear me, Priscilla?" He stopped pacing and stood in front of her. "I want you to ask Jesus Christ to forgive your thoughtless ways. You know good and well this ain't the way to act, this ain't showing proper respect for your future husband and your Christian upbringing. Good Lord, what will your Mama say if she hears about this? That woman worries enough as it is." Running both hands through his hair, taking a deep breath. "I need to cool off, that's a fact, so I'm gonna drive around until my head's clear. Then I'll come back here and we'll take this dang car back to the dealer and get your money back. That's what we'll do. You hear? You go in there and close your eyes and pray to the Lord to guide you in His ways. You hear?"

She nodded, knowing the sound of her voice would only rouse him more.

He turned his back on her and stomped out the door, banging it shut behind him. Tears leapt into her eyes. She hadn't told a single lie, but this had gone all wrong all the same.

Priscilla, shaking, made her way to a dim corner of the front room and slumped into an old wing chair. It was worn, warm. She sat back and closed her eyes: *Dear Lord, Why do I make him so mad? I knew this car thing was* a problem, and I guess it was vain on my part to take it, Lord, but it's true: I meant no harm. Help me, Jesus. Help me find a way to make it up to Kendall. He's right, I know he is: I shouldn't make major decisions without talking to him first. I'll do as he says, Lord. I guess the point is that I was being deceitful, in a way. A Christian woman can't be deceitful with her husband. That's the lesson here, isn't it, Lord? So I'm going to have to tell the whole truth. He's gonna find out that this car was a gift. That's what I had to learn, isn't it, Lord? Not to try to hide anything from my future husband. Thank you, Jesus, for leading me in the path of righteousness.

She paused. And Lord, if you can find a way to help Kendall with his temper, I'd be beholden. Thy will be done. Amen.

Priscilla opened her eyes, a weight lifted from her heart. That's what she'd do when he came back and said it was time to return the car. She'd tell him the truth, that one of the patients at the diet clinic gave it to her. She couldn't tell him who, he'd understand that, but she'd have to tell him that it was a gift. And they'd have to take it back. He wouldn't permit her to accept gifts like that from some other man. That car had been nothing but trouble from the first, she could see that now. She was at peace about it. She'd gladly take it back for Kendall.

"You in there, Little Darlin'?" Kendall's voice called from the front hall. The room was dark. She must've dozed off. What time was it?

He rushed in, fell to the floor and hugged her around the knees. "You not mad at me, are you?" Kendall rubbed his head in her lap.

Disoriented, Priscilla patted his thick hair. "Why would I be mad at you?"

His dark eyes stared into her face. "That Mustang is some car. I still can't believe you went out and got that Mustang on your own." He raised up and kissed her, just a quick energetic smack on the lips. Her brain was clearing somewhat, and she remembered: Kendall had been furious with her about the car. "That was one crazy thing to do, Priscilla. That's a fact. But I shouldn't a gone off on you like I did. Forgive me?"

"There's nothing to forgive. I coulda guessed you'd be mad. You have every right." It came back to her now: she was gonna tell him where she really got the car, and agree to return it. She pushed a strand of his hair behind one ear.

Dear Lord that was one fine-looking face. He was as happy now as he'd been enraged before. One thing about Kendall: he was passionate all right. Only she could never predict what turn that passion was going to take.

"I drove on down to the Ivy, and some of the guys were there, and they like to messed their pants when I pulled up in that red Mustang convertible." He took both her hands and dragged her out of her chair. She still had on her coat and gloves. "Come on, Priscilla, let's you and me take it for a spin. Why not?"

She followed along behind him this time as he pulled her to the door. "You're absolutely right, Kendall. A woman has got no business doing something this big without getting the okay from her fiancé. It was wrong of me..."

He turned and hugged her to him, rubbed his hands all up and down her back while her front was pressed into his body. "You just a silly girl, is all. You didn't mean no harm. Lord knows you're bout as sweet as they come." He kissed her again, this time a more lingering kiss. "That's one thing I love about you, Priscilla. You just a sweet little thing without a ounce of bad in you." And he laughed his big hearty let's go have some fun laugh and turned back toward the door. "I've got my work cut out, that's a fact."

"So you like the car?"

"Like it? Good Lord, girl, if I didn't know better I'd say that car was custom made for me." He stopped. "Just promise, swear, you won't never do nothing like that again without talking to me first about it. Even to make me happy. You swear?"

"Course I swear, Kendall. No way in this lifetime I'll ever do anything like that again."

Trailing down the porch steps behind him, her tiny hand snug in his strong slender fingers, she had to laugh, too. That was one promise she wouldn't have any trouble keeping. If she ever saw Elvis Presley again it'd be on TV, and he wouldn't be giving away cars.

Priscilla
January 10, 1973

Priscilla stood, glass of watery Pepsi in hand. The whole place rocked for the Lynyrd Skynyrd set. Nobody sat down. Kendall boogied down in Ronnie VanZant's position as front man. Frenzied women nearly wet their pants when he launched into "Freebird." Most of the regulars bragged how they'd seen Skynyrd right here at the Ivy at least a dozen times, every time they came through Durham. They went wild when Kendall's band covered their boys. Course some of the college kids whistled and stomped no matter what they played. Sometimes Kendall would do a few chords of "Rock Around the Clock" as a joke, and those Tarheel preppies would start clapping and squawking the Rebel Yell. Sent the band into hysterics. Those preps stayed roaring drunk the entire evening – probably the entire weekend. The guys and the gals, too. It was nothing to see one of the dates in Pappagallos, a cashmere sweater, and matching slacks leaning over the toilet in the Ladies' Room retching her guts out. Plus the middle-aged townies always elbowed up front like the place belonged to them. The women ogled Kendall, the men rubbed the women, they all swayed up against one another like they were about to have group sex right there on the floor. Priscilla hated everything about the Ivy.

Next to her Evelyn was attempting to move in time to the music, but her lack of rhythm must've been some kind of birth defect. Priscilla was embarrassed for her, but Evelyn certainly didn't notice. Her face was shiny red, glowing, like she'd just been crowned May Queen. Probably the beer. Evelyn drank from the pitcher right along with the guys whenever they took a break, never noticing that they talked around her like she didn't exist. Priscilla hadn't even tried to count how many glasses she'd gulped down while she nodded and pretended she was part of the gang. Evelyn drunk wouldn't be a pretty sight. Priscilla couldn't stand the thought of holding her limp hair out of her face while she threw up.

"Kendall is sooooo cooooll!" Evelyn screeched in her ear, like she was announcing the Academy Awards. Priscilla faked a smile, lifted her glass in a silent toast. The place was so loud she didn't even try to talk. Small blessing.

Kendall looked over at her from the bandstand and winked, right in the middle of the song. Priscilla smiled back at him, connected. Praise the Lord. She still found it hard to believe she was his girlfriend — his fiancé! — in this room full of women, any number of whom would slip him their phone numbers during the course of the evening or try to waylay him on the way to the men's room (Gents at the Ivy). Some of them way prettier than Miss North Carolina. And about a hundred times as sexy. Lots of times, after a gig, when they'd go back to her place or just ride around talking, he'd say, "Them gals at the Ivy are plumb disgusting, the way they throw their bodies up against me and the guys and say nasty, sinful things they got no business saying." Then he'd cuddle her and tell her how much he loved her, respected her Christian ways. He despised the place every bit as much as she did, called it his cross to bear, but didn't he have to work to make money, and playing nights gave him plenty of time to write gospel songs days. And put a little aside for the wedding. He'd break through with a recording contract, she knew he would, and then they would never have to set foot in a bar again in their lives. He'd promised. Priscilla could put up with the Ivy for him for now, but the place still made her sick to her stomach.

Plus the smoke made her eyes burn like crazy. Way over half of the customers were smoking: smoking, drinking, yelling, dancing, screeching along to the songs. How did they do it all at once? How could they think it was fun? Priscilla put her glass on the table and started nudging her way through the crowd to the front door. Cold as it was outside, she had to get some fresh air or she'd throw up herself.

The icy air smacked Priscilla as she stepped out the door, took her breath, like riding on a roller coaster jolting down the first hill. She turned her face to the overcast sky: was it going to snow? Hadn't heard anything about it on the news. Gasping from the freezing air, she moved toward the car, wishing she'd picked up her coat. She shivered in her pullover sweater, no gloves, no hat. She'd just sit in the front seat for a little while, turn on the heater, try to relax till she was sure the band was taking a break. The roar from inside was considerably quieter out here, but she could still hear the muffled racket.

When she got to the Mustang – my Mustang! – at the back of the lot, she realized Kendall had the key. Go back? Huh-uh, better frozen than fried. Not that many people were outside – just a few couples making out like crazy and two guys sharing a cigarette – and none of them were paying the slightest attention to her. But still, she felt like some show-off, or worse, some phony who was just imagining she belonged with this car. Like people probably thought she pretended Kendall was winking at *her* back there inside. Fat chance. Why would the lead guitarist/singer in Cool Water wink at a plain Jane like her? Why would a natural-born nobody have a red Mustang convertible?

Priscilla sucked in the cold air, made herself shut her eyes and think about something pleasant: Elvis, calling her his Little Miss Priss. Elvis, saying what sweet bitty hands she had. Elvis, insisting she feed him his rice, her and nobody else. Saying grace before he ate. "Dear Lord, Make me grateful for the food I'm about to eat, even if it is nothing but a piddly bowl of rice without even a single spoon of sugar. Amen." Without even trying he could make her laugh in a heartbeat, the way he said the silliest thing like that. Those things really happened. Didn't that mean he thought a lot of her? He really gave her this car, that's a fact. She touched the shiny surface. It felt like a cold glass to her fingers, like a ice tray. Elvis liked lots of crushed ice. He'd chew an iced tea glass full of ice, but he wouldn't drink any water. Said it didn't taste like anything. Why should he drink something that didn't have a bit of taste? He longed for a chocolate milkshake, or a Pepsi full to the top with crushed ice. He'd crunch his ice and they'd pretend he was drinking a Pepsi. For a second she imagined her and Kendall doing something silly like that.

Thinking about the pretend Pepsi made Priscilla thirsty, too, but she didn't want to go back inside that noisy, crowded room yet. And she wouldn't go to the bathroom. She always went before she came, so she wouldn't need to go to the Ladies. It was hard, since between set-up and breaking down Kendall was usually there at least four hours. Then he sometimes liked to sit with the guys and unwind, have a beer or two after the place cleared out. He claimed beer wasn't a sin, even though the Assembly had a strict rule against spirits. Didn't Jesus drink wine? Plus it was getting drunk that was wicked, not drinking and keeping your head. Respecting your body as a temple. And Kendall kept his head, most all the time. So usually she'd be there four or five hours without going to the bathroom. But the Ladies' Room smelled like Pinesol and puke, and even if she was a nurse she couldn't stand being closed up in a tiny restroom with the rank smell of boozy vomit. It made her think of all those Sunday car trips with her family. Made her practically heave, right now, just the idea.

    The whole family would go to church and Sunday School all dressed up. Mama always sewed her Sunday dresses extra pretty, even if her school clothes were nothing special. After, they'd sit down at home to a big Sunday dinner: fried chicken, gravy, mashed potatoes, green beans with ham, hot rolls, applesauce, usually pound cake or some kind of pie. Then they'd go for a Sunday drive. Only Priscilla got carsick. Every Sunday. They'd pile into the old Chevy station wagon, the tan one they had for years before Daddy got the Corvair, and she'd have to sit in the middle in the back, since she was smallest, with Bud on one side and Paul on the other, her feet perched on the hump. She'd take along paper towels and two big brown grocery bags, one inside the other. And before they were out of town good she'd throw up into the bags. In front, her Daddy would holler, "Don't you get any of that mess on the car, you hear?", then he'd turn to her mama and say, "We can't even go for a drive without the girl getting sick. What in the world's wrong with her?" Never Priscilla. "The girl." Her mama would just shake her head. And Bud would lean over and whisper, "You get a drop of that crap on me and I'm gonna have to slap you silly." Only Paul ever acted like he kinda understood, kinda felt bad for her. He'd sometimes give her a tiny pat, maybe on the hand, maybe on the shoulder. But he wouldn't look at her, and he wouldn't say a word. If they stopped at Tastee Freez for ice cream cones she'd get out and shove the bag in the trash can and climb back in the car, close her eyes, try to fall asleep. Her Daddy would yell, "You want a cone?" and when she'd shake her head no he'd say, "Guess that means we can get a double, Buddy-Boy. Whaddaya say?" She still couldn't ride in the back seat of a car without getting sick as a dog.

    Priscilla shivered; she'd have to go back in. Her hands and ears felt like they were frozen, like she couldn't move her fingers. She put her hands up under her hair, covered her ears. At least she couldn't hear the band or the screaming crowd, even if she was a human Popsicle.

"You got a light?"

Priscilla jumped like she'd been shot.

"Hey, sorry, didn't mean to shock you or anything."

The man standing in front of her reminded her of her brother Bud, only Bud had been dead five years. This guy was big, burly, with a round face. Not good-looking, not ugly. Just big. He didn't have on a coat, either. Probably didn't need one.

"Oh. Goodness. I mean, I don't smoke or anything . . ." Priscilla tucked her arms together so her hands were under her armpits.

"No problem. I shouldn't be smoking anyway. This your car?" He pointed with the cigarette.

"Uh-huh. I just got it. This week."

"It's a beaut. Oh. What am I thinking? My name's Jared. Jared Falkner. No U. The *disgraced* side of the Falkner family." He stuck out his other hand, grinning. Lots of white teeth. His Southern accent was thick, not North Carolina. Reminded her a little of the way Elvis and his boys talked. Maybe Mississippi.

"I'm Priscilla," she answered, head down, and offered a quick handshake. His hand was warm.

"Saaaay, Miss Priss, those little fingers of yours feel like ice cubes. We better go inside before you freeze to death." He held on, turned toward the door still holding her hand, tugging her just the slightest bit.

Priscilla jerked away. "I needed to get away from the smoke in there."

"I see." He dropped the unlit cigarette in his other hand, crushed it with his boot. Not like a cowboy boot. Like a workman's boot. "Nasty habit. Keep meaning to quit."

"Plus people act so crazy in there, making so much racket they can't even hear the band. After a while the noise gets to be too much, you know?" She blew on her fingers, tucked them up under her armpits again.

"Band any good?"

"They're terrific. Really popular around here. My fiancé's the lead."

"You don't say. Your fiancé." He smiled that big-toothed smile again. "I heard from some of the guys on the job that this Cool Water is pretty slick. Thought I'd give 'em a listen."

"You won't be able to hear much tonight," she said through chattering teeth.

"Since I'm here might as well go in. You better come on. You shivering all over."

Priscilla noticed that the sound had tamped down a notch or two. Band must be on break. Kendall would be looking for her. Plus she *was* freezing. "Yeah. But I better go to the Ladies first, you know?"

"Mind if I wait for you? I'd like to meet the band, if you wouldn't mind introducing me."

"Well . . . you know, they kinda like to keep to themselves on break." How could she come right out and say no to this Jared guy? That would sound so . . . rude. But Kendall would be mad enough to spit if she walked in with a man. A stranger.

"I ain't gonna be no trouble. Promise. C'mon." He started for the building.

She walked along a couple of steps behind Jared Falkner, wondering how in God's name she was gonna pull this off.

The guy held the door for her. That was a surprise. As she edged past him the sweat and heat and smoky haze formed a gray cloud. All Priscilla could see were blurry heads and dim bodies. She had to walk in front, to lead the way to the table. The jukebox blared some country song she didn't recognize. "No need even trying the Ladies," she yelled over her shoulder, pointing to the line that snaked all the way to the bar. He just nodded as she shoved through the crowd, the side of his hulky warm torso pressed right against her side. He was much taller than Kendall — maybe six two or six three to Kendall's five seven — and had to outweigh him by a good fifty or sixty pounds. That solid meatiness reminded her of her father and older brother.

Finally she could see the shape of the guys huddled around the table up front. Usually they'd go outside to the alley on break, but tonight was way too cold. And the Ivy didn't have a back room. People were pressing up to them, which Kendall would hate. He was pouring a beer. She watched as he took a big drink and then looked up toward the door just as she was getting close to him. Good thing she couldn't see his full face. His eyes were enough. She waved a little wave and tried to hustle, but there was no hurrying in this crush of people. He kept staring at her, those dark eyes two shiny warnings. Jared Falkner leaned down, "That your guy in front of us? Cause if it is, he looks mad enough to bite a rattlesnake."

"That's him. He was just worried, is all."

"If that's worried I'd hate to see mad." His mouth brushed her ear. Jared Falkner laughed, a man's laugh, deep and from the gut. Priscilla didn't find him a bit funny.

Kendall stood. "Where you been?"

Out of breath, though all she'd done was walk across the room, Priscilla started explaining, "I went outside cause of the smoke, you know, and . . ."

Jared Falkner pushed around her and stuck his hand over the table toward Kendall. "How ya doing? I hear you're Priscilla's main man."

Kendall looked like this stranger had tried to kiss him, he was that stunned. "Say what?" Like a trained dog he put out his hand, though, and shook, glaring toward Priscilla. "You know this guy?"

"We just met. Outside. Like I was saying . . ."

"I was looking for a light and this lovely lady here told me she was engaged to you, so I begged myself along so's I could meet you and the guys in the band. I play a little guitar myself. Hey there." He shook hands all around the table.

"Where's Evelyn?" Priscilla wanted to make peace, so she put her arm through Kendall's. He plopped down in his chair, forcing her to let go. She knew if there was one thing he couldn't stand it was some hanger-on who bragged about what a great musician he was. This whole evening was going from bad to worse.

"I told her to get lost." Kendall smirked. The other guys grinned.

"Come on. Really. Where is she?" Much as he couldn't stand Evelyn, Kendall would never be outright mean to her. Unfriendly, yes, mean, no.

"She went to take a piss."

Priscilla's face flushed. He never talked like that around her.

"Say, let me go find a chair for Priscilla. Be right back." Jared pushed his way back through the mob lurking around the table.

"Take your time," Kendall said, loud enough for everybody at the table to hear. He gave Priscilla a hateful look and started talking to Eddie, the bass guitarist, next to him.

She wiggled around behind him, started rubbing his shoulders. "Look, Kendall, I didn't do a thing wrong. He just kinda followed me in here."

He ignored her so she just stood there massaging his tense muscles. Kendall hunched toward the guys and drank his beer, like she didn't exist. Priscilla

Charlotte Morgan

wanted to cry, or pray, but she couldn't imagine doing either standing next to the stage at the Ivy with a crush of drunk people practically in her lap.

Jared Falkner materialized holding two chairs up over his head like they were bottles of soda. "Here you go, Miss Priss, let's make a place at the table for you."

The members of the band pushed their chairs closer without looking up, and Jared squeezed in the two he'd confiscated as close as he could get them. He held Priscilla's while she sat and was about to sit himself when Evelyn appeared out of nowhere, her face white as a nurse's cap.

"You need a hand, Miss?" Jared asked, steadying her as she lumbered toward Priscilla.

Evelyn didn't even look at him, headed straight for Priscilla. "I am sooooo embarrassed," she said, putting her head on Priscilla's shoulder.

"It's okay," Priscilla murmured, patting her damp hair, bracing an arm on her shoulder, standing. She and Jared eased Evelyn into a chair.

"Ooooh, I feel so awful," Evelyn moaned.

Priscilla hunkered down beside her. "No problem. You'll be fine. You want me to drive you home?"

"No!" Evelyn looked up with startled eyes, begging. "I gotta stay for the last set. What'll the guys think if I leave now?"

They won't even notice, Priscilla thought. "You sure? I could have you home in ten minutes. Get you some coffee and aspirin on the way."

"If my parents saw me like this . . ."

"Okay. I'll get you a ginger ale." Priscilla turned to go to the bar. "Oh, sorry, this is Jared Falkner. Evelyn Walsh."

He eased into the chair beside Evelyn, turned his face toward Priscilla. "I'll look after her. Don't you worry. Take your time." One wide hand reached up to Priscilla's shoulder and stayed there a few seconds.

She was wedged in by the crowd. "This might take more than a minute," she called over her shoulder, hoping Kendall would look up. He didn't.

Evelyn plopped her elbows on the table and dropped her head into her hands like she'd been charged with homicide.

"You know a sure cure for the bad head and the rolling stomach?" Jared asked, looking from one to the other.

Evelyn shook her head no without making a sound.

122

"You stand on your head and count to a hundred."

Priscilla and Evelyn both stared at him like he didn't have a grain of sense, and after a couple of seconds he burst out laughing.

"Don't knock it till you've tried it," he hollered between laughs. Everybody close by looked at them like, *What did we miss?* Even Kendall. Jared Falkner's round face lit up like a spotlight. Evelyn grinned, too, pale as she was.

"Hey, don't try it till I get back, okay?" Priscilla yelled, forcing an opening through the bodies.

The third set the raucous mood subsided to a steady buzz. A lot of the Skynyrd groupies left, and most everybody else stayed at their tables and drank, no doubt anticipating last call. Cool Water performed a variety of songs, everything from Gene Autry to the Everly Brothers. Some gigs Kendall would try out one of his own gospel tunes somewhere in the middle of the last set, but he hadn't so far tonight. He hadn't looked toward Priscilla once, either. In fact, when he and Eddie were crooning "If You Don't Know Me By Now," he kept staring at this blond who'd been eyeing him all night long, pretending he was singing to her. She was slumped down in her booth, eyes half closed, moving to the music like she was gonna have sex with him right then and there. Priscilla thought it was trashy. She knew Kendall was acting that way to get back at her for bringing Jared Falkner to the table. He probably thought she'd been flirting with him, too, and that was why he was so all-fired jealous. Still, it was no call to act so raunchy out in public.

Meanwhile, Jared had been downright good company to her and Evelyn the entire hour. She'd been right: he was from Mississippi, just like Elvis. In fact, his grand-daddy had moved from Oxford to Tupelo to preach at the First Baptist Church, but mostly to get away from the drinking, non-church-going Faulkner relatives. That's why he'd changed the spelling of their last name. "Funny thing," Jared told Priscilla and Evelyn: "my side of the family got to be no count, and the cousins with the U back in Oxford got all famous and uppercrust. Don't that beat all?"

Priscilla had to ask him what he knew about the Presleys, since he was from Elvis' hometown.

"Lord, people in Tupelo don't have much good to say about ol' Elvis. You all fans?"

"I got every single he ever made," Evelyn gloated. "I bought 'Don't Be Cruel' with my very first allowance when I was eleven years old. Seen him two times in concert, too." She held up two fingers and poked them in the air, proud as if she'd been on two dates with Elvis himself. She'd perked up considerably since her ginger ale. Plus Jared Falkner was paying her a lot of attention.

"You don't say? How 'bout you, Priscilla. You a fan too?"

"I wouldn't say a *big* fan. I've always liked the Beatles songs better, to tell you the truth. My Mama likes Elvis a lot, though, and I grew up with his music in the house. 'Cept when Daddy was home. Daddy couldn't abide him. Thought he was, what would he always say? Thought he was common as dirt and twice as filthy."

"I like his music good enough." Jared took a sip from his Miller High Life bottle. "People back home call his family white trash, I guess you know that."

"That's so hateful," Evelyn pouted.

"Yeah, I read all about that in the movie magazines." Priscilla stared into her glass, dying to say what Elvis was *really* like. "Seemed like the Presleys loved their boy, though, from what I've read."

"I'll say. Rumors about that mother of his – what was her name? Gladys Love? Don't that beat all? – anyway, people said she never let him out of her sight. Like to ruined him the way she doted."

"*Ruined* him?" Priscilla blurted. "Fan or no fan, that kind of talk bothers me, everybody so full of jealousy they have to say hateful things." She sat up straight. "How can anybody claim something like that, when he's one of the most popular people in the United States? When he probably makes more money every year than the President, himself."

"Easy there, darlin," Jared tapped her wrist, leaned in. "Word has it he ain't never got over his Mama dying, that he's bad into drugs."

Evelyn and Priscilla looked at one another – not a word about drugs on his chart – both shouted, "No!"

"Hey, hey." He held up both hands in mock defense. "I ain't the one saying so. Rumors, that's all. His Mama was a drinker, that's for a fact. And people around town who keep up with his kin say he pops pills, anything he can get into his mouth. Especially diet pills."

"Oh I don't believe that for a minute." Priscilla shook her head, turned to look at the band. Kendall couldn't stand it when folks talked while the band was performing, and she realized they'd gotten pretty loud, but he wasn't paying a bit of attention to them. Why was all this Elvis gossip getting to her anyway? Wasn't like they were big buds or anything. Probably cause it wasn't the Elvis she'd known for that little bit, and she couldn't let on. And he did give her a car. That was some personal connection, wasn't it?

Cool Water finished "Nights in White Satin" to earsplitting applause and whistles. The people might be sitting down now, but they were no less into the music. Kendall had his back turned, prepping the guys for the next song, when somebody hollered out, "How 'bout 'Rocky Mountain High'?" That tune had been on the radio non-stop all month. Kendall had sworn to Priscilla it made him gag, it was so sweet, and he labeled John Denver a prissy little fag. Plus he never did requests anyway. Anybody who followed the band knew that. A woman in the back hollered loud enough to scare a ghost, "Do some Elvis. Do 'Burning Love'!" Kendall swung back around to face the audience, hit a loud chord, and the band launched into an all-out rendition of "Layla." He'd sworn he'd never sing an Elvis song, that he'd rather cut off all ten fingers than cover that fat, vulgar has-been.

Jared tapped her shoulder. "Your boy's good, Priscilla. He can play, that's for sure."

"I know. He's way too good for this place."

Evelyn offered, "They're ALL too good, the whole band."

They sat and listened, all watching Kendall while he pulled his Eric Clapton cool-rocker routine. "Hey, did you ever run into Elvis yourself?" Priscilla turned to face Jared again. She had to ask.

"Naw. By the time I went to school they'd already moved to Memphis. Besides, they come from East Tupelo. The wrong side of the tracks. My cousins and all, we were bad boys, you know, but we weren't white trash. We come from Tupelo proper."

"You don't say." She wasn't even gonna get into what Jared was doing right this minute and what Elvis was up to. Somewhere in Hawaii getting ready for some major concert big deal. That white trash stuff burned her up. "Well, anyway, I still don't believe that about the drugs."

"Like I said, it's just rumor." Jared drained his beer and sat the empty on the table.

Kendall was talking into the mike, thanking the crowd for being so fine, thanking the boys in the band for their talent and hard work, inviting everybody to come back next weekend. She watched him, so poised and confident up there, the crowd eating out of his mouth. He raised his hand, hollered, "God bless," and then the boys started their closer, "Green River." Every single time Kendall sang that first line, "Well, take me back down where cool water flows," he smiled at her. Their little secret. They were both soooo glad the gig was over. Only tonight he didn't look her way. Not even a glimpse.

"You all gonna hang around a while?" Jared asked, looking from one of the women to the other.

Good grief. Couldn't he feel the tension radiating down from Kendall, Priscilla wondered. "Kendall and I will probably head on out soon as they pack up."

"Well. Some other time then. You need a ride, Evelyn?"

Priscilla jerked her head in Evelyn's direction. Evelyn could've won the Green Stamp bonus award, she was that tickled.

"I haven't called anybody to come get me yet," she answered. "I was kinda hoping one of the guys in the band would offer, but since nobody has . . ."

"Come on then, let me take you. You'll have to give me directions, though. I'm still learning my way around Durham."

Dear Lord, Priscilla thought. Evelyn has the social skills of a walrus. And this Jared seems nice enough, sure, but should I let her get in his car? We don't really know him. Maybe he's some kind of hobo murderer. Still, Kendall's not-talking mad; if I ask him to drive Evelyn home, who knows how long he'll give me the silent treatment? Or worse. Throw one of his fits, maybe. She looked up at him again, singing gentle as a angel. No, he wouldn't blame her for this Jared thing once she explained. And besides, Evelyn was a grown woman. Couldn't she handle herself with a guy? Women went home from the Ivy with guys they'd just met every night of the week. Standard operating procedure. Her mama made her skittish about living in a big city like Durham, that was all. Evelyn was on her own.

The guys finished "Green River" and bowed as everyone in the room stood and clapped and cheered. The house lights came up. Cool Water never did an encore. Kendall claimed that was for concerts, not bar gigs.

Priscilla searched around the chair backs for her coat. Evelyn was already pulling on her plaid parka. Good grief, how long had she had that ugly thing?

Since high school? "Y'all look out for the police, you hear? They're all over people leaving the Ivy on weekends." Let that be a double warning.

"Not to worry, Little Missy." Jared put one hand on her shoulder. "It's my lucky night, meeting you folks."

Priscilla wasn't much for the John Wayne routine, but this Jared had a smile in his eyes. Nothing shifty about it. And she'd gotten a good feeling talking to him.

"I'm off tomorrow, Priscilla. You too?" Evelyn bubbled like it was her birthday.

"Yeah. Kendall and I are gonna go see Mama after church. So I'll talk to you Monday evening. Okay?"

"Sure thing." Evelyn pulled up the hood to her parka and took her homemade red knit gloves out of the pockets. "Don't worry a bit about me, Pris. I feel fine now." Evelyn gave her a big hug, the fake fur trim of her hood tickling Priscilla's cheek. "Thanks for inviting me. You know how much I love Cool Water. Tonight was fabulous."

"I'm not worried." She hugged back, sat down, didn't bother to mention the fact that she hadn't invited her. "Bye now. Take it easy, you hear?"

"You bet," Jared replied, patting her shoulder. "You take it easy, too."

Priscilla watched as he led the way to the door and Evelyn lumbered along behind him. In a way she wished she'd left with them. Cause she was. Worried. About Evelyn leaving with this man they'd just met. Worried, especially, about what Kendall was gonna do once they got inside the car. He'd never say anything ugly to her in front of the guys. He'd ignore her, sure, but he wouldn't say a single nasty word. But what would he say – or do – once they were alone tonight?

She crushed her coat against her chest, closed her eyes tight. Dear Lord, don't let him be mad at me. Please, I pray, I know it's thy will be done, not mine, but what good could it possibly do for Kendall to lose his temper? When I didn't do a thing wrong? This place is sinful, I know, it's a temple of wrongdoing and temptations. But Kendall's a good man, a Christian man, you know he is. Guide him in the way of your son Jesus, in the way of forgiveness. This I pray in His holy name. She sighed. Oh, and watch over me, Lord. Make me pleasing in His sight. Amen.

Priscilla opened her eyes, looked around at the shabby room, almost empty now except for some guys wiping the tables and the band clearing the equipment onstage. Could God even hear a prayer coming from a place like this? Surely Jesus, who walked among us, surely He'd understand. She had to trust and obey, like the hymn said. She fumbled under the table for her pocketbook. That's what she'd do, trust and obey in Jesus' loving care. Plus she'd borrow a page from Elvis' book, too. She'd Take Care of Business. Priscilla had to smile, thinking of Elvis saying that. He was so much fun to be around, no matter what Jared Falkner said about him. He had a extra big heart, that's for sure. No, she wouldn't get all fretful. She'd comb her hair and put on a little lipstick, and as soon as they got to the car she'd let Kendall know he was the one and only man on earth for her. Her Special Angel. Looking in the mirror, thinking about Elvis and Kendall, she hummed that old sweet song to herself, "You are my special angel, sent from up above . . ."

Priscilla
January 10, 1973, later

The car was freezing. Kendall turned on the ignition and the heater, fiddling around to find the controls. They were both still figuring out where things were on this fancy-schmancy Mustang. Priscilla huddled in her bucket seat, looking straight ahead. He hadn't spoken since they'd walked out of the Ivy. He'd held the door for her, like always, then packed up the trunk while she waited, about to pop. The windows were cloudy with the cold. She thought about reaching up and making swirls on the windshield with her fingers, but instead she forced herself to be still.

"Look here, Priscilla, give me your hands." His voice was quiet, prayerful.

She turned to him, pulled off her gloves. Kendall never wore gloves, no matter how cold it got. Course it wasn't usually this cold in Durham, even in January.

"Let us pray."

His hands weren't the slightest bit chilled. Those long slender fingers were warm as toast. How'd he do that? Priscilla bowed her head and closed her eyes, so much a habit that it was only after she'd done it that she was struck by how peculiar it must look, two people sitting in a red Mustang praying.

"Dear Lord," Kendall paused, took a deep breath. "Lord, I come to you with a troubled heart tonight. Troubled by the wanton behavior of my precious Priscilla."

Wanton? She hadn't even come close to wanton. Had she?

"And Lord," he continued, "give me the strength to follow in thy son Jesus' ways, to seek thy guidance, to walk the one true Christian path of love and forgiveness. This I pray in His name. Amen."

"Amen," she whispered. It was dead wrong to be distracted during prayer, but she couldn't help it. He wasn't being fair.

Kendall squeezed her fingers extra tight, stayed like that for a few seconds before he loosened up. "Now you. You pray for your sins, Priscilla."

She opened her eyes and looked up at him, but he still had his head bowed. What was she to do except try to pray? Again, she lowered her head, shut her eyes, striving to make that Christian connection, to find solace in that promise: I am always with you. "Lord God, I don't know what to say . . ." She really didn't. Kendall held on, waiting in silence until she continued. "I've upset my future husband, and I know you expect better of me." She'd done nothing wrong, though. "Jesus teaches us: Bear all things. Endure all things. I strive for the right, Lord. You know I do." She took a deep breath. "Help me to be acceptable in Thy sight; keep my feet on the path of righteousness. This I pray in Jesus' Holy Name. Amen." Would that do?

"Amen." Kendall's voice was hearty. He hugged her, held her so tight she could barely breathe. "You can't begin to understand how upset I get when I see you with some other man like that, Priscilla. You can't *imagine*." He was talking into her hair, his voice all thick like he was testifying. In the Spirit.

"I would never deliberately do a thing to make you mad, Kendall. Don't you know that?"

He took her by the shoulders, held her back against the window. "Darlin', ain't never been no woman in my life I could trust. You know that good and well. You the first pure woman I've believed in, had faith in." His eyes were tearing up. "When I saw you walk in with that, that nut-case, I like to lost my mind."

Priscilla reached up to touch his cheek. He nuzzled into her hand. "Oh, Kendall."

"Even my own mama was next door to a tramp, right in front of my pitiful excuse of a daddy."

"I know, Kendall, I know." She pulled him to her chest.

"Drives me wild to see you acting like that, paying all that attention to some big-butt stranger, knowing it's bound to drive me to distraction." Tears were streaming down his cheeks now. "Drives me to sinful thoughts."

Kissing him on the forehead, Priscilla started singing in that lullaby voice mamas use to soothe fretful children, "I come to the garden alone, while the dew is still on the roses." They both loved that old hymn, would harmonize to all the verses while they drove around town.

Kendall jerked up, so that the word "roses" broke off in a kinda gasp. "I mean what I'm saying, Priscilla. That made me crazy-mad. Like I could've done something I'da had no business doing. You hear?" His eyes had that out-of-control look that scared her half to death.

"I do. I hear." Again, she touched his face. He kept on staring at her in that frightful way for a few seconds, then he leaned forward and kissed her, gentle as a daddy kisses his new baby.

"I love you, Priscilla."

"I know you do."

"Today's been too weird, babe. First you going off and buy this car on your own like that. Then bringing some strange man into the Ivy, like it's a normal everyday thing . . ."

"I didn't want to . . ."

"Let me finish." He raised his voice the slightest bit. "Crazy day like that, I'm too much on edge anyway, you hear? What with worrying about them songs I sent out to that record company, and worrying 'bout making enough money for our wedding, to settle down and all, and having to play at the Ivy week after week, I'm too much on edge these days. You gotta understand me."

"I do. I truly do." She loved Kendall so much right this second, like Jesus must've loved his own disciples. He loved her. He *needed* her. Now she kissed him on his forehead, his eyelids, his damp cheeks. "I promise I won't ever do anything foolish like that again. I swear on the Holy Bible."

"You the best, Priscilla. Makes me nuts, thinking I could lose you."

"That'll never happen. Never in all eternity."

Finally he smiled, brushed his hands through her hair. "So let's get out of here, whatcha say?"

Priscilla let out a breath, like she'd been holding it for the last two hours. The car was almost too warm now. That was some heater. "Want to go to my place for a while? I could make some hot chocolate. Maria's working a double, and Angie said she'd be spending the night out." Kendall had no respect for

131

Maria and Angie, couldn't wait till she didn't have to live with them, though Priscilla told him they'd been nothing but nice to her.

"Angie spending the night out. I can guess what that means." Raising his eyebrows, he put the Mustang in reverse.

Priscilla leaned back against her comfy seat, relaxed for the first time in what felt like forever. She rolled her head in Kendall's direction. Gosh he looked handsome driving this sporty car, the collar of his jacket up just the slightest bit, that shiny wavy hair of his hanging to his shoulders, his dark eyes all sparkly. Like they belonged together, him and the Mustang. Some car commercial. Sooooo cool, like Evelyn said. "This sure is some car, isn't it?"

"That it is, little darlin. That it is." He turned and smiled at her.

She touched his arm. "Listen, Evelyn left with that guy. You think she'll be all right?"

He shrugged. "Evelyn ain't none a my trouble."

"I know that. But I was a little worried when he offered her a ride, to tell you the truth. She's so . . . so . . ."

"Stupid is what she is. Stupid as a cow. And bout as big."

"Oh, Kendall, come on . . . she's not that bad. And I'm feeling kinda responsible, you know?"

"No, I don't. She's a grown woman. She can make her own decisions, right? It ain't like you made her go with that nutso guy."

"You're right. Still, I hope she's okay. She's not exactly experienced with men, you know?"

"She'll be fine. If he gets a little too feisty she can just sit on him." He smirked at his own joke. "Yessireebob, she can sit on his fat ass."

"Kendall . . . that's not kind at all."

"Maybe not. But it's the truth and you know it."

She had to laugh. More because she was relieved that they were talking easy than because of his nasty kidding. "You shouldn't be so hard on poor Evelyn. It's not like she's popular with the guys."

"I'll say. Hey, enough about Evelyn. Come on over here next to me." He patted the gearshift.

Now she raised her shoulders. "Guess I can't. Sorry." As she spoke she reached over and put her hand under his hair and rubbed his warm neck.

"Dang. That's the one thing that ugly Corvair of yours had on this here Mustang. Least you could sit right up next to me where you belong."

Priscilla leaned over and kissed his prickly cheek. "Guess we'll just have to wait for that till we get home."

"Guess so."

He looked so happy now, like a guy with his first guitar. For the first time this evening Priscilla got that flushed feeling, that warmness all over she got sometimes when things were perfect between them. Oh, she couldn't wait till she and Kendall were man and wife. She knew, without any question, that he was the one and only man God intended for her.

"Hey little darlin, why don't you see what's on the radio? Let's have some tunes."

She reached for the knob. Yes indeed, every now and then life was absolutely, positively perfect.

After gigs Kendall could be hungry as one of her fatties just off the rice diet. She'd fixed him half a dozen eggs, scrambled with Velveeta and sausage like he liked them, and four pieces of toast. He drank Pepsi like it was water. Kendall wasn't one for hot drinks, so she hadn't bothered with the hot chocolate just for her. Bustling about fixing for him, she didn't even think about eating anything herself. She wasn't hungry anyway. Too worked up, her stomach fluttery. What a strange night it had been. Kendall was right. A strange week, really, but she couldn't talk to him about all that. About Elvis and the car. Maybe once they were married. That part, keeping things from him, felt wrong, even if it was her professional promise. Could nurses share confidential information with their husbands? She didn't think so. It would be peculiar, though, keeping secrets from her husband. When they were one. Late as it was, Priscilla was wide awake, all these thoughts running through her head like some tape recorder on fast forward. She was used to this time of night; it was her regular shift. Though it was sure hard getting up in the morning for eleven o'clock church, she loved the times like this when it was just the two of them here at the apartment. For a little while she could pretend it was *their* apartment. Almost like they were an old married couple.

"Next to your mama you're bout the best cook I've ever known. They can't make a breakfast at the Top Hat good as yours." Kendall patted his non-existent gut. "Ain't nobody can cook like your mama, but you run a close second. Yessiree. You likely to have me fat as a hog before I'm thirty."

Priscilla looked over her shoulder and smiled at him, sitting there all satisfied. She was finishing up the dishes, which included all of Angie's for at least the last five days. She never had minded washing dishes, the warm sudsy water making the glasses and plates shiny clean. Back home usually she got to be all alone, cause everybody else would go in the front room just in case her mama might tell them to dry. Nope, washing the dishes was a pleasing task. Cleanliness being next to Godliness.

"You bout done, girl? I'm ready for that hugging you promised in the car." Wired, he called it. He'd say he was wired after playing three sets. Hungry, wired, and ready to have a little loving.

She hung the damp dishtowel on the handle of the stove to dry. "Want anything else?"

"Wouldn't mind a little cuddling and kissing from my best girl. That'd top things off fine. Come on over here." He held out his arms for her, a big grin on his handsome face.

"Do I need to fix my hair?" She'd pulled it back in a low ponytail while she was cleaning up, and loose strands straggled around her face. She didn't feel all that glamorous.

"Sit on my lap, darlin, let me do it."

She snuggled into the natural curve of his body. He untwisted the hairholder and let her ponytail loose, sticking his nose into it.

"What do you put on your hair that makes it look so clean all the time? Even after a night at that nasty Ivy. Lord knows I wish I didn't have to work there, wish I didn't have to subject you to that place."

"Same as you. Prell." She'd washed it that morning.

"My hair don't look like this." He pulled a few strands out to its full length in his fingers. "Look how shiny yours is."

"Yours is way shinier. You just teasing me and I know it." She turned around and ruffled his wavy thick hair with her hands. He could make her feel almost pretty.

"Let's put on some music and sit on the sofa where we can stretch out." He stood, still hugging her close to his body. "You my doll baby, that's a fact." He kissed the top of her head.

"You pick a record, okay? I gotta run to the little ladies' room."

As she pulled away from him he held on, pretending he wouldn't let her go. "Don't fall in. Promise."

"Really," she laughed, and he let loose. She hated the way the men in her family talked about using the bathroom: take a whiz, take a dump, get a load off. Her daddy and Bud would say those things and laugh every time. Not so much Paul. What an ugly word: bathroom. She'd always been modest about that. Even when she was little. Even now, when Angie left the door open and talked back and forth it still got to her, though, as Angie said, they were both "girls." Really, all she wanted to do now was brush her hair, put on some Jergens lotion and lipstick, and freshen up for Kendall.

When she came back into the living room he was lying on the couch, boots off, arms behind his head, eyes closed. Credence. The *Green River* album. She could've picked it herself. Kendall had to admit John Fogarty could do it all. Claimed he looked and sounded right much like Fogarty, which was true. He'd cut out the lights, left the kitchen light on so she could see her way to him.

He didn't say a word while she sat in the spot next to his waist, just turned sideways and pulled her down beside him. They lay like that, him nuzzling the back of her neck, his feet wrapping around her feet, her massaging his wiry arms. He pulled her hair to the side so her neck was bare and rubbed his beard against it. She giggled, flushed having all of him up next to her. After a few minutes he whispered, "Come here, baby," and turned her toward him. Her breathing hurried, Priscilla moved against him and wrapped her arms around his head. They started kissing one another, both kissing, lips, cheeks, neck, lips, forehead. Kissing like their lives depended on it.

Kendall's hands moved from her hair to her shoulders down to her waist, caressing her all the while. They gravitated up under her sweater. When they touched her bare back she startled, those slim fingers a jolt. That sensation. They'd laid down together here before, but he'd never touched her like this, not so . . . naked.

"I . . . love . . . you . . . so much," he said, his hands moving all over her bare back now, shoving her sweater up.

Priscilla kept kissing him, pushing toward him, clutching his hair, his shoulders, his shirt. They were both breathing fast, panting almost. His hands opening, spreading, rubbing up and down all over her back.

"I want you, . . . Priscilla," he murmured, those fingers at her sides, now, touching places he'd never touched before, so unbearably sensitive there under her arms, the feeling agitating, unnerving. She could hardly catch her breath.

"I . . . want . . . *you*," she gasped, sure that the hard swelling against her leg was him, his longing for her. "I want . . ."

He groaned, pressed against her till she could barely breathe, then jumped up so fast he almost threw her on the floor. "What?!" he yelled, steadying himself, his hands pushing down on the front of his jeans. "What is *happening* here?"

Shaking, Priscilla tried to sit up, pulling her sweater down. Losing her balance, she fell against the arm of the sofa. "Kendall, I . . ." She reached out a hand to brace herself, to touch his arm, but he jumped back from her.

"Yield not to temptation!" he screamed. "What are you *doing*? What's happening?" His eyes were wild, glaring at her like she was some rabid animal he'd tripped over.

"I thought . . ."

"You thought *what*? That we'd *do* something here . . . that we'd have *sex*, for God's sake . . . right here on the sofa . . . like . . . like those whoring roommates of yours? Is that what you thought?"

Priscilla froze. What *was* happening?

Kendall flopped into the bean bag chair beside the sofa, head dropping into his hands. "Dear God, dear God," he kept saying, almost crying. When he looked up at her the anguish in his face was unbearable. "I thought you were different. I thought you were pure of heart."

"But, Kendall, you . . . you yourself said . . ."

"Dammit, Priscilla. Dammit all to hell." Now he was screaming again, standing over her. "This wounds me, Priscilla. Don't you understand? Bringing that guy to the table, that was bad enough . . . but *this*, this sinning in the flesh . . . this whoring talk . . . good Lord, what am I supposed to do?"

Priscilla squeezed her eyes shut, put her hands up to her ears.

Both his hands grabbed hers and jerked them away from her head, held them in a tight grip. "Listen to me. I mean it." His face was right up next to hers, those eyes crazed, his voice the voice of a mad man. She shook her head yes, yes, yes. He pulled her up, dragged her by both hands into her bedroom. "I want you to get that Bible right there by your bed . . . and I want you to get down on your knees . . ." he was having a hard time getting the words out, "and I want you to open to the Book of . . . of . . . Corinthians, . . . Paul's first letters . . ." He threw the Bible onto the bed, forced her to her knees. "Do it now!"

Shaking, she could barely turn the thin pages. Her fingers were like Popsicle sticks.

"What is wrong with you? First Corinthians, the seventh verse!" He grabbed the Bible from her and flipped the pages to the passage he wanted, stabbed it with his fingers, shoved it back to her. "Right there. Read it out loud. Now!"

Her throat was so dry she didn't think she'd be able to force a word out. Swallowing, she started, "Now concerning the things whereof ye wrote unto me: . . ."

"Louder. Read it louder, Priscilla. I mean it."

"I'll try." She cleared her parched throat again. *Dear Lord, let me do this. Make this end.* "It *is* good for a man not to touch a woman."

"You see. You see what he's saying there. No touching." He poked her shoulder with a finger. "You hear that? Keep on."

"Okay." *Please, Lord, help me out here.* "Nevertheless, *to avoid* fornication, let every man have his own wife, and let every woman have her own husband."

"That's it. Clear as day. Avoid fornication! I told you, Priscilla. I told you all along. The Lord tells us clear as day through his messenger Paul: we are to *avoid fornication*. We are to stay pure until we're married. You KNOW that." He slumped onto the bed, seized her shoulders, shook them in time to his words. "Why are you tempting me? Why are you seducing me with your wicked ways? WHY?"

Paralyzed, Priscilla could only stare into those dark eyes, hypnotized. Was he going to cry again? Or would he lose it completely? He'd never hit her. Would he? Could he?

"I will tell you why." He pointed his finger in her face, stood again. "Satan is trying to get hold of you. I can see it clear as day." He started pacing behind her. She could only squeeze her hands together, bow her head, pray for him to calm down. "That's it. The Devil is happiest when he tempts the pure of heart. THAT . . . IS . . . IT!"

He sat on the bed and grabbed her shoulders again, forcing her to look up at him. This time he was smiling. She didn't know which was worse: his angry face or this excited, grinning face. "Don't you see? He's been tempting you, Priscilla.

Tempting your innocence. Your purity. That car. That stranger. Your . . . wickedness tonight. It's Satan trying to claim you for his own. His very own."

Quick as a cat he kneeled beside her. "We got to beg God for His forgiveness, Priscilla. We got to beg Him to send His army of angels to watch over you, to keep you safe from the depraved wiles of the Devil. Pray with me now, Priscilla. Pray for forgiveness and protection." He clenched his hands together, closed his eyes, and lowered his head to his hands.

Drained, scared to death, she couldn't pray anymore, but she stayed there beside him in a prayerful position, too numb to move. Why was he acting this way, like they'd sinned, *she'd* sinned? Like all the sin was hers? Hadn't he started it, been just as desirous? Just as . . . involved? He'd been mad at her before, yelled and carried on, but he'd never been so out of control, so . . . cruel to her. That's what he'd been . . . cruel. She just wanted to be alone, wanted him to go away. Lord, don't let him scream at me anymore. Don't let him touch me again. There, she'd prayed. Please, make this end. She waited.

Finally: "Amen." He touched her shoulder, gentle as a newborn kitten. She flinched as she turned toward him. "God's gonna see us through this, darlin. He is. You can always turn to God in prayer. He'll always be at the center of our home, the center of our hearts. He'll watch over us until we're one in His Holy name."

She could only nod.

"Now I'm gonna leave you, Priscilla. I'm gonna go back to my room and continue to pray. I want you to cleanse yourself, you hear? I want you to read Paul's letter over and over again, and pray, and cleanse yourself."

Again, she shook her head yes.

"And in the morning we're gonna go to church, like always, then to see your Mama, and I think we need to talk to her about our wedding plans. I think the Lord's saying we shouldn't wait. Shouldn't leave the door open to temptation and the devil. That's His message to us tonight."

"Okay." Wedding? How could he be talking about any wedding right now, tonight, before she'd even been able to catch her breath from this . . . this . . . this shameful, awful *thing* that just happened.

He stood, pulled her up, too. She wanted to recoil from the touch of his hand, but she made herself stay steady, willed herself to be still. "What we're gonna have to do is, we're gonna have to stop all this kissing and such. It only leads to . . . to temptation. It invites sinful thoughts. Okay?"

"Yes." She folded her hands together in front of her.

"So I'm gonna just say goodbye." His voice so sweet, so easy. "I'm taking the car. You shouldn't be driving it. And I'll pick you up at 10:30, same as always. You be ready out front, okay, so I don't have to get out." He patted her shoulder, like a mother comforting a sad child. "Take solace in the Lord and His promises, Priscilla. You only have to ask God for his forgiveness, and ask with a loving heart, and He'll wash away your sins."

"I know. I will." Go. Please just go, she thought.

"Ten thirty, then." And he walked away.

When she heard the door close she ran to the bathroom and heaved into the toilet. Sour Pepsi and slimy strands of bile and, finally, still heaving, nothing.

The lights are out, the door's closed. It's dark, all dark, like a cave. Like a grave. She's huddled in the tub, hugging her legs, the scalding water all the way up to her shoulders. Priscilla rested her head on her knees and cried till she didn't have a drop of salty water left in her body. She'd taken off her clothes, then the gold cross she always wore around her neck – the cross her parents gave her when she was baptized – then her birthstone ring she got when she graduated from nursing school, and last his ring, the promise ring from Kendall. The whole time praying. Father forgive me for I have sinned. Father forgive me for I have sinned. Stepping into the hot water, naked as the day she was born, all Priscilla wanted was water, water as fiery as she could bear it. After she'd thrown up she'd rinsed her mouth over and over, unable to swallow but needing to get the taste out, needing to wash away those terrible words. I want . . . *you*. Just thinking them made her weep with humiliation.

And Kendall. Kendall who loved her and wanted to marry her. How could she get in the car with him? Drive to her Mama's? Talk about a wedding? She shivered. Shame? Was that it? Pride? Was she guilty of the sin of pride now, too? Cupping her hands, she splashed her face, lay back so the water came all the way up to her chin. She didn't want to move from this tub. He'd said cleanse yourself. Be reborn in the Lord's forgiveness. But what had she done that was wrong? The image of his frenzied face, the feel of his hands shaking her. She couldn't get those out of her mind. He had a temper. She knew that. But such *rage*. She knew that rage. She'd lived with it all her life, until she went away to school. She'd watched it boil over on her mother, her brothers. She'd felt the hands of rage against her shoulders, her back, her legs, her face. Never burning itself out, gathering strength each time it appeared. No matter how many Sundays they went to church. No matter how many times they blessed the food. No matter how many times they said their bedtime prayers at night, in the dark. "Deliver us from evil." That rage lived inside their house, ate at their table, slept in their beds. She knew its face. And now it wore Kendall's face.

But she loved Kendall. She did. With all her heart. And all her soul. And all her body? What had she done that was wicked, that sent for Satan? Nothing he hadn't done, too. Nothing he hadn't wanted just as much as she had. But he'd insisted *she* had tempted *him*. How? She'd never so much as kissed another boy. Never been on a date. Never even slow danced. Against the church. The Assembly banned dancing. Sunday Christians, many of them danced and smoked and drank liquor, even. Not her mama and daddy. Never. Her mama clung only to her husband, like the Scriptures said. Did she love him all those years? Had she loved him once? Had she seen his temper before she took her vows?

Priscilla clung to the edge of the tub with her hands, didn't want to so much as touch her hateful skin again, not even with a washcloth. Kendall said, "Cleanse yourself." Was he washing himself clean now, too? Was he reading Holy Scripture and praying without ceasing? Did he despise his own skin right this minute, too?

Truth was, she didn't want him to touch her again, either. Her own husband to be. The thought made her break out in goosebumps, even with the water still so hot.

Breathing fast, Priscilla pushed herself upright, shaky. Was she baptized in the Spirit? Had God forgiven her? Lord knows she'd asked for forgiveness, begged even. But was her heart impure, still? Had she come to God like a child, asking forgiveness? Or did she doubt her own sin, still? Did doubt mean she wasn't in the Spirit? She felt around in the dark for her towel, hanging an arm's length away. Wobbly, she put one foot onto the bath mat, then the other, sank to the floor hugging her towel, crying again. Where did these tears come from? Dear God, give me strength. She stood, wrapped the towel around her, forced herself to open the door. Even though the hall light was out and all the lamps were off in the entire apartment, faint light seeped in through the blinds and curtains. She squeezed her eyes shut and felt her way along the wall to her bedroom door, slammed it. Inside, Priscilla leaned against her dresser and prayed. Help me here, Lord. Help me know the true path to righteousness. I know I'm not perfect. I know I'm guilty of keeping secrets from Kendall. And going places I've got no business. Am I guilty of sins of the flesh, Lord? Have I sinned against your Holy Name? Is there lust in my heart? Dear God, am I a wicked woman? Please cleanse me, make me pure in Thy sight. This I ask in Jesus' name. Amen.

Holding the towel tight around her body with one hand, she pulled open the top drawer and took out a clean, folded granny gown. She shook it open and maneuvered one arm in, her neck, then let the towel drop and stuck her other arm through the hole. The nightgown smelled of Tide and Chlorox and the baby powder sachet she'd made for her dresser. Was she cleansed? Or was that a devilish image, like when Jesus went to the wilderness and Satan appeared before him? Kendall had said read the Scripture. But she wouldn't turn on the light. She couldn't. Making her way to the bed, Priscilla tried to remember the verses he'd had her read. "Avoid fornication." That word made her throat constrict, begin to water. No, no. She wouldn't think that vile word. Hadn't he said that the Devil comes after the pure of heart? Didn't that mean he thought that she was pure. Had been pure . . . before tonight? She dragged the covers back, crawled under them, pulled them up over her head, completely, so the dark enclosed her. Total dark. Best. She lay stiff, still, until her breathing eased and her arms and legs relaxed a bit.

Evelyn. Was Evelyn all right? Dear Lord, look after Evelyn. Please. I know your son Jesus cares for every one of His sheep. Maybe Evelyn needs Him more than I do right now, Dear Lord. Look over her. Please. Amen. And Elvis. What about Elvis? He had to be in Hawaii. When was that concert thing of his? Had it been tonight? Oh, she hoped not. Tonight was a bad, bad night. Surely the Lord protected Elvis from evil, sad as he was. Heartbroken as he was. His Mama dead. His own beloved Priscilla leaving him, taking his little girl, seeing another man. Oh that man had suffered. She'd never seen a man cry like he did, like a little child. Kendall had cried in her arms tonight. Just for a second. But he'd tried to hold back, tried to keep from doing it. Not Elvis. He cried like a three-year-old. And he prayed the same way, with a heart open to the Lord, full of faith. Innocent. Kendall said those awful things about Elvis, ran him down every time his name came up, when he was a decent Christian man. A sinner? Of course. All humans sinned. But a faithful Christian to the core.

That's it. Priscilla turned the covers back to her shoulders. Hazy light seeped from the curtains. Of course she'd been cleansed. "Ask and it shall be given you." She'd asked. She wanted God's forgiveness for any sin she'd committed, for anything unpleasant in his sight. Truly. She only had to come to him as a child, like Elvis. And Kendall? His prayers were between him and the Lord. Had he asked for forgiveness, too? For what? It wasn't her concern. Hadn't his anger been at himself, too, at least partly? She wanted to believe that. Wanted to think he saw his own desire in the same light he saw hers. Exhausted. Too exhausted to sort it out. New day. "If I should die before I wake, I pray Thee, Lord, my soul to take." Hated that prayer. Scared her every time she had to say it out loud, a little girl kneeling. With her daddy. "If I should live another day, I pray Thee, Lord, to guide my way." Better. Not much better. Live another day. If. Kendall. In the morning. Church. How would she feel? No lustful thoughts. That's for sure. Love? No lust. Please Dear Lord. Amen.

Priscilla
Sunday, January 12, 1973

Priscilla stood on the sidewalk in front of the apartment complex, shifting from foot to foot, anxious. The bitter cold from last night hadn't let up. She could smell the snow in the air, that heavy, damp smell. Maybe Kendall would still be angry; maybe he wouldn't want to chance a trip to Henderson if it started to snow while they were in church. Her mama counted on their once-a-month visits, had no doubt started cooking yesterday, but they could go another Sunday. She wouldn't want them driving in bad weather.

The red Mustang rounded the corner, slowed down. As Priscilla stepped toward the curb, reaching for the handle with her gloved hand, Kendall jumped out of the driver's side. "Let me get that for you, darlin. Ain't nobody gonna say I ain't a gentleman with my little lady. Nosirree." He patted her on the shoulder before he reached down for the door. Big smile. Eye contact: I love you, love you, love you.

"Thanks, Kendall." Head ducked. As she settled in her seat he slammed the door and hustled back around to get in himself. On the radio, Reverend Ford from First Baptist was reading scripture. Priscilla didn't recognize the verse. Something about rebuilding a temple. Had to be Old Testament; they were always rebuilding temples in the Old Testament.

Arm on the back of her seat: "Saaay, would you take a look at you with them glasses on. I ain't never seen you in glasses before, Pris." Kendall grinned like she'd brought him an early Valentine.

"I almost never wear them any more." This morning her eyes hurt too much to put in lenses. "You know how it goes, other kids always called me four eyes..."

"I like them. I like them a lot. Makes you look about twelve. Like a sweet little girl." Still grinning to beat the band. How could he be grinning, like nothing at all happened? He started up the engine and eased out into the street.

The First Baptist choir launched into the Doxology. ". . . from whom all bless—sings flow . . ." They'd be at First Assembly before Pastor Ford started his sermon. Thank goodness. She wasn't ready for any preaching just yet. Priscilla let the hood of her car coat down, pulled off her gloves. Kendall had gotten the car all toasty. Driving to church together, like every Sunday for the last year, except they were in the Mustang instead of her Daddy's Corvair. The same, though, like none of this week had happened. Is that how God's forgiveness worked? So everything felt the same? But it didn't. She didn't.

"You get any sleep last night?" She had to ask. Maybe she wasn't supposed to mention what happened last night, but it seemed wrong to act like this was every other Sunday since they'd known one another.

"Hardly slept a wink. Guess what?" His voice sounded joyful enough to be telling her he'd had a direct vision from God. He looked at her like he was about to make her Angel for a Day.

"What?" She had to look back at him, act like it mattered, even though she was feeling curious as a piece of cardboard.

"Would you look at that ponytail? If you ain't cute as a bug!" He whistled through his teeth like guys will do when they see what they call a tough-looking woman. Not a mousy one in glasses.

She reached up and touched her hair. "Yeah. I went to bed with wet hair."

"This new look suits you to a T. I swear it does." He patted her shoulder again.

She didn't like all this patting. "Anyway, you won't believe this, but I wrote a new song last night. This morning, really, I guess. Pris, I'm not kidding, I think this one is it."

Her mouth gaped. He wrote a song last night? While she gnawed herself alive from the inside out?

"You know how the Lord tells us to turn to Him in our hour of suffering, turn to Him in our hour of need? How He'll make us whole again? That's what I did. And He sent me a song."

Priscilla stared, couldn't say a word.

"Bless His Holy name, He sent me a song. Divine inspiration, that's what it was. That's how it come to me."

Was it true? Had the Lord visited Kendall last night, while she lay in bed agonizing over her so-called sins? Had Kendall been righteous, in the eyes of the Lord? Had she been wanton, after all? Her hands started shaking. She squeezed them together in her lap.

"Ain't that a miracle, Priscilla?" He reached over to grab one hand. "Goodness, you're shivering. Let me turn this heater up for you. Don't want you to take a chill." He grinned at her. "You are my sweet little girl today, ain't you? Just look at that ponytail. That and them glasses, you look like you're in 'bout the sixth grade. If you ain't the cutest . . ."

"I didn't roll my hair in curlers last night, okay? So I had to put it up. I was hoping it wasn't too ratty, that it wouldn't matter much at church."

"Matter? I'm nuts about it." He squeezed her clutched hands, pulled the car into the church parking lot. "Listen, when we get to your Mama's I'm gonna sing the new song for you. It'll knock you out, I swear it will. This one's gonna make it, Priscilla. I can feel it in my heart. In my *soul*."

Priscilla nodded yes.

He cut the engine, turned to face her. "Plus I'm gonna talk to your Mama today about the wedding." He smiled, put both hands on her shoulders. "I prayed on it last night, and it come to me, how we could make it all work. The Lord guided me in this, Priscilla. He walks us through the valley. Then into the light. I'm a happy man this morning. Happy in God's grace."

"It's s'posed to snow." She bit her lip.

"Don't you worry 'bout a thing. God's hand's in this, I can feel it. So let Him work through you this morning, Priscilla. It's going to be a glorious day." He jumped out of the car and ran around front, opened her door, held out his hand for hers. "I'll see you after the service, okay? Praise the Lord, this is His Holy day."

"'Kay." She pulled up her hood. "I'll meet you here after." She stood by the car while he grabbed his guitar case from the back seat, slammed her door, and started sprinting toward the side entrance to the church. He turned and waved once, and she raised her hand in his direction. She was glad she didn't have to sit with him in church this morning, glad he'd be up in the music section

Charlotte Morgan

on stage, glad the Youth Choir was singing so she could be by herself in the congregation.

Whatever it was she was feeling, it wasn't God's glory working through her, she was sure of that. Confusion. Anxiety. Fear? Priscilla trudged toward the front door of the sanctuary. Maybe God would come to her like he'd come to Kendall and help her see. Right now it was like the scripture said, through a glass darkly. That's what she'd pray for: to see face to face; to know and be known. Since she'd met Kendall she'd never felt such . . . uncertainty around him. And dread. That's what she was feeling today: dread. She didn't want to go with him to her Mama's. And the wedding? Talk about the wedding today, like he hadn't screamed those awful things at her? He was thinking about last night as some holy revelation. Maybe it had been a revelation for him, but she certainly wasn't feeling God's blessing this morning. Not a shred of God's charity. That's what she'd pray for in church: faith, hope, charity. "And the greatest of these is love." Okay God, get busy, she thought. I need You here.

Still overcast. Heavy air. Hands deep in her pockets, Priscilla huddled by the passenger side of the car, shifting her feet back and forth. Colder, if anything, and clouds so close you could touch them, but still no snow. Sundays they planned to go to her mama's they never went to the social hour, but Kendall couldn't get away fast. People always stopped him to thank him for his music ministry. Today he'd had a solo verse of "Jesus Calls Us O'er the Tumult," and surely half a dozen people would grab him and say his singing had helped them re-dedicate their lives to Christian service. He had been inspired, that was a fact. His voice had never been purer, stronger. But that lift she always got when he sang, that chord somewhere inside that he touched, that transported her: nothing this morning. Not so much as a flutter. Like she was listening to him sing some TV jingle. Drive your Chevrolet through the USA.

A couple of boys ran over and started circling the car. "This yours?" they asked, Ahhing and Man-oh-manning. She nodded. Would they ever flip if she told them where she got it. What would Kendall say if she told him the truth? While they were driving to her mother's? Would he go ape, accuse her of lying? Would he think she'd done something nasty with Elvis to get it? The thought made her stomach roil. Was that it: he'd think the worst of her? He couldn't think any less of Elvis.

"Ma'am? Mind if we look inside?" one of the boys asked.

"Sure. Just open that door. Go ahead."

They stuck their heads into Kendall's side and about flipped, looking at the dash and bucket seats. "This thing is loaded!"

Why did she call it Kendall's side? It was her car. Elvis liked her. Thought she was a nice woman. Her name the same as his own dear Priscilla. A good nurse. So he gave her this car. That was it.

"How's my girl?" Kendall kissed her on the cheek. She jumped. "Heeyyy, take it easy there. I ain't gonna bite, you know." He opened her door and slid his guitar in back. "You guys like this Mustang?"

"Yes sir!!" they answered, "it is one hot car! Thanks," and ran off toward the Sunday School building.

"You gonna get in, or you gonna stand out here in the cold awhile?" Kendall asked, holding her door for her.

"Sure. Thanks." She sat. Was he always doing that, thinking the worst of her? Her mind wouldn't go back any farther than last night. It was like she could picture them together, on a picnic by the river, eating supper at the Top Hat, at the church social hall, but the volume was off. She couldn't make out what he was saying to her. Just last night. Loud, clear, hateful. Sinning in the flesh. Whoring talk. That's all she could hear.

"Looks like we might get that snow." He cranked the heater all the way.

"I think we might."

"What you reckon your mama's cooked up for us for dinner? I'm 'bout to die I'm so hungry."

"Same as always."

"You think she'll have a ham today?"

"Probably."

"Good Lord Almighty what I wouldn't give for one of her rolls with a slab of ham right this minute. And a pile of that macaroni and cheese."

Priscilla leaned back against the seat and closed her eyes.

"Cat got your tongue?" Kendall reached for one of her hands and gave it a squeeze. She didn't have the urge to squeeze back. She just shook her head.

"What's the matter?"

"Just tired's all."

"Keep me some company, okay? I'm too revved up here, from the service and my new song and all. I'm filled with the Spirit, 'bout to jump out of my skin. So I need some company, okay?"

"Sure. I won't go to sleep on you." She kept her eyes closed.

He drove for a few minutes, tapping out a tune on the steering wheel. "Say, I was wondering, why'd you stand up for the prayer of healing touch this morning? What was that about?"

She shrugged. "Just, you know, God's touch is all." Her throat felt like she'd swallowed glue.

"You ain't sick or anything are you? You coming down with something?" His voice sounded all concerned.

"Nothing like that. No."

"You ain't mad at me? I couldn't stand it if you were mad at me."

"I'm not mad." She rolled her head toward the window, opened her eyes, stared out at the bare, gray trees, the sky the same color. Sad, confused, worried . . . but not mad.

"Thank the Lord. You okay, darlin'? Something bothering you?"

"I'm okay. Tired's all, like I said."

A bit of an edge in his voice: "You ain't on about last night? You prayed, right? Asked the Lord for forgiveness, right?"

"Right."

"Cause that's behind us. God's blesséd grace has cleansed you. I can feel it working through us today."

Priscilla didn't say a word.

"You rest, then. I'll turn on the radio for company. If it won't bother you."

"No. Go ahead." She closed her eyes again. When was she gonna start feeling like herself? When was she gonna want to talk to Kendall? Or even be in the same room with him? Was he right? Was she holding a grudge? Why hadn't she been able to turn it over to the Lord this morning? The hymns didn't put her in the Spirit, not the slightest little bit. She'd gone through the motions, praying and singing and even standing for the prayer of healing touch, but she hadn't felt a thing. Except maybe sadness. Deep down sadness. But even that was more like it was somebody else's sadness, maybe Mary at the tomb, not hers. All she felt was empty. Alone. Sitting right here by Kendall in her brand new car.

Kendall found a gospel station, drove for a while singing along while she stared at the countryside. He'd written a song. That thought nagged. She was supposed to be cleansing herself of sin while he wrote a song.

Elvis singing "Amazing Grace" came on, and Kendall switched the station.

"Why'd you do that?" she snapped.

"Do what?"

"Switch off Elvis. I love that hymn."

"Fat fart can't sing."

"Don't talk like that around me! And stop saying ugly things about him. Why do you go on about him anyway?" She glared at Kendall.

He glared back. "Him? Since when you a Elvis fan?"

Priscilla turned red, looked ahead. "That's not it. I just like that hymn is all."

"All right Miss Elvis Presley groupie, have it your way." He found the station again and left it on through the end of the song. "That satisfy you?"

"You don't have to be so hateful."

"You the one been pouting all morning, not me."

"I'm not pouting."

"Call it what you want."

They drove on, big fat snowflakes falling now against the windshield. Only a few more minutes till Henderson. Then what? She cut a look at Kendall. He was mouthing the words to "Rock My Soul in the Bosom of Abraham" along with some black gospel group. Was he truly a better Christian than she was? More righteous in his faith? She was so confused about all this. He'd dedicated his gifts to Jesus, his singing and songwriting. Had she truly dedicated herself? She'd been blaming him for being so . . . scary last night, downright mean, but had she been wrong, too? Had he asked for forgiveness with a true heart, and she hadn't? But he'd only talked about *her* sins, not his. That's what upset her so much. And the way he . . . grabbed her. Made her feel so dirty. Was that right? Was she thinking all this through, or just pouting? Should she turn to him in love, not anger? Turn the other cheek? She couldn't sort out her feelings.

He reached for her hands again. "Hey, Pris, I'm sorry I swore at you, okay? I don't want us to fuss."

"Neither do I." That was the truth. She let him hold her hand, wrapped her fingers around his. Should she talk to him about her feelings? Or should

Charlotte Morgan

she just pray more? He seemed so at ease, himself, with what had happened between them. Like it was over. Like it was no big deal.

"Looks like this weather's serious, don't it?"

All she could see out the window was blowing snow. "It'll be good to get to Mama's."

"Fun taking this car on the road. Drives like a dream, don't it?" He put his hand back on the steering wheel.

Priscilla nodded. "You reckon I ought to try Evelyn when we get to Mama's?"

"What for? No sense making a long distance call when you can phone her tonight when we get back if you need to. She ain't going nowhere."

"I was just worried a little."

"Still thinking about that slimeball she left with?"

"Not him, Kendall. Her."

"Evelyn might be a waste of space, but she's big enough to take care of herself. Don't you worry, you hear?" He smiled that sparkling smile. "Don't want my little darlin' to worry about a thing."

She made herself smile back. "You pay attention to the road, you hear? Don't want you to wreck this new car."

"Like I said, don't worry about a thing."

"Good Lord, I was worried sick when it started up snowing. Thank the dear Lord you're here." Her little mama, Neva Jane Johnson, was standing in the doorway, peering out the storm door, when they drove up. Priscilla should've known. She was talking as soon as they got to the stoop. "Y'all get on in here before you let the cold in."

"Hey, Mama, how you feeling?" Priscilla hugged her around the tiny shoulders, kissed her mama on her still-smooth cheek. They were the same height, had been since Priscilla was twelve. "You look real good. You lose some more weight?"

"Bout the same, Priscilla Jane. Can't complain." She opened her arms to Kendall. "Lookee here, young man. You were careful driving over here, weren't you?"

Kendall hugged her tight, stood back. "Mama, you look prettier every time I see you. What'd you think of that new car of ours?"

"Lord have mercy, that's your car? I figured you must've borrowed it. Where's Daddy's Corvair?" She looked at Kendall, then Priscilla.

"What smells so good? You didn't bake a pound cake this morning, did you?" Kendall hugged her again. "Bless your heart, you know that's my favorite."

Priscilla tugged at her gloves, then her coat. "Kendall, give me your coat, let me hang it up." Why hadn't she even thought about her Daddy's car? Course her Mama would want to know about it.

Mama peeked out the storm door again. "That surely is a handsome-looking car, Kendall. What'd you say about Daddy's car, Priscilla Jane?" She shut the front door.

"Mama, Kendall's mighty hungry. Can I help you get the food on?"

"Course he's hungry. Bet neither one of you ate a fit breakfast." She rubbed her hands on her flowered bib apron. Her mama always wore a dress and apron, year in year out. She was only sixty, but she'd been dressing like this as long as Priscilla could remember. The only difference, now, was her hair was completely white, instead of the brown it had been when Priscilla and her brothers were little. "Let me just see about the sweet potatoes. You all wash your hands and come on to the table."

After she scurried into the kitchen Kendall walked over to Priscilla and kissed her forehead. "What're you gonna tell her? She's gonna bring it up again."

"Oh, don't I know." She took the coats to the hall closet and hung them up. "I can't lie to my mama. What am I gonna do?" She plopped on the sofa – same brown and gold plaid sofa they'd had her whole life.

"Could you tell her it's in the shop? That wouldn't be so much a lie as a shading of the truth. I'm sure it's in the shop getting fixed up before they try to sell it, right?"

"You think?"

"Course I think, or I wouldn't a said it. Want me to tell her?"

"Would you? You really think that would be okay? Mama would be heartsick if she thought I sold Daddy's car. You know how she holds onto every little thing of his like it's some sacred relic."

"I'm putting the food on the table, Priscilla Jane. Y'all better come on. It won't be a bit good if you don't eat it while it's hot." They could hear her walking back and forth from the kitchen to the bitty dining room.

Kendall stood, took Priscilla's hand to pull her up, too. "I don't mind doing it one bit, for the time being. But then we're gonna have to figure out what to tell her later. This ain't gonna go away."

"I know. Thanks, Kendall. I don't know how I'm gonna eat a bite of food, worrying about this."

"Don't worry. I'll handle it." He gave her a hug. "You my best girl. I'm gonna take care of my best girl." He pulled her toward the opening to the dining room. "We're coming, Mama. I hope you've got plenty to eat, cause I'm bout to starve."

"We'll see if I can fill you up. You mind saying Grace over the food?"

"Not at all, Mama. Not at all."

Afternoon nap time: Priscilla had always loved the quiet, the privacy, even as a child. She was stretched out on the single bed in her old room, glasses folded on the matching maple nightstand. Everything looked fuzzy, like one of those French paintings. The snow was pouring out of the sky. She felt like she was down inside a Christmas snow globe, her Mama's house the little tiny house, her inside even tinier. Quiet. Still. Like time had stopped. She'd been so tired she could hardly lift her fork while they were at the dinner table, but now she was wide awake. Wide awake and clear-headed. That song. When Kendall sang that *She Devil* song for her and her Mama, he could've been driving hot nails into her heart. This was what he had written last night, after he'd accused *her* of fornication. Wasn't he saying *she* was the devil? If she'd heard that "Free from the devil,/ free from sin,/ free from temptation,/ Don't let her come in" one more time, she'd have had to run out into the snow screaming. Oh, it had wounded her.

But now, now it was like some kind of icy calm had taken over, like he'd opened a window to her mind. She could see plain as the toes on her feet: Pure as she'd kept herself, chaste as she'd always been in thought and deed, Kendall didn't trust her one bit. But this is what came to her, clear as Paul's vision on the road to Damascus: it was for some whacked-out reason of his own. Whatever made Kendall go ape like he did, it wasn't really about her. She was his target, his safe target for his own hurt and pain. She could see that now, like looking into some crystal ball and reading the inside of his head. Or his heart. Hadn't he called his own Mama a hussy? All this built-up anger, it wasn't about her. She was the one who could help him, her and the Lord. He *needed* her. Oh that was a blessèd realization. Prayer came easy: Thank you, Sweet Jesus, for bringing me to this understanding. I been holding a powerful grudge against my husband-to-be for his shortcomings. I tried to pray for forgiveness, but my heart wasn't open to Your power and mystery. Now You've revealed my duty, Dear Lord, and I embrace it with open arms and thankfulness. All glory and praise to Your Son's Holy Name, Amen.

Eyes closed, Priscilla could feel her entire body start to relax, like those relaxation exercises they used to do in nursing school. What was that class called? Fundamentals of Movement? Something like that. They'd lie on the floor on mats and . . .

Tap, tap, tap at the door. She sat straight up. "Yes?"

"It's me, Priscilla Jane. Mind if I come in?"

Priscilla fell back against the pillows. "Course I don't, Mama."

The door opened and her little Mama tip-toed into the room. Was she shrinking, Priscilla wondered? She'd always been small, but small and sharp-edged, like the outlines in a child's coloring book. Now it was like she was hazy. Probably just cause she didn't have her lenses in. That was all.

"It's okay. I wasn't asleep. Just resting my eyes."

"Lord knows you've got circles down to your chin. And you hardly ate a bite at dinner. Ain't you getting enough rest, Priscilla Jane?" She sat at the edge of the bed, took her daughter's hand. Her face had that blurred look, too. Everyone was always saying Priscilla looked just like her Mama, but she didn't see it.

"Mostly. I been kind of tired lately. But I'm okay, Mama. Really."

"You been saying your prayers?"

She nodded. "Of course. All the time. I couldn't get by without saying my prayers."

"That's a comfort. I pray for your Daddy and your brother all the time, pray they're at peace in the Lord's loving arms."

"They are, Mama. You know they are."

"I don't know, Priscilla Jane. Sometimes I think about Bud dying over there in that heathen country and I fret something awful."

"Bud took Jesus as his Savior long before he went to Viet Nam, Mama. You don't have to worry about him."

"I know. But I always had a sense Bud drifted in his faith. I hate to say it, but I did. He had his ways I didn't approve of, some of that cursing of his. And I know he took to drink, though I never saw it myself. I just knew. I pray hard for Bud's salvation every day."

Priscilla could feel her Mama's deep sadness pulsing through her hands. Bud's death had been a bad blow. The worst. "Listen, Mama, what do you think about Kendall's faith?"

"Goodness, Priscilla Jane, he's the Lord's man all right. I give praise you've found a Christian man like him. That's one burden off my shoulders."

"You reckon he loves me, Mama?"

Her mother looked toward the window, stared for a few moments like the snow was hypnotizing her.

"Mama?"

Still staring out the window: "He's devoted to you, Priscilla Jane. Anybody can see that."

Was that an answer?

"He told me he wants to marry you soon as possible, maybe just have a small ceremony here at a Sunday service."

"What do you think, Mama?"

"I never was one for all that spending and showing off a lot of people go for. Your Daddy and I married at a Friday night Praise and Prayer meeting. That was good enough for us. God's blessing on your union, that's all you need."

"So you think we should do something like that? Soon?"

She looked back at Priscilla, leaned closer, took both hands in hers. "If Kendall says so. You got a stubborn streak, girl. Always have. You got to learn to defer to your husband. That's the Lord's way." She squeezed hard, dropped her daughter's hands.

"Did you ever have any doubts about Daddy? Ever worry if he was really the partner God had chosen for you?"

Her mother stood, folded her hands in front of her apron. "What kind of question is that? You ain't been listening to them feminists ranting on about women's rights, have you, girl? All that sacrilege?"

"Course not, Mama. I just wondered, is all. Sometimes I feel so confused."

"Confused? Pray to the Lord, Priscilla Jane. You gotta feel plain lucky Kendall Kennedy has chosen you. The Lord has brought you a Christian man who cares for you and intends to marry you. You gonna question God's judgment? You gonna turn your back?" Her voice had an irritated edge.

Priscilla sat up, swung her legs over the side of the bed. "Mama, I won't trying to get you upset. It's just that, well, Kendall has a kind of a temper, sorta like Daddy's..."

"Don't you dare go criticizing your Daddy, you hear?" Now her voice was plumb angry.

"Mama, please, I didn't mean that for criticizing. You know Daddy could get mad at us..."

"Never without a reason. *Never.* 'Spare the rod and spoil the child,' that's what the Bible says, plain as can be. You children needed a stern hand." Her cold stare cut Priscilla more than her words. "Your father was a good provider, a strong Christian man who put his family before everything but his God, and you know it. Shame on you, Priscilla Jane. Shame on you for speaking ill of your own dead Daddy." She turned her back, walked toward the door.

Priscilla stood, grabbed her mother's tiny hand. "Oh, Mama, please don't be mad at me. Please? I meant no harm. I'm just scared a little bit, I guess."

Her Mama turned her face toward Priscilla, her expression still icy. "That don't give you any right to disrespect your Daddy. I won't have it."

"I'm sorry, Mama. That's the Lord's truth. I only wanted some help dealing with this temper of Kendall's, that's all."

Turning to face Priscilla, her voice that punishing voice her daughter had heard almost every day of her growing up: "You tend to your own flaws, missy. You ask God's guidance for dealing with your own imperfections. The Lord'll look to Kendall. You just ask for help with yours."

"You're right, Mama. You're absolutely right." Again she kissed her mother's soft cheek.

They were close enough so that Priscilla could see every fine wrinkle in her mother's face, the sadness in her brown eyes, the slight tremble of her lips. "Girl, God don't promise being a woman and a wife is easy. He promises to be with you is all. And He promises you rest from your labors. Kendall will walk with you in the Lord. That's all you can ask. Ain't a thing confusing about that, you hear?"

"I do, Mama. I surely do."

"Well, then." Her mother let loose, rubbed her hands on her apron. "I suspect Kendall's bout ready for another piece of my pound cake. He says he'd like me to bake one for your wedding, and I told him I would."

Priscilla watched her tiny Mama walk down the narrow hall to the living room, a sight she'd seen more times than she could count. Had her shoulders always been so slumped? Had she always walked so slow?

They always ate leftovers for Sunday night supper. They'd been doing this in her family Priscilla's whole life. She used to prefer the cold supper: leftover rolls, ham or cold chicken, whatever Jell-o salad they'd had, green beans from the pot, not even warmed over. Plus they didn't all sit down together, just came in and ate and washed their own plates and stuck them in the dish drain. She'd read, eat slow, enjoy the food served up without tension. Now, since her Mama had so little company, the three of them ate together at the table. And after supper, her Mama would wrap up whatever remained and send it with them back to Durham. Said it would just go to waste if she kept it.

"You ain't gonna try to drive back tonight in this mess, are you, Kendall?" her Mama asked.

"No reason not to, Mama. Won't be a soul on the road but us. And this little Mustang's low to the ground. It'll be fun, won't it, Pris?"

Priscilla was terrified of driving in a storm, any kind of storm. The idea of sleeping in her own small room here while the snow piled up outside was comforting. But she'd promised her Mama she'd defer no more than an hour earlier. "Kendall's a good driver, Mama. Don't fret. If he says it's safe then it must be all right to go."

They both smiled at her. "I reckon he knows what he's doing."

Kendall swallowed. "After we finish supper, I'm gonna shovel the front steps for you, Mama. It's piled up pretty good already. Maybe you won't get too much more tonight. And I'll put some salt down. That way it won't be so hard on you in the morning."

"That's mighty thoughtful, Kendall. We don't usually get this much snow. I guess Daddy's got a shovel out back in the shed. I can't remember, but he must."

"Don't give it a thought. I'll take care of it."

Priscilla pulled a little piece off her plain roll. She'd been fiddling with her food, not the slightest bit hungry. Her Mama had only taken a few bites, too.

"I better warm up the car. We ought to leave pretty quick after we eat, right, Pris?"

"Sure. If you think so."

"In fact, Mama, would it hurt your feelings too much if I excused myself right now and got busy with them steps? And you wrapped up some cake and rolls for us to take back?" He wiped his face with his paper napkin, stood. "I wouldn't mind a few slices of that ham, either."

"Not a bit. I think it's probably a good idea for you all to get going sooner instead of later, son. Priscilla can help me with the food and dishes." She looked from one to the other.

"Of course." Priscilla stood, too, picking up her plate. "You go ahead and shovel the snow. I'll finish here with Mama. Maybe get the front walk, too." She smiled at him.

"Thanks, ladies. You two are the best. That's a fact." Kendall practically ran to the coat closet. A blast of freezing air pushed through the door before he could slam it.

Priscilla shivered. "It's mighty nasty out there, isn't it?" She began stacking the dirty plates. Kendall surely behaved in a considerate, Christian way to her Mama.

"Hope he don't catch cold out in this storm in just that jacket of his. Boy don't ever wear a hat." Her mother went to the kitchen, got wax paper and a brown grocery bag, came back to the table. Priscilla didn't mention that cold air didn't cause colds, germs did. Her Mama'd just think she was being a know-it-all. "No sir, we don't often get this much snow in Henderson." She started wrapping packets of food and putting them in the bag for Kendall and Priscilla to take home.

The two women worked in quiet harmony. Clearing the dishes and putting away the food had always been their shared chore, and it showed. Priscilla usually volunteered to do the dishes, and her Mama usually let her, but tonight she wanted her mother's company for these few private minutes, so she didn't offer. When her mother began running hot water into the sink Priscilla said, "Want me to get a clean towel and dry?"

"That would be a help."

Glasses first, then silver, then plates. Finally, cooking utensils and pots and pans. Priscilla could do it in her sleep. She didn't think she could wash any other way. As she was hanging the damp dish towel over the stove handle she asked, "You still got them Elvis records you used to play?"

"Child, where do you get your ideas? You have always been a mystery to me, that's a fact." Her mother took off her apron and hung it on the hook by the refrigerator. "If Paul didn't take them, I guess they're still in there in the hi-fi cabinet. Lord, I ain't seen them records for years."

"Mind if I look?"

"Help yourself. You want some hot tea before you start out?" Her mother was filling the kettle with cold water, another nightly ritual. Tea and evaporated milk and two spoons of sugar.

"I'd love some, if Kendall isn't in a hurry to get going."

"I'll put the cups out."

Priscilla opened the mahogany cabinet and flipped through the albums, mostly gospel, some Eddie Arnold and Kitty Wells. Then there they were, those two record albums she'd heard at least a hundred times each, "Elvis" and "Elvis Presley." Gracious, look at him, he was just a boy.

"I found 'em, Mama," she called out from the front room. She could barely hear her mother's "That right" from the kitchen.

She pulled them out, hurried to her mother's side. "Look. I can't believe we still have these."

Her mother was wiping the porcelain top of the kitchen table, didn't look up. "They belonged to Bud, you know."

"Really? I always thought they were yours."

"Mine? Why in the world would you think such a thing? Bud brought them into the house. I was surprised your Daddy let him keep them, to tell you the truth. But then he never could say no to Bud."

"But you were the one played them."

"Your brother lost interest pretty fast. Plus he got that old junk car. Remember? He was out working on it all the time, or running around who knows where with those friends of his. He won't that interested in Elvis Presley after that first big deal about him."

"I always remembered you playing these, Mama. That's how I remember it."

"I might've played them some."

"And singing along. I don't remember a thing about these and Bud."

"Didn't I just tell you them were his records?" She shook the damp dishrag in Priscilla's direction. "Them things won't nothing but trouble from the day Bud bought them."

"Can I take them with me? You wouldn't mind?"

"Lord no. What in the world would I want with them?" The tea kettle started to whistle; she walked to the sink, rinsed the dish cloth, wiped her hands on her apron. "You want me to fix you some tea or not?"

Priscilla
January 12-13, 1973

Trembling down to her toes, barely able to lift her foot to the next step, Priscilla made her tedious way up the stairs to her second-floor apartment. The snow had continued to fall, blizzard-like, the entire drive from Henderson to Durham. A drive that should've taken no more than an hour and a half, at the outside, took over four terrifying hours. She and Kendall had stopped talking after the first fifteen minutes, stopped listening to the radio after half an hour, and for the rest of the drive they both just strained their eyes to see, prayed and willed themselves inch by inch over the invisible highway home. Now, safe, Priscilla couldn't stop shaking. She couldn't remember being so frightened. Well, she had been that scared, for a fact, but that was behind her now. Forgiven. Soon forgotten.

Durham lay silent in the storm, no cars on the streets, falling flakes blurring visibility all around, everything humped over with white snow. Parts of the city were blacked out, but when they finally got to her neighborhood lights were on in some windows. She could see to make her way to the building. Random footprints had been snowed over, but they were still visible enough to guide her, clutching the two Elvis albums to her chest, to the door and warmth and safety. Still, she couldn't stop shivering. Bed, blankets, sleep. She'd pray for sunshine in the morning. Then she'd be fine.

A burst of energy propelled her from the top step of the second landing to her door. Fiddling for her key, gloved fingers quivering, she could hear, faintly, music. Laughing. Angie and Maria? Still up? Sunday nights they were usually in bed by eleven if they were home. The car clock, lit in that eerie blue light, had hummed 11:47 when Kendall eased the car to a stop in front of the apartment building. She could see those hands pointing to those numbers clear as the door smack in front of her. She'd been so thankful to make it home, had silently memorialized the moment of reaching shelter as some magical number series, some Holy mystery: 1-1-4-7. They'd prayed together, given thanks to God for guiding them along the treacherous way. She'd added a quick prayer for Kendall's safety the little way he still had to go to The Estate. He'd kissed her forehead and she'd gotten out into the cold and blowing snow, catching her breath. She hadn't even thought about her roomies being up.

Priscilla knocked, unable to put her clumsy hands on the keys somewhere down in her purse.

"It's open!" Laughing, like it was some Saturday Night Live joke. All the insomniacs at the clinic watched SNL. Even Elvis.

When she opened the door the aroma of popcorn and some sweetish-smelling candle and wine engulfed Priscilla.

"Heeeyyy, Priscilla, we been wondering where you were," Maria saluted, causing Angie to hoot like there was no tomorrow.

Angie, between laughs: "Are you dressed for Halloween? I've got it – Buddy Holly! Am I right?" Making Maria double over.

Priscilla shrugged. Guess they'd never seen her in her glasses before. Burning candles covered every surface, but the kitchen light was still on, so Priscilla could see their ruddy faces clear as day. She had to smile, in that way you have to when everybody around you is laughing at some joke you haven't heard. "What's going on?"

Angie, still laughing: "It's a Blizzard Bash. Haven't you heard?"

"Heard what?"

"Durham's shut down." Both howling.

Priscilla leaned her albums against the wall. Then she pulled at her gloves, tucked them in her pocket, started taking off her coat and scarf. "Shut down?"

"What in the name of God is that on . . . your . . . feet?" Angie, pointing at her boots, almost fell off the sofa.

"Oh." Priscilla stuck out one foot toward them. "Galoshes."

The word "galoshes" sent them both over the top. Priscilla started laughing, too. The black rubber boots were pretty ridiculous, she had to admit.

"My Mama made me wear them. In case we got stuck in the snow."

Protecting Elvis

Tears running down their faces, as if on signal they both jumped off the sofa and ran to her. They were wearing long flannel nightgowns: When had either of them ever worn anything so demure? Priscilla had no idea they even owned such garments. And fluffy slippers. They could be a TV version of freshmen in a woman's college dorm, they were that innocent looking. Still, their faces broadcast some sassy demeanor. No one would really mistake them for schoolgirls, even in their current get-ups.

"Let me try them on, Pris? Please???" Maria wanted the galoshes. Her curly dark hair was in a crooked ponytail on top of her head, making her look younger, more girlish.

"Can I have the glasses? Just for a sec?" Angie begged. Face washed of make-up, blond hair brushed straight, she was still gorgeous. "You are sooo 'Bad Baby Doll' porn queen in that outfit."

"What?!?" Priscilla couldn't remember being so . . . overrun. Like being set down in the middle of a litter of gigantic puppies. "Sure . . . the boots are pretty wet. Maybe the glasses will make you dizzy, Angie. They're right strong." Maria was dragging her over to the beanbag chair, while Angie picked up her coat and threw it toward the sofa. It missed, but they didn't seem to notice. Angie scurried toward the bathroom. Priscilla was aware of her own bedraggled appearance: Baby Doll porn queen? Hardly.

"I gotta see how these look on me!" she called as she ran down the hall.

"You just sit right here and I'll pull your boots off . . ." while kicking off her pink scuffies. Maria fell back on the floor but only laughed and grabbed for the slick boots again. "Where in the world did you get these?"

Priscilla thought: I was about to ask you the same thing about YOUR costume, but she shrugged and said, "They used to be mine, you know, when I was in maybe sixth grade. My Mama never throws away anything." Everything was a blur.

"They are AWESOME," Maria insisted, rolling around on the floor trying to push her size seven bare foot into the size five and a half galoshes.

Angie shuffled back in the living room wearing the glasses. She was fumbling like a person trying to find her way in the dark. "You are blind as a bat, Priscilla. I couldn't even see myself in the mirror. How do I look?" She struck a guitar-playing pose.

"Like . . . like . . . an IDIOT!" Maria yelled, falling back against the sofa, one boot half on her foot, the other still by Priscilla.

"Take these before they make my eyes cross permanently," Angie held the specs out to Priscilla. "Want some wine?"

"No thanks. Hey, seriously, what did you mean about Durham being . . . what did you say? . . . shut down?"

Angie plopped on the sofa. Maria sat cross-legged on the floor, failed boots next to her. "Nothing but emergency vehicles on the streets. People are supposed to stay home unless they're crisis designated." She poured herself a half glass of red wine. The jug was almost empty.

"So won't you two have to go in to the hospital?"

"Nope. The radio said Code A personnel only, and I'm a C and Maria's a D, so we figure — tra la — no work for us tomorrow, anyway."

The Stones stopped singing. Priscilla hadn't noticed that they were singing, really, until they stopped. Just background to Angie and Maria's foolishness.

"Music! We need more music!" Maria said, raising her empty wine glass.

Glasses readjusted, Priscilla stood in the middle of the floor. Clearly she wasn't going to get any sleep just yet. "Want me to put on a record?"

"Sure." Both voices piped, almost together.

"I found these old Elvis albums at home. Want to hear them?"

"Why not?" Angie said. "God, I had such a crush on him when I was ten years old."

"Priscilla's got a boyfriend," Maria started chanting.

Priscilla held up the *Elvis Presley* LP, with the handsome young duck-tailed singer strumming his guitar. "He was plenty cute, wasn't he?"

"Lemme see!" Maria demanded.

"Me too!" Angie chimed in. They both held out their hands for the album cover. Priscilla slid out the record and handed the empty jacket to Angie, who was fake fainting. "He was such a doll, wasn't he?"

"He's still way too pretty for a guy," Priscilla answered, balancing the record on the turntable. "And sweet as can be. You can't even imagine."

Strains of "Blue Suede Shoes" filled the room.

"Ohmigod, remember that?" Maria screamed. The roomies jumped up, like they were on a spring, and started bopping in place. "Come on, Priscilla. You can't just stand there when the King's rocking out."

The music did make Priscilla want to bounce and swing, no doubt about it. But she'd never danced in her life. It was against the Assembly.

Angie and Maria grabbed her hands, like the three of them were gonna play Ring Around the Rosie. Only they were gyrating and twisting and shaking their shoulders. "You can do anything but lay offa my Blue Suede Shoes," they hollered along with Elvis. Their dipping and swaying forced Priscilla to dip and sway along with them, and before she knew it she was singing and hopping around the room, too.

When the song ended the three of them fell in a heap on the floor, laughing and holding their sides. The tempo shifted to "I'm Counting on You," and the three women looked at one another, laughs easing to giggles. "Good Lord, that Elvis could always make me go crazy. He was my absolute first heartthrob." Angie caught her breath. "Remember him on Ed Sullivan, how cute he was? When was that, back in 1956? Good Lord, I was only 11 years old."

"I didn't see it," Priscilla said. "My Daddy wouldn't let us watch, that first time, so my brother Bud went to one of his friends' houses."

"You have got to be kidding," Angie stared at her like she was some kind of freak. "Everybody in America watched that show."

"I know. We didn't even ask after that." Priscilla reached for a fistful of the cold popcorn. "When Bud bought these albums, my Daddy 'bout had a heart attack. Said he better not ever hear them or he'd break them in two. But he didn't. Bud got away with murder."

"Guess I did, too," Angie grabbed her cigarettes off the coffeetable. "My Mama didn't much care what I did, long as I didn't bother her." She lit one of her Marlboros. "Heck, my mama had me when she was sixteen, so she was not much more than a girl herself when Elvis made this album." Taking a long thoughtful drag. "Lord, I'm a year older than she was then! Imagine that." Blowing out smokerings: "I can see her now, dancing in the living room with my Daddy to 'Heartbreak Hotel.' God she loved that song."

"You wild child, you," Maria punched Angie's shoulder. "My Mama thought the Pope wrote the Bible, and believe you me we weren't allowed to listen to Elvis or go see his movies or so much as mention his name at home." She poured the last of the wine into her glass, took a swig. "Course we managed to sneak into every movie he ever made. And listen to the records in Gina Tamborini's basement every afternoon after school. What you don't know can't hurt you, right?" She held up her glass.

"Right!" Angie clinked a fake glass.

"My mama used to listen to the records in the daytime, too," Pris added. "I remember coming home from school and hearing her sing along to 'I'm Gonna Sit Right Down and Cry Over You.' She'd never admit it, but she did."

"Lord he was hot." Maria sighed. "Oh, hey, I almost forgot. Your Mama said for you to call the minute you got home. No matter how late. She was worrying herself sick over you driving in the storm."

Priscilla jumped up.

"And that Evelyn called, too. Wanted you to call her tomorrow first thing."

"She sound okay?"

"Whiney as usual." Maria held her nose. "'If it wouldn't be too much trouble, could you please have Priscilla call me.' Good grief she is a pain."

"Evelyn's not that bad. Just kinda – I don't know – lonesome, you know?"

Angie started singing "Are You Lonesome Tonight?" over the song on the stereo, and Maria jumped in.

"You two are nuts!" Priscilla laughed, going to the kitchen for the phone. They just turned toward her and sang louder.

Her mother answered after the first ring. "Priscilla? That you?"

"It's me, Ma. Sorry to call so late."

"You home?"

"Yes ma'am. Got here just a little bit ago."

"Goodness. I like to worried myself to death. Couldn't even think about going to bed."

"Still snowing in Henderson?"

"Good heavens yes. It hasn't let up a bit."

"Here either. You have everything you need?"

"Talked to Paul. He's coming in the morning. He'll shovel the walk and the steps. Says he'll try to make it to the store for some fresh milk and eggs."

"I wish Paul had come over yesterday. I sure would've liked to have seen him."

"Well, I tried to talk him into coming for dinner. You know how stubborn he is. Like all the Johnsons."

"That's not it and you know it, Mama."

"Well it don't make a bit of sense, him not caring for Kendall. But he's got his ways. You know Paul."

She did know her brother. And she did know he didn't like Kendall one bit. Hadn't liked him the minute he set eyes on him, and that was that. "Well, tell him hi."

"I'll do that. You ain't going out in this mess, are you?"

"No, Mama. Angie and Maria say Durham's on shut down or something."

"Heard that on the radio. This whole half of the state is shut down. You stay put, you hear? What's that racket?"

"Angie and Maria singing, if you want to call it that. Listen, I'll talk to you tomorrow. You give Paul my love, okay?"

"I will. Say your prayers, now. Good night."

"Bye, Mama." Priscilla hung the receiver on the wall unit, kept her hand on it. Should she call Evelyn? She looked at the clock. Almost one. She'd be asleep. Phone ringing would probably scare her parents half to death. Pris'd have to wait till morning. It struck her: Dang. I sure would like to know what she wanted. At least she was home, so I have to think Jared Falkner didn't do her any harm. But what *had* they done? Probably he just drove her straight home and that was that. What had he said to her? She'd just have to wait and see.

"Get on in here, Priscilla. Angie says she wants to play Truth or Dare."

"What's that?"

They lost their breath laughing. "You never played Truth or Dare?" Angie finally managed, like she'd told them she'd never been outdoors. "Damn, Priscilla, did you grow up in a bubble?"

"I didn't think so," Pris said, falling into the beanbag chair. "So how do you play?"

Just then the lights went out. Even with the candles, it was eerie to have the power go off. The music stopped, the whole building got quiet.

"Freak-eeee," Angie whispered. "Is that freaky or what?"

Maria crawled up on the sofa, sat on her knees staring out the picture window. "Look out there. Not a light anywhere. Like we're down in a cave . . . or a tomb!"

"Don't say that!" Angie whined. "Get back down here with us."

"Scaredy cat," Maria laughed. "Let's tell ghoststories!" She picked up one of the candles and held it under her chin. "Oooooouuuu. Remember the one about the hook?"

"Stop it right now, and I mean it!" Angie insisted. "I am so scared of the dark it's not funny."

"All right, scaredy cat. I won't sneak up on you and say . . . Boo!" and Maria fell on top of Angie, tickling her all over.

"Stop! You're gonna make me wet my pants if you don't STOP!" Angie laughed.

"Listen, you two, have you got the flashlights out?" Priscilla looked around the room. "And maybe we should get our quilts and all and bring them in here together, since if the power stays off all night it's gonna get really cold."

"Cold?" Maria looked at Angie. "I cannot stand being cold." Both gals looked to Priscilla.

"Tell you what. Go get your quilts and blankets and a sweater and socks. We'll make a great big pajama party here in the living room. Okay?"

They both jumped up and got busy, Maria heading for the room she and Priscilla shared, Angie going toward her room. "Oops. Forgot a light," Angie said, running back to grab one of the candles on the coffeetable, slowing down to keep the flame from going out. She grinned at Priscilla. "Silly me."

"I'll look for the flashlights," Priscilla called.

She carried one of the candles into the kitchen and found the drawer with the matches and more candles and a flashlight. She tested it: it worked. When she came back into the living room Angie and Maria were squabbling over how to make a giant bed.

"Tell you what: Why don't we make three sorta sleeping bag/bedroll things close together? Wouldn't that work? I'll go change. I feel like I've had on these clothes forever."

"The floor's gonna be *hard*," Angie complained.

"Sissy," Maria countered.

Priscilla changed into a granny gown and sweater and socks as fast as she could, not even stopping to hang up her skirt and blouse or put her dirty underwear in the hamper. She always put her clothes up, but tonight everything was different, all turned inside out by the storm. She'd never been to a pajama party with girlfriends. Would she tell Angie and Maria that truth, if they dared her? Is that what their game meant? She'd gone to youth camping trips at church, and all night prayer meetings, and young peoples' lockdowns, but she'd never been invited to a p.j. party with just girlfriends. Wouldn't they laugh if she told them that? She started to go into the bathroom to brush her teeth but changed her mind and dragged the quilt and coverlet and blanket off her bed, picked up her candle, and went back into the living room.

"We can't make any more popcorn – Duh; no power – but I found a bag of chips and Maria had hidden some Oreos on the top shelf of the pantry – which I made her cough up – so we've got storm supplies."

"There's always peanut butter and jelly," Priscilla added, shaping her bedding into a kind of sleeping bag form and tucking herself in.

"Ugh. I hate peanut butter and jelly. My Mama thought it was an all-purpose meal: breakfast, lunch, and supper. I couldn't eat another peanut butter and jelly sandwich if I was starving in prison."

Maria passed the Oreos. "So, we gonna play the game?"

"Forgot my pillow." Priscilla scooted to her dark room, grabbed both pillows off her bed, was back in a sec. "You'll have to teach me how," she gasped, snuggling into her covers, plumping her pillows behind her.

"It's easy," Maria said. "We take turns. Two of us ask the third one a question. That person can either answer – the truth only, nothing but the truth – or take a dare."

"What kind of dare?" Priscilla didn't think she'd have any problem telling the truth about her all-too-undaring life, but she needed to know what she was getting herself into.

"Oh, nothing dangerous. Just silly stuff. Like knock on your neighbor's door and ask if the refrigerator's running, or call your boyfriend and sing 'Row Row Row Your Boat.' Goofy stuff like that."

"Okay. I'll play." That sounded more idiotic than daring.

"Good." Maria nudged Angie. "Want to do a practice question?"

"Sure. Let me ask Priscilla an easy one: Did Elvis make you feel all hot and bothered?"

Priscilla blushed while the two of them fell into one another cackling. "Hot and bothered? No." They laughed even louder. "No, really, I swear. I mean, he's sexy handsome, just like on TV and all, but mostly he's sweet, like I said." "Awwww" they both moaned, in a mocking way. "And he talked a lot about his Mama. He had these pet names for her, like Nungen and Satnin, and he'd get tears in his eyes whenever he so much as mentioned her. And she's been dead for about seven or eight years, now, but talking about her still makes him cry."

"Awwww," they both said again, but this time without the sassy tone.

"Who's gonna go first for real?" Maria asked, looking around at both of them. "I will, I guess. That way Priscilla can get the gist."

"Okay," Angie grinned, almost leered. "Lean over here, Priscilla, let's decide what to ask her."

Priscilla leaned toward Angie, who cupped her hands against her ear and started whispering so fast Pris could barely understand her.

"Let's ask something about boyfriends? Okay? Like how old she was when she got her first kiss. Oh, she'll answer that in a second, no problem." She put her hand over her mouth, shook her head. "I've got it!" She snapped her fingers, didn't even consult Priscilla. "Who was the first boy you had the real hots for?"

"That is sooo easy," Maria crooned. "That is not even slightly daring, Angie, you wimp. You must've had too much wine to drink. It was Robby Lovelace, from sixth grade."

"Well what did you do with him?" Angie almost lost her balance.

"No way. One question. You blew it." Her face was all cocky in the candlelight. "Now Priscilla and I get to ask you."

Priscilla was thinking that this was all pretty dumb and boring. She wasn't even all that interested in boys in sixth grade, for heaven's sake. And besides, even if she had been, she wouldn't have called it *the hots*. These two were what her Mama called boy crazy, that was a fact, but then she'd known that. No big truth there.

Maria leaned against her shoulder, whispered, "How's about how old she was when she got her first top feel . . ."

Priscilla leaned back, raised her shoulders, like Huh?

Maria grinned, wiggled her finger for Priscilla to come close again. "You know, had her boob felt the first time."

Priscilla glared at her.

"Okay, that's it. You wanna ask or you want me to?"

Priscilla pointed: You. What in the world would she say if they asked *her* something like that? She felt all goosebumpy. Kendall *had* rubbed her up there. And she had felt . . . *hot*. At first.

Maria nodded, grinning. "Okay, here goes. Angie: How old were you when you had your first top feel?"

Angie looked from one to the other: "You two are so . . . nasty!" She pointed a finger at Maria, laughed. "This is your question, isn't it? You've got a little boy's dirty mind, Maria, that's what you have." She shifted on her blankets. "Aren't these supposed to be Yes or No questions?"

"Huh-uh. And you know it," Maria answered.

"I swear, whenever I play this game with guys they never start off with something so . . . nosy. They'll ask, like, Do you wear a D cup? Women are the worst. And some women are worse than others." Her face lost its cheerful glow. She glared at Maria. "Any more wine?" She stared at the empty bottle.

"Come on, Truth or Dare," Maria smirked. "Bet you were all of . . . what? . . . thirteen, maybe? Twelve?"

"That is totally . . . it's like . . . too out there."

Priscilla didn't like the prickly edge sneaking into their voices one bit. "Whoa, here. This is supposed to be fun, right? Why don't we ask a different question? That one is upsetting Angie. Or play something else. Twenty questions?"

Angie ignored her, stood up over the both of them, half crying now. "You want to know the truth, Maria? You sure?"

Priscilla jumped up, too, tried to put her arm around Angie's shoulder, but Angie shook her off. "Come on, you don't have to answer that. Really. It's a stupid question."

Pushing her hair back from her face: "I'll tell you the truth about my first feel, Miss Gotta-Know-It-All. I was *six years old*. How do you like that?" Maria looked like somebody had slapped her. Priscilla froze.

Rubbing her cheeks: "And you wanna know who it was? My Uncle Timmy. That's who. My Mama's baby brother. Who lived with us and was all of sixteen himself. And started feeling me up when I was in first grade. That's how old. You satisfied?"

Six years old? Priscilla gagged, wrapped her arms around her waist. Maria covered her face with her hands. Priscilla couldn't tell if she was crying or hiding, thinking Angie might hit her. Angie was definitely crying and shaking all over.

"Come on, y'all. Please don't y'all do this any more." This time Angie let Pris take hold of her shoulder. "Come on, Angie, sit down, okay? This is a stupid game. You don't have to say another word, you hear? You okay?"

Angie climbed back into her covers, stared at Maria, who hadn't moved or made a sound, who still had her head in her hands. Priscilla went over to her, ruffled her hair. "Come on, Maria. Let's just do something else, okay? You didn't know. All right?"

Maria looked up. Tears covered her face. "I am such a frigging dope. I am so sorry, Angie. I don't know why I do such asinine things. Forgive me?"

"People have no idea. They just have NO fucking idea."

Priscilla sucked in her breath. She'd never heard anyone say that word in a conversation. Not a woman, anyway. Sure, people talked like that at the Ivy. Strangers. But not the people with her.

Maria scooted over. "Come on, sweetie, say you forgive me. Please? I just wasn't thinking straight, you know? All that wine and pot. My goddamn dumb brain just wasn't working right."

Pot? Priscilla looked around. She didn't see any pot. But she had smelled that weird sweetish smell when she first came in.

"You can say that again," Angie said, quieter, her voice still shaky.

"My goddamn dumb brain wasn't working right!" Maria yelled.

Angie softened. "Okay. All right. Enough. I was kinda out of it myself, I guess. Losing it like that. I can't believe I told you all that." Looking at Priscilla. "You don't think I'm a slut or anything, do you?" Reaching a hand up.

"Heavens no!" Priscilla squeezed her hand, nestled down beside her. "You? You were just a little girl. Stuff like that isn't your fault. Good Lord, I don't know how you stood it!"

"There are plenty of sick people in this world, that's a fact."

Maria teared up again. "I am a major dope."

"No, really, it's probably better to get it out into the open." Angie reached out and squeezed one of Maria's shoulders. "I was in nursing school, you know, taking one of the psychology courses, abnormal, I think, and I don't know, the professor was lecturing on types of sexual deviance, and I lost it. I hadn't even thought about it in years, and I just went to pieces."

"You poor thing," Priscilla said.

"And they sent me to the clinic, to one of the therapists, and it just poured out of me. Like some volcano erupting, I swear." The three of them huddled together. Angie sighed. "It was a relief, really. To talk about it."

"What did your Mama do?"

"I never told her. I never told anybody but that therapist. And now you two." She looked away. "I was too ashamed."

They sat without speaking for a few minutes. Priscilla wanted to ask: What about Timmy? What happened to him? But she thought that might sound wrong, like she was maybe accusing Angie or something, and she didn't want to add to any of her bad feelings.

"Mama loved Timmy. She tried to take care of him. See, their Mama had died before she was forty. Drank herself to death is what they told us. Anyway, Mama took responsibility for Timmy. She had no idea what he was doing to me all those years."

"What happened to him?" There. Maria said it. Almost in a whisper.

"He overdosed. Right before his twenty-first birthday. Mama was planning this big bash, and a couple days before it he o-d'ed. Like to killed her, too."

"Good Lord," was all Priscilla could say. Her Daddy's yelling, and Kendall's temper, didn't seem all that bad, compared to this.

"Me? I cried for days. Mama thought cause he'd died. She never knew. I mean, what's the sense of telling her? Causing her more hurt?"

Priscilla nodded agreement. "You were so *strong*."

"He always came in my room in the dark, after everybody else was asleep. Or passed out. And . . . you know, he didn't stop with just feeling me up."

The three women were quiet, like they were each holding their breath.

"And I thought my Daddy beating us was bad," Priscilla said.

"Yeah, and my Daddy hollered and cussed at us all the time, like he hated us. But nobody ever . . ." Maria looked from one to the other.

"So," Angie said. "That's the dirty story. Didn't mean to dump on you two tonight. This was supposed to be fun. I swear, I don't know what got into me."

"I'm glad you told us," Priscilla said. "I had no idea. You're always so . . . confident. So . . . together."

"Yeah. You better believe it." Angie laughed for the first time. "No man's EVER gonna make me feel like a helpless worm again. I can promise you that, for a fact."

"I believe you," Priscilla nodded.

"Me too."

"How do you do it? How do you make sure a man doesn't . . . take advantage? Or do something . . . wrong?" Priscilla hadn't known she was going to ask. The questions just popped out.

Angie, hands shaking, lit a cigarette. "I stay a mile away from the Timmy types, for one thing."

"Timmy types?"

"Yeah. Guys who talk sweet and butter you up and bring you presents and act like they're God's gift to women. I can spot the type a mile away."

"Really?" Priscilla was trembling now, herself.

"Men like that, it's all about THEM, their needs. You know the type, don't you, Maria? You're pretty savvy about guys, except where Dr. G's concerned."

"Had to get in your dig, didn't you, Angie? Guess I had that coming." Maria, squirming, had a wounded puppy look. "Gordy's nothing like that and you know it."

"Now Kendall, he's a flirty type," Angie took a deep drag, "but he's got the Lord holding him in check. Otherwise I might say look out for him."

"Kendall's so considerate you wouldn't believe it." Why did her voice sound defensive like that? It was the God's truth.

"Yeah, he's a sweetheart, all right. But I wouldn't be a bit surprised if he had a temper." Angie was thoughtful for a minute. "But who could ever get mad at a nice gal like you, Priscilla? I swear."

Priscilla looked down, now. She wasn't used to compliments. Plus Angie saying that about Kendall having a temper . . . that flustered her.

"Hey, let's lighten up, okay? Wanna put on another record?" Maria asked.

"You ARE a dope. The power's out, remember?" Angie laughed, finally.

"Right. I forgot." Maria looked around the room. "How's about we paint Priscilla's fingernails. Can we do that? And toenails, too?" She looked at Priscilla, who looked up, surprised.

"MY fingernails?"

"Sure. I've got this amazing new orangy shade."

Angie stood up. "I've got it. Let's give Priscilla a makeover. Wouldn't that be cool?"

"A make-over?"

"You know. The full make-up deal. By candlelight." Maria latched onto the idea, ran with it. "We could style your hair . . ."

"No hot rollers, dummy." Angie interrupted.

"Right. Well, we could still tease it. And do SOMETHING."

"Okay." This wasn't what Priscilla wanted to do. She really wanted to snuggle down under the quilts and try to get some sleep, but if this would cheer up Angie she'd go along. "I've never had a make-over."

"I'll bet you haven't, if you'll pardon me for saying so. Get the nail polish, Maria. And your make-up. I'll get the hair stuff and my make-up kit, too. This'll be a lotta fun."

They both took candles and hurried to the bedrooms. Priscilla sat there, stupefied, in the glow of the darkened room. Where did they get all that energy? What a crazy night. Really, what a completely crazy day. Kendall hadn't called. Did he make it home okay? Kendall: Could he be the Timmy type? NO, her brain shouted. Kendall's NOTHING like that. Maybe, her brain whispered, just maybe she ought to think about it after she'd gotten some sleep. It'd been a long, exhausting day. Maybe she ought to pray about it, ask God's guidance. Kendall loved her. Wanted to marry her. Soon. And she loved him. Wore his promise ring. But he DID have a temper. She knew that for a fact. But he'd promised. He'd sworn he'd never hurt her again. She believed him, with all her heart. With all her soul. Why, then, why had what Angie said bothered her? Planted such an outlandish notion.

Her head fell to her chest, she closed her eyes. Good grief, she needed sleep in the worst kinda way. Dear Lord, Could you help me out here? Why is all this getting under my skin? Is it just cause I'm so upset about Angie and all? Or does it have something to do with Kendall and me? Lord, I know I'm weary. And I'm trying to follow your Son's example of forgiveness and loving like I want to be loved. But everything that's happened in the last twenty-four hours, it's all crazy and confusing to me. I'm turning to you in my hour of need cause I don't know what else to do. What made so much sense this afternoon feels all twisted into knots again tonight. I'm praying for help in the name of your Son Jesus Christ. Please. Tell me what to think. What to *do*. Thy will be done. Amen.

"Don't forget the hairspray," Maria called, scuffies shuffling back down the hall. "And cottonballs. We'll need cottonballs." She stood in the entrance to the hail, beaming. "Oh, Priscilla, you are gonna look soooo gorgeous, like Natalie Wood, I'll bet, when we get through with you."

She sighed. "Since you're going all out, why don't you try for Elvis Presley's wife? Her name was Priscilla, too, you know."

Course she knew. Everybody in America knew. 'Cept maybe Kendall.

Priscilla
January 13, 1973

"Somebody gonna get that?"

"Huh?"

"Somebody gonna get that phone?"

Priscilla's eyes opened. The lights were all on. The phone was ringing. Stale popcorn and expensive perfume odors mingled, not in a pleasant way. She jumped up. Her face felt stiff, like she was wearing a rubber mask two sizes too small, with twigs sticking out of her eyelids. Mascara. Foundation. The makeover. That was it. Lord she felt exhausted, exhausted and weird.

Stepping over blankets and the two mute bodies, she made her way to the kitchen. "Hello?"

"Morning Sleeping Beauty."

"Kendall?"

"What other guy'd be calling you first thing in the morning?" His voice all perky.

"When did the power come on?"

"We never lost power over here."

"Oh. What time is it? Our clock says 2:14."

"It's 9:30. Whaddaya want to do today?"

She shifted the phone to her other ear. All kinds of bobby pins were holding up her hair-do, and one was poking into her ear on that side. "Do? I thought we had to stay inside. Angie and Maria said only critical vehicles, or something like that."

"I don't have to give any lessons, everything's cancelled, so I thought maybe we'd do something. For fun. Maybe go sledding or something like that. I ain't worried about driving."

"I never was one for sledding. Always too cold. Too scary."

"You are such a fraidy cat."

"I guess." She leaned against the kitchen wall. "Right now I'm soooo sleepy. Can't think straight. We stayed up and talked half the night. You want to practice some and then call back in a couple of hours?"

"We? You stayed up with those two? There won't no men there, right?"

"Of course not."

"They weren't smoking no wacky tobaccky, nothing like that."

"Kendall." She turned her back to the living room, lowered her voice. "Why do you always think the worst of Angie and Maria?" One of them had said something about pot, but she hadn't actually seen any.

"Why do you think? When's the last time either one of them went to church? You got any idea?"

"No. I don't. But where's your Christian charity? Remember: 'Judge not, lest ye be judged.'"

"I just hate to think of them telling you a bunch of crap, putting nasty ideas in your head is all."

"They're not a bit like that. They're super neat gals. And fun. I like them a lot."

"Since when? You'll have to ask them to be your bridesmaids if you love them so much. I can see them walking down the aisle at the Henderson Assembly of God right this minute. Can't you? Maybe your brother would ask one of them for a date."

His sarcastic voice was grating. "Listen. I'm about to fall asleep standing here. Will you call back in a couple of hours? Please?"

"Okay. I had no idea you didn't go right to bed when we got home." All hurt. "I'll talk to you later."

"Bye." She hung up. That irritated tone. What was that about? Just cause she didn't like to go sleigh-riding? Cause she'd talked to her roomies? He could be downright bossy. And so self-centered. She stumbled back to the living room, crawled into her quilt nest.

"God I need a Pepsi. Is there any Pepsi in the fridge?" Maria rolled over, her eyes still closed.

Angie didn't move.

"I don't know. Want me to look?"

"Naw. I gotta pee anyway. Who was that on the phone?" Maria stretched her arms over her head.

"Kendall."

"Good Lord, that man can't stand to let you out of his sight, can he?" She sat up. "I wish Gordy acted that way."

"Really? He calls here for you right much."

"I guess." Maria stood. "Somebody PLEASE trade heads with me." She stumbled toward the bathroom. "And turn out the lights."

Priscilla rolled over on her stomach. Was that it? Was Kendall so crazy about her that he couldn't stand to let her out of his sight? This morning – Who knows? Maybe it was 'cause of what Angie said last night – this morning she couldn't help feeling like he was trying to push her around. Lord, she was bushed. Bone weary. She wasn't in any mood for that huffy act of his.

"You want anything?" Maria climbed through the living room clutter toward the kitchen. "Damn this place is a mess. We're gonna have to do some major cleaning. When did the lights come on?"

"I don't know. We musta all been asleep."

"What time is it anyway?" she called from the kitchen.

"Around 9:30 I think."

Maria came back drinking from a tall bottle of Pepsi. "Now that's the ticket." She snuggled down into her blankets. "Nothing like aspirin and a Pepsi to cure what ails you."

"Mmm-hmmm," Priscilla mumbled, half asleep again already. Elvis loved Pepsi. Wouldn't touch a Coca-Cola. As she was drifting off she wondered: Why hadn't she just gotten in her bed, now that the heat was back on? This was cozy, though, having Angie and Maria close like this. When had anybody paid as much attention to her as those two did last night? They were neat gals, no matter what Kendall said.

The banging at the door finally got through Elvis singing "Tutti Frutti, Aw Rootie," with Maria and Priscilla wailing along at the top of their lungs. The living room was spotless. They were both dressed in jeans and sweaters, folding the last of the blankets. Angie was in the shower.

"Ohmigosh, that's Kendall!" Priscilla said, freezing in place. Her face was scrubbed clean, her hair brushed straight.

So? Maria's eyes flashed to Priscilla. "Come on in! It's open!" she yelled, smiling.

The door opened and Kendall strode in, his face a scowl.

"Let me turn this down," Priscilla said, dropping the blanket, scurrying to the hi-fi. "We were just singing along while we finished up our housecleaning."

"Hollering along is more like it." Kendall stuck his hands in his pockets. "How ya doing, Maria?"

"Fine. Wish you'd come up with Priscilla last night. We had a blast. Did a make-over..."

"We didn't know you two were gonna be up, right, Kendall?"

"That's for sure. Plus we were ragged out from the drive. Least I was."

"Oh, I was too. But Angie and Maria were having a — what did you call it? — a Blizzard Bash."

"Uh-huh. Thought you were gonna meet me out front, Pris. So I wouldn't have to park." That tone again.

"Sorry. We still haven't set the clocks. Plus I guess the music was kinda loud."

"Kinda."

Maria finished the folding and set the blanket on the coffee table. "So what are you two up to? You sure you oughta be driving in this? You could stay here and we could all play *Sorry*. Or charades."

"Lots of trees down. Can't make it down some roads. But Mangum's fine. Thought we'd head out 158 to the diner in a while."

"Everything's closed though, right? You don't have to go in to the clinic, do you, Priscilla?" Maria put her hands on her hips.

"I wasn't scheduled in till eleven tonight, anyway. So we'll see. I'll call later." Priscilla opened the closet and took out her coat. "Kendall just wants to ride around. Durham hasn't had this much snow in over a hundred years, he says."

"Yeah. It's something out there. And that Mustang glides through like it was made for the snow."

"Mustang?" Maria raised her eyebrows.

"Priscilla didn't tell you?"

"Tell me what?"

Protecting Elvis

"She bought us a Mustang last week. Friday, was it? You oughta see it. Look out the window there." He pointed to the picture window.

Maria looked at Priscilla, eyebrows raised, Priscilla shook her head yes, and Maria edged over to the sofa and stared out. "That's YOUR car?" she said, turning back to Priscilla.

"You bet," she answered. "Plus Kendall's too, of course." She was pulling on her galoshes.

"Of course," Maria echoed. "What in the world possessed you to buy a red Mustang convertible? That sounds like something Angie would buy."

"It's a long, kinda complicated story."

"I reckon. I mean, nobody could blame you for not liking that stinky Corvair. But a Mustang? A convertible?" Maria looked from one to the other. "Priscilla, you're a woman of mystery. Here I took you for a quiet little country gal . . ."

"That's exactly what she is, really," Kendall stepped to her, put an arm around her waist. "My little country bumpkin."

"I didn't say bumpkin, did I?" The smile went out of Maria's voice. "Priscilla's sharp as a tack about lots of things."

"Nobody said she won't sharp. She's a A-1 nurse. But my little country gal for sure ain't no woman of the world, and that's a fact." He pointed down to the rubber boots, chuckled.

Priscilla looked no more like a woman of the world than a flying cow, and she knew it. She had to smile: Maria thought she was sharp? Or maybe she was just saying that, to bait Kendall.

"Anyway, let's get going before all the snow melts," Kendall's smile twitched.

"You want a ride anywhere? Maybe to the hospital?" Priscilla asked. She realized she wanted Maria to come with them, even if Kendall didn't.

"Nah. I better hang around here. I'm kinda hoping Gordy will call."

"Okay. Well. That was a lot of fun last night. Tell Angie thanks, too, okay?"

"Sure thing." Maria stepped up and gave her a hug. "Mind if I listen to your records some more? It's a trip, hearing Elvis sing those old songs."

"Help yourself."

The 158 Diner, just past the "Welcome to Durham, Diet Capital of the World" sign, was wall-to-wall with truckers. Most of them were smoking and

181

talking on the phones on the wall beside each booth, huge plates of food in front of them. Kendall fit right in, in his leather jacket, boots, and jeans. Priscilla stuck out. She was one of the only women, besides the waitresses. She wondered: How did these gals get to work today? Were they considered critical employees? But Kendall was right, this place never closed.

He was digging into the North-South Special: two eggs fried hard, pancakes, Polish sausage, creamed chipped beef over toast, and homefries. He could eat enough to feed a family and still stay slender. Her patients would hate him. She'd ordered oatmeal with brown sugar and hot chocolate, one of her favorite all-time breakfasts.

"Evelyn called last night," she said.

He looked up. "Huh?"

The jukebox was playing some country song she didn't recognize loud enough to wake the dead. "I said, Evelyn called last night, so I called her back this morning. She got home okay."

"That creep you dragged in didn't put any moves on her, did he?" Kendall managed, still chewing.

"She was perking like a coffeepot. Said that Jared Falkner was the nicest guy. He came in and met her Mama and sat down and ate a sandwich with them. Said he was homesick, is all, and he was tickled to death to meet all of us."

"Well you can count me out of his fan club." He shoved a big piece of biscuit in his mouth.

"Maybe he'll take her out. Wouldn't that be nice?"

"Uh-huh. Fat chance." He laughed, went back to working on his platter of breakfast. He ate fast, like her Daddy. Plus he'd cut everything up and then eat. She remembered her Mama telling her, when she was little, just cut the bite you're going to eat. That's what she did, when she ordered pancakes or French Toast, which wasn't too often. But her Daddy ate just like Kendall, slicing and dicing everything on his plate first, then shoveling it all in as fast as he could. At least Kendall ate his eggs fried hard, so the yolk wasn't running all over everything else. Her Daddy used to say, "Gimme my egg as close to when it came out of the chicken as you can." She'd never eaten a fried egg in her life.

The hot chocolate was perfect. The waitress brought it to her in a little aluminum pitcher, so she actually got two cups. She held the warm mug, sipped, enjoying the rich Hershey taste. Like a melted kiss. She started to tell Kendall,

This cocoa tastes like a melted Hershey's Kiss, but she decided not to bother him. The place was always so smoky it took her appetite, but this morning, crowded as it was, for some reason the cigarette smoke didn't bother her. She just kept her mug close to her face, the warm porcelain soothing her hands, the cocoa fumes filling her nose, and she was comfortable.

"Cat got your tongue?" Kendall was wiping his mouth with his napkin, taking a gulp of hot coffee.

"Just enjoying my hot chocolate is all. Your food good?"

"Super. Hit the spot." He leaned back in the booth, patted his flat gut.

"Sure is beautiful out."

"Yeah. Ain't never seen nothing like it."

"You get off school for snow much when you were a kid?"

"Lord, if a flake hit the ground they let us out. But we hardly ever had much snow. Can't remember a white Christmas."

"Me either." She set her cup back in its saucer, and Kendall reached for her hand.

"This is nice, ain't it, just the two of us together like this?"

"It is."

"You never said too much about my song yesterday. We didn't get to talk much in the car, what with the storm and all."

"Right." She shifted in the booth.

"Your Mama really liked it. Said she thought it would go right to the top."

"Mama loves gospel, that's for sure."

"Yeah, but she ain't so much for the rock part of it, usually, but she said this one caught her up, right off."

"It's catchy, that's a fact."

"So what'd *you* think, Priscilla? You still ain't said." He tugged her hand.

Lord, he's like a little boy, sometimes, wanting pats on the head. "It's like you said, Kendall. It's a winner." She hadn't lied. She didn't see any virtue in telling him she didn't like the whole idea of women being portrayed like the devil one bit. Or telling him what it made her think of. Why bring up that whole horrible night, anyway? They both wanted to put it behind them. But would she think of it every time she heard that song? If it became a hit? For some reason he didn't put the two together. Or if he did he wasn't letting on.

"Really?"

"Really."

"This morning after I talked to you the first time I went back and worked on it some more, the music, and I swear, I think I've got it down. I think I'm ready to get the guys and make a demo."

"No kidding."

"Strike while the iron's hot."

"That's something."

"We'll have to practice hard, of course, but I've made up my mind. I'm gonna go for it."

Dishes hit the floor, and Priscilla startled, pulled her hand away. All of a sudden the smoke was getting to her. "Listen, you think we could go?"

"Sure thing, darlin. Let me get the check." He looked around, but their waitress wasn't in sight.

Priscilla tucked her napkin beside her bowl, took a last sip of cocoa. It tasted more like chalk, now that it wasn't hot. She set her mug down.

"Thing is, your Mama and I think there's no point in waiting, for the wedding and all. Even if this song makes it, it'll take a while, you know?"

"I know."

"So maybe we ought to look at some dates."

Somehow sitting in the 158 Diner wasn't the place Priscilla had envisioned making plans for her wedding. Not that she'd had some big romantic notion, but this felt wrong. She was getting jumpy, jangled, probably from the lack of sleep and the noise and the smoke. It just didn't feel like the time to talk about this. "Can we do that when we get home?"

"Didn't you say Angie and Maria were staying home today?"

"Yes, but . . ."

The waitress slapped the ticket on the table. "You want anything else?"

"No thanks," Kendall said, not looking at her, staring at Priscilla. "But what? You don't wanna go back there, do you? I ain't gonna sit around all palsy walsy with them two, even if you got the hots for them."

"I guess not. But where can we go? Everything's closed." Really, she was pooped, ready to go back to the apartment and take a nap.

He put the money on the table. "Let's drive. We can talk while we're driving. We can park, leave the heater on, if we want to."

184

"Okay." But not for too long, she wanted to say. She'd say that, once they were rolling.

"I got an idea." He stood, took her elbow. "Let me help you with your coat. You need to go to the little girl's room?"

"No. I'm fine. But we're not gonna drive too far, right?"

"Ain't this God's glorious day?" He pecked her on the cheek, right there in front of all those truckers. "Don't you worry 'bout where we're going. I got a plan." Cock of the walk.

The drive north on 15 was clear except for the occasional truck. Quiet. Priscilla almost fell asleep. Kendall didn't say much, just drove with a satisfied smile on his face, humming off and on. It wasn't till they came to the Lake Michie sign that she figured that was where he was headed. "They won't have the roads into the lake cleared."

"What's that?" He turned to her, smiling, like his mind had been a million miles away. Probably on that song, him getting a gold record.

"We're headed for the lake, right? All I said was, they won't have the roads in cleared."

"Oh." He looked confused. "Let me worry about that, okay? You get some rest." He patted her knee.

"Sure." Priscilla closed her eyes. So very quiet. The snow created a kind of cotton-ball world. And the Mustang really did glide along like one of those figure skaters in the Icecapades.

In a few minutes: "Damn."

She opened her eyes. Snow was piled high at the entrance to the lake, from the plow clearing the highway, no doubt. No way the Mustang could turn in. And even if it could've, the road to the gate must've been covered with a foot of snow. She couldn't even identify the road.

Kendall's eyes started darting from one side of the highway to the next. He wiggled his fingers on the steering wheel, like he was tapping out a song. "Damn," he repeated, staring ahead. "Gotta find a place to turn around."

"This is nice, riding along in the snow. It's so quiet, just like that Winter Wonderland in the Christmas song."

"Ain't what I had in mind, though. I wanted to find us a place to park."

"Maybe you'll come to a place where the snow plow turned around."

"When'd you get so all fired smart?" His tone wasn't playful any more.

Priscilla felt everything tense all over, from the back of her neck down to her ankles. In just that instant all that cocoa calm turned rigid. "I was just thinking out loud is all."

He was leaning forward, like he could see a wreck in the road ahead. They drove on for a few minutes in tense silence. "I been thinking some myself, Priscilla, and one thing I been thinking is you ain't been yourself. You been different these last few days. Kinda high and mighty, to tell you the truth."

She stared at him. He was serious. Hadn't been herself? Who had she been? She didn't know whether to scream or cry, so she just stared.

He hit the dash with one fist. She startled. "That's exactly what I mean, dammit. Look at you. Glaring at me like I'm some kinda monster or dummy or something. Where you come off looking at me like that?" He clenched the wheel with both hands, gave her a edgy glance, turned his eyes back to the road.

She gazed down at her own hands, gripped together like someone praying for pardon, afraid to look up at Kendall again. What had set him off? She had no idea. Her suggestion about the turnaround couldn't have been enough to bring on such anger, such . . . venom. At any rate, she knew better than to say another word. What would her mother want her to do? Or Jesus? She floundered around in her jumbled brain . . . defer . . . the Lord's man . . . the Lord's way. Turn the other cheek.

"We got to get this straight, Priscilla, once and for all. I'm the man of this family, the husband, the head of the household. You got to look to me as your master. These sly ways of yours, running me down, just cause you went to nursing school, that's gotta stop. You going out and buying this car, staying up all night with them two sluts you call roommates, them filling your head with nasty ideas, it's gonna stop. You hear me? Here and now."

He jerked the car around all of a sudden. The back wheels lost traction, and for what seemed like an hour the landscape spun. When they finally stopped, facing the other way in a cleared turnaround, the world rearranged itself, white tree by white tree, snow-mounded bush by snow-mounded bush, icy fence post by icy fence post.

Priscilla sat, frozen, her hands still clenching the dash. Had she screamed? She didn't know.

"You all right, baby?" He put his arms around her, pulled her to him. He was shaking, too. His breath smelled distinctly of old syrup and coffee. She gagged. "I swear, I didn't mean to do that. The back tires must've hit a patch of ice is all. We're fine, okay? The car's fine. We just spun out there for a minute is all."

Priscilla swallowed, pulled away. "I'm fine. I need to get some fresh air." She opened her door, stepped out into the crisp, cold, clean air. What had Angie said? Timmy types . . . a helpless worm. She clenched her sides, squeezed her eyes shut. Dear Lord, What's happening here? Help me, Jesus. This man, I swear, I think he's nuts. He's scaring me to death. My Mama says to obey him, Lord, but I'm thinking maybe I been listening to her and not to you. So help me, Lord, help me know Thy will. Amen. She felt less trembly, but still her heart pounded.

Kendall came around the car, lifted her chin. He looked worried half to death. "You just shook up is all, right, baby? You don't need to go to the hospital, do you?" Frosty mist puffed out of his mouth with each word.

"I'm feeling kinda sick to my stomach, Kendall. Would you take me on home? I think I need to lay down."

"Sure thing, darlin. I'll get you there in no time flat." He opened her car door, helped her in, like he was helping a fragile old granny.

She lay her head back on the leather seat, closed her eyes.

"You just lean back and rest, okay. I made that turn too fast, is all. You don't have to worry about a thing. I'll get you there safe and sound in just a few minutes."

She shut out his voice. She didn't want to be in this car with him. Inside her head she thought about Elvis, pictured him in his silk karate outfit that he liked to wear in bed. He'd told her his wife Priscilla had taken karate, too. How strong she was for such a little bitty gal, and then he'd started crying, wailing like a child afraid of the dark. He *was* afraid of the dark. They never turned the lights off in his room. They'd talked all night every night. She'd never known a person who slept so little. He'd bawled and said, "She was my Nungen, my Satnin wife, and I ain't never gonna be the same without her." There he was, Elvis Presley, one of the most famous people in the world, and he was weeping for his wife he'd loved and lost. Like one of his sad, sad songs.

Kendall eased the car against the curb. "Let me walk you up, okay?"

"No!" She sat bolt upright. "I'm better. Really. I can walk by myself."

He leaned toward her, as if he were going to kiss her. She turned to her door, opened it, then looked back to him. He smiled, ran one hand through her hair. Priscilla jumped.

"You still scared, baby? I couldn't stand it if I'd hurt you back there. Listen, you call me if you have to go in to work, and I'll come pick you up. Okay? I'll even pick up Evelyn if I have to." That grin.

He could be so sweet. She stared into his concerned face. "We probably won't have to go in. But I'll talk to you later." She got out of the car, leaned back in to say goodbye. "Look, I need to go in now." When had she ever wanted to get away from him? Needed to?

"Okay. Sure. Sorry about the scare." He blew a kiss. "Love you."

And she ran.

Satnin
April 1973

Quit that weeping and carrying on right this minute, Bitty Boy, you hear your Mama? That pretty face don't need to be doing all that crying.

You know sure as sin I ain't one for buttin in your business, sonny buck, but somebody's gotta tell you what's what. Ain't a thing but all them diet pills making you carry on like this. Ain't you. That ain't my pretty Satnin son. I done said before and I'll say it again, I don't want to hear another word about fat. You her beautiful Satnin Boy. Not another single word, you hear?

Her yuvs her beautiful bitty one, yuvs her Nungen better'n breath, that's a fact.

Them pills you been taking to help you lose weight, them's the devil's own pills. Who give you all them pills, Nungen? Who done this to you? You complaining you can't see that good, and your stomach bout to kill you. Take a good look: see for yourself what them pills're doing to you.

Truth be told, I did some things I shouldn't've done, back there when I was at Graceland and you was running all over the place, them girls grabbing at you night and day, never giving you a minute's peace. You not sleeping. Me there by myself in Graceland worrying. I did some things to help me sleep, too, Itty Bitty. I ain't saying I didn't. Me and Notary, we got the same weakness, but it's sadness makes us turn to it, son. Goodness knows we tried turning to the Lord, tried so hard, but sometimes we was mortally frail. I got right bloated, that's a fact, used to be so bitty but them Schlitz tallboys made me all swelled up, but I got to a lowdown place where I couldn't help myself. I felt so shamed. You never did think your Itty Mama was anything but your gorgeous Satnin, now

Charlotte Morgan

did you? I see you all puffy like that now yourself, your face swelled up so awful: Don't I know what that means? Suffering, pure and plain. Brokenhearted. I see you lonesome as dark in that mansion, no matter who's there with you. You never could abide the dark. Don't nobody know that like you and me, Satnin.

What I wouldn't give to be back on our porch swing on Old Saltillo Road, Jesse close by, back in our little house Daddy Vernon built with his own hands. All that money ain't bought you a thing but suffering. Killed me, like to kill you, too, Baby Boy. Listen to what I'm telling you. I ain't proud of what I did, and I'm telling you to take a hard look at all that and stop it right now. Right this minute, today, before it gets too far out of hand. While you can. You never said a single word, sweetness, about the sinful things I was doing, but I could see the sad look in your sparkling eyes, that look when you come home off the road. You knew it won't right, me turning to that devil drink. Them pills ain't right for you either, Satnin. Take a long hard look. Pray for strength.

There, there, Baby Boy. There, there. His Mama's gonna get Alberta to make him a sweet potato pie. Satnin Mama's gonna send him big bunches of wuv and kisses, kiss his itty-bitty hands, every single pretty finger, yes her is. There, there.

I ain't gonna hide nothing else from you. I can see I gotta tell you what's bothering me, to try to help you find your way: Satnin, I like to worried myself sick that whole time you was out there in Las Vegas. I don't want you going back there, you hear? That place is the devil's own schoolyard, take my word. Bad enough you have to get on a airplane. You know I can't stand that. But going all that way over the ocean, to Hawaiya. Don't never do that again, Sonny Buck. Promise your Satnin Mama you won't. Promise her this one thing. That won't right, that whatever you want to call it on the TV, nothing about it right: You singing up there in Hawaiya, people in China looking at you right that same minute. How in God's name can that be right? Only God and His angels got the power to see all over the world at one time, can't you see that? Got to be the devil's hand in something like that. It ain't good. It's making you heartsick, don't you see?

Daddy Vernon ain't got the sense God give a mule, so it's not a bit of use talking to him. He don't mean you no harm, but he ain't got sense enough to help you out with this stuff going on. He never could ease my fears for one minute, so I know he ain't a bit of use easing yours. He calls hisself managing

190

your personal affairs, but from what I can tell he ain't doing a thing to help you out. Helping hisself is all. Mr. High and Mighty. You know good and well how he used to get upset with me, what he done. Bad things. Sins of the flesh. He just ain't got the sense to handle anybody's personal affairs. Can't handle his own.

Don't cry. I'm just telling you all this, Satnin Boy, so you'll see I know exactly how you been feeling, so blue, so blessed blue. Broken hearted, all alone in that mansion even with them so-called friends all over the place and that false conniving hussy right there up in the bed with you. Don't nobody know that like you and me, Bright Eyes. Him's her Nungen, her very own heart and soul.

Please don't get on with me about that Linda woman, please, Bitty One. She ain't the one for you. Ain't nobody right in the eyes of God but Little Satnin. Priscilla won't my choice. You know I loved Anita like my own daughter, like your baby sister, but you married Little Satnin in the eyes of God and that's for all eternity, Satnin Boy. You got to make things right with her if you're gonna get better. You ain't ever gonna feel right with that Jezebel in the house there with you, I can see that clear as the world. You ain't gonna get well, her in your bed, them pills in your belly.

Go on down to the kitchen now, you hear. Talk to Alberta. Talk to Notary. Have them make Nungen a bacon sandwich just the way him likes it, all crispy and thick with plenty of mayonnaise. Have them get down on their knees, right there in the kitchen, and say their prayers with him. Pray for peace of mind, beautiful Satnin boy. Pray to God.

And hear me, don't get up yet: Throw them damned pills down the stool. Get that woman outa your bed, you hear me, and get your wife and little bitty girl back there at Graceland with you where they belong. Stop all this doping and sinning. Her can't stand to see him so sad. Her grieves to see him so sad, so sick at heart.

191

Notary
July 1, 1975

"Go on, Precious," Notary yelled through the door, "stop that scratching, you hear your Mama talking?" Notary scrambled around in her purse for the house key, her bony rear end pushing the screen open. "Er-nest! Come get this dog 'fore she scratch all the paint off the door. Er-nest!"

Can't never find no key when I need it, she fretted. That man sitting in that car watching – What his name? – his pointy face poking out the window there, hollering at me am I okay. Got the dog on one side the door, that man out there hollering – don't like this new driver Mr. Vernon got, don't like him one bit, him sitting in that Cadillac staring at my behind. Enough to frazzle a alley cat. "Precious! You hear your Mama? I said stop dancing around that door. Er-nest!" That man deaf as a tomb. Thank the dear Lord here the key. Can't get in this house soon enough to suit me.

Notary let the screen slam as she bent over to pick up Precious. "Don't wet me; don't wet on me, baby. Take it easy now. Where's your Daddy? Outside cleaning fish? Gonna have us a fish fry tonight, is we? Your Daddy gonna cook us up some fresh fish? Won't that be good? Um-um!" Precious wiggled so much he was almost impossible to handle, with Notary's pocketbook hanging open on one arm and her sack of leftovers on the other. The small black fireball kept trying to lick Notary anywhere he could find bare skin, on the neck, on the arm, struggling to reach her chin or cheek. "Lord, don't them greens smell good? Let's go find your Daddy, little Precious, let him know his Sweet Mama's here, finally. Bet them greens cooked down just right. Bet your Daddy gonna cook us up some cornbread, too. Ain't nothing better, is it, little Precious, than Ernest's cornbread? You know you gonna get some."

She walked through the dim house, stopping just long enough to drop her bags on the white kitchen table. Ernest had two places set at one end. "That man, if he ain't the best man on the earth I'd like to know who is. Got that table set so pretty, don't he? Er-nest!" She petted the dog's head and scratched under his scrawny neck where he had a little white patch of fur. "Problem is, he can't hear worth a damn. That a fact. Won't hear old Gabriel blow his horn come judgment. Have to grab him by the shirt collar and drag him into heaven, don't you reckon, Precious?"

Notary opened the back screen and put the dog on the cement stoop. The squirmy mutt still didn't run out into the dirt yard. He kept jumping up on Notary, scratching at the hem of her uniform, like he was trying to leap back into her arms. "Go on now, Mama's bone tired. Go on now. Shoo!" She fluttered her hands at the dog, but he blocked her way to the steps, insisting she take him up again. "Mama's weary, you hear?" Still, she leaned and picked up the demanding dog. "There your Daddy, see? He still ain't know I'm here."

Ernest Midgette had an old enamel sink set up against the back fence, sunk into a wooden cabinet he'd salvaged from the garbage dump one day about ten years before, right after he and Notary married and moved into her house. Had to have himself somewhere to clean fish, he'd declared. Don't do to clean fish in the house. Notary watched him, his broad back bent. Had on a apron, of all things. He was a clean man, neater than most women, that was a fact. Not like Walter one bit in that regard. Rest his soul. Walter track dirt in, not even know it. Wouldn't care. Drip fish water on the clean kitchen floor, laughing bout how many he catch, not notice the mess. Walter messy to beat the band, no doubt, but Lord what a grin. One thing sure, though, both them men crazy bout her ol black butt.

Notary carried Precious down the rock path to the fence. Leaned over, kissed Ernest on the neck.

He turned toward her and beamed. "Fixin these trout for you. Sure glad you home, baby." His dirt black eyes smiled, every wrinkle in his handsome face smiling, too.

"Save them heads and tails, you hear. Cats gotta have something."

"Don't I always?" His wide, caramel-colored forehead was beaded with sweat. Ernest had good color. Notary loved his skin, that lightish milky shade. Loved holding her arm up against his, saying, "What you doing with a old black bitch like me?"

Ernest kept gutting his fish, his hands sure, like he could do it blind. Notary put Precious down. He immediately went to the fence and lifted one leg, the size of a chicken wing, and peed against the metal webbing. Overexcited like always, he went sniffing around the edge of the yard, quick as a bumblebee.

"How your day go?" Ernest asked. Good thing for him he won't much of a talker, Notary liked to say.

"Lord knows Miz Gladys turning over in her grave, all that mess going on over there these days." Notary pulled up one of the yard chairs, flopped in it.

"You want a glass of tea?" Ernest looked over at her.

"In a minute, maybe." She pulled a man-sized white handkerchief out of her pocket, wiped her mouth. "Antwan coming for supper, you reckon?"

Ernest shook his head no. "Ain't seen him."

She pulled the handkerchief back and forth between her hands. "He love a good fish fry, better'n hard candy. Wish he'd come on. He phone?"

Ernest only shook his head again, kept on working his fish.

"Anybody call?" Precious bounded to her, tongue lolling out, and she picked him up. "Too hot out here for a little old black-assed dog all over me. You gonna die of a heat stroke, you keep running around." The spoiled dog nestled in her lap.

"Evonne call this afternoon."

"What she say? You gonna make me drag it out?"

"She gonna come for the fourth. Bring the kids. Carl ain't coming."

"Big surprise. She want me to call her back?"

"Didn't say so."

"Reckon Antwan come? He know we always have a picnic on the fourth."

Ernest rubbed his hands on his apron, picked up the gut bucket. "Lemme take these to the alley. Be back in a minute."

Notary rubbed Precious, stretched out and panting on her lap. *How I gonna tell Ernest I probably won't be here for the cookout on the fourth? Not till early evening, anyway. He got all them people coming, mostly my kin, too, planned all that food, I gonna have to be up at Graceland waiting on Mr. E.*

Ernest gonna be upset, that's for sure. Can't do a thing about it. Mr. E. say he gonna be home, gonna have people over, we gotta be ready, that that.

"Lord, them alley cats think they got theirselves a crab feast back there. Won't hardly a thing left before I turned around good."

"They need a treat sometime too."

Ernest set the bucket back in the sink, picked up his plate full of shiny fish. "Who you reckon gonna eat all these?"

"I got my guess, you eat till you pop, Mr. Midgette." She pronounced it midget, the way he hated, instead of mid-jet.

"Ain't no midget live in this house," he came back, for at least the thousandth time.

"Don't I know," she laughed. "Man 'bout as big as Gorgeous George. Twice as good looking, too, I'm thinking."

He grabbed her hand. "Come on baby, let's have us a feast. I'll come back out and hose down the sink after dark."

Notary set the dog down and pushed up from her chair. "What you want me to do?"

"Not a thing, baby. Slaw ready. 'Tater salad in the fridge. Tomatoes sliced. All you got to do is pour the tea while I fry up these fish."

The bones of all eight fish were piled up on a plate in the middle of the table. Ernest sat back, rubbing his hard rounded stomach. He didn't have an ounce of flab on him. "Ain't nothing better than fresh trout, you think, Notary?"

"Sure up there with the best, Ernest." She patted his hand. "Beat a cheeseburger all around the block any day." Ernest was a good man, calm, easy-going, not even a speck wild like her first husband Walter. Walter could dance and drink rye all night and still go to the plant in the morning laughing. Ernest, he cook and clean while she work, make her life easy, treat her like a black queen.

"You sit, baby, talk to me while I put all this up." He started scraping the plates. "What all going on up at Graceland, you say?"

"Mr. Vernon, he ain't been hisself of late. I tole you that. But these days he's acting like they broke, complaining this and that about the household accounts. Saying he gotta let so and so go. Everybody all anxious, him acting like that."

"I guess. He ain't talking bout house staff, is he?"

"Course not. We's family. Don't he know good and well Mr. E. wouldn't tolerate him saying so much as a cross word to me and Alberta and Mary? No sirree. But them friends and cousins, Mr. E.'s so-called boys you know, they all skittish."

"Why that?"

"Don't nobody know. But I tell you what I think. I think something bad going on behind the scenes. Mr. E., he don't want nobody upstairs, not a one a them buddy boys of his, cept his feeble cousin Billy. That Linda woman, that cheap white hussy – you know I didn't like the looks of that woman first time I laid eyes on her – she act like she running the show, but you ask me, I say he's just using her, too. Whore, if you ask me. Something going on up there, and it ain't good. Lord, he hardly come out the bedroom any more. Don't even come down to play the piano, they all say. Even late at night." She stood, got a Schlitz from the fridge, handed it to Ernest to open for her. He gave it back without a word and she took a long, cold drink. One thing sure, she and Miz Gladys both liked their Schlitz tallboys. "Dr. Nick over there every other minute, in and out, giving him shots, Ol' Uncle Vestor say. How he know, out there at the gate? Mr. E. only talk to him once in a blue moon." Notary picked up Precious, rubbed him slow and easy. "No sir, Miz Gladys wouldn't wanna see a bit of this mess."

"Poor soul."

"You right about that, Ernest. Poor sweet soul in heaven. Praise be. Ain't nobody gonna blame her for drinking her tallboys, no sir. Not a soul in this world. Not in front of me." She drank down some more of the beer. "That the biggest part of the problem, way I see it. Mr. Vernon and Mr. E. two banty roosters done lost their hens. That the deal goin on them two can't handle. One just like the other, you ask me, only Mr. Vernon ain't got a pot to piss in. He depend on Mr. E. for his last nickel."

"That boy sure do love his Daddy, though."

"That the truth in this world. Mr. E. got a big heart where family concerned."

"Humh. Like somebody else I know." Ernest never changed his quiet tone, but Notary got his message.

"You know Antwan gonna get next to me, Ernest, so you might as well not make any picky remarks, you hear?"

"Won't pickin."

197

"All the same, don't sneak up on that subject. Just say what you got to say. Come on out with it, stead of pouting."

"Not sayin a thing." He poured the grease from the iron skillet into a coffee can, started rubbing it out with newspaper. "Just wish he'd call you once in a while, that's all. Come by the house."

"Lord have mercy, don't I know?" Notary put her elbow on the table, leaned her face onto her hand. "Why that boy gotta keep to the streets like he do?"

"Why he gotta break his Mama's heart, all I say. The rest of it ain't my concern."

She was thinking: You ain't got no idea, Ernest, not a single idea in that nappy head of yours. You claim you know about a black hole inside your heart. I say you got no notion. That day Andruw drown, Antwan come home crazy in the head, say his brother go down, come up one time, yell his very own name, Antwan, then gone, just like that. You ain't know. Lost two boys that day, one drown, one gone to hell. Just in that minute it take him to scream and cry and say to me Andruw gone, Mama, Andruw drowned in the river. Them twin boys, one breath, one bulge in my body. Both gone just like that. Miz Gladys, she the only one begin to understand how a mama love her boys. And look what it done to her. Lord have mercy, look what it done to her.

Notary stood, cradling the dog up to her chest like an infant. "Ain't no call to hold blame against him and you know it, Ernest." She glared. "Some things in the hands of the almighty. Ain't no cause to blame that boy."

Ernest wiped his hands on a dishrag, slow and deliberate, turned to Notary and put them both on her waist, easy. "Ain't trying to give you more heartache, baby. God knows that. Just wish he'd come on by and sit a while with you."

"Some things ain't gonna change, Ernest. That a fact." Her eyes had lost all their smile. Now they were the color of the murky river water.

"Hate to see you so tired, baby. That big house dragging you down. Working you too hard."

"That ain't it a bit, Ernest. Mr. E. on one a them crazy diets of his. Dr. Nick say no fried food, Mr. Vernon say give the boy what he ask for, Mr. E. send down for watermelon and Pepsi. Won't let nobody in upstairs to clean his rooms. No sir, ain't the housework dragging me down. Something crazy wrong up there. I can feel it." She forced herself to smile at her husband, he so worried. "Just old, I guess. Old and plumb wore out."

"Fifty-seven just getting going good, woman." Both Ernest's hands shifted down her back to hug her flat rear end. "I the one's old." He kept rubbing her butt with his strong, firm hands.

"Humh. Don't seem to me sixty-six exactly round the bend." She grinned wide and easy now.

"Tell you what, old woman. Let's just get in bed and see if ol Ernest can rub away some a them aches and pains? What you say to that, gal?"

She kissed him on his cool cheek. How he stay so cool, this the first day of July? Hot enough outside, still, to bake biscuits on the pavement. "That'd be nice, Ernest. That'd be real nice."

Phone ring in the dark, send chills. Keep on ringing. Notary stirred: Ernest don't move. Can't hear. Could ring till Judgment he wouldn't know less he sitting right up side of it.

Notary roused her tall thin body from the tangle of bed sheets, reached to hold onto the bedside table. Trembling. Phone ringing off the hook. "Coming," she muttered to no one. Just had to say something, crawling out of her skin like she was. Hand against the wall, she made her way down the short hallway to the front room, reached in front of her for the black receiver, feeling in the dark like a blind woman.

Her bony fingers grabbed the cool receiver, lifted it to her ear. "I'm here."

"Mama? Something wrong, Mama?"

"That you Antwan?"

"Who you think it be, Santy Claus?" He laugh that high giggle laugh he only laugh when he nervous. Or messed up.

"What time is it?"

"Damned if I know. You up?"

"Won't till just now. Where you at?"

"Not too far. Ernest home?"

"Course he home. Middle of the night. He sleeping, like most sane people ain't working graveyard."

"What the huff about? Thought you'd be glad to hear from your baby boy." That giggle again. He drunk. Or high as a kite.

199

Charlotte Morgan

"You know I glad to hear your voice. But still. Scared me."

"Why that? You getting scared of the dark, Mama? I little, I didn't think you scared of the devil hisself." Teasing like.

"Maybe not. Maybe the devil ain't scary enough to worry me these days."

"Don't go talking like that, Mama." That sugar voice he use when he want something. "You getting ready for the fourth? Ernest gonna get the fireworks and all?

"You know that. You coming by?"

"Don't reckon. Thought I'd come by in the morning, though."

"Gonna have to be early. I leaving for work right around seven."

"Damn. Why you gotta go in so early?"

"Mr. E. got big plans for the fourth. Gotta start the cooking and cleaning. He gonna have a big party hisself."

"Why don't you quit that nigger job, Mama? You ain't nobody's step 'n fetchit."

"Listen to you, boy. Didn't Mr. E. put food in your black stomach for eighteen years?"

"Cause a you, Mama. You paid the price, day in day out. Cookin and cleanin for the white massah. How come you don't quit now? Just you and Ernest. Get some a that gov'ment money they giving out. Ernest, he can tell you how to do it. Don't see his black ass working."

"Get off that crazy talk. You know Ernest got a bad back. Shut up about that right this minute. None a your concern." She flopped in the easy chair by the phone table. The slipcover scratched against her bare butt. "When you coming by? Why ain't you coming for the fourth? Evonne and the kids coming. Marsea and Fontana driving down from Jersey. You gotta come see your sisters and their kids. When the last time you seen them? Lord knows, you didn't even come by Christmas."

"Mama, I ain't called you for no sermon."

"Just wondering. They all looking to see you. Ernest gonna barbecue ribs. He already got more fireworks than the President, prob'ly. And I plan on making banana pudding and a pound cake. Evonne say she bringing two or three kinds a pie." She catch her breath. Antwan don't say a word. "And the girls bringing some a that Yankee food, too. Them potato-cake things everybody so crazy about."

"Bound to be good. Making my mouth water just hearing you talk. But like I say, I got plans already."

"What kinda plans? None a them plans start with a capital T, I hope."

"Just cooking out with some of my homeboys, Mama. Why you always gotta look for trouble? I swear."

"Don't wanna hear that word, Antwan. Sound trashy. Come on round and see your family. You know I miss seeing you."

"That why I calling, little Mama. Love you best. You know that."

"So how come you coming by in the morning, son? Gonna have a bite a breakfast?"

"Little short, Mama. Thought you might have a little extra put by."

"What happen to that hauling job you had? Thought you was keeping up with that steady."

"That guy crazy. Five minutes late, he crap his pants." The boy laugh, not natural. Nervous.

"Ain't I told you a thousand times you gotta be on time, work hard, you want somebody to keep you on?"

"Ain't you, Mama? At least a thousand times." That goofy giggle. "But you know your Antwan need his beauty sleep. Gotta sleep in if I gonna run with the big dogs. Can't play and work, seems like. And you know I gotta play some." Pleading, like when he four, want a sucker. "That boss man, he act like man's s'posed to work round the clock. That ain't me, that a fact."

"How much you need to tide you over?"

"Couple hundred oughta keep me going till I find some work. I'm thinking one a them jobs where things get going around lunch time, you know? Maybe shift work at the dock. That make sense to me. Then that old devil clock ain't gonna sic me. I be rolling soon, give you every nickel back and then some. Buy you a new Sunday hat."

"You allergic to work, seems like." For the first time in a long time Notary wished for a cigarette. She hadn't smoked in over ten years, ever since she'd married Ernest. She was feeling fidgety, didn't wanna hang up, lose contact. "Might try the glove factory. Hear they's looking for people."

"Ain't going to close myself up in no factory, Mama. Couldn't breathe. You know that."

"Guess I do." She pursed her lips. "I'll put some money in a envelope, stick it in the mailbox. You better get here 'fore the mailman come by, though, all I got to say."

"What time he come by these days?"

"Round two, two thirty Ernest say."

"Not a problem." He didn't say anything for a bit.

She wait. Voice different when he did talk. Quiet-like. "Member, Mama, when Daddy alive? How he'd take us to the river on the fourth? Throw us in the water like we was fish, swim around and duck us? Girls laughing? Me and Andruw taking turns standing on his shoulders? Member that?"

"Lord yes, Antwan. You think I likely to forget a single thing about your Daddy?"

"Guess not." Quiet again. "So tell the girls hey. And put some a your banana pudding in the fridge. Never can tell when I might drop by, you know?"

"Wish you would, son. You take care of yourself, you hear? Don't get in any mess."

"Just hanging with my running buddies, Mama. That all. And some women bout to tie me in knots."

"Any one in particular?"

"You know I gotta spread the good looks around, Mama. Ain't no woman gonna make me set still. Not any time soon."

"Reckon not. You change your mind, come on by, Antwan. Bring one a them gals. I won't be here till late, so come on by in the evening, you hear?"

"Why's that? You ain't working on the fourth, Mama? Not with your family coming."

"Just part the day. Be home around six, after we get the food ready up there. Alberta gonna stay the night, Mary gonna come early in the morning, so we got it worked out."

"Damn, Mama. That ain't right."

"Not your business, Antwan. Mine to worry 'bout." She didn't want to preach to him, like he said. Didn't want this to turn bad like it could. "Glad you called, son. Good to hear your voice. Always is."

"You too, Mama. And thanks. You my main gal."

"Night now." She put the receiver back like in slow motion, stared at it, leaned back in the scratchy chair. Her naked body was shivering even though it had to be at least 80 degrees out. And muggy as mud. She wasn't ready to crawl back into bed with Ernest, not yet.

Precious came wagging into the room, jumped up on her lap, scratched her thighs so bad she hollered "Get on down," pushing the dog away. Precious whimpered at her feet. With one bare skinny foot Notary nudged the dog away. "I said get on back in the bed now. Ain't studying about you right this minute."

She stood, walked into the kitchen, opened the refrigerator and felt around for a beer. The light made her blink. Why'd that boy have to rile her so, calling in the middle of the night? Ernest would stiffen his back when she told him Antwan had called again for money. What could she do? She felt around in the dark kitchen for the church key, opened the drawer by the sink, got what she was searching for. The beer tasted good, running down her throat all cold and sharp.

Me and Walter used to drink beer half the night, she thought, then fall into bed and make crazy love till I couldn't even remember falling asleep. Wake up grinning, all tangled together. God that man was proud of them twin boys. Like the two of us'd done something out of this world when we had two brown baby boys, so much alike couldn't nobody tell them apart, not even Walter half the time. He'd loved his girls like a mad man, but them twin boys was his eyeballs. That a fact. Called 'em his Sugar Babies when they was born, neither one of 'em any bigger than the palm of his hand. He the one insist on naming them both Walter: Walter Andruw, first born, Walter Antwan, the boy that come second, not even a whole minute later, fore I even took another big breath.

A thought hit her, almost took her breath: Thank the dear Lord he never know Andruw drown, never see Antwan like this, bandanna tied around his head, gold chains all over his neck. Hangin with them guys act so tough-like, ranting whitey this, whitey that. Getting fired every job he try. Walter, he work hard every day the Lord send, bring every penny to me. Sure, he like his spirits. Stay up late. Like Antwan say, gotta play. But Walter a big-hearted man, know when to do what. And Ernest treat her right, take care of the house, make life easy as he could. Hadn't she prayed to the Lord every day the last ten years to look after her last living boy? Don't she know in her gut Ernest right, that boy racing toward trouble like it a prize?

Heaven help us, that all I got to say, she prayed to herself, heaven help us all. And Mr. Elvis, too, she added. Lord says look out for others. I ain't the only one with troubles, that a fact. Even Mr. E., rich and famous like God, even he got a pack of problems.

Notary
July 2, 1975

Bangin at the front, like somebody shootin down the door. Bangin, bangin, bangin. Coffee smell. Ernest up. Why he don't get it?

Notary sat up, old skinny breasts hanging, trying to clear her head. Didn't she just talk to Antwan? Feel like ten minutes ago. Didn't he say he couldn't come by so early? She looked at the bedside clock. Hands say just after six thirty. Light out. Antwan never been up that early in his whole life. What he? Twenty-six? Never been up that early in twenty-six years, cept maybe when she was nursing him. Then he go right back to sleep.

Bangin, bangin, bangin, bangin, loud enough to wake the dead. She stood and took a cotton housedress from the closet, wrapped it on. Where Ernest?

She pulled the curtain back from her front window, could partway see two strange guys standing on the stoop. Stretch shirts. Cornrows. More chains than Mr. Elvis. What them two doing bangin on her door this early? Got no business . . .

Antwan! Something wrong with Antwan! She stumbled down the hall fast as she could make herself move, still felt like running in molasses. Open the door, there stand these two nasty-looking guys, bout Antwan's age, hard looking in the face. "What you want?"

"Tootie here?" the tall one asked, leaning like he looking around her.

"Tootie? Ain't no Tootie live here." Getting her breath. Thank the Lord. Then mad. Mad as hell. "Why you come bangin on my door so early?"

Tall one looked at other guy, one got a white patch on half his face. Look mean, too. "What Tootie's name? Tootie Pettiford? That it?" Other guy shrug.

"No Tootie Pettiford here. Get on." Mistake. Wrong house. Praise be. Some other Pettiford mama got heartbreak coming.

They stared her down. "Need to see Tootie."

"Antwan," the short one say to his buddy. "That his name. Antwan."

Notary's heart stopped. Back screen slam. That it. Lord, Lord. Ernest out picking tomatoes in the back, to fry up with eggs. And biscuits. Can't hear. Notary grabbed at normal things in her mind. Eggs. Tomatoes. Breath. "Antwan ain't live here. What you want with him?"

"Need to talk to him. Today. Yesterday. Gotta see him sooner stead of later. That's a fact." The tall one talked like an automatic pistol, bam, bam, bam. Short one just stood there, staring, them eyes stupid like a chicken's. "Where he staying then?"

Ernest walked up behind her, moved her to the side with a firm push of one hand. "You two need something?"

Without so much as a blink the tall one say, "Need Antwan. You know where he hangin?"

"Ain't heard from Antwan. You best be moving along."

"He call, tell him Dawg tired of waitin." They don't move yet, like they froze.

"Don't 'spect we'll be talking to him any time soon. You best look somewhere else."

"Be a good idea you find him quick, cause like I said, Dawg's tired of waiting." They both slide back, like some funky dance step, move half sideways, half facing the door, out to the sidewalk. They turn together, slow-like, slouch on down the walk.

First Notary noticed, a car at the curb. Got another guy in it, driver. Big car. Four doors. Not black, not blue. Expensive car, like one a Mr. E's.

Ernest shut the door, even though it's already heating up in the house. Walked back to the kitchen. Notary stand there a minute in her housedress, trembling. Must be past time for her to get ready for work, eat breakfast. Car be here for her pretty quick now.

"You gonna eat, Notary? Food ready."

She think she gonna say Ain't hungry, you go on. But can't say a thing. She think she gonna hustle on back to the bathroom, clean her face, brush her teeth, go iron a fresh uniform. Don't move.

Ernest stood in the kitchen doorway and stared at her. She's already tired of people staring at her today, want to tell him Get on yourself, don't wait for me. She still don't speak a word.

"Sound like Antwan got hisself in some trouble again."

That the best you can say, Antwan got hisself in some trouble again? Ain't I already heard that, seen them so-called running buddies of his with my own eyes? Tootie. Who Tootie? Ain't he got a Christian name, Walter Antwan? Ain't he my last living boy? Then *you* got to say something like Antwan got hisself in some trouble again?

Notary flopped into the same nubby armchair she'd sat in the night before, when Antwan called. Drug money. That's what he was after from her. Drug money. Why'd she buy this slipcover anyway? Won't nothing but a irritation, plain and simple. She could feel the sweat behind her knees, at the crease in her neck, in the cracks at her elbows. Sweat pouring down from her armpits. This chair damn uncomfortable. Day already hot.

"What you want me to do?"

Shut up the first thing.

Sound come out of her throat, like somebody far away moaning, like the moan come from deep down in the earth somewhere.

Ernest right at her feet, kneeling down, grabbing her arms. "Notary! Notary baby, you gotta let me help you . . ."

Moan turn into a shriek, like shriek from some haint, shrieking, shrieking from the grave.

Ernest leaned up, put his one hand on her mouth, pulled her up to him with the other. "Baby, baby, you can't let this beat you down. Turn to Ernest, baby. Turn to your Ernest who gonna help you get through this."

She fall against him, now, like all the breath gone from her body, like the strength drained down through her toes into the floor. He pull her to the sofa, pull her up onto his lap like a child, hold her close, his own heart beating like a tractor engine.

"Baby, baby, don't you be scared, you hear? Don't you be scared of a thing. We gonna take care a this together. We gonna do something, make it right. You hear? We gonna do something. I swear."

Far away she heard a car pull up to the curb, honk. She tensed. They back? They back already for her one living baby boy?

207

Charlotte Morgan

"Hush, hush now, Notary, you hear me? That just the car come for you, come to take you to work. I gonna go on out and tell him you ain't coming today. You sit here, still, I be right back." He started to ease her to the sofa, to stand.

"No!" she hollered. Where'd that come from? Why she say that? She grab at his hand, pull on it. "Go tell him I be a few minutes, you hear?" Voice panicked.

"You can't go up to Graceland today, baby, not like this. 'Sides, we gotta find Antwan, find out what's going on, see what we need to do."

She stood, her legs wobbly. Gotta go, all she know. Gotta get up there to Graceland, figure this all out. Ernest, well-meaning, ain't a thing he can do. See that plain as clean sheets. "Tell that driver I be there in a minute, hold his horses."

Ernest tried one more time to hold her back with his strong arm, but she pushed at him with her other hand.

"I ain't foolin." Strong-like, now. "Lemme loose, I mean it. Gotta press that uniform and get going."

Get that slapped look off you face, man. Ain't about you. About Antwan. So might as well stop looking like a kicked dog and get on out the door like I say.

She hurried back to her room and grabbed a gray uniform from the ironing stack. She'd tell Ernest something to do, make him feel like he could help her out. Send him down to Beale, maybe, to ask around at the joints. Anybody seen Antwan? But still won't nothing he could do up against this Dawg person. How her boy get messed up with all that? Drugs for sure. Gotta get some help from somebody who knows the streets, knows how to handle these dope things. Her head get dizzy-like; she got to steady herself against the ironing board, make herself straighten up.

Mr. Red, Mr. Sonny, they bound to know more about the streets than Ernest. He want to help, but fact is, what use he gonna be? She ain't never ast a single one of them up at Graceland for a favor, not a single thing. Mr. E., he always good at Christmas, but she ain't never ast nobody in that house to do a thing extra for her. Been there through it all. Miz Gladys dying, God rest her sweet soul. That chile coming over here from Germany, so crazy over Mr. E. Him ignoring her more often than not. Mr. Vernon bringing that woman and her three wild boys into the house. Never did a thing but look the other way, keep the place just like Mr. E. want it. Cook, clean, look the other way. Been what? Near on twenty years. He say what, more times than she could count? "Alberta, Notary, Mary – they're my girls, my family. They belong right here at Graceland with me." Time she ask a favor of that family. Swallow her pride. Pride goeth before a fall. Ain't that what the good book say? Ain't about to let Antwan fall.

Lord, direct my feet in the right path, she prayed. See if somebody up there can help me with this Dawg. Help me get my boy outa this deep trouble he in. 'Fore it's too late. Amen.

Made the potato salad, lots of sweet pickle juice like Mr. E. like it. Made the pans of baked beans, ready to stick in the oven day after tomorrow. Fixed three dozen devilled eggs with bacon. Don't know how, just kept on working. Watching. Waiting for some sign.

Alberta said, "What's wrong, Notary? Ain't singing, ain't saying a word. Something wrong?" I shake my head, keep my own counsel. Don't do to talk about it. Shamed, too. Alberta's had a hard row, that a fact, but still, think I'd fall to the floor if I tried to say a word.

Hit me while I'm putting the dishes up: Didn't leave no money for Antwan. Him in all this mess, them two hoodlums coming to the door, I forget all about that cash I promised. Call Ernest, catch him 'fore he go out, say get my hide money, shoebox in my closet, you know, put three hundred in a envelope in the mailbox. He want to know, You hear from Antwan today? You know where he at, so I ain't gotta go over to Beale asking around? I say no, just do what I'm asking, can't explain now. Help don't s'posed to tie up the phone at Mr. E's, you know that. Talk to you later. He agree, huffy like. I ask myself: What two hundred dollars gonna do if drugs involved? Three hundred, for that matter?

Wiped down the chair pads on the patio. Swept the leaves. Keep on. Mr. Sonny, Mr. Red, they sleep late like always, come in the kitchen joshing around bout eleven or so, wanting us to cook up some cheeseburgers, fry some 'taters, how 'bout some cabbage and apples? Mr. Jerry come on over, they all plays pool. That Linda woman ring about two, want to know can she have a grapefruit and pot of coffee, and send Mr. E. plenty of watermelon and a quart of milk. Not a word from Mr. E. hisself. Like he can't talk? Like he can't ast for

Charlotte Morgan

what he want? He always do before. Nothing wrong with him but her, you ast me. Put the tray outside the door, she say. I go up, leave it by the door, hear the teevees going, that all. Even if I try to leave a note, that Linda gonna get a hold of it herself, I'm thinking. Ain't gonna get to Mr. E., even if I say private on the outside. She act so high and mighty, like ain't a one of us can help him but her. Look right through us in the kitchen when she come down, ordering this and that for the picnic. I say think about this: When he get so sad? I want to ast her: When he get so sad?

Mr. Sonny, Mr. Red, Mr. Jerry bring their plates up, teasing around, crazy stuff, "You been behaving yourself, Notary?" Like that. I try to figure how I could ast Mr. Red about this Dawg person. Mr. Red the one to know, I figure. He the one act the most street-wise. Trashiest, to my mind, even if he do act in the movies, play the guitar sometimes on the records. So what? Maybe he do some a that dope hisself, I think on more than one occasion. Miz Gladys say, "Elvis think the world a that Red. He kinda shifty, you ast me." Get him to the side, just ast him if he ever hear about a guy named Dawg, badass here in Memphis? But then I think: He gonna know it got to do with dope if he know anything. Then what I gonna say? Gonna say my boy Antwan in deep with this Dawg? Mr. E. won't have a thing to do with any drug mess, no sir. Head a mess trying to figure it out, whole body like it gonna pop wide open. Jumpy jeebies. Then I got to say yes, tell him that the thing worrying me: My boy involved some way with dope. That the thing I need some help with. Fast. So what? Swallow my pride. I would, I think, I get the chance. But they leave the house. Where they going? What if Mr. E. need them? Things strange around here these days, no ignoring that.

Mr. Vernon come up to the house to get some lunch, Miz Patsy, just jabbering bout what we gonna have for the fourth? All that. Mr. Vernon ast after Ernest, has he caught any fish yet this summer, all like that. He sweet, Mr. Vernon. Not a bit uppity. Miz Gladys love that man, but she know the story. Least he didn't bring it in the house while she alive, I'll say that for him. Think for a second maybe I get him to take a note to Mr. E. Or even I ast him for some help. But Mr. Vernon never one to decide a thing. He more like a chile than anybody up at Graceland. He take it, never give it to Mr. E. Can't deal with no troubles. Never could. Don't want to worry him. I sure of that, once I think about it good.

210

Wish Miss Priscilla still here. She one smart woman, that for sure. Didn't she have to watch and wait, watch and wait all that time? She quiet like a cat, figuring who to trust, who to keep at a distance. Still, she know what Mr. E. need, know how to cheer him up. Know who's good for him, who not. And that precious Lisa Marie. Never seen a man crazier bout his wife and precious baby. That Colonel keep him on the road, out there in Hollywood, Las Vegas, keep him surrounded by these so-called buddies, don't want him too close to Miss Priscilla, you ast me. She too smart. Almost smarter than that Colonel hisself, and he know it. That snake. He the cause of that marriage ruination. Miss Priscilla, she got a kind heart, too. She here, she wouldn't keep Mr. E. away from me. She always nice to the house help.

Running the vacuum in the parlor it strike me like a stick: I gotta take the note to Mr. E. myself. Just knock on the door and say, I got a message for Mr. Elvis, got to give it to him myself. Stare that Linda woman down. Don't like the thought, don't like it one bit, but that the way. Gotta do it for Antwan. Gotta make myself do it for him.

Only problem, by the time I think of this, round four o'clock, Mr. E. bound to be sleeping again. So I know I can't do it today, since I gotta leave at five and he never be up again till ten, eleven at night. Mary say most of the time he ain't even getting up then, that what she say when I see her last week. Say he holed up in there eating, sleeping, not even taking a bath. Them diet pills, sleeping pills, all that mess he putting in his body stead of food. Reading them books that Mr. Larry bring, bout spirits and all that. That ain't him. No sirree. But ain't no use in me going up there when he's asleep. That Linda just take the note, throw it away, that be that. She a damned witch for sure. Working her hateful ways on that sweet, broken man. He gotta collect hisself, get hisself together. Don't know if he can with her running the show. Ain't like him, ain't like him a bit, to let that woman take over his business.

He bout as kind as they come when he's in his right mind. Give his Mama a 'lectric mixer one week, give her another one the next day. Say she need two, one for each end of the counter in that big ol' kitchen. Kiss her all over the face, grab her up and dance her around the house. Sit down at the piano with her, play ol time hymns like she love, from that assembly church back home she talk about all the time, and the two of them sings so pretty must've made the angels smile. Lord she had a pretty voice. Got all shaky, at the end, but she did

211

love to sing. He'd call her his Itty Bitty, his Satnin Mama, voice like a child. Them two talk they special talk. Ain't never seen a boy care bout his Mama so much.

Me and Miz Gladys, we used to be prayer partners. We'd read Bible verses together whenever I stay here at night, say our prayers, pray out loud for the living and the dead. Good Lord bound to hear. We'd talk right much about our boys, too. She'd tell me how blessed I was to have both my twins alive and fit, sweet Christian boys that go to Sunday School every Sunday the Lord send. What good boys we both had. She liked to say Elvis strong because Jesse's spirit moved into him first breath he took. Said she could always feel Jesse with them, too. That woman, ain't never a woman loved her boy more than she loved Mr. E. Killed her, him on the road all the time, her closed up here at Graceland. Said this big house the loneliest place in Tennessee most a the time. Mr. Vernon no company, he so high and mighty running the place. Who knows where he go at night? Don't wanna know. Dodger had her ways, like to talk to Aunt Delta. Two of them ain't spend that much time with Miz Gladys, for some reason. Probably they all out of sorts about her tallboys, but don't Jesus hisself say not to judge? Some people Sunday Christians, you ask me. Not Miz Gladys. Didn't nobody make her day like Mr. E. when he home. He got a kind heart, just like her. A deep down sweetness. He bound to help me. All I got to do is ask. He bound to step in. Big question: Tomorrow be too late?

Notary made the driver let her off at Evonne's. Ernest called just before she left Graceland, said let's meet at Evonne's. She want us all to eat over there tonight. Just for a second Notary had to feel pride when she got out the back of the car: Driver bound to see her daughter doing well. New brick ranch house, yard got grass, a bird bath, and petunias along the front. Clean as a pin. Had to feel proud, just for a breath, that he see how her girl making a good life for her family.

Trudging up the clean-swept walk, not a stick on it, Notary felt her worry take hold again. Evonne came to the door, called, "Come on in the house, Mama. Here, give me that bag." Came down the steps and gave her Mama a tight hug, took the sack of leftovers. "You didn't need to bring these, Mama. I'm cooking us a nice summer supper."

"Ernest here, honey?"

"Been here a while, Mama."

They stopped at the steps. "Nothing bad about Antwan, is it? No bad news?"

"He ain't called. Nothing much new, Mama, Ernest say. Antwan ain't hurt, that what you thinking. Come on in the house." She led her mother through the open door into the spanking clean crowded living room. Ernest, seated in a arm chair, stood up when the women came in the room. The two grandkids ran and grabbed Notary around the knees.

"Hey there, Carl Junior. Hey Tenosha." Notary managed to pat each child's head. "Don't y'all knock Granny down now, you hear? Granny's kinda shaky today."

"You kids quit pulling on your Granny, I mean it." Evonne grabbed Carl Junior by the elbow. "Leave her be. She been working all day."

"They okay, honey," Notary said, taking each child by the hand. "Come over here on the sofa and crawl up with me." Hard to be worried sick with your grands pulling at you.

"Bring me something sweet, Granny?" Carl Junior, six years old and bright as brass buttons, asked, fidgeting. Didn't he look more like her own brown boys than his dark black Daddy Carl? His face not so fat like Carl's, either.

"Think they's some chocolate cake in the bag, boy. And maybe some leftover coconut cake, too. Mr. E. ain't eatin no sweets these days, but we still making them. Never can tell when he want some."

The boy ran after his Mama into the kitchen, Evonne saying "You know good and well I ain't gonna let you spoil your supper," as Notary pulled Tenosha, three, bird-tiny for her age, up to her lap. "How's my baby girl?" Tenosha just stuck her finger in her mouth and sucked, snuggled into her Granny's soft chest. "You a darling girl, Tenosha, you know that? Don't know how your Mama had such a quiet, sweet girl."

"I heard that, Mama," Evonne said, coming back into the living room, wiping her hands on a fresh tea towel. "Sent Carl Junior out the back to play with Damian. Supper be ready in a bit. He been 'bout to drive me crazy all afternoon, picking on his sister." She pushed her straight hair away from her face, sat in a arm chair. She the only one of the children to have good hair. Evonne thin like her Mama, but she sure had Walter's fire, that for sure. Don't know where she get that hair. "What's all this Ernest been telling me about Antwan, Mama? What kinda trouble he get hisself into now?"

Notary looked down at the girl, looked back at Evonne.

"It okay for her to hear, Mama. Ain't keeping no secrets from the kids. They gotta know some time. Maybe keep them from acting stupid like their Uncle Antwan one day."

"You say so." Notary turned toward Ernest. "You find out anything today? You hear any more from him?"

Ernest rubbed his hands together. "Didn't get much, and what I got ain't good."

"He pick up that money?"

Shook his head: "I check the mailbox 'fore I leave to come over here. Still there."

"He ain't got the money? What you reckon that mean?" She looked from one to the other. "He say last night he coming by in the afternoon to get it. When Antwan ever miss picking up money?"

Evonne had that look she got, face stern, whenever Antwan's name come up these days. "You talk to him, Mama? Ernest didn't tell me that."

Ernest give her a hard look too. Won't like Ernest, even though he didn't like her giving Antwan money, to shoot her a strong look like that. Didn't like her keeping secrets even worse. "Forgot to say, is all. Won't no secret. He call last night when I was dead asleep. You sleeping too, Ernest. Call and say he got plans for the fourth, lost his job, want . . ."

"He lose another job, Mama? How many that make?" Evonne's voice had that nasty tone Notary never let her use when she a girl. Now nothing she could say. Girl grown, had her own kids. Kept kids. Made good money. Didn't let none of them use a smart mouth. Still, she use that smart aleck mouth herself where Antwan concerned. One more pain in Notary's gut.

"That not the problem right now, way I see it, Evonne. Worse row to hoe now, I'm afraid." She rubbed Tenosha's soft head, neat little curls in tight bands all over that tiny head. Felt good, like when her own girls small.

"You ask me, Mama, he got hisself into this hole, Antwan gotta dig hisself out. I don't see why you giving him money. You always do that, look where it got you."

How you get so hard-hearted, girl? Not from me. "Can't do that, Evonne. Ain't the way it works, least not for me. That boy in trouble, his Mama gotta . . ."

"Gotta what, Notary?" Ernest stare hard. Won't like Ernest to interrupt. He so quiet all the time. Ain't one to fuss. "Gotta have crooks banging down the door? Listen to blackass dope dealers making threats inside your own house? That what a man gotta do?"

He riled, plain to see. Feel like she stand with Antwan, her own family gonna stand against her. That what this about? "Never saw that coming, Ernest. Know Antwan mixed up, shiftless, never saw none a this mess coming." She lean her head back against the sofa, close her eyes, Tenosha burrow into her. "It's okay, honey. Granny fine. Just tired."

"Better check after this meatloaf. Bout ready, I think. Tenosha, you coming with Mama to wash your hands, baby?"

The little girl shake her head no. Granny pat her tiny shoulder. "I take her in a minute, 'Vonnie. You got enough to do."

Evonne's big sigh say plenty. Ernest come over to the sofa, sit down heavy, after Evonne leave the front room. Just sit, don't say a word. Notary wonder how she gonna put a bite in her mouth, her throat so tight. Hear Carl Junior hollering, laughing out back. Him and that neighbor boy Damian put her in mind of her own boys playing. Fenced yard, plenty toys. Evonne got everything so nice here. Hear her call, "Get on in here, Carl Junior, wash your face and hands for supper." Gotta eat, Evonne's feelings get hurt if she don't.

"Asked around Beale about this Dawg, Notary." Ernest's voice soft again. He never one to stay mad. "You ain't gonna like what I hear."

"Go ahead. Ain't asking you to pretend, Ernest. Ain't never asked that."

He reached a big hand to her knee, lay it there. "That the truth, baby." He sit another little bit, quiet. Woman need patience with Ernest. He a good man, but he sure demand a load of patience. "Good places, bartender look at me like I some crackpot, some ol crazy uncle, you know? Ain't never heard a no Dawg, less it Hound Dog." He force a smile. "Heard that plenty."

Notary waited.

"Y'all come on. Wash your hands. Food on the table," Evonne call from the big eat-in kitchen. Even got a dishwasher. Big Carl right proud hisself of that dishwasher.

"Coming," Notary call back. "Come on, Tenosha. Let Granny carry you to the bathroom, honey." She stand, lift the baby on her hip. "I gonna take Tenosha to get washed up, Von. Be right there." She look at Ernest. "Gotta say what you know right now. Don't want to rile Evonne. She hate good food to get cold."

"Them bars down on the river, ones where we say the river rats hang?" She nod. "That's where this Dawg run drugs."

"Lord have mercy," Notary say. Bad go to worse.

"Need to pee, Granny." Tenosha, three years old, still never talk above a whisper.

"Sure you do, sweetheart. Come on." She walk down the hall, Ernest follow her into the bathroom while she lift Tenosha's little sundress, pull down her bloomers, hold her bony body on the toilet to pee.

"Went on back up to the junior high school, where them boys Antwan used to run with before he quit school play ball. Some of them still there every day, playing ball. Wait around, talk to Jerome. You remember him? Tall, skinny, got funny looking eyes, kinda crossed?"

"Course I do. He real polite child whenever he come to the house." She looked down at Tenosha, sittin there quiet. "Wipe your bottom, girl. Then we gotta wash your hands right quick fore your Mama have a hissy fit."

"Jerome live in the projects, his Mama raise them kids alone, you recall that? Anyway, he still living with her, know what all's going down on the street. He say this Dawg move here from D.C. Bad news. Selling dope all right, pot, little cocaine. 'Ludes. Talk tough, rant about whitey, all that mess."

Notary turn on the faucet, dangle Tenosha over the sink. The child flutter her tiny fingers in the spray. "Could be worse, I s'pose."

"That ain't all. Jerome say word is Antwan running for this Dawg, hanging with him pretty steady. Last week or so, ain't paid his share. Kept it all."

"Mama? Tenosha? Y'all come on now." Plain to see Evonne at the end of her patience.

"Wiping our hands. Be right there."

Tenosha wrap both skinny arms around Notary's neck, cling tight. "Let's go on and eat, baby. Mama got some applesauce on the table for you, I bet." Child didn't eat much more than applesauce. Sometimes a little rat cheese. That about it.

"Notary." Ernest take her elbow. "This big. This Dawg might be small change, but Jerome say he mean. Say he looking for a fight."

"Guess Antwan know that." Notary rocked the little girl in her arms. "Come on, sweetie pie. Let's ask Granddaddy Ernest to say the blessing, what you think?" She looked Ernest straight in the face. "Need Granddaddy to bless more than the food right this minute. Think you can do that for us, Mr. Midgette?" This time she pronounced his name right. "Think it might be a right smart idea if Granny say a little prayer along with him, too. Think she need to do that, for sure."

Notary
July 3, 1975

Middle of the night, Notary sat at the kitchen table trying to figure out what to say in her note. Precious sound asleep at her feet. Hard to write. Not the letters. Right words. She'd left school after ninth grade — won't a bit of use her going after that. She second of nine, too many mouths need food, too many feet gotta have shoes. She live at home, wait tables at the hotel coffee shop, bring in good money. Good in school, always made good grades. But Mama say got all the 'rithmetic, spelling a girl gonna need by ninth grade. Her handwriting perfect, too. Still, handwriting not the holdup. What to say? Gotta be right words. Only get one chance.

Been up half the night, she figured, still ain't put the first word on this pad of paper. When Mr. E. ring for his breakfast – rather, when that Linda woman call down – she gonna insist on taking up the trays. Gonna knock at the door, no matter what that witch say. Note gotta be right. Gotta be perfect.

Mr. E. no dummy, that a fact, Notary thought. Lotta people think he some country bumpkin, got no more sense than a pissant, but he plenty smart. He read all the time. Maybe read too much, some say. That Mr. Larry, s'posed to cut his hair, he bring him all these books about psychic powers, get Mr. E. all riled up about that mess. He a Bible boy, that how his Mama raised him. She turn her worries over to the good Lord, that bound to be plenty. Mr. E. religious, too, say his prayers like she taught him, but he open to all this mess cause his heart broke in more pieces than a picture puzzle. Never the same since his Mama pass. Knock him off his wobbly feet when Miss Priscilla leave, take that child.

219

What she gonna do, though? No choice. That fat Colonel got him under some kinda spell. Miz Gladys never did like that Colonel, didn't trust him one bit.

Notary no dummy herself, she know, but she sure perplexed about what the best thing to say. Read more books than her whole family put together. Even after she left school. Never one to worry about how she say what, but this note maybe Antwan's only chance to get outa this mess. Sound like he broke the bank on stupid this time. Sound like this Dawg mean business.

Maybe forget the note, get Mr. Red first thing, take him aside and explain. Somehow that don't feel right. Mr. Red, with all his joshing and glad-handing, he ain't nothing but Mr. E.'s colored boy. He don't jump less Mr. E. say how high. No, best shot at the top.

And look like she gotta take this in her own hands. Evonne no help. God knows Notary love Ernest, he as good a man as the Lord ever gave breath, but he not much help at a time like this. He too gentle, if there any such thing. Too good. Walter, he a church-going man, he a angel to his children, but he tough, he come from the streets. Antwan never be in this mess, Walter around. She got no business thinking such thoughts. Make her skin warm, hungry. Make her see that man clear as the kitchen counter, make her almost smell his breath. She like working at that hotel, didn't miss school a bit. Fourteen, girls grown back then. Men flirt, pay her mind. Fun, going to the clubs at night, dancing, wearing pretty things. First meet Walter there, Lord knows she'll never forget, him buck dancing. Good Lord that man could dance. She tall, not much butt or chest, but she pretty good dancer herself. Both laugh to beat the band, dance half the night. Start running together. Walter a catch, that a fact. Good looking big man, work steady at the train yard, not married. Her Mama need her at home, but she still got plenty of time to go with Walter.

When she got pregnant with Marcea, he hold her flat belly, want to marry her that minute. Walter not one to stand back.

She shook her head, like shaking away flies. Don't do a bit a good thinking bout things nobody can change. Gotta get busy, write this note out, get some rest.

She put pencil to paper. Gotta write first with pencil, she think, face facts. Copy it in pen when she get it the way she want it to read.

Dear Mr. Elvis –

Antwan in trouble bad. Need help. Hoodlums down at the river after him. Some guy named Dawg the main one.

What you think I should do? Any way you could help, or get Mr. Red to help?

Hate to say, but guess it gotta be fast. I'd sure be grateful, since he my only living boy.

You know ain't a day go by that I don't pray for you and Miz Gladys and Mr. Vernon.

Yours in Jesus,

Notary Pettiford Midgette

Mr. Elvis first know her, first hire her to help out at Graceland, she Notary Pettiford. Walter alive then, back in 1956. Don't even know if he recognize name Midgette. Mr. Vernon sign all the paychecks. Gotta write it out, Notary Pettiford Midgette. Course, what other Notary he know?

She looked back over it. Bone weary. Have to do for now. Maybe when she copy it, first thing in the morning, she make a change here and there. For now, gonna put it up. She think: Oughta say something like If I done something out of place by asking this favor, please don't think I trying to reach above my station. Just what any Mama probably do. Something like that. Notary pick up her pencil, make a note on the paper right that minute, 'fore she forget.

Some reason, she don't want Ernest to see. Wound his pride, he see her turning to Mr. E. for help. Still, can't wait around for him or that boy Jerome to figure out some way to stop this Dawg. Ain't got much stock in that. Got to do what she can do. Got to try. Worried sick Antwan ain't come for that money. What that mean? She stand, fold the paper, stick it in her pocketbook hanging on the kitchen door handle. So tired she can hardly move, but no doubt soon as she lay down in the bed she won't be able to sleep a wink. Say her prayers again, maybe that help. Ask God. Ask anybody can hear: Please keep Antwan safe.

"Mama?" Scritch scratch, like Japenese beetle at the screen. "Mama? Gotta wake up, Mama." Scritch scritch.

Notary dreaming. Gotta be dreaming. That Antwan calling, plain as day.

"Mama? Get up, please. Over here." Scratch scratch.

She pulled the sheet up over her self, skin same color as the dark, rolled over toward the sound. That Antwan?

"Mama."

221

Voice louder. That Antwan, for real? She dragged the sheet around her. Ain't one for spooks and such. Lord knows she tired, murky in the head, but still...

"Ma-maaaaa," long moan. "Please, Mama, wake up."

She leaned toward the window screen. "That you, son?"

"Come out here, Mama. Gotta talk. Fast."

"Lemme get a robe, boy. Come round the back." Ernest ain't moved. That man sleep like a baby, sleep through world war. Put her face to the window, whisper. "Come on in the kitchen, Antwan, lemme fix you a plate." Precious stand up, start licking her arm. She pick up the dog, let it lick all over her, keep him from barking.

"Can't. This gotta be fast, Mama. They looking for me."

All her insides jelly. Ain't never been involved in no mess like this. How Antwan get to this place? She carry the dog, take her housecoat from the hook in the closet, feel her way to the back door, step out into the muggy night. "Antwan? Where you at?" Put Precious down, watch him head to the camellia bush.

"Shhhh. Hush up, Mama." His voice scratchy, like the screen. Child sound frantic.

Notary follow the sound, watch the way the dog go. See her boy all crouched down, hunkering up against the house on the other side of the tall bush, Precious wagging all over him to beat the band. "Hon-nee..." She reach down to touch his shoulder.

"Shhhh," he say again, finger up to his mouth. "This bad, Mama. Real bad." He take her hand, drop it, glare into her face. "Gotta have more than the two hundred I asked you for..."

She kneel her bony self down close to him. Yard smell like cut grass. When Ernest cut the grass? Her boy sweaty, not work sweaty, either. Smell like panic. "I already put three hundred in the envelope, son. You get it out the mailbox?"

"That ain't gone do it, Mama." His voice all raspy.

"What you need?"

"Little over a thousand." She catch her breath, he wait a second, breathe hard out his nose. "Still, even with the money, it still gonna be too hot for me to hang around town."

"What you talking about? Who this Dawg you all tied up with?"

"How you know about him?" His eyes cut at her, wild like the devil clawing at his back. "None a your concern, you hear? This shit ain't none a your concern." He shove Precious off him, dog go running to Notary. "Wish I didn't have to come here. You got that much in the house?"

She gotta say the truth: "Don't think so, son. 'Fraid not."

Antwan drop his head in his hands. Shake it back and forth. "Sorry ain't the word, Mama, for what I got to say to you. I crazy-sorry to bring this mess to you, come begging. What else I gonna do?"

"You hush. Ain't begging when you come to your own Mama." Pick up her Precious baby, pet his tiny wiggling back. Wanna pet Antwan, he all strung tight as a tick. Never seen him this agitated. What she gonna do? Didn't keep that much in the hide money. Maybe six hundred, tops. Already took out three. Ernest have some, but not likely to have four hundred in his pants pocket. Her eyes getting used to the dark, she see her boy's face a little better when he look up at her. Never did like that doo-rag he wear. Face too skinny. His dark eyes jumpy-like, mouth all tight, trembling. "You on some kinda drug right this minute, son?"

"What you talking 'bout, Mama. Ain't got enough for a nickel bag. Ain't nobody on the street gonna give me a thing, either."

"Can't give you that kinda money tonight, son." She rest the dog on her chest, still petting. "Try to get it together in the morning. Bank closing at noon, for the holiday, but maybe I can get Ernest to go."

"Gimme what you got now, Mama. Don't know what else to do. If I can't get things straight with Dawg, I gotta take off now. Tonight."

"What you mean take off?"

"Leave Memphis. Stay away till Dawg and his boys move on."

"And if they don't?"

"Can't worry 'bout that now. They after me, Mama. Ain't kidding. I owe him that money. Plus, you know, man can't mess over the boss."

She shook her head. "Lemme get what I got. You wait here." She stand up, bony knees creaking, sound like a tree branch breaking.

"Shhhh, Mama. Pleeeease," Antwan whisper. "They been watching this house, I figure,"

"Watching my house?" Notary scanned the back stoop, the dark windows, the outline of the rickety metal chairs she'd had since Noah. "Don't believe it for a minute. Think I'd know." She holdin Precious so tight he whimper. "Hush

223

now. Quit it, you hear?" Feel like somebody drain the blood out of her body. "I go get what I got."

Inside the kitchen she go first to her handbag, count out what she got there by the little bit of light coming in at the window. Used to the dark now, don't need much. Thirty eight dollars is all. Hadn't been to the store all week. Ernest go. Precious follow her down the hall. In the box in her closet she feel around for the money, tuck all the cash in the pocket of her housecoat. Ernest turn over, don't make a sound. Reach around for his wallet on his dresser. Take out the bills. Walk back to the kitchen, lean over the counter, count it all. Not even five hundred. Four hundred seventy nine. Even if he put that with the three hundred in the envelope, not enough. Could call Evonne. She'd give it to her. Wouldn't want to help Antwan, would fuss at her something awful for giving him her hide money, but she'd let her have it if she ask. Ain't gone solve the problem, though. Gotta get this Dawg off Antwan's back. Gotta fix it so he ain't after him.

Notary open the screen door, let Precious run out ahead of her. "Scoot on off the stoop now, baby. Mama gotta hurry." She walked over to where Antwan squatted over, handed him the cash. "Not quite five hundred. Put this with the other, you close to eight. That help?"

He stare hard at his hand. Don't say a word.

"You ain't gonna take that money and buy drugs now, Antwan? Promise me you ain't."

"Tole you Mama. Ain't nobody gonna sell me no drugs, even if I want it. Dawg got the word out." His voice flat.

"How come you don't just take this and go to Jersey, stay at Marcea's some?"

He shake his head back and forth, don't stop. "This big, Mama. I think about that very thing, but ain't gonna do no good. Dawg gotta prove hisself on the street. Make his name in Memphis, you know? Can't let nobody get over on him. Won't work." Precious tried to lick his face but he shoved him away.

"You eat?"

"Ain't hungry. Gotta go now. Gotta catch up with his boys, send Dawg what I got. Today the last day, he say. That the message."

"Tell you what: you come on by the back gate at Mr. Vernon's round two. Come in on Dolan Avenue, all right? Won't nobody be there. Lemme see if I can get the rest for you. Lemme see what I can do."

"Twelve hundred what I owe him, Mama. This here too short, ain't gonna work. How you gonna get that kinda money in the morning?"

"You let me figure that, son. You just take care of yourself, don't let nobody hurt you. We gone put this mess behind us."

For the first time Antwan stood. Lord, Notary thought. He skinny all over. Where his muscles? Where her cocky boy? She like to cried out, seeing him so bad off. Precious paw her legs. She reach out to grab one of her boy's hands, it all clammy. Lord, Lord, help me Jesus.

"Ain't what I wanted, Mama. Ain't started out to let you down."

"Hush, child." She take his head, cradle it against her shoulder. He let her, like he don't have the strength to stand on his own.

Notary gotta stay busy. Cutting up the apples for the pies. Thinking: Made the crust. Gotta make four pies. Plenty cinnamon and butter. Want Mr. E. to be satisfied. Can't bake until the morning, though. Crust gotta be flaky, apples warm, when Mr. E. and his people ready to eat. Be ready to go in the oven after the beans done. Whole kitchen smell like ham; baking two hams for ham salad. He love that almost better than peanut butter. Put the rolls to rise in the morning, bake the coconut cakes.

Waiting for that phone to ring, bout to jump outta her skin. Told Antwan two o'clock. Almost half past one. Red and all them downstairs. Ate. Mr. Vernon come over early, too. Everybody all fired up 'bout the party, teasing me, say they gotta taste this, try that, why I don't make some turkey too? Say Mr. E. gotta come down tomorrow, be his ol self. He love the fourth. Ride go-carts, have fireworks, have a good time. Still ain't told Ernest I gotta come out here a good part of the day. Too much on my mind.

Mind racin: Ernest don't like it one bit when I ask him to get the money. Say, Anything I got you got, Notary, but ain't right you giving it all to Antwan when he just go from bad to trouble. He right, I tell him, but look like Antwan in way over his head this time. Look like he gotta pay up or something God-awful coming down on him. Ernest say Let's pray, and we do, but I tell him that ain't enough. Lord helps those who help themselves. I gotta help my boy. No ifs, ands, or buts.

Most people look at Antwan, probably see nigger hoodlum. See the gold chains, the jive get-up. Think drugs. They right about that. But Antwan got a good heart. Don't I know? Ain't I raised that boy? Just got too many scars is all. He go astray after his brother call his name, drown. Ain't got no Daddy to keep him straight. Boy never did like Ernest. Won't Walter, he couldn't get beyond that. Gotta help him find the path back. Nobody else see he broken all to pieces inside, can't help it. That a Mama's role. Evonne, Ernest, what they think ain't my trouble. They can help me or not. I gonna do what I need to do to help my only living boy. Long as I got breath myself.

Phone ring, Notary like to throw the bowl of apples in the air. Alberta answer, say yes ma'am this, yes ma'am that. She stand, set apples down nice on the counter, start washing her hands. Look up at the clock. Say one twenty six. Lord, Lord.

"Miss Linda upstairs, say Mr. Elvis want the same today. Want cut-up watermelon, milk. She gonna have poached egg, wheat toast, no butter, thing of coffee. You wanna fix it, you want me?" Rolled her eyes. Gotta say Miss Linda in the house.

"Don't mind doing it, Alberta. Got plenty time to make this pie filling. You go on with what you doing, I fix the tray nice."

"That suit me fine." She smiled. She don't like that Linda woman a bit better than I do. Don't none of us in the kitchen want her in the house. Can't say, though.

Notary 'bout ready to pop, thinking, Got the note in my pocket, wrote out in my best hand. Added them parts about sorry if it's trouble, all that. Found a envelope in the Christmas card box, wrote To Mr. Elvis Presley on the front. Licked it closed. Been waiting for this minute. Yes, Lord, this my one chance to help Antwan outta this big mess. I singing, "He got the whole world, in his hands, He got the whole world, in His hands, He got the whole world, in His hands, He got the whole world in His hands!" Giving glory while I fix the food. She gotta ask for poached egg today, don't she? Can't fret over that.

Step out the back, cut couple yellow roses for the tray. Mr. E. like things pretty. Get the cloth napkins. Everything nice. Don't care if egg get cold.

Going up the steps Notary sing some more, "Move On Up A Little Higher," giving praise where it belong.

Her body vibrating all over, like electric shock. She still singing when she get to Mr. E.'s door. Can't hardly hold herself still. Her mind racing: I s'posed to knock, put the tray on the floor. She rest the tray 'gainst one hip, knock, still singing. Keep singing, wait, knock again.

Miss Linda open the door, face ugly-like. "I declare, Notary, long as you've been here you'd think you'd know to leave the tray by the door." All exasperated. She reach for the tray.

"Mr. Elvis!" she yell. "Got a note for you!" Loud as she can holler. Hold tight onto the tray like holdin onto child about to be kidnap.

"What has gotten into you, Notary. Hand me that tray and get on downstairs. You know you're not s'posed to disturb Mr. Elvis!" Her voice sharp like a butcher knife. She grab hold of the tray herself.

"Please, Mr. Elvis! Please, Lord, got a secret note here for you!" They playing tug of war, both holding onto that tray. That Linda shooting mean looks, looks would kill a rat.

"Mr. Presley's gonna hear about this," she say.

"Notary? That you, Notary?" His voice sound like a boy's, sweet, timid.

"Yes sir. It me. Got something for you, sir."

"Linda, bring it here, please baby girl."

Notary let go the tray, reach into her pocket, put the note leaned up against the little rose vase. Smile. Can't help that smile, giving praise. Mr. E. gonna read the letter. That Linda hopping mad. "I'll bring it to you, honey bunch. Just you stay put and your baby girl will be right there with it." She give me a look, Notary'd be drop down dead if looks could kill. That woman meaner than a snake, and don't she know it. Don't care one bit. Mr. E. gonna read my note. Thank you, Lord Jesus. Praise be.

Back downstairs, Alberta asked, "What all that commotion going on upstairs?" Notary grinned, said, "That hussy throwing a hissy fit. Ain't know why. Maybe egg cold." They both laugh.

Notary gotta look at the clock. Right at two. "You mind if I get a breath of air? It got right hot upstairs, you know what I mean."

"Don't mind a bit. Everything under control here. 'Bout ready as we gonna be for tomorrow. Least what we can do ahead of time." Alberta love Mr. E., don't think much at all of this woman he carrying on with. Miss Priscilla the favorite, next to Miz Gladys. Mr. E. not in his right mind, kitchen staff whisper, only reason he let this Linda woman come to Graceland.

Charlotte Morgan

Notary take off her apron, hurry out the back toward the gate that open onto Mr. Vernon's place. He and Miss Patsy in the office building, ain't nobody back here these days. Used to have the horses here, have Miz Gladys' goat, chickens, all that. Ain't hardly got any animals at all these days. Pony for Miss Lisa Marie, that about it. Dog ain't even around. Sick. Staying at some vet all the way up north. Got some strange sickness don't no vet here in Memphis know how to fix. Too quiet around here these days, you ask me. Not a bit like the old days when Miss Priscilla here, little Lisa Marie living here. Sad feeling. Still, Notary can't wait to tell Antwan she got help on the way. Sure, he gonna go on and on about her toadying to white folks. That his problem, way she see it. Mr. E. a kind-hearted man. Got connections. Don't care if he purple.

She look around, thinking: Ain't see Antwan where we s'posed to meet. Probably hiding till I get up to the fence. That smart. Boy scared silly last night, ain't gonna be standing out here in broad daylight. Probably in them bushes up against the fence.

"Antwan? Got the money, son." Whisper voice, like kids sneaking around, don't want Mama to know. She remember his face, think, Boy shushing me last night, like he scared outta his skin somebody listening. Clear to me, can feel it in my bones: Ain't nobody here. No breeze. Hot as blue blazes out here. Stop at the gate, exactly where I say to come at two o'clock. Course Antwan be late for his own funeral.

Lord, Lord, why I think something like that. Ghost crawl over my grave, give me such a chill thinking some stupid saying like that. Ain't thinking right.

Look back at the house, the yard, the stables. Member that day Mr. Elvis bull-doze down the chicken house. That man decide to do something, it done. That a fact. He decide he gonna help Antwan outta this fix, don't have to give it another thought. He get Mr. Red to talk to me, probably think I just want money. I glad to say No sir, don't need a penny. Just want you to get somebody to make this Dawg back off my boy, that all. Not the sheriff. Lord knows Mr. E. know every sheriff in the state of Tennessee, but can't get no law involved in this. Not for a second. Antwan liable to end up in prison. But Mr. E. know plenty of people off Beale, plenty people in the projects. Didn't Miz Gladys tell me her own self how they used to live in the projects? Won't a bit ashamed. Said many a time she wished they was back in Tupelo in that little two-room house where Mr. E. born. That about the saddest woman I ever know, there at the end, when she trailed after her boy to Texas, her so sick she could hardly sit up in her chair. Won't a bit surprised, myself, when they bring her back here to the hospital to die. Mr. E., he shocked, wouldn't believe his own eyes, that his Mama dying. Didn't I know?

No sign of Antwan. Gotta be fifteen after. That boy oughta come on, now. Know I can't wait out here all day.

Didn't Miz Gladys say herself, more times than I could count: This the loneliest house in the state of Tennessee, Notary. Everybody think it so grand. It just a big, empty house most of the time, like a great big broken heart, that's what this place is. We prayer partners, me and Miz Gladys. Can't say how often she call me to her room, that pretty purple room Mr. E. fix up so nice on the first floor so she don't even have to go up and down the steps. Call me in, say, Stay and talk to me. Let's pray a little bit, sing a few hymns, talk about our boys. She want to know what Andruw, Antwan doing. Mostly, though, we talk about her boys. Jesse and Elvis. Like she got two living boys, too. Woman love them boys better'n breath.

Antwan better come on now, next minute or two, she think, hands wringing. I gonna have to go back to the house, no foolin. Alberta good to me, we help one another out, but I ain't gonna take advantage of her generous heart. Wouldn't be right. Mr. Vernon come in the house, I ain't there, he start to puff up. What if Mr. E. already sent for Mr. Red. What if he looking for me? Antwan say he got till today to get the money together; ain't no need worrying that Dawg done something bad already. No sir. Ain't gonna think about that.

Start singing: What a friend we have in Jesus, all our sins and grief to bear, What a privilege to carry every thing to God in prayer. Miz Gladys love that hymn, sing it in her sweet shaky voice. We drink our tallboys. Sometimes she finish, pour a little vodka into the can, say, Notary, you want some sweetnin' for your drink? I say No thanks, Miz Gladys. Ain't never liked no vodka. No ma'am. She say she prefer white lightnin, like back home, but Mr. Vernon told all the boys to stop bringing it to her. Say it bad for her liver. What Mr. Vernon care about my liver, anyway, she ask. Don't even hardly come in to say good night any more. Why he gotta cut out her pleasures? Now and again I'd get Walter to get some for her. She sure did appreciate that.

Lord, when Walter died, didn't Miz Gladys bake a coconut cake herself and send it to the house? Didn't Mr. E. order the biggest heart made out of roses I ever seen in my life? Gave me some comfort, it surely did, knowing they praying for my sweet Walter's soul up in heaven.

Don't know what to do now. Gotta go back up to the house. Can't wait another minute. Can't leave no envelope of money settin here on the ground. That'd be pure-T stupid. Don't need Evonne around to know that. Oughta leave something, though. Let him know I been here. He bound to figure I got the money if I leave him some sign. Ain't brought no pencil and paper. Didn't even think about it. Sure he'd be here like he say. Why that boy so damned unreliable? How that happen? Ernest say I too soft on him, but that ain't the problem. Didn't he used to get honor roll in school? Do his chores right along with Andruw, two of them racing to see who finish first? He go the wrong way cause of all the sadness spilling out of his heart. Ain't got no room for joy. Maybe we get him out of this mess, maybe he be grateful, find a way to go straight. Please, Lord, help my boy put his feet on the path of righteousness.

Them yellow roses over by the fence there right pretty. I break off a couple, twist them on top of the gate, he bound to notice. Miz Dee set a lot of stock by them roses when she live here. Ain't sorry to say she gone. Good riddance, I say. Ain't nobody trimmed them in some time, that plain to see. Better watch out for them big thorns, they bound to hurt.

Okay, Antwan. Mama going now, soon's she fix these roses.

Dang, thorn stick my finger anyhow, hurt like hell. Better suck the blood, clean out the dirt. Hope the Heavenly Father help you see them two roses twisted there on top of that gate, son, help you know your Mama been here waiting for you, bring the money you need. You better come on and get it, even if you late.

Alberta washing up serving pieces. "You feelin a bit better, Notary?"

"Some better. Not so hot." She wash her hands in cold water, try to stop the bleeding.

"You hurt yourself?"

"Just sticker bush out back. Gotta finish up these pies, get them ready to bake in the morning." For the first time she notice ain't no voices coming up from the pool room. Music playing loud, like always, but ain't hearing no loud talk. "Mr. Red and them leave out of here again today?"

"No. Funniest thing. Right after you go out Mr. E. ring downstairs, ask for them boys to come on up. Ain't done that in how many days? Long time, that's for sure. Anyway, they hustle on up like Christmas, ain't come down yet."

Notary bout to pop, wiping her hands on paper towel, holding it tight over the place where she got stuck. "How 'bout that. Reckon he getting ready for the fourth, after all. That Linda call down, or he call?"

"Don't know. Rang the phone in the other room. Didn't talk to nobody myself. Just heard them talking is all."

"You don't say." Notary smiling to beat the band now. "Mr. Elvis make up his mind, that that. And that a fact."

"Don't I know." Alberta grinned. "Quiet ain't the same as peaceful, though, no ma'am."

"Ain't that the Lord's truth." They smile at one another. Both had been employed at Graceland since the day the Presley family moved in. They'd cooked with Miz Gladys. They knew her recipes by heart. Knew what Mr. Elvis liked, what he didn't. He'd come in the kitchen, kiss his Satnin Mama on the cheek about a half dozen times, tease with Alberta and Notary. Call Alberta VO-5. Ask Notary when she gonna eat enough bacon to fill out them bird legs of hers. Won't no Rock and Roll King then, nosir. Just Miz Gladys' boy is all. Said Ain't it the truth, Mama? The kitchen the heart of the house? Couldn't nobody smile a happier smile than Miz Gladys, days like that. House ain't had no heart, kitchen or otherwise, since Miss Priscilla and Little Lisa Marie left. Heart ain't in no bedroom. Mr. E. know that better'n anybody. That Linda think she can make him happy holed up up there in that bedroom, she don't know him one bit. Alberta and Notary know. "Just glad he wants his boys around. Maybe he gonna snap outta this rut. Maybe he gonna come down and act like hisself again."

"Could be. Never can tell where he concerned." Alberta wiped the big bowl they always used for potato salad. "Lord knows I been praying for that boy, praying for him to find some peace."

"Better pray for us all, Alberta. We could all use some of the Lord's peace."

"Amen to that."

Ernest in the living room, got the front door open, when Notary get home. Precious wagging her tail, watching out the screen. "You reckon it ever gonna cool down?" she ask, stepping in the room.

He stand, walk to her, put his hands on her waist. "See Antwan?"

She put one hand on his shoulder. "He ain't come for the money." Kiss his cheek. Aftershave smell good. Ernest one sweet-smelling man.

Ernest just shake his head, follow her in the kitchen. Smell of collard greens take over the kitchen, they so strong. Usually she could eat the whole pot. Tonight, ain't got much appetite. Kitchen sweltering. "Want me to fix you a glass of tea? Got it all ready."

"That be mighty good, Ernest. Mighty good indeed." She set her bag on the table – "Brought Precious some leftover bacon, little bitta ham" – reach down, pet the dog. "Gonna go change first, that be all right with you. This uniform probably stand on its own, it so sweaty."

Ernest moved around the kitchen, easy, like a granny. Shooed Precious outside with his treat.

Notary don't hurry. She step out of her uniform, throw it in the hamper. Stand in her slip. That just as bad. Ease that off over her head. Bra and drawers sticky. "Think I get in the tub a minute," she call. Pull off the underwear, walk naked to the bathroom.

"Here you go, baby." Ernest stand in the door, hold out a big tall ice tea glass to her. "Made it with some mint from the yard, like you like."

She lean over the tub, start the water. "Swear, don't never remember it being this hot. How 'bout you?" She take the glass, hold it up against her head – "This gonna save my life" – swallow down half the cold tea.

"Want me to wash your back, baby?"

"That might be fine." She set the glass on the edge of the tub, step in, settle.

Ernest come on over and perch on the edge. "You still one fine-looking woman, Notary." He got that besotted look on his face, only mean one thing.

She pour water all over herself, splash her face, her front, her head. Feel cool and good.

"Lean forward, let me get the wash rag, rub your back."

Notary grab her knees with both arms while Ernest rub the cool rag back and forth, up and down, along her bony shoulders and back. "That cooling you off?"

"Um-huh. Keep on. So relaxing." Tension easing out, pouring off like syrup.

"Evonne call, say call her when you get a chance."

"Guess she wanna find out what's what."

"Reckon. Rosa call, say she ain't coming tomorrow."

"Say why?"

"Guess they gotta go to Sammy's."

"She coulda told you that before." Notary thinking: Ain't the time to tell him I got to work part the day. Better wait on that.

"You know your baby sister. She spoiled. Plus Sammy say jump, she bound to say how high. Least she call this time." He squeeze the rag. "Lean back, baby. Rest. Let me get the front."

She slide down in the tub, close her eyes, lay her head back against the smooth edge. Ernest start rubbing the front easy. Rub her neck, her shoulders, first around one titty, in circles like, then the other. She bout to moan it feel so good.

"Them black titties of yours like a girl's, baby. Sit right up so pretty like a girl's. Make a old man rock hard, just lookin at 'em."

Notary don't open her eyes, just lay back, feel like a black queen. He rub her belly in slow circles, too, then drop the cloth in the water. "Lemme get some soap for this here sweet place." He tickle her furry spot, easy. "Don't want to rub that sweet place too hard."

She can hear him lathering the Ivory between his hands. Then he slide one hand down between her legs, up on her hilly place, soap it up. Slow, soft. She moaning out loud for sure, now. Cool water, Ernest rubbing. Damned if she don't feel like she floating up, up, on up to glory. See colors, red, shiny, on up past goose bumps, slow easy circles in that place make her shiver, tense, cry out, see colors so brilliant behind her eyes, like firecrackers.

"That good, baby? That what you like?" He move his hand away, slow, rest it on her flat, wet belly.

Notary don't want to open her eyes, just want to slide down in the water, stay here. Feel cool, loose, empty in the head.

Ernest stand. "Lemme get a towel here, baby, dry you off." His voice still soft, dreamy. He waiting.

She gotta move, gotta open her eyes, gotta let her husband rub her dry, lead her to the bedroom, love him, too, like the good man he is. She know that. One more instant she stay still, though, eyes closed, water covering up to her neck, so easy, so safe, in the dark cool place ain't nobody but her.

233

Notary
July 4, 1975

Notary held a glass of ice water in her lap, sitting out in the back yard trying to catch the breeze.

Antwan ain't called. That's all right. She slept good for a while, woke up, so hot in the room had to come outside for some air.

Looked around. Ain't much moving. Even birds still. Better, though, than inside. Heat hanging heavy in the house like a damp quilt.

Ernest almost on top of her, snoring to wake the dead. Body like a stone, he so deep asleep. Damp with sweat. Couldn't hardly breathe. Had to slip outside.

Thinking 'bout last night. After supper, he cleaning up the kitchen getting ready for the cook-out, she finally tell him she gotta work in the morning. "How long?" first thing he ask. Not mad. Ernest ain't one to flash a temper. "Never can tell," she say. Ain't he been 'bout as sweet to her as anybody on earth? Wouldn't do to say probably have to stay up there most of the day; after all his cooking and planning. That'd take the air right out of him. "Hope you back by noon, at least," he say back, voice still calm.

"Can't promise, but do my best."

He look at her hard, then: "Girls driving down all that way, wouldn't be right if you miss a good visit with them 'fore they have to turn around and go back." Voice right next door to riled now. No foolishness.

She knows he right, figures, I get home late, he gonna be peeved. Plus don't never get to see Marcea and Fontana enough. Them girls understand about work, though. They just like me in that regard. But still, Antwan the lost sheep. Can't help but dwell on him.

Charlotte Morgan

Tiny hope: Maybe Antwan sneak by again. Maybe he holed up in the daylight, scared to come out, but maybe he come by the house again tonight for that money. Do her heart good to give him some relief, tell him Mr. Elvis gonna look into it, maybe, gonna get some of his boys to make this Dawg back off.

Memphis a funny place, no doubt about that. Even if she anywhere else in the world, if she close her eyes she could bring back the night smell of Memphis. Ain't nowhere else like it. River. Big muddy. Got its own smell for sure. Dank. Rich like chocolate puddin. Sweaty like a man's armpits – not old smell, strong smell, fresh. Air moist, too, like clothes on the line. Carry echoes, all them blues, almost hear the air vibrate. Black folks live good in Memphis. But ain't Dr. King got shot here? Ain't there some mean white people, hate colored, hate the'selves? Not a bit like Miz Gladys and Mr. Elvis. Gotta spit foul words to whoever listen? Got niggers, too, bad as the river rats, gotta stir up meanness. Memphis got blues, got ribs, got honkytonks for black and white alike. Why Antwan gotta search out the trouble? Why he gotta hang with no-counts like that Dawg?

Hear tell that some people call Mr. E.'s boys the Memphis Mafia. Ain't a joke. More guns up there at Graceland than down at the sheriff's, she betting. Every one of them boys packing. Mr. E., too, though he don't let on. Them boys ready to give him their skin, he need it. Some say he even think about getting one of his cousins to shoot down that karate teacher Miss Priscilla run off with. Don't know that for a fact, but some will say it's so. One thing she do think: Mr. Elvis want that man dead, he be dead by now. Lord knows the boy like to lost his mind when his pretty wife leave Graceland and take that child with her. He act so high and mighty for the public, but he like to grieved hisself to death. No sir, ain't worried for a minute bout him getting a job done when he make up his mind. Only thing, maybe he don't think it a good idea to get hisself involved in my mess. Plus it a holiday. He ain't nothing but a big baby when a holiday come around. Love the fourth. Anything rally him, that be it.

Course Alberta say he send for the boys right off, soon as she come back downstairs. That happen just after she give him the note, but she ain't about to tell Alberta that. VO-5 faint if she know Notary stick her big mouth into Mr. E.'s room, defy that Linda woman to her face. Still, Alberta say he start calling outside while she's out back lookin for Antwan, say the ones ain't at the house come on over quick as hot grease.

Protecting Elvis

'Fore Notary leave yesterday that new Dave what's his name come over, one make everybody uneasy. That quiet one, look like he just as soon hit you in the head as say hello. Eat like a field hand, no better manners than a goat. He probably one of Mr. Sonny's low-life friends, she gotta think. Glad he come, for once. Bet he, Mr. Red, Mr. Sonny knock some sense in this Dawg's head if Mr. Elvis tell them to. Hope that mean he taking care of business, like he say all the time. Ain't no coincidence he jump up and get a move on right after she send in that note. Couldn't be. Miz Gladys raised him up proud, but neither one of them ever the kind to get stuck-up, forget where they come from. His Mama talk to her day in day out like her own cousin or next door neighbor. Us two pray together like sisters. That woman don't seem to see colored, neither do he. They both got soft hearts, no doubt about it. Don't like to see nobody they care about down and out. It a fact Mr. Elvis even meet the President of the United States, but around here he don't act like no King, no sir. He Miz Gladys' boy, that all he want to be.

Still, she know in her heart, sure feel a heap better if Antwan had come by the gate to get the last of that money. Make her rest easier to think he'd at least paid off this Dawg. He take money out of the situation, maybe that fool dope head won't be so mad, stop acting crazy, claiming he got to teach Antwan a lesson. Ernest say that Dawg gotta save face, he ain't about to back off, even with the money. She thinking maybe he get the cash, that enough face saving. Lord, wouldn't that be a blessing?

Ain't no way in the world to know what gonna happen when the sun come up. That's the Lord's own truth. Ain't no need to get flustered, again, though. Prayed for strength. Prayed for Antwan's safety. Can't say Thy Will Be Done, though. Just can't bring myself to say it. Ain't ready for my last living boy to be taken, don't care if it is God's will. Done prayed to Jesus for help, asked Mr. Elvis to step in, ain't another thing to do. Worrying ain't never paid a bill. Best thing: Go on back in the house, get some sleep. Be ready when the day break.

Walkin in the door at Graceland on the fourth of July like going to Disneyland, Notary thinks. Glorious morning, like God smiling. Bound to be a glorious day. Praise the Lord. House sparkle. Kitchen smell better than anywhere in town, she s'pect. Got a whole different feel today, like the fun about to start, that a fact. Not creepy-quiet like it's been for a good while now. Almost three weeks since Mr. E. go upstairs, ain't come down. Man pure exhausted, all them concerts the Colonel plan. More than that, though: Can't stand being forty, hate all them papers saying he fat. Just bloated, is all. Ain't eat right. Ain't he won that big Grammy for his gospel music this year? He still a star. He tired, upset, is all, plus must be out of his head to let that Linda woman take care of him 'stead of people here at Graceland who been knowin him since when.

Makes her pleased to realize Mr. E. his old magic self again. She say to herself, Soon as I walk in the door today I can tell the place lively again. Even them glass peacocks looking perked up this morning. Praise God, that bound to be a sign things changing all over for the best.

Notary goes on in, ties her apron. Mary still there, in the kitchen, ain't left. Family need us both, she say. Alberta coming in at noon.

Mary round and soft like Alberta, she notice, got the kindest face she ever see, like a black angel. She think: I the only one skinny as a alley cat. Ain't nobody up yet, Mary say, but big crowd stay up half the night. Reg'lars sleep over. Gotta freshen up for the party, she say, after all the carrying on last night. She smiling, though, not complaining. We all glad this place coming back to life.

Notary ask, "Mr. E. come down?" She feelin like crickets hatchin under her skin: I ready to pop, she think, anxious to get some hint he sent some of his boys out to deal with this Dawg. Her mind reelin: Mary bound to figure I still worrying about the boss, 'fraid he won't gone leave his room for the fourth. That happen, he worse off than we ever seen. But I know better, already know he rallied yesterday. Mary don't know about my family troubles. Keep my own business to myself over here.

"Lord yes. He look good, too. Laughing, carrying on the way he do. Call everybody, play go-carts, start shooting off the fireworks. Like old times."

"Praise be." Wonder: Did he see about Antwan?

"Yes sirree, them boys all here, some I ain't never seen, plus plenty girls. Mr. E. come right in the kitchen, hug me, say 'If it ain't no trouble, Mary, could we have some supper in a bit?' That big grin of his. Not near as puffy as the last time I laid eyes on him. Teasing, just like always."

"You don't say."

"I fix up meatloaf, gravy, plenty of mashed potatoes, bake three sweet potato pies. Don't you know 'round midnight they eat every bite, then ice cream, too. Start singing at the piano after they eat. Can't nobody in the world sing 'How Great Thou Art' like Mr. E. Bring tears to my eyes. I giving thanks to the Lord over and over the whole time, bout to pop to see Mr. Elvis his ol self."

"Today gone be like old times, I guess." We both pleased; ain't no pleasure working in a house hanging heavy with worry, even if that house Graceland. "All the boys here for supper?" Try to dig some dirt without showing my shovel.

"Far as I could tell. Mr. Vernon come up this morning, say we gotta be ready for maybe fifty people today. I figure we 'bout right with the food."

Beans baking in one oven already, ribs in the other. Mary stacking serving dishes on the counter. "Want me to start making light rolls, or you reckon we gonna need 'em?"

"Guess we better after all. I got the tea on, making plenty lemonade, got the soft drinks cold. That Miss Linda say gotta have chicken, too, 'long with the ribs and cheeseburgers and hotdogs. I ain't say a word, just take the chicken out the freezer. Reckon we better fry it late this afternoon."

Mary don't roll her eyes like me and Alberta do about that woman sleeping up there with Mr. E. day and night, acting like she his wife when she ain't. Mary think the same as us, bound to, but maybe she a better Christian woman. "I'll put the rolls to rise, then make a couple coconut cakes. You reckon two be enough?"

"Oughta be, with the pies. Mr. E. say last night he want to have plenty, but that sure to be enough. Maybe make one chocolate sheet, too. Some of them boys don't eat no dessert, anyway, they so busy drinking beer."

I lower my voice; still ain't heard nobody get up, but don't hurt to be quiet 'bout some things: "How that Miss Linda act last night? She behave or show her tail?"

"Like she won Miss America." Mary smile. She always manage to get in her digs one way or another. We all know that woman ain't won no Miss America. Just Miss Tennessee is all. Mary whisper too, now: "She the queen of the place, for sure. Least she think so. Then Mr. Elvis go in the jungle room, call Miss Priscilla out there on the West Coast, talk more than a hour – you know how he talk and talk to her – beg her to let him send the plane, her and Lisa Marie come on and spend the fourth at Graceland. I won't snooping, mind you. He just talking right there plain as day, so I could hear most every single word."

"Ain't no secret he always gone love Miz Gladys, Miss Priscilla. Any other woman better be ready for third place, that the best she can do." Me and Mary move about the kitchen, getting our work done for the party, ain't hardly got to talk to one another 'bout what to do. Done it more times than either one of us can count. Sometimes we talk, sometimes we don't. I busy taking out my bowl, flour, Crisco, try to act regular, keep my voice calm. "That Mr. Dave here?"

"Don't know if he sleep over, but he here last night some time, that a fact. Pretty sure he eat. He and Mr. Red all buddy-buddy, but Mr. E. don't seem to pay him much mind." Mary shake her head. Mr. Dave give us all the heebie-jeebies.

"Don't say." Gotta wonder: Did Mr. E. send them out to find this Dawg down at the river where he hang, give him a talking to, maybe rough him up enough to let him know they ain't foolin'? Know Mr. Red love to do that kinda thing. Wouldn't put nothing past that Mr. Dave. He got a strange look, like he ain't right.

"What your people doing for the fourth, Notary? Your girls coming down from Jersey?"

"Marcea and Fontana driving down today, say they plan on leaving early, maybe still dark, to get ahead of the traffic. Oughta be here by noon, they thinking. Evonne bringing the kids. Ernest cooking up a big picnic for late this afternoon. How 'bout you?"

"Ain't got a thing planned. Told Mr. E. I could stay on if he need me. Wouldn't seem like fourth of July if I won't here, you know?" She wiping the counter, getting set to put out breakfast stuff, be ready when all them guests wander in. "You go on ahead home early this afternoon, be with your family. Me and Alberta can handle things here."

"We'll see how it go." I gotta think about that. Ernest want me home, girls coming, grands. Few of my sisters and brothers. Still, wanna find out what I can here. Can't rest easy till I know something. Don't s'pect Mr. E. gonna say a thing to me directly, ain't like him, but wouldn't be a bit surprised if he ain't told Mr. Red to let me know what he gone do about Antwan. Could be over and done already. But maybe he gotta ask me some question or two first, don't know where to find this Dawg. Torn about this. Go home early, maybe miss out. Still, could go home, Antwan be there, all this behind him. Fixed up last night. Merciful Jesus, seem like my head gonna split in two. Ain't gotta think about it right this minute, though. Only just close to nine. Mr. E. won't come down till early afternoon, even on the fourth. Them boys of his won't be up much earlier, from what Mary say. Ernest say he'll call when Marcea and Fontana get there. So I just gotta bide my time, do my cookin and cleanin, trust in Jesus and Mr. E. Start singing, cooking, take my mind off all this: "Sowing in the morning, sowing seeds of kindness, Sowing in the noontide, and the dewy eve . . ."

Out back sweeping the patio when Mr. Red sneak up on me, tap me on the shoulder, make me jump like I seen a ghost.

"Lord, Mr. Red, ain't no sense in scaring me like that." He grinning. Mr. Red grin all the time. He ain't nobody's pretty thing, you ask me. Don't seem right, red hair, blotchy red skin. Been with Mr. Elvis from the first though, and ain't nothing Mr. E. do he don't know about, seem like to me. Even went to Germany with him. Always carrying on a bunch of foolishness, playing football, bringing in girls, though he got the nicest wife you'd ever want to meet. He a wild one, that a fact.

"Didn't mean to scare you, Skinny-Minnie." He cross his arms on his chest, smirk at me all goofy. Sometimes I think he usin pot same as Antwan, his eyes get all red like his face. Hard to tell, though. He always been rowdy. "The Boss asked me to see what I can do for you, said you might need a little help."

I can't hardly breathe, I so glad. "That a fact, Mr. Red. You be sure and tell Mr. Elvis I grateful for his kindness."

"You know good and well he don't wanna let one of his special girls worry, Notary." He act like he flirting with me, which is exactly the kind of foolishness he always putting out.

I got to act calm, don't do to act riled. "You know anything about this Dawg? Any of your buddies ever hear of him?"

"That ain't a name that strikes a bell. When the Boss read that note of yours, though, he started laughing out loud. Ain't heard him laugh like that in I don't know when. He'd called me and Sonny up to the room – first time since the Memphis concert we even been up there, you know – and he said 'You boys gotta read this. You reckon Notary's talking 'bout a Hound Dawg'? Got to him, for some reason. I didn't think it was all that funny, but the Boss sure did. Me, I'm just glad to see him laughing, so I gotta laugh too. Linda, she was sittin there on the bed, not even crackin a smile. Guess she got a little bit jealous of you, you sexy thing."

"You don't say." Don't want to say the wrong thing. Best wait, see what Mr. Red's leading up to.

Charlotte Morgan

"That bitch. Please pardon my French." He glare at me, like am I gonna say a thing about that Linda woman. Don't I know better? "Anyway, Elvis is laughing so hard, I'm laughing, too, then I hand back the letter, he reads it again to hisself, he starts crying like a baby. You know how he gets when he thinks about Miz Gladys. Must've been that Mama line got to him, all I can figure."

"Don't I know." When he gonna get to the punch line? Sun glaring down already, it only something past eleven. A few of Mr. E.'s boys already making a racket carrying on in the pool. Course he ain't come down yet. Too early. 'Bout to jump outa my skin, waiting for Mr. Red to get to the part about Antwan. "Didn't mean to cause him no grief. Lord knows he's had a rough enough time lately."

"Ain't we all?" Mr. Red right selfish sometime, you ask me. Gotta have a part in the movies, be Mr. Big Shot playing football in the yard. Karate, guitar. Everything Mr. E. do he gotta do. Sometimes seem like he wish he Mr. Elvis hisself. Don't do to say something like that out loud, though. Not even to Alberta or Mary.

He rub the back of his neck with one hand, only time he don't grin. "Where's Antwan, Notary? Be best if I talk to him myself, get the straight stuff."

I gotta shake my head at this. "Sure wish I knew, Mr. Red. Ain't seen him these last couple days. Ain't got no idea where he's at."

"What about this Dawg? He got a last name?"

"Not that I know of. Only heard Dawg."

"Boss told me to check on it today, before things get going good. Don't see what I got to go on, though, to tell you the truth."

I wanna scream at that. He ain't gonna give up that easy? Can't let that happen. "Far as I know this Dawg hang out down at the south end of the docks, near them strip joints and nigger bars. You know the ones I'm talking about?"

He screw up his face. Don't know which worse, stupid grin or ugly glare. "This ain't got to do with drugs, does it Notary? Cause if it does you know the Boss don't want to touch it."

Mr. Elvis hate drugs like the devil himself. Even got the President to make him some secret drug agent. I know if I say drugs involved that be the end of it. "Ain't got to do with money or drugs, Mr. Red. No sir. Don't need a nickel from Mr. Elvis. Got to do with colored boys pissing around the fence, see who's top dog, you know what I mean?" I gotta roll my eyes, act like some black clown.

Lord forgive me for telling a flat out lie. Maybe send me straight to hell. But I ain't got no choice, way I see it. Not if I gonna save Antwan.

Mr. Red laugh like a hyena. He that way. "Guess I could round up Dave and Sonny, head on down there. Maybe get one a them massages while I'm at it." He roll his eyes, too, making a mockery. My stomach bout to heave, but I gotta grin back. That the way it works.

"I'd sure be beholden, Mr. Red. That make this fourth of July Christmas for me, that a fact." Talk that Uncle Tom talk, do everything but tap dance. Feel ready to puke.

"Yes ma'am, that sounds like a right good way to get things underway this morning." Now he hot to trot. "Don't you worry 'bout a thing, Notary. After we give him a talking to this Dawg gonna be tucking his sorry black tail." He laugh at his own joke, like he funny as Milton Berle. Ain't a bit funny, you ask me, but I gotta laugh too. "Yessir, the Boss'll think that's a riot hisself."

"You get on outa here, Mr. Red. I'll cook you up something special before you get back." Wink like I think he as handsome and clever as Mr. E. Do what I gotta do. He eat up all that attention. Want him fired up to get this thing done.

"I'm gonna count on it. Let me get Sonny's lazy ass up, get a move on. Don't want to be gone when the Boss rallies."

"No sir, that wouldn't do."

He scrambles along into the house. I gotta sit a minute, feel like somebody let the air outa me. Flop into one of the patio chairs to catch my breath. Mr. Red used to play football at the white high school, Alberta tell me. That where he meet Mr. E. He work out, stay muscular, even when Mr. E. gain all that weight. He right vain, I reckon. Don't care, long as he tougher than these rats this Dawg got crawling around him. I ain't never liked Mr. Red all that much, but if he handle this bit a business for Antwan, I'll include him in my prayers every day from now till my last breath. That a promise. Course I don't even know if God gonna listen to my prayers anymore, me a lying sinner. But I ready to lay down my everlasting soul if it give Antwan another chance. And ain't that what Jesus say: Bring the sinners to me, let me give 'em God's own forgiveness? Ain't He died for my sins? I gotta believe that's the truth, cause Lord knows I need it.

Kitchen like Grand Central, guys wandering in asking for this, that, the other. Alberta taking care of them, me and Mary still fixing for the picnic.

Soaking the chicken in salt water, shaping the rolls for the last rise. Boiling some more eggs: look like we ain't gonna have enough devilled eggs, and that won't do. Place like all the holidays, now. Everybody buzzing around, laughing, waiting for Mr. E. to come down. Plenty guests out in the swimming pool, guys playing pool downstairs, people in the jungle room playing records. Ain't nobody up in the music room, only go up there when Mr. E. say. He ain't called down yet, so doubt he even awake. Only a little after one. Ain't seen no Dr. Nick here yet. That Mr. Larry ain't been by to give Mr. E. a haircut. Might be a while.

Outside phone ring, I pick it up right away. Could be Mr. Red. "Graceland kitchen. This Notary."

"You 'bout done up there, baby? Marcea, Fontana here."

Can't hardly hear Ernest, place so busy. "Still got some cooking to do. Shouldn't be too much longer."

"Girls look good, tired, though. Can't wait to see you. Gonna rest a bit. Others coming 'bout three. You be here by then?"

"Try my best, Ernest. Most likely."

"Okay, baby. You come on, let Alberta handle things up there. Ain't no party without you."

I hang up the phone, feel like a worm in the ground. Ain't even told Ernest Mary staying. That man couldn't tell me a lie if somebody stuck a knife to his back. Couldn't even shade the truth. Crazy thing: Antwan ain't ever gonna know 'bout this, neither will Ernest. Jesus say: You wanna pray, go in the closet. So maybe secrets ain't always a bad thing. Or maybe I just tryin to justify my own sneaky ways. Don't matter. One way or the other, I gotta be sure Antwan safe.

Little after two Mr. Vernon come up to the house, look around the kitchen, see everything in order. He say, "Ain't no use all three of you staying. Look like the picnic ready. You want me to call the driver for you, Mary?" Mary explain she staying, ain't got no party to go to, so he say, "Okay, Notary, I'm getting the car." And he call the house phone, get that new chauffer guy, the pointy-faced one, and I ain't got no choice but to go on home. Ain't even seen Mr. E. to give him a look, let him know I 'preciate his help. Wouldn't dare say a thing, but he'd get my drift. He know how much I think of his Mama. That mean a lot to that boy. He know we pray together when she livin in this house. He ain't about to forget a thing about his Mama. I fretful, though: Mr. Red and his boys still ain't back. That bound to be good. Bound to mean they hook up with that Dawg. I'd rest easier if I heard it from Mr. Red, though, before I leave.

I get home, Marcea and Fontana scurrying around the kitchen helping Ernest, jibber-jabbering like they kids. Them girls both lively. Marcea look a lot like me, people say. She tall and skinny-like, but child got plenty a curves, too. Fontana more chunky, got size on her. More like Walter in her looks. Lord, I glad to see those two. Hug, kiss, talk up a storm. They follow me into the bedroom while I change, show me pretty new opal ring Fontana buy herself, new watch Marcea get. Give me a present – them girls always gotta bring me a gift, every time they come, even if it ain't my birthday or Christmas – got a heart necklace, little bitty diamond chips all over. Lord, I ain't never had nothing so nice. Bring little something for Tenosha and Carl, Junior, too. Got big hearts, both them girls. Wish they'd marry. Gotta think losing their Daddy and their one brother, both so sudden-like, made them shy of getting tight with a man. Maybe not, maybe they just independent type women.

Ernest call back, "Ain't no time for a hen party. Need help in here getting this food on." He laughing. Man love it when the house full. Won't nobody but him and his Mama and his first wife, Alma. He nurse both them women through cancer, do for them like a angel. I know Ernest from church for years, everybody think he a gentleman. But sad, both them women so sick. He and Alma never did have a single child. Which worse, I gotta ask: preparing, watching your loved ones waste away, doing for them day and night, or laughing one minute, drinking coffee, taking a bite of toast with blackberry jam, and next minute down on the floor screaming it ain't so? Can't know the answer, can't figure God's ways. Ernest a deacon at the church, always good-hearted. When Walter die he come to the house with other deacons, sit with us all. He know Andruw and Antwan from Sunday School, know Antwan a sweet-natured child, not one to run with no street trash. He come after Andruw, too. Keep coming. Pulled me up out of grief.

"We coming," I holler. I put on clean white pedal pushers, old sandals, plaid cotton shirt. Love fresh, cool clothes.

"Here, Mama, let me hook your necklace," Fontana say.

Marcea grinning. "Look like a girl, Mama. Looking more and more like a girl every time I see you. You going backwards." Both them laugh. They happy children, seem like, despite the sad times. How come some turn out so level, 'nother one lost? Life a mystery, that a fact.

"Ernest spoil me is all," I say. "Making me fat, too, don't you think?" I stick out one bony hip, they grab me, hug me some more.

"Ain't hardly enough here to love, Mama. Need to eat some more if you gonna have anything to grab onto." That Fontana.

"You all coming, or I gonna have to come in there and drag somebody to the kitchen?" Ernest want to be a part of the laughs. He standing in the door now, smiling, got his apron on.

Front screen slam, Carl Junior come hollering into the house, Evonne hollering behind him to stop. Sisters run out, oooh, aaaah, all talk at once. Ernest come over, rub my cheek. "Let's us have a good fourth, what you say, old woman?"

"You right, Ernest." I grab his hand, squeeze it. "Look here what the girls bring." Lift up my diamond necklace.

"That sure do sparkle pretty on your neck. Them girls crazy 'bout you, Notary. You a good Mama." He squeeze my hand, tug me to the front room where most a my family waiting.

Everybody here, almost. Precious bout to have a fit, running all over the back yard begging for scraps. Can't make up his foolish mind what to eat: rib bone? chicken skin? piece a hotdog? Marcea and Fontana taking turns carrying Tenosha, can't let her go. She all dressed up in yellow sun dress, white sandals, got yellow barrettes all in her hair. She 'bout the sweetest child ever born. Carl Junior hanging onto his big cousins, eat hotdogs till he pop. Ernest and the girls got the big table with all the food set so pretty: flowered tablecloth, daises in a blue mason jar, clean tea towels over all the food. Look like a picture.

Evonne's Carl ain't come. She said he won't all along. Said he gonna go playing golf with some of them mens he work with. Whoever heard of such? Cousin ask Evonne, "He too high tone for this fam'ly?" She insist no. Say he gotta do all this and that to move up in his insurance company. "'Sides," she laugh, "Big Carl ain't never knowed how to have fun like us."

My closest brother Earl Junior here with his fat wife Carletta. She laugh like a half-wit, we all say, but she sweet, bring the best homemade devil's food cake you ever put in your mouth. Next older brother here, too, Marcus and Lurlene. They live right here in Memphis but we don't hardly ever see 'em, 'cept maybe at Christmas. Go to a different church. Both Earl Junior and Marcus bring kids, grandkids. Yard full. Kids out front blowing bubbles, writing with chalk on the sidewalk – Ernest think of everything when he throw a party – nieces and nephews in the front room talking, playing cards. Some got nursing babies. House full, too.

"Where Antwan?" Marcus ask. "Ain't seen him in don't know when. What he up too?"

"He be by in a bit, prob'ly. Say he got plans. Got a date. But say save him some a my banana pudding, so he bound to be here before the fireworks get going."

Marcea and Fontana ain't asked a thing about Antwan. Ernest must've filled them in before I got home. Or they been talking to Evonne. Just as well. When he get here it'll be just like the Bible say: feast for the prodigal. My heart 'bout to pop, looking for him at the gate every few minutes.

Lurlene wanna know all about the goings-on up at Graceland. She like that mess, read all the movie magazines. I tell her what-all we fix, how Mr. E. have a big to-do last night, how he got upwards of fifty people coming today. She drink it all in like lemonade. Don't tell her a thing about him, though. Wouldn't be right. He due some privacy from people close.

"You still coming and going in one of them Cadillacs?" she ask.

"Lord yes. Too far out for me to ride a bus. Mr. E. kind-hearted to his help."

Don't I know that for a fact. I drink my Schlitz, glad I got home for all this. Look over, smile at Ernest turning ribs on the grill. Smell charcoal, spices, Lurlene's musky perfume. Relax for the first time in days. Cooling off, tiny breeze blowing, perfect weather for the fourth. Be dark soon.

"Aunt Notary?" One of the nieces yellin from the back stoop. "Anybody seen Aunt Notary? She got a phone call."

I look up: Neva standing there holding a crawling baby on her hip, looking around the yard for me. "Right over here," I say, edging through my people to get to the back door, tripping over the uneven path. "Coming, Neva."

She smile, – Neva, Lurlene's oldest girl, got a pretty, wide smile – say, "Sound like some white man, Aunt Notary. I tell him you got company, call back tomorrow, but he insist."

"That all right, sweetheart," I say, brush by her, pat that baby's soft head. Gotta be Mr. Red. Ain't expected him to call.

247

"This Notary," I say, picking up the phone. Young nieces and nephews all over the kitchen and front room, stop talking, stare at me. Just being polite, I guess, quiet.

"We found Antwan," all he say.

"Antwan?" I can't hardly hold onto the phone.

"Don't look good," he say.

I can't say a word, barely breathe.

"You there, Notary? I said we found Antwan down by the docks."

He can't be drowned. He can't be dead. Not my last living boy.

"Notary: Listen here. When we found him it was too late. He'd been knifed. Bad. Lost a lot of blood. We paid some black guys to take him to Memphis Baptist. You better get on over there fast."

I drop the phone. Can't faint. Gotta get to the hospital. Fast, he say.

Somebody screaming and screaming. Loud like horror movie. Can't be real.

Ernest come charging into the house like a bull, grab me by the shoulders, start shaking and shaking. "It Antwan?" he yell. Funny, I think: Ain't never heard Ernest yell.

I pull away, start yelling myself. "Gotta go. Gotta go right this second, fore it's too late. Gotta get to Antwan."

And she ran.

Satnin
July 1975

Glory be. "How Great Thou Art." We did love singing to God's glory, me and you and Daddy Vernon, didn't we, Nungen? We'd sing together so pretty. Back there in Tupelo, do you remember any of that, Bitty Boy? At Assembly of God? Them was happy times. Our voices was right nice together, singing them hymns, if I do say so myself. And now you got another one've them big prizes for singing God's own songs. Like a angel. Ain't no angel got a voice prettier than that, Satnin Boy. I can tell you that for a fact.

But I gotta tell you this, too, no matter how hard it pains me, no matter how much you don't wanna hear it: That so-called Colonel ain't doin right by you, Bitty Boy. Me and Jesse's worried sick. He's gettin worse all the time, making you go out on the road so much, looking the other way with all them pills you been taking night and day. Them drugs cloud your judgment, Nungen. It's plain as the nose on your pretty face: it's the money, sonny buck. Much as I hate to say it, much as I can see it pains you, somebody's gotta say it. He's a fool for money. You the one with God's own gifts. Didn't we know it from the first? He ain't nothing but a hanger-on. Let the scales drop from your eyes.

Like to scared me into eternal damnation, you hiding up there in that room all that time with that woman ain't fit to wipe your feet. She don't know a thing about my sweetness. You need a higher opinion of yourself, sonny buck. Don't his own Satnin Mama know that? Him needs to stand up proud in the sight of the Lord, not hide away with some harlot. Her ain't throwing stones, no her ain't. Her don't judge. Don't God know the Nungen's own family had crosses to bear? His Daddy ain't been no saint; His Nungen Bitty Mama won't wearing no halo, either, during her days on earth. Lord knows. But ain't it the Lord's own truth that serpents come wearing disguises, some luring to the eye, some with honeyed tongue? Him can't ever forget that.

Don't your Satnin Mama know what's chasing after you like a rabid dog? You scared half to death of that number 40. Who else knows that but you and me, Nungen? You and me and Sweet Jesse. Your Daddy Vernon don't have no idea. He ain't been no comfort to you in your hour of darkness, in your valley of despair. Reading all them books on the spirit this and the aura that ain't gonna help one bit, sweet boy. Ain't but one God, the Father Almighty, and his Blessed Son Jesus Christ. Him know that in his heart. Turn to the true Christians in your pain and sorrow; you got Notary right there, 'bout the purest Christian heart I ever did meet that side of Glory. Lord knows many's the black night we'd read the good book and pray together. Won't no churchifying prayers, either, Precious Boy, but prayers like hymns, rising straight up to God's own holy ghost. That woman helped your Satnin Mama through many a valley. Ain't nothing gonna save your earthly soul, give you relief from pain, but re-dedicating yourself to God's own service, sweetness. Ain't that prize a sign? Not a one a them rock and roll songs ever did bring you a prize that high. The Lord's sending you a message to lift you up to His holy service, to use your gifts in His name. To bring sinners to the one true way.

Ain't your time yet to come to be with Jesus and me and Jesse and all the little children, black and white. Can't you see that, Nungen? Much as his Satnin Mama wants to hold him in her arms, to see his pretty face, to know all the torment's dropped away, she knows it ain't his time to depart this earth yet. Time to give back to glory, sweet boy. Time to serve the Lord, bless his holy name. Don't matter 'bout your fleshly frame, sweet boy. Don't do for you to be prideful cause you ain't the slip of a child you once was. You gonna shed that earthly body one a these days. Lord knows that don't matter one bit to me and Jesse and your brother Jesus. We're all beautiful every one in the eyes of the Lord. Remember that, Son, when them papers and magazines make so much of your appearance. That's just another way Satan's trying to wedge his way into your spirit, your Christian soul. Say: Get thee behind me. Lift your face to glory. Sing hallelujah in His holy name. "How Great Thou Art." Don't be afraid, Sweetnin. We'll be together when your time comes, when God says come on home to Glory. He'll lift your burdens like he lifted mine. Til then, Fear not. Jesus is right with you, right there at Graceland. Turn from them devils in your midst. Walk tall with the Lord.

Graceland
August 18, 1977

Notary sat beside Mr. E's casket, dressed all in black from Peau de Soie hat to patent leather high heels. She still had the diamond heart around her neck, hadn't ever taken it off. These days she was skin and bones. She hadn't been back up to the house since July 4th two years earlier. Hadn't worked a single day since her own boy Antwan died in her arms that very night.

Miss Patsy Presley herself called, insisted she was sending a car, said Notary was family. Mr. Elvis would want her here. Alberta and Mary were in the kitchen, cooking one last time for Mr. E, a big summer supper with all his favorites, for all his people after they laid him to rest. Both cooking and crying steady. They'd each hugged Notary like she was their own child, held her close and cried. She hadn't shed a tear. Notary hadn't hardly been eating all these months, much less cooking. Ernest fixed for her, but she could barely swallow even the mildest warm soup. Her girls had been easy with her at first, gentle. Then Evonne got plain mad, told her off for ignoring Carl Junior and Tenosha, turning her back on the good man who loved her better than breath.

Now she sat here, alone, black purse on her lap, hands twisting the straps, looking at Mr. Elvis' peaceful pretty face. All the worry washed away. Miss Priscilla wanted each of the house staff to have a time to say good-bye before the family and friends came crowding in for the funeral at two. Notary always had liked Miss Priscilla. Trusted her. Even in her grief that gal thought of others: Insisted Mr. Elvis loved his people at Graceland like family. They needed their private time with him. Won't even giving that to the movie stars who showed up. Yes indeed, Miss Priscilla a wise woman, young as she is. Guess she'd suffered plenty of sadness herself.

Notary leaned forward toward the beautiful white copper casket, stared straight at Mr. Elvis' closed eyes. "You the last of the twins to leave us. That make all four of you boys gone to heaven now. Lord, when Miz Gladys was here we ain't neither of us ever pictured the day when all four of our boys would be with the heavenly Father. Just sweet Jesse there, waiting, till the others lived out their time. Sure to live longer than their mothers, we both think." She opened her purse, took out a white crocheted handkerchief, leaned toward the open casket again. "Miz Gladys give this to me one time, right after we'd prayed together for God's grace, right after we'd asked the Lord Jesus to help us bear whatever cross he send us." She squeezed the white handkerchief in her dark-gloved, slender hand. "Want you to take this on home with you now, Mr. Elvis, to Miz Gladys and Jesse and Andruw and Antwan." She stood, swayed the tiniest bit, steadied herself as she put one hand on the white cool metal. "You take this on to glory with you, Son, and tell Miz Gladys I ain't gonna ever forget her sweet faith. Gonna trust you and your Mama and your brother to take care of my beautiful boys till my time come. Gotta let go of this burden, now, Mr. E. Gotta send it on up to God with you." She tucked the delicate square under his arm, smoothed the sleeve of his creamy white jacket. That child looked real pretty and neat. His Mama gonna be so proud when she see him dressed so fine. One thing sure: Heaven ain't divided into black and white. Jesus loves all his little children, red and yellow, black and white, don't the good book say so?

"I'm gonna say good-bye now, Mr. Elvis. Ain't gonna grieve no more for you or the ones gone ahead of me up to heaven. Gonna walk on out of this room – ain't never seen so many flowers in my life, Mr. E., not even when your Mama pass – and give glory to God for the blessings he send. Gotta go back on home, tend to the living. Know you at peace, sweet boy. Antwan at peace now, too." Standing tall, her face serene, Notary walked from the music room of Graceland for the last time.

Priscilla was asleep when she got the news a little after 3:30 on the sixteenth. Evelyn called weeping like her own brother had died. At first Priscilla couldn't understand her. She was finally able to gasp out, "Elvis . . . ohmigod . . . Elvis is dead. Turn on your radio." Priscilla stood, numb, as she listened to the soft familiar ballad, "Love Me Tender." Followed by the solemn announcement: "At 3:30 this afternoon Elvis Presley was declared dead at Baptist Memorial Hospital in Memphis." Elvis, dead? She'd seen the pictures on the magazine covers of him all bloated, his eyes so sad, though she refused to read that garbage about him. She couldn't ignore the nasty black headlines while she was waiting to pay for her groceries, but she'd never buy one of those tacky tabloids herself. Everybody knew they were packed with sick, sinful lies: Woman Claims Her Twins Were Fathered by Elvis. What hateful stupidity. Or that spiteful book that had just come out by his so-called trusted friends. She'd never ever read that. So many people wanted a piece of Elvis, any way they could get it. Even if it killed him.

She knew the real Elvis, the sweet, funny, Christian, generous Elvis. The one who talked and laughed and cried all night, and sang hymns and prayed like a child. The one who loved Eskimo Pies and peanut butter but wanted to stay young and beautiful forever. Ask anybody with half a grain of sense: He was still going strong up till that very day. He'd appeared in Greensboro in the spring. Evelyn and Jared got her a ticket, tried to talk her into going with them, but she didn't want to see Elvis like that. She preferred her memories and records. He was hardly a has-been, like Kendall liked to say. He couldn't be dead, just like that, in the middle of a normal summer day. Not Elvis. He always made a comeback. Didn't he? She sat on the sofa in a daze, the radio playing his music song after song. In no more than five minutes, the phone was ringing again. Angie and Maria were leaving the hospital, coming home to comfort her. She couldn't even remember if she'd spoken to them.

Before long Evelyn and Angie and Maria were sitting around the living room lighting candles and listening over and over to Priscilla's Elvis albums. Evelyn there with Angie and Maria: one more weird aspect of a totally weird day. She talked about the King non-stop, like he'd lived next door to her: "While he was at the clinic he never ever one time acted like a big shot, like most of the so-called stars who come to lose weight"; "One time Elvis teased me and said if I'd sneak him in a Hershey bar he'd marry me"; "I never can decide which is my favorite Elvis song. Don't you love 'Suspicious Minds'?" On and on. Priscilla hardly said a thing.

Who had the idea? Nobody remembers. But they all decided to get into the convertible and drive to Memphis. It would take most of the night, but so what? They'd take turns driving – except for Evelyn, who couldn't drive – and be there in the morning to pay tribute to the greatest performer of their lifetime. "Of *anybody's* lifetime," Evelyn insisted. Priscilla noticed that the others were talking in past tense. Was it true, then? Was he really dead? Somewhere along the way they planned to get some flowers. Maria suggested buying a teddy bear. They'd each write a note. Priscilla rallied. Maybe if she went to Graceland she'd know it was real. And if it was, she needed to say good-bye. Plus she'd never actually thanked him for the car.

The next morning the air hung in Memphis so hot and muggy that they said over and over how lucky it was that Priscilla had a convertible. The night had been surreal, driving through the dark lonely mountains of North Carolina and Tennessee listening to every song Elvis ever performed. Only Elvis, on every single radio station. When they parked along Elvis Presley Boulevard, in some used car lot blocks and blocks from Graceland, as close as they could get, they raised the top and locked the doors and blinked at one another in the sunny glare: This unlikely foursome was here, in Memphis, on August 17. They were all supposed to be at work. Their clothes were rumpled, they hadn't brushed their teeth, they'd hardly slept at all. Angie pulled a lipstick from her purse. "I don't intend to look like a hag when I say good-bye to the King of Rock and Roll." As if it mattered. But it did. They all stood on the hot asphalt parking lot and brushed their hair and put on varying degrees of make-up. "Now let's find a Pepsi machine and get something to drink, before I pass out," Maria said, "and then we need to get on over to his house."

That's how Priscilla came to be in line, still, at 5:30 that evening when the four of them finally made it to the front door of Graceland. They'd waited all day, taking turns going back to the car and going for drinks, food, a bathroom break, inching their way in the weeping crowd closer and closer to the music gates. Once in line, they couldn't leave; they were compelled forward by some sense of belonging, some need to be in this very place at this very moment, no matter the discomfort. Many of the thousands of motley pilgrims carried transitor radios. Elvis songs blasted on rock stations and Christian stations and country stations. Priscilla had the fleeting thought: They're not playing Kendall's "She-Devil" song today. Won't he throw a hissy fit: Elvis knocked him off the air. She had to smile. Word eventually passed through the crowd: Fans may pass by the casket, in groups of four, between three and five o'clock this afternoon.

Then, close to five: The hours will be extended. Elvis always had the greatest respect for his fans, and wouldn't want to let them down, even today. Especially today. When their foursome got to the music gates they'd placed their teddy bear, flowers, and notes in the mountain of tributes. Priscilla, swooning from the heat, exhausted from lack of sleep, was almost to the grounds before she'd written anything. Then, near the entrance, she'd scribbled the first thing that came to mind, folded it, and tucked it down in the withering bouquet: Dear Elvis – I will never forget meeting you. Your mother must've been proud of you every day of her life. Thank you for the Mustang. Maybe you don't even remember giving it to me, but I'll never sell it. I never expected it to bring me to Graceland for this. You're in my prayers. Your friend in Jesus, Priscilla Jane Johnson.

The bodyguards, dressed in dark suits, looked weary and downhearted standing close by the white casket. As the four women stepped through the front door into the entrance hall, Priscilla swayed at the sight of Elvis lying there so still. They gripped hands, and Angie whispered, "Dear Lord. Let's say a prayer for him," and Evelyn started praying out loud, but Priscilla just stared. He was gone. His face was waxy, his eyes closed, the pulpy lips still, those jittery hands immobile. That whole week she'd known him he never slept, and what little he did he twitched and fidgeted. So he was dead. Gone to God. The other three women whispered, "Amen." Priscilla, lifting her shoulders, looked directly at his tranquil face and said "Good-bye, Elvis. Thank you for the car. It's perfect."

They slept on the pews of the church next door to Graceland, people all around telling Elvis stories, playing guitars, singing Kumbaya. A few hippies swore they'd gone to Washington that cold November day, had done the exact same thing when President Kennedy was assassinated. Angie and Maria met people from Texas and Virginia and Louisiana and South Carolina. By morning they'd invited half a dozen guys to come visit. Evelyn and Priscilla mostly watched and waited, stunned by the previous day's events. When they got up in the morning the four nurses took turns washing at a nearby White Tower, then returned to wait by the side of the road until the funeral procession passed, well after two in the afternoon. Even Evelyn didn't say a word until the last of the fourteen white limousines had gone by. Those masses of fans, many swooning in the heat, silent except for the occasional restrained sob; the cloying smell of roses and carnations and sweat; helicopters buzzing overhead; rescue workers passing through the crowd, giving out water and ice: Priscilla knew she'd never forget a second of it. Finally, as the street emptied, as they admitted there was nothing else to see, nothing else they could do, they trudged back to the convertible for the last time, to head home to Durham. Exhausted, Priscilla mumbled to no one in particular, "Elvis never knew it, but he changed my life."

Velis sat at her desk until late on the sixteenth, answering phone call after phone call, keeping her voice steady. Yes, it was true what the radio was saying. The King was dead. Weary and heartbroken as she was, she wouldn't dare let the phone ring unanswered and disappoint a fan club member at this hour of need. When Marc got through, when she heard his unexpected "Hello, Vuh-lis?" after her "Tupelo Fan Club, Birthplace of Elvis," that was the first time the entire evening she almost dropped the phone.

"Velis? You okay?"

Her throat tightened. "It's been an awful day."

"Is anybody there with you?"

"No. Hal was here earlier. The officers are coming over. Patsy's chartering a bus."

"Don't go on the bus."

"What?"

"Please. Go with me. And the boys. They're here with me, for vacation. I've gotten us a flight into Charlotte, and I've rented a car. We won't get there until early tomorrow morning. But I'll drive down to Tupelo to get you. Wait for me. Okay?"

The wretched feelings she'd held in check all day, since Hal had come over from next door and told her that horrible news, were threatening to tear her into tiny bits. It took every shred of her strength to swallow and speak. "Is the magazine sending you?"

"*Rolling Stone*? Yeah, I'll have a press pass. Things are crazy down there already, from what we hear, and I'd feel better if you were with me."

"I'm not sure . . ."

"Plus the boys're coming."

Gavin and Gabe? In that crush of people? Course they were older now, but . . . "Is that safe? For them, I mean."

"They're setting up a press section at the cemetery. I know I can get in. I'll try to get you and the boys in, too, but that might be iffy. If I can't I'll be sure you're somewhere close by. Out of the crowds. I'd feel better if you were with them. Especially Gabe."

"Of course." Velis pictured his tiny body in that crush of people, Gavin so perfect, so strong, precious Gabe forever smaller, overshadowed.

"So be ready early in the morning, okay? We're leaving here in a couple of hours."

"I'll be here."

Velis had actually gone to Memphis four years before, to Graceland with the fan club. After that morning Helen had her heart attack, she started going out again, little by little. At first she'd go to supper with Hal once a week or so, after dark, to get him out of the house. Besides, neither of them were much good at cooking; that had been Helen's job, even if it wasn't exactly her talent. Then Velis started going to early service at Calvary Baptist with him. Hadn't the church members been good to her Mama when she was so sick, and hadn't they lifted up Hal when his beloved Helen went on ahead of him? Plus more than one of the powdery-smelling widow ladies wasted no time setting her cap for Hal. He begged Velis to come along and help him ward off their none-too-subtle invitations to home-cooked Sunday dinners.

So she'd given in, in the end, and gone on the bus trip with the Tupelo Fan Club. What a day that had been. All those dear friends she'd known all her life, singing Elvis songs at the top of their lungs and passing around their concert programs and movie magazines and every Elvis trinket ever made. Meeting fan club members she'd only known as telephone voices. She was breathless the whole way. The hour there and back passed in a blink.

At the mansion, Elvis came down, just for a little bit, and let every single one of the club members take pictures with him. All those years she'd seen every snapshot and promotional picture the club owned, but she still couldn't have imagined how gorgeous he was in person. He was beautiful, that was the only word that suited. But down to earth, somehow, still a hometown boy. He asked all about Tupelo— the hardware store, the new baseball field, his home place the club was restoring and opening to the public—and when he found out she was Velis – "You really Nelly's girl, sweetheart? No kidding? I loved that

259

Nelly like crazy" – he'd kissed her on the cheek and given her a big teddy bear hug. He'd squeezed her to him, tears in his shiny eyes, and whispered, "Ain't nothing in this world hurts like losing your Mama." How long since she'd been kissed? His skin and lips were silky soft, like an infant's. His Brut, strong as it was, couldn't mask some other unique scent, what she ever after thought of as Elvis's own sweetness. That whole day was a treasure.

To her surprise, Marc brought Gavin and Gabe to Tupelo to stay next door once every spring and for a week in the summer, like he'd promised. Hal taught them all to fish, and the boys spent time with her at the house just like she'd imagined, working puzzles under the dining room table and learning Elvis songs. They even took day trips to the beach, and cool evening picnics to the state park. Marc was a good man, a doting father, just like Helen said. Gabe was her heart now. Of course she'd go to Memphis to be with him. And to pay her respects.

The press box was no more than a raised platform off to the side of the Mausoleum, more like scaffolding. Some of the big papers, Memphis reporters Elvis had trusted, had permission to ride at the end of the procession, to go inside for the short service. Somehow Marc claimed two chairs at the back of the press viewing stand for Velis and Gavin. Marc was up toward the front with Caroline Kennedy and the other out-of-town reporters, shouldering behind the cameramen to get every glimpse possible of the cortege when it arrived. Gavin leaned against her shoulder, groggy in the heat, exhausted from the wait. She held Gabe on her lap. "Either one of you want a sip of Pepsi?" They both barely shook their heads. "No thanks, Aunt Velis," Gabe managed. In the past four years Gavin had shot up, slimmed down, turned into a miniature Marc. Gabe looked no different than he had in his astronaut picture, except maybe his face was a little more solemn, at times. He leaned against her chin, his sturdy body sweaty, his stubby legs not reaching the wooden scaffolding. Waves and waves of flowers, as far as the eye could see, rose up from the ground, giving off a dizzying, Sleeping-Beauty hypnotic smell. Hound dogs, crowns, broken hearts, guitars, teddy bears, arrangements from all over the world, even from President Carter, for this Tupelo boy who went to grade school with her Mama. But it was all the bows that shimmered in the sun that held Velis' gaze: red, yellow, white, baby blue, sparkling gold like one of Elvis' own elaborate jumpsuits.

The silver Cadillac turned into the roadway leading to the Mausoleum. Velis could see it gleaming, a magical car bringing a country boy to this castle of a burial place. "Look boys, can you see? You want me to hold you up, Gabe? Gavin, you want to stand on your chair?" They only shook their heads no, too dazed to move in the August heat, too unconcerned to want to see even a fairy tale car. So she sat still with her twin boys up against her, while every other person stood to watch the King pass by this final time.

Satnin
August 18, 1977

Her knew her Bright Eyed Boy'd come home to his bitty Satnin Mama one day. Praise God from whom all blessing's flow, Nungen's come home to glory.

Come here, Bitty Boy. Come here and give your Satnin Mama who wuvs you a great big hug and sweet, sweet kisses.

See Jesse, see your pretty precious brother?

Glory, glory, praise the Lord, my baby boy's come home at last.

She Devil

When Satan rears her wily head
    And turns her lustful face toward me,
I crave to kiss her tempting lips –
    Dear Lord, please set me free.

Chorus

Free from temptation,
Free from sin,
Free from the She Devil,
Don't let her come in.
Don't let her come in.

When money sounds her siren song
    And lures me with her sultry spell
I long to join the greedy throng,
    Lord, please block that crowded road to hell.

Chorus

When drugs and drink seduce my mind
    And dare me to one time imbibe
She says, "Come on, take one small chance,"
    Lord, stay right here by my needy side.

Charlotte Morgan

Chorus

Salomé sways before my eyes
    And twists her seven silky veils
I almost grab her wanton thighs,
    Dear Lord, God, please – don't let me fail.

Chorus

Charlotte Morgan
Protecting Elvis
© 2013

Acknowledgements

"The king is dead; long live the king."

Frankie and Jimmy Apistolas have made a home away from home for me and my writing at Nimrod Hall every summer for twenty-five years. The Virginia Center for Creative Arts "launched" my writing all those years ago. Paule Marshall told me "the work must be done," Lee Smith helped me find my voice, and Tom DeHaven showed me how to pare away the precious. Greg Donovan took a chance on me. The "writer women" at Nimrod Hall have been my writing family, my support system, my goddesses, especially Cathy Hankla. Laura Gabel-Hartman has been my friend and writing partner for thirty years. And finally my husband John Morgan always knew I could. I stand on their shoulders.

CPSIA information can be obtained at www.ICGtesting.com
Printed in the USA
LVOW08s2000050614

388791LV00005B/574/P